# INTO YOUR WORLD

MEENA

**BLUEROSE PUBLISHERS**
India | U.K.

Copyright © Meena 2024

All rights reserved by author. No part of this publication may be reproduced, stored in a retrieval system or transmitted in any form or by any means, electronic, mechanical, photocopying, recording or otherwise, without the prior permission of the author. Although every precaution has been taken to verify the accuracy of the information contained herein, the publisher assumes no responsibility for any errors or omissions. No liability is assumed for damages that may result from the use of information contained within.

BlueRose Publishers takes no responsibility for any damages, losses, or liabilities that may arise from the use or misuse of the information, products, or services provided in this publication.

For permissions requests or inquiries regarding this publication, please contact:

BLUEROSE PUBLISHERS
www.BlueRoseONE.com
info@bluerosepublishers.com
+91 8882 898 898
+4407342408967

ISBN: 978-93-6783-980-5

Cover design: Shubham
Typesetting: Sagar

First Edition: December 2024

# Acknowledgements

This book would never have been written, let alone published, without the incredible people who supported and believed in me.

Thank you to my family, especially my sister for her endless love and unwavering belief in me—your support has meant everything.

To my wonderful mother, my greatest inspiration. Your encouragement and faith turned this dream into reality. I couldn't have done it without you.

To my best friend, Minakshi, for always standing by me, cheering me on, and being my constant source of strength.

To my fictional boyfriend, who kept my imagination alive and my creativity thriving, for being a constant source of inspiration.

And finally, to everyone who believed in my story—this book exists because of you.

Thank you.

# *Trigger Warning*

This story explores sexual content, violence, abuse, grief and loss, PTSD, and trauma—with moments that may be unsettling, including graphic depictions of murder, gore, and raw emotional struggles.

And, just to keep things interesting... there's a touch of ✹ magic ✹

Before you turn the page, remember—I can slip right into your world too. Are you sure you're ready for that kind of risk?

# Contents

Chapter 1
  Pilot ................................................................. 1

Chapter 2
  The Indestructible Book ............................ 14

Chapter 3
  Awakening Rift ........................................... 24

Chapter 4
  Rachel Greene ............................................ 33

Chapter 5
  Unexpected Alliance .................................. 40

Chapter 6
  The Looming Threat ................................... 47

Chapter 7
  The Turbulence of The Past ...................... 61

Chapter 8
  Absent .......................................................... 76

Chapter 9
  A Night Out ................................................. 92

Chapter 10
  Whispers of Confessions ......................... 113

Chapter 11
  Archon Astralis ......................................... 120

Chapter 12
  The Six Tomes .......................................... 129

Chapter 13
Flames and Taffeta ................................................................ 139

Chapter 14
Dazzling Desires .................................................................... 152

Chapter 15
Masquerade Ball .................................................................... 158

Chapter 16
Zephyr's Shadow ................................................................... 170

Chapter 17
A Love Unspoken .................................................................. 185

Chapter 18
The Crucible of Truths .......................................................... 189

Chapter 19
The Breaking Point ............................................................... 205

Chapter 20
Caught in The Crossfire ........................................................ 214

Chapter 21
Shadows of impending doom ............................................... 224

Chapter 22
The Cost of Envy ................................................................... 237

Chapter 23
In the Wake of Flames .......................................................... 247

Chapter 24
Irrevocably mine .................................................................... 255

Chapter 25
    Maybe not ............................................................................ 264

Chapter 26
    Beneath the Viel of Fear ...................................................... 272

Chapter 27
    Wicked Justice ...................................................................... 279

Chapter 28
    Ceremonial Reckoning ......................................................... 290

Chapter 29
    Petals of Despair .................................................................. 303

Chapter 30
    Rookie Blunder .................................................................... 314

Chapter 31
    The Price of Pretence ........................................................... 328

Chapter 32
    Run Run Run ....................................................................... 338

Chapter 33
    Cooking Together ................................................................ 350

Chapter 34
    The Sacrifice ......................................................................... 366

Chapter 35
    He's Alive .............................................................................. 383

Chapter 36
    Confession ............................................................................ 395

Chapter 37
   Did I scare you, Miss Kirby? ................................................... 409
Chapter 38
   Walmart .............................................................................. 418
Chapter 39
   Shameless ............................................................................ 431
Chapter 40
   The Evil Zephyr Valtor........................................................... 448
Chapter 41
   Hidden Chest....................................................................... 462
Chapter 42
   The revelation ..................................................................... 475
Chapter 43
   The Final Chapter................................................................ 493

# Chapter 1

## Pilot

*Liza's POV*

I used my sling bag to cover my head as I rushed to the university through the rain. The sun isn't down yet, but the dark clouds above make it seem like it's night. I came out here to get myself a cup of coffee because my machine broke down. I could have brought my car but the cafe wasn't too far and I don't use my car for places that aren't too far and can be covered on foot. When I got out, the weather was absolutely fine. Though some white clouds were blocking the blue sky but there was no hint of rain. It was just a pleasant warm evening.

I fastened my pace, avoiding puddles as I walked down the uneven sidewalk, and took shelter under an old bus stop to save myself from getting entirely soaked. I checked my purse to see if everything inside was alright and to my good luck, everything was dry and fine. I took my phone out of my jeans pocket and checked the time. It flashed half past four. *God, why does this always happen to me?*

Hello, my name is Liza Kirby. I'm 26, and I've been living on my own since I was 14. My life follows a monotonous routine: I wake up, go to college, come back home, eat, sleep, and repeat. This cycle has persisted for years. The only change is that I was once a student, but now I teach English to high school students.

Throughout my college years, I never made friends. I was antisocial and people intimidated me. Even now, when my colleagues invite me to hang out, I invent some excuse to avoid going. However, there's one person I wish would ask me out: Nate Wilson. He's the most handsome man at our college, kind, humble, and respectful. I've been attracted to him since I was 16 and have known him since childhood. He used to be my neighbour.

But Nate has a girlfriend, and she's stunning in a way I can never be. I see myself as anything but attractive. My grey eyes feel out of place on my face, and my skin is far from flawless, with freckles dotting my cheeks and nose. My hair is as dry as sandpaper. I don't have curves, nor do I have good height. I mean, did God have some kind of problem with me that he didn't give one good thing?

Flashes of lightning lit up the darkened sky followed by cracks of thunder as though in reply. I took a shaky breath in and stepped back, hoping the light would not fall on me and cook me alive. I also hoped that the wind would not blow the roof away. It's the only thing saving me from the rain.

Suddenly, a car sped by, hitting the dirty water pooled in the gutter and splashing it all over me. I gasped, spreading my hands wide as I looked down in shock. My clothes were ruined, caked with mud. I shot a glare at the car and was about to yell, but another car passed and did the same thing. My blood boiled, anger rushing through me, but instead of letting it out, I decided to bury it. They were gone anyway. What could I do?

I rubbed my arms in an attempt to send some warmth to my trembling body. It was getting colder by the minute. I looked around, hoping to find someone but there was not a single soul. My heartbeats increased. Now, if somebody kidnaps me, my screams will not reach anybody.

*But the question is, who will kidnap me?*

I sighed and spotted an old stool beside the advertisement. It lacked any ad, so I approached cautiously and took a seat. My legs found relief, the stool sturdy beneath me. A smile graced my lips but it was gone when the stool broke down, sending me tumbling backward with a grunt of pain.

"Ah," I groaned, clutching my back, "What an awful day!"

Attempting to rise, I froze as my gaze fell upon a book nestled behind the bus advertisement shelter, catching the faint light filtering through the rain. The book seemed to defy the very elements, its sleek grey and silver cover gleaming under the dim light that barely pierced through the downpour. It was as if the rain parted around it, refusing to tarnish its pristine surface. Compelled by an irresistible force, I reached for it, my hand trembling slightly as I lifted it from its resting place. The cover felt cool, almost otherworldly, in my grasp. Not a single drop of rain marred its surface-it was untouched, impossibly dry, and perfectly preserved as if the storm had never dared to lay a finger on it.

I inspected it closely. The title, "Arcane Flame," adorned the cover, yet there was no author or publishing information to be found. No ISBN, no blurb-nothing to hint at its contents.

*Hmm, interesting...*

I couldn't help but wish to keep it. It was a novel and I love novels. Maybe I should take it home. Without another thought, I tucked it carefully into my purse, its weight a comforting presence against my side. I felt a strange sense of satisfaction as if the universe had aligned just right to bring this book into my hands.

Eventually, the noise lessened and the drops faded into a musical chime. The rain hasn't stopped but it's not as heavy as before. I sighed and stepped out of the shelter and headed back to school to get my car.

At home, it was all the same. Silence and loneliness. I dropped my bag on the table and went into the bathroom to get a shower. Water has a way of making everything sticky, making it hard to get undressed. It took me 10 minutes to take them off and 10 minutes for the hot water to take the chill.

When I got out of the shower, it was pouring outside, the thunderstorm echoing in my hallway like a background sound from some scary movie. I put on my flip-flops and went out in the hallway to make something for myself. I was starving and shivering.

Wrapping myself with a shawl, I went to the kitchen and took out the pack of raw chicken from the fridge.

While the chicken was being cooked in salted water, I decided to make some herbal tea to prevent myself from catching a cold. I checked the time on my phone and it flashes half past six. I sighed and put it back inside. After the chicken was ready, I roasted it and served it on my plate. My stomach was screaming for it. With the plate in my hands, I quickly took my place on the sofa and turned on the TV.

Impatiently, I sliced a bite and shoved it in my mouth. As soon as the juicy chicken met my taste buds, I moaned in delight. Its simple pleasure was enough to momentarily overshadow the day's frustrations. With a contented sigh, I opened Netflix and queued up an episode of "The Big Bang Theory," my perennial favorite. Despite having seen every episode, the show never failed to entertain.

Midway through the episode, a nagging realization tugged at my consciousness. I still had a mountain of test papers from last week's exams awaiting my attention. Despite my hectic schedule, I couldn't afford to neglect them any longer. Hastily finishing my meal, I washed my plate and retreated to my bedroom, exhaustion weighing heavily on my shoulders.

Though every fiber of my being yearned for the solace of sleep, duty called. With a weary sigh, I settled into my chair and began the arduous task of grading papers. The clock ticked past eleven by the time I finally completed the last one, a yawn escaping my lips. I methodically organized the papers, tucking them away in a drawer before allowing myself the luxury of finally surrendering to sleep's embrace.

But then, the sound of water droplets dancing echoed through the house, drawing my attention away from the stack of papers. Following the sound, I discovered a troubling sight- a leak in the roof. "Oh my god!" I exclaimed, rising from my chair to assess the damage. Water pooled on the floor, inching its way toward my furniture, its path illuminated by the dim light filtering through the rain-soaked windows. "Why didn't I notice this sooner?" I wondered aloud, hastily rearranging the furniture to protect it from the encroaching water. With a heavy sigh, I located the source of the leak and positioned a basket beneath it to catch the relentless drip. Armed with a mop, I set about cleaning the sodden floor, the rhythmic drip of water a disconcerting backdrop to my efforts.

Exhausted, I went downstairs to sleep, knowing full well that the relentless sound of water dripping nearby would keep me wide awake if I stayed. Even though I have twenty rooms in this house, I've never used them. I never needed to. This place, a grand and imposing estate, was gifted to me by my grandmother on my 16th birthday.

The only time I ever explored its vast halls and hidden corners was the day I first moved in. It's an enormous house, almost too big for someone like me, complete with a personal garden and a swimming pool large enough to host a party for the entire town. None of my neighbours can boast of anything close to this. From my windows, I get the best view in town- an unbroken panorama that stretches far beyond the town limits.

This house has stood here since the first war, its walls holding secrets and stories I may never uncover. If I ever decided to sell it, I could easily fetch billions. But it's not just a house-it's a legacy, a gift from the only person who truly understood me. No matter how much I might want to sometimes, I could never bring myself to part with it. It's not just the money; it's the connection to my past, to her, that makes it impossible to let go.

With a sigh, I lay down on my couch, hoping to drift off to sleep, but couldn't. Restless, I sat up and glanced around the room, my gaze eventually landing on my purse. A flicker of recollection stirred within me-the novel I'd found earlier was still tucked inside.

Eagerly, I retrieved it, the memory of its mysterious appearance adding to my anticipation. I flipped open the pages and began to read, instantly drawn into the world it revealed. The story begins with a wealthy man, burdened by his father's towering expectations, yet determined to rebel, to disappoint with his unconventional choices. It wasn't what I expected, but something was captivating about it, something that resonated with me in ways I hadn't anticipated.

I kept reading, engrossed by the plot as it unfolded. When the female lead finally entered the story, I couldn't help but feel a connection. She was deeply in love with the protagonist, caring and fiercely possessive. But Adrian-the protagonist-didn't seem truly invested in her. Despite this, he was set on marrying her, convinced that she was the only one who truly understood him.

As I turned the pages, a familiar pang of jealousy stirred within me, an ache that had nothing to do with real life but everything to do with the longing for a love that existed only within the confines of a story.

I turned the next page and the lights went out, distracting me. It was all dark. Power outages are a very common occurrence during heavy rain. I stood up, turned on my phone's torch and looked for the candles in the kitchen. After I found one, I lit it and placed it on my table. The only place which had some light was my couch, the rest of the house was covered in dark shadow. If someone else was here, he'd have run out but because I've lived here for years, this house doesn't scare me at all. However, I do sometimes end up thinking of getting murdered and no one getting to know about it because of my antisocial nature. I have no one who'd care about me if I go missing. One day, I'll die and nobody will even shed a tear for me. But the big question is, who'd kill me? Well, when the thief finds nothing here but dirt and spider webs, he definitely would.

I shook my head, trying to clear my mind, and headed to the kitchen. Grabbing an apple, I sliced it into pieces, the simple act grounding me in reality. Returning to the couch, I settled back down, putting the plate on the table next to me as I continued to read. As I delved deeper into the story, the protagonist's character became increasingly complex, almost unsettling. One moment, he was charming and playful, the kind of person who could light up a room with just a smile. But in the blink of an eye, his mood would shift-he'd turn cold, rude, and arrogant, pushing everyone away. At times, he seemed so full of life, as if nothing could bring him down. But then, without warning, darkness would seep into his words, revealing a desperate need for light, for something-anything-that could pull him out of the shadows.

"I have to read more to understand him better," I muttered to myself, flipping eagerly to the next page. Outside, the weather raged on, thunder reverberating through the house while lightning illuminated the hallway in jagged flashes. Yet, it didn't bother me at all. It's not new to me. I've seen worse weather here.

With my eyes fixed on the book as I reached for another piece of apple, I ended up reaching for the knife. I hissed and immediately retrieved my hand, sitting up and seeing blood coming out of my finger. *Oh shit!* I sit up and scoffed as I saw drops of blood on the candle and table. I went to my kitchen and put a bandage on it.

I went back to my table with a cloth in my hand to clean my blood, but before I could, my attention was drawn back to the book. A strange unease settled over me as I noticed something off-the cover page now bore cryptic sentences, symbols that didn't resemble any language I recognized. My brow furrowed in confusion and curiosity, a strange mix of intrigue and unease pulling me back into the book's enigmatic grip.

I picked it in my hand, bringing it closer to the light. The words on the page were dark, almost ominous: It was Latin. *"Ad omne quod scelestum est, peto ut mihi des potestatem perducendi non existentem ad vitam!"* The moment the words left my lips, an eerie silence fell over the room, heavy and suffocating. I swallowed hard, my instincts screaming at me to put the book down and step away.

But before I could act, a sudden gust of wind roared through the room, snuffing out the candle and knocking me off my feet. Every window in the house flew open, the curtains whipping violently in the stormy wind that had seemingly come from nowhere.

"Okay, that's new," I murmured, my heart pounding as I tried to make sense of this. The room fell silent just as quickly as the chaos began. My hands trembled as I placed the book on the table and hurried to close all the windows, locking them securely one by one. The air still felt charged, as if the house itself was holding its breath.

When I struck a match to lit the candle, the light was back. I sighed and blew it out. But when I glanced at the time it appeared past 3 am. My eyes widened, "Oh my god! I should sleep now," Panicked, I hurried toward my sofa, but a sudden noise from the kitchen made me stop dead in my tracks. My breath hitched, and I felt a cold shiver run down my spine.

Afraid, I grabbed the baseball bat that I keep beside the couch for moments like this, "Who's there?" I called out with courage.

*Silence.*

My throat tightened as I forced myself to take small, cautious steps toward the kitchen, my heart pounding so hard I could hear it in my ears.

"I know karate!" I shouted, my voice wavering as I raised the bat, mentally preparing myself for whatever horror might be lurking. Though, deep down, I knew I wouldn't last a minute against anything truly threatening. My grip on the bat tightened as I finally stepped into the kitchen, expecting the worst.

Instead, a mouse darted across the floor, scurrying away from a toppled box of chips. Relief flooded through me, and I let out a shaky breath, lowering the bat. I set it on the counter and quickly picked up the chips box, returning it to the cupboard. My heart began to steady, the tension easing from my muscles.

"You scared the shit out of me little mouse." I said and turned around only to froze on my spot, my blood running cold. A man stood there, watching me with calm, steady eyes. I gulped.

"Who are you?" he asked gently, the calmness in his voice only amplifying my terror.

Taking a deep breath, I screamed at the top of my lungs.

"My god, stop screaming!" he exclaimed, covering his ears. Ignoring his plea, I screamed even louder and bolted. Fear propelled me as I leapt onto the four-foot kitchen counter in one fluid motion. I never knew I could jump that high-apparently, the fear of death can make you do anything.

He pursued me relentlessly as I dashed through the house, my mind racing with panic. I had never experienced anything like this before, I didn't know what to do to handle this situation.

"You need to stop running and listen to me!" He yelled, following me like I was his prey.

*Actually, I was a prey.*

I screamed again and raced upstairs, my breath ragged, when suddenly, I felt a sharp tug on my leg. My eyes widened and heart stopped when he pulled me down hard. A rush of dread flooding my senses as he hovered over me. In that terrifying moment, I could almost see my life flash before my eyes, imagining all the horrific ways he might use to end it. But even as fear tightened its grip, a fierce determination burned within me-I wasn't going down without a fight.

I screamed, the sound raw and desperate, as I hit him with all my strength. My hands flailed wildly, pushing and clawing at him, trying to drive him away. Every instinct screamed at me to fight, to do whatever it took to protect myself. In the chaos, my movements were frantic, driven by sheer terror.

"You need to stop hitting me, girl," he shouted, his tone exasperated but not threatening.

Desperation twisted my words into a frantic plea. "You're in the wrong place, sir. I have nothing to give you. I'm broke. Really. You'll regret killing me. I'm broke, man. I'm very poor. Please, just leave me alone! I'll move out, I swear, I'll never come back to this town. Just leave me!"

His confusion was palpable as he looked at me, brows furrowed. "What? I'm not here to kill you or rob you. You've summoned me. Now, it's your responsibility to send me back!"

I stared at him, my mind reeling, trying to comprehend his words. Summoned him? What was he talking about? I couldn't even form a response, just blinking at him in stunned silence.

"I'm Adrian Scott," he said, his voice firm. "And I want you to send me back."

Unable to make sense of the situation, I acted purely on instinct. My hand groped frantically in the darkness until it grasped something solid. Without a second thought, I swung it with all my might and hit him on his head. The impact was immediate-a dull thud as the intruder crumpled to the ground, knocked out cold. My chest heaving as I stared at my hand in disbelief. The object I had used as a weapon was nothing more than a sandal-an utterly bizarre choice, but it had been enough to protect myself in the chaos of the moment.

"Psycho," I breathed out.

# Chapter 2

# The Indestructible Book

"Let go of me!" he roars at the cop, his voice echoing with a desperate ferocity as he thrashed against the restraining hands. Cuffed and held by three officers, his fury burns brighter than fear. Brave or simply unhinged?

"Get in!" The officer shoves him into the squad car with a final, forceful push. He casts an evil glare at me before the door slams shut, making my heart pound.

"My god, he's scary," I let out, my hand on my heart.

"Don't worry, Miss Kirby. He won't disturb you again. We'll take care of him from here!"

"You should take him to a hospital or something. He seems mentally unstable to me," I suggested, my voice trembling slightly.

"I AM NOT SICK!" he bellows from inside the car.

My eyes widen.

"Don't be scared, ma'am. He won't trouble you again. Please try to get some rest."

I nodded, "Thank you, officer."

As the cop walks away, I retreat inside, the familiar comfort of home suddenly feeling foreign and unsafe. That night, sleep eluded me. When morning finally came, I dragged myself to the shower, got dressed, and headed to school, the clear blue sky and warm sunlight doing little to lift the shadow over my heart.

At school, the first face I saw was Nate's. My cheeks flush. "Hi, Nate."

"Hey, Miss Kirby. How are you doing?" His smile dims, concern etching lines of worry across his features as he tenderly lifts my chin, his gaze probing for the truth beneath the facade. "You okay? You look tired."

*See, how well he sees through me.*

"Yeah, last night wasn't the best."

"Why?"

"Uh, I've been busy. What about you? Don't you have a class?"

"Yeah, but I'm not attending today. Exams are close. I need to make preparations."

"Yeah, I checked last week's test papers. The students are doing well this year."

"In English, Miss Kirby. There are more subjects they need to excel in to pass the year."

I chuckle. "Don't worry. I believe in them."

"Nate?" Our conversation is interrupted by Miss Kavanagh, his girlfriend. She wraps her arm around his possessively and says, "Hi, Liza. How have you been?"

"I'm doing great, thanks."

"Good to know," she smiled, "Nate, babe? Can we eat out tonight?"

"Sure. Would you like to join us, Liza?" he asked, his smile kind but unaware of the silent struggle within me.

"Oh, I wish, but I'm busy. Maybe next time?"

*I would rather die of hunger than watch them feed each other.*

Nate nodded, "Next time then."

The day drags on relentlessly, a blur of teaching, lunch, and endless classes that seem to stretch into eternity. Exhaustion grips me like a vise. I couldn't sleep last night and the blame rests squarely on the shoulders of that psycho. His haunting presence refusing to release its grip on my thoughts. His fierce green eyes flash relentlessly in my mind, a constant reminder of last night's terror.

But amidst the fear and unease, a flicker of something else ignites within me. That psycho. Despite the chaos he brought, there's no denying the undeniable allure of his appearance-light blonde hair cascaded in soft, shining waves that framed his face with effortless elegance. A perfectly sculpted jawline added to his striking features, while his full, symmetrical lips held an understated allure. But it was his eyes—vivid green, like emeralds catching sunlight—that commanded attention, their piercing clarity contrasting beautifully with his fair complexion. Ah, if only he weren't a psycho, but a man who found me captivating, perhaps even worthy of his affection.

*A handsome guy falling for me?*

The notion is laughable, absurd in its impossibility. In another universe, maybe, but not in the harsh reality of my existence.

When I reached home, I collapsed onto my bed, feeling the mattress embrace my tired body. Just as sleep begins to claim me, the doorbell rings.

*Fantastic!*

I reluctantly drag myself from the comfort of my bed and opened the door. The plumber I had summoned earlier to address the persistent leaks has arrived, his presence a stark reminder of the myriad repairs my mansion requires. I guide him through the labyrinthine corridors, each step a testament to the neglect that has befallen my once grand home.

As if on cue, an architect and his team materialize, their arrival heralding a thorough inspection of the aging structure. The need for repairs is undeniable, and the cost exorbitant but unavoidable. My wedding savings will have to be sacrificed. After all, what's the point of saving for a wedding when no one wants to marry you?

"We'll start tomorrow."

"Sure," I say, shaking hands with him before he leaves.

I headed straight to the kitchen, my stomach growling in protest. Exhaustion clung to me, but it never dampened my enthusiasm for cooking. I whipped up a feast of Chinese food, the fragrant aromas lifting my spirits. Humming a tune, I danced my way to the bedroom, balancing the steaming plate in my hands. Happily, I sank into the bed, eagerly digging my fork into the food. I ate, did some school work, and then don't know when sleep took over me on the table.

I awoke to the sound of wind rustling outside and my curtains dancing violently. Sitting up, I glanced around, my back and neck aching due to the uncomfortable position I've slept in. Don't know why but everything seemed off, and I couldn't shake the odd sensation. I yawned and peered out the window, heavy wind was blowing, giving me a message that it's gonna rain again tonight. I rose slowly and dragged myself to the mirror, observing my tired reflection with swollen eyes.

With a weary sigh, I went downstairs, retrieved the food from my refrigerator, and placed it in the microwave. While it heated up, I checked my phone and discovered the welcome news that school was closed tomorrow due to the heavy wind. Relief washed over me, grateful for the unexpected day off. I needed one. The microwave's bell chimed, signalling that my meal was ready. I retrieved it and began to eat, savouring the comforting warmth amidst the unsettling stillness of the wind outside.

I wandered through my silent house, eating my meal while making mental notes of what I was going to do through this day off and I found myself looking at the weather from my glass window.

The scene that greeted me was one of tranquil beauty. The sky was painted in darkness, a gentle darkness that hadn't yet fully surrendered to the night. The trees stood like silent sentinels, their outlines sharply etched against the dusky backdrop. The towering cliffs of the mountains loomed in the distance, their rugged profiles softened by the fading light. The landscape was bathed in a dusky glow, a perfect balance between light and shadow that lent an air of mystique to the view. It was a sight that demanded contemplation, urging me to pause and drink in the natural splendour before me.

The whisper of a breeze rustled through the leaves, creating a soft symphony of sound that complemented the visual feast. It was a moment of perfect stillness, where time seemed to stretch and bend, allowing me to lose myself in the quiet magnificence of the scene. The beauty of the night, the serenity of my home, and the comforting ritual of my meal merged into a single, harmonious experience.

I stood there, my mind still, simply absorbing the peacefulness that surrounded me, feeling an overwhelming sense of gratitude for this rare and precious respite from the busyness of everyday life.

Watching, as I raised a spoonful of food to my mouth, my gaze fell upon the car parked in my garden. The spoon froze in mid-air as confusion washed over me.

*How on earth did it end up there?*

The doors were securely locked, and there was no way a car could have entered without my notice. With a growing sense of unease, I turned to call the authorities. After the events of last night, I couldn't risk venturing out alone and unarmed. I turned, making my way to the telephone but-My eyes widened and I halted in my spot. A sudden chill ran down my spine and I stood there, my breath picking up.

Slowly, I glanced back at the car, my heart pounding in my chest. The number plate read '1010,' sending another wave of shiver down my spine.

Without a second thought, I dashed upstairs, leaving my half-eaten meal behind on a nearby surface.

When I reached my bedroom, I frantically scanned the room until my eyes landed on the book lying on the table. Snatching it up, I flipped through its pages with trembling hands, desperation mounting with each passing moment. The sound of my own heartbeat filled my ears, drowning out all other noise as I searched for answers within the pages of the book.

Reaching the page I sought, my eyes widened in disbelief, and an audible gasp escaped my lips. The book slipped from my trembling fingers, landing with a soft thud on the floor. I swallowed hard, my palms slick with sweat, as a wave of dizziness washed over me. At that moment, it felt as though the world around me dissolved into nothingness, leaving me suspended in a void of uncertainty and fear.

"No, no, no, no, no, no," I placed my hand on my forehead, "It can't be. This isn't possible. How can it be possible?" I looked down at the novel and gulped hard. The number plate the car had is the same as the number plate of Adrian's in the book.

*Is it some kind of coincidence?*

*Or I'm losing my mind?*

I nodded, "Definitely a coincidence," I told myself. But deep down, doubt gnawed at me, refusing to be silenced. I picked up the book, determined to reassure myself by returning to the page to recheck the number plate. However, when I flipped to the page, it was no longer there. Panic surged through me as I realized the car had vanished, leaving behind a space.

I frowned and paused. Gathering my resolve, I flipped to the first page of the book once more, but as I looked up, the ground seemed to shift beneath my feet. Adrian was gone, just like the car, leaving nothing but a space in his wake.

"Oh my fucking God!"

My world shook. I felt lightheaded. I couldn't grasp it.

"Is-Is this true? Is this really happening? I actually summoned a fictional character into the real world?" I slammed my palm on my mouth, my eyes wide and shocked, "Fuck!"

An hour had passed, and the book lying on my bed as I stared at it without a flicker of movement. My heart rate had returned to normal, and the gravity of the situation began to sink in. I had unwittingly summoned a fictional character into the real world, and now he is in jail. The book, it seemed, possessed a strange power to bring its characters and contents to life.

As I grappled with the enormity of my mistake, a sense of urgency gripped me. I wasn't supernatural; I have no idea how I have managed to perform such a feat. But one thing was clear, I needed to rectify it before things spiralled out of control. If Adrian and his car are out, who knows what else from the book would follow?

I rose from my seat, determination coursing through me as I gripped the book tightly in my hands and made my way to the kitchen, the weight of the book a constant reminder of the task at hand.

I ignited the stove, the flames dancing eagerly as if sensing the impending sacrifice. With a steady hand, I put the book onto the flames. But to my astonishment, the flames failed to consume it. The book lay in the fire, untouched by the hungry flames. I increased the heat, desperate to see some sign of destruction, but the book remained unscathed, its pages pristine.

Refusing to give up, I retrieved the book and attempted to tear its pages, but they resisted my efforts with unyielding strength. In a last-ditch effort, I reached for my ink box and poured its contents onto the book, hoping to mar its pristine pages. Yet, to my dismay, the ink simply slid off, leaving the book untouched and unharmed.

Shocked by the book's resilience, I couldn't help but recall how it had remained unharmed even when submerged in water.

*Does it mean it is indestructible?*

The realization sent a chill down my spine. If the book couldn't be harmed, then how could I ever hope to undo what I had unwittingly set in motion?

"No. There has to be a way," I muttered to myself, refusing to accept defeat.

"I'M NOT SICK!"

Adrian's voice rang in my ears and I saw no better option.

# Chapter 3

# Awakening Rift

*Liza's POV*

Despite the itchiness in my hands and the tight grip of anxiety constricting my chest, I plastered a smile on my face as I greeted him, "Hi," The word felt forced, almost foreign, as it left my lips. His jaw clenched, his muscles tensing visibly, and his eyes bore into me like daggers, sharp and unyielding. The intensity of his gaze sent a shiver down my spine, a reminder of the chasm between us.

The frustration and confusion etched on his face mirrored my own turmoil. I know what I did was wrong, dragging him into a world where he didn't belong and then sending him to jail. But what else was I supposed to do when a complete stranger materialized in my house out of nowhere? Offer him a warm greeting?

I lifted my hand, gesturing for him to step out. "Please," I said, my voice awkward and uncertain. His expression remained stoic, heightening my apprehension. Without a word, he walked out of the station, leaving my hand hanging in the air. I pressed my lips into a thin line and retracted my hand, trying to calm my nerves. "He's spent an entire night in jail, Liza. Give him some time," I whispered to myself, following him silently.

As we walked side by side in uneasy silence, the enormity of the situation weighed heavily on me, pressing down with an almost tangible force. Here was this incredible being from another realm, and I was not fascinated or thrilled, I was overwhelmed and frightened. I didn't know what to do, say, feel, or believe. He had come out of a different realm, thanks to me, but how am I supposed to deal with this now? Nobody taught me about how you handle someone who's from an entirely different realm. I have no guidebook for this, no instructions on how to navigate the chaos I had unleashed. Hell, I didn't even know this was even possible before now. A fictional character into reality. I'm still trying to grapple with the fact that I summoned him.

I don't know what I'm going to do next, how I'm going to send him back but I will try-try my best. So, here I am, bailing him out.

"What did you tell the cops?" he asked, his voice startled me, and I blinked, not believing he had actually spoken.

"Uh, I said you were my friend's boyfriend, you came to surprise her last night. She had already left before you arrived, so you found me instead. I freaked out because I'd never seen you before. That's the story I gave them."

He raised an eyebrow at me, "Didn't they ask about my girlfriend?"

"No."

"Thank you," he said, and I tried hard not to melt at the sound of his voice. It was so damn hot. But the sarcasm that dripped with that word didn't go unnoticed by me.

"You don't need to thank me," I smiled, trying to mask the effect of this whole situation on me. I was nervous and scared. So many questions were bubbling within me, but, I pretended to be cool, or at least, I tried to, "I was just fixing my own mistake."

"Right. And you still have a bigger one in hand to fix."

"Yeah, I need to find a way."

He paused, "Find a way?" his tone didn't sound like before. It sounded sharp and bitter.

I nodded, hesitate, "Yeah, I mean, I don't know how to send you back," I reached for my car door, but before I could grasp it, his hand shot out, seizing my arm in a vice-like grip.

My heart skipped a beat as he yanked me back, his sudden movement causing my breath to catch in my throat. Our bodies were so close now, the air thick with tension as his piercing gaze bore into mine. His jaw was clenched, the muscles taut with frustration, and I could feel the intensity of his emotions radiating off him in waves.

"What are you doing?" I managed to choke out, my voice trembling with a mixture of fear and confusion.

His grip tightened on my arm, the pressure sending a jolt of pain shooting through me. I winced.

"What do you mean, you don't know?" he demanded, his voice low and menacing. I couldn't speak. My head was jammed with fear, "I've asked you something," He grits out.

"Uh, I mean, I-I don't know how I brought you here," I stuttered, feeling small under his towering presence. I leaned back against my car, trying to put some distance between us, but his gaze pinned me in place. My heart raced as his eyes bore into mine, filled with anguish and urgency.

*Alright, now he's scaring me.*

"Listen, Liza Kirby," he spoke, his voice firm but tinged with desperation. "You summoned me here, and I need you to send me back. I don't belong in this world. You've messed with reality, and now it's up to you to fix it."

"See, I'm just an ordinary person trying to comprehend all of this. It still feels like I'm trapped in a dream. Please, try to understand," His only response was a tense inhale, "And you're hurting me," He glanced at my arm and released me slowly. For a moment, I thought I saw a flicker of guilt before it was replaced by coldness. I rubbed my arm, trying to soothe the pain.

"You better find a way soon because if you don't, you'll face the ugly consequences of your mistake," Saying this, he silently got inside my car. I stood there, still reeling from the surreal turn of events, unable to shake the feeling that I had unwittingly unleashed forces beyond my control. But I have to find a solution. A way to make things right, no matter how daunting the task seemed.

As we pulled up to my home, he wasted no time in making his way to the door, his determination palpable as I followed timidly behind. Once inside, I hurried to fetch him a glass of water, hoping to offer some small comfort amidst the chaos that had engulfed us. He accepted it with no expressions.

I sank onto my couch, exhaustion washing over me like a tidal wave. Just as I began to close my eyes, his voice shattered the fragile peace that had settled over the room.

"What are you doing?"

Startled, I blinked open my eyes, meeting his gaze with a mixture of frustration and weariness. "Resting," My reply was tinged with a hint of defiance.

His response was swift and uncompromising. "You can't rest, Liza. Not until you find a way to send me back."

Feeling the weight of his expectations bearing down on me once again, I sighed deeply, the exhaustion threatening to overwhelm me. "I will," I assured him, "I just need a moment of peace." But his resolve remained unyielding.

"How did you summon me?"

Resigning myself to the inevitable interrogation, I shifted into a more comfortable position on the couch before responding with a weary sigh, "Honestly, I don't know."

He scoffs, looking frustrated, "Okay, tell me about everything that happened last until I came."

"Well, I was reading-

"In detail. I need to know every small detail of last night."

I nodded, understanding the gravity of his request, and proceeded to recount every moment from the previous night. From the discovery of the mysterious book to the leakage, the accidental cut on my finger, and the strange lines that appeared on the pages, to me reciting them. I left no detail unmentioned, hoping to provide him with the clarity he sought. When I finished, he regarded me with squinted eyes.

I lifted my shoulders, "What?"

"You don't just casually read anything that appears magically, Miss Kirby."

"I-I got curious. I couldn't stop myself," I defended myself, though he was right.

"See where your curiosity got you," he retorted, his smile tight and mocking. "It was a spell."

"A spell?" I echoed, the realization sinking in like a lead weight. He nodded solemnly. "But incantations typically work with witches and supernatural. I'm a human."

He sighed tiredly, "A non-existent creature is standing before you, and you still think you're an ordinary human?" he quipped, his tone laced with bitter irony.

I faltered, struggling to come to terms with the magnitude of his revelation. "I-"

"Where's the book?" he demanded. I handed him the book and sat back. As he inspected the pages, his expression grew increasingly grim. "This book has nothing to offer. It's useless."

"So, what do we do now?" I asked, feeling a sense of desperation creeping in.

"We read," he declared, his tone resolute.

I frowned in confusion. "Read what?"

"Everything," he said, "Ancient texts, arcane manuscripts, obscure folklore-anything that might contain clues about summoning rituals or magical phenomena. We'll need to visit libraries, consult experts, and scour online forums dedicated to the supernatural. Maybe then we'll find a way to send me back."

My head began to spin at the magnitude of the task ahead. "Wait, so we're doing all of this and there's still just a 'maybe'?"

"Girl, I'm the one who doesn't belong in this world, not you. Let me worry about the uncertainties." I fell silent, processing his words. "And if you want something to worry about, think about how you managed to bring a fictional character into the real world."

Offended by his continued rudeness, I couldn't help but snap, "You have to stop being so rude to me, alright? I know I made a mistake, but it wasn't intentional. It's not like I was trying to do something and ended up with the opposite result. Whatever happened, happened without my knowledge. So stop being rude to me. And for the last time, it was all just a coincidence, okay? I don't have any powers. I'm just an ordinary human being."

He sighed. "I'm sure by the end of this, you'll also learn about yourself because you certainly don't know what you're capable of yet."

"Right. Now, do you happen to know the author of your book?" I questioned. He shook his head, disappointing me, "Do you think Google might have the answer?"

We both turned to my phone. I searched for any information about the book online but to my disappointment, the search yielded no results. I sighed heavily, feeling the weight of defeat settling over me.

"So, I guess we'll have to start by scouring forums and books?" I proposed, trying to muster up some semblance of optimism. He nodded in agreement, "By the way, don't you think you should freshen up? You've spent the entire night in jail. A shower might do you some good," I suggested.

He glanced down at himself, then back at me. "I don't have any extra clothes."

"Oh," I said, "Why don't you stay here while I go get you some clothes?"

"I'll go with you," he announced, cutting off any protest before I could voice it.

We headed out and bought clothes for him, picking up something to eat on the way back. Once we returned, he went to shower while I started cooking, following his preferences.

While I was setting the trays on the table, I heard footsteps approaching. I didn't need to look up to know it was him. As he drew nearer, the fresh scent of his shower hit me, making me glance over despite myself. There he was, the epitome of hotness, focused on fastening the button of his cuff, completely oblivious. He wore a crisp white shirt and beige pants with boots. The upper buttons of his shirt were undone, revealing a glimpse of his chest, still glistening with droplets of water. His hair was damp, with water sliding down his neck and onto his chest, accentuating his ridiculously handsome looks.

My eyes trailed down, taking in his perfectly toned body. I couldn't help but wish I could touch it. I pressed my lips together and my grip tightened on the plate as I let the sight of him sink in. He was drop-dead gorgeous.

*Focus, Liza. Control yourself.*

My subconscious snapped me back and I quickly drifted back up to his face, only to realize that he was looking at me.

*Fuck!*

My heart skipped a beat and my cheeks flushed in embarrassment.

I tried to find my voice. "Uh, why are you wet? I left a towel and hair dryer for you."

"Maybe I didn't notice."

I nodded. "It's alright. The food's ready. Please, sit," I gestured to the table, and he complied with a smile. It was the first time I saw a true, genuine smile from him. And it was beautiful.

# Chapter 4

# Rachel Greene

*Liza's POV*

In the serene atmosphere of the library, we gathered a substantial stack of books, each promising a potential solution to our quest. Without library cards to check them out, we found a quiet corner, claimed a table, and dove headfirst into the pages spread before us. The scent of aged paper filled the air as we turned page after page, immersing ourselves in the wealth of knowledge contained within each volume. We read about famous cases related to summoning, captivating stories, and mythological tales, each offering a glimmer of hope, only to be dismissed as irrelevant to our peculiar situation. The hours melted away as we poured over the texts, our focus unyielding despite the growing exhaustion gnawing at the edges of our minds.

As the sun dipped below the horizon and the library grew quiet around us, we pressed on, fueled by sheer willpower and the hope that somewhere in these pages lay the solution we sought. And even as fatigue tugged at our eyelids, we continued to read, driven by the belief that perseverance would eventually lead us to success.

I yawned and glanced at Adrian. He was engrossed in his fourth book, reading at a pace that seemed almost unreal. As I gazed at him, a surreal thought crossed my mind: a character from the pages of a book was now walking among us. Would anyone believe such an incredible tale if I dared to share it?

"You're staring at me, Liza," Adrian's voice broke through my reverie, his attention still captured by the book.

"Yes, I am. I mean, you're made of ink and paper, yet here you are, in the flesh. It's baffling," I was unable to contain my wonder.

He met my gaze and sighed, mirroring my own perplexity, "Honestly, I've been pondering that myself."

"Really?" I pressed, eager for insight. He merely nodded before diving back into his reading, leaving me to my own thoughts. But another thought captured me again. I leaned over and pinched him. He hissed, retreating his hand, giving me a look of disbelief and confusion. I softly chuckled, "Sorry, I was just checking if it will hurt you."

He smiled tightly, "You hit me with a sandal the other day. Could have thought about that too to be assured?"

I chuckled again, "Right," And then I went back to reading again. A few minutes later, Adrian grabs my attention.

"I think I found something."

"What?"

"See this," he said, turning the screen of his laptop toward me. "This is Rachel Green. She's deeply involved in witchcraft and the occult. I watched many of her videos, and they seem genuine. She calls herself a psychic and has a reputation for helping people in need. Her book, which I've been reading, details numerous unsolved cases related to summoning and sacrifices."

I leaned closer, examining the image of Rachel Green on the screen. She had piercing blue eyes and an aura of mystique that seemed to jump out of the monitor.

"How do you think she could help us?" I asked, my curiosity piqued.

"She's documented cases where she's successfully contacted spirits and entities from other realms. If we're dealing with a summoning, she might have the knowledge we need to understand how to reverse it and send me back."

I nodded slowly, trying to absorb the implications. "But do you really think she would help us?"

Adrian shrugged. "It's worth a try. From what I've read, she's pretty open to helping those who are genuinely in need. We could reach out to her, explain our situation, and see what she says."

"Explain our situation? Adrian, you're not a Satan, spirit, demon, or something supernatural. You're fiction. You're a very different case."

"She deals with the inexplicable all the time. If anyone can make sense of this, it's her."

"Can we believe her? I mean, what if she's a fraud?"

"She could be. But we can't sit and read forever; we have to take risks too."

I nodded, agreeing with him, "Right. How do we get in touch with her?"

"I found her contact information online. It turns out she's based in New Orleans".

I froze, my heart pounding. "New Orleans?"

"Yeah. We might need to go there to meet her in person."

The mention of New Orleans brought a flood of memories crashing over me.

*"Mom, please. Don't do this to me. I will never disappoint you again," I cried, begging her not to throw me out of the house.*

*"No. You are a disappointment. I won't work my ass off for an abomination like you. You belong to the streets, not my house." She gripped my wrist so tightly I felt my bone crack. "If you can't help me, then you can't live with me," I kept crying, begging her. But she didn't stop. She dragged me to the door and threw me out of the house.*

*"I'm your daughter, Mom. Where would I go?"*

*"That's your problem to figure out. But if you ask me, go to your dad," She shut the door in my face.*

"Liza?" Adrian's voice brought me back to the present.

I blinked, "Yes?"

"Have you ever been to New Orleans?" he asked, his tone gentle but insistent.

I took my time before replying, "New Orleans is my home. So many memories are attached to that place."

Adrian looked at me, a faint shade of concern flashing on his face, "Is going there going to be a problem for you?"

I hesitated, feeling the weight of my past pressing down on me. "Maybe. But if Rachel Green can help us, it's a risk I'm willing to take."

"Alright. We leave tomorrow. Let's hope she has the answers we're looking for."

I nodded.

As we packed up our things, the prospect of returning to New Orleans filled me with a mix of dread and hope. The past might have its hold on me, but finding answers and solving this mystery was the priority now.

With that shared understanding, we walked out into the evening, ready to face whatever challenges lay ahead. The future was uncertain, but at least we had a direction-and perhaps, a chance at uncovering the truth.

As we returned home, Adrian went straight to my couch and lay down, clearly exhausted. We had been reading since morning, and the fatigue was evident in his every move. I didn't have the heart to disturb him. Instead, I went to the washroom to freshen up, hoping a splash of cold water would clear my head. Afterward, I headed to the kitchen to make him something to eat. He hadn't had anything since breakfast, and I knew he must be starving.

The kitchen felt like a sanctuary, a place where I could momentarily escape the weight of our recent discoveries. I busied myself with preparing a simple meal, the familiar actions of chopping and stirring grounding me. But when I returned to the living room, I found Adrian fast asleep on the couch. He looked so peaceful, the lines of stress smoothed out on his face. For a moment, I stood there, conflicted. He needed to eat, but he also needed rest. The couch wasn't the most comfortable place to sleep, yet waking him felt almost cruel. After a few minutes of silent debate, I decided to let him sleep. I placed the meal on the table opposite him, hoping the aroma might wake him gently, and then retreated to my room.

Sleep, however, was elusive. I tried to sleep but my mind was a whirlwind of thoughts, questions without answers, and a gnawing sense of urgency. Despite the glimmer of hope we had found in the woman who might offer assistance, a deep-rooted skepticism lingered within me. Could we truly depend on her to unravel the mystery that had engulfed us? As I tossed and turned in bed, the questions multiplied. What if Rachel Green couldn't help us? What if her knowledge fell short of what we needed? What if we are left stranded in this surreal predicament with no way out? And what if she's a fraud? The very thought worried me deeply.

Determined to find more information, I grabbed my laptop and settled back on my bed, diving into the world of online research. I scoured interviews, forums, stories, videos, and the works of creators passionate about magic and spells. I meticulously jotted down notes, hoping for a breakthrough. Hours slipped by unnoticed as I delved deeper and deeper, but every lead ended in disappointment. I learned about countless summoning rituals, and intricate descriptions of demons, spirits, and even angels, but nothing addressed our peculiar situation-nothing about a spell tied to fiction.

Frustration settled in. I felt utterly lost. I know nothing. I don't know how I brought him here, nor do I know how to send him back. I don't even know about the consequences of this situation. I felt like I was grasping at straws in the dark and this was only growing my frustration. But I kept looking.

As the night wore on, my eyelids grew heavy. I struggled to stay awake, my vision blurring as fatigue crept in. Questions continued to swirl in my mind, mingling with the frustration of hitting endless dead-ends. Why had the spell chosen me? Was there a deeper purpose I had yet to understand? These thoughts danced on the edges of my consciousness, teasing me with their elusiveness. Eventually, exhaustion overtook me. My fingers stilled on the keyboard, and the laptop's glow faded as I drifted into a restless sleep, the unanswered questions and my mounting frustration haunting my dreams.

# Chapter 5

# *Unexpected Alliance*

It was 7 AM when I finally stirred from my slumber, the early morning light filtering gently through the curtains. Blinking away the remnants of sleep, I glanced around my room, taking in the familiar yet chaotic scene. My bed was a sea of scattered notes and an open laptop, remnants of my late-night study sessions that had stretched into the early hours. It has been a week since Adrian entered my life. We've spent our time reading, scouring the internet, and trying to untangle the web of our situation. And *barely* talking. Today, we are heading to New Orleans to meet Rachel Greene. We discovered that Adrian, lacking any identity, is at risk of getting into trouble since he doesn't exist in our realm. Being an introvert and generally a rule-abiding person, I had to compromise my morals to find a fraudulent way to create a passport, visa, and other identification for him. Last night, we finally secured the documents, though it came at a steep cost.

Despite the late hour at which I had finally succumbed to sleep, my internal clock had roused me early. I reached for my phone, hoping for a distraction to shake off the lingering grogginess. As the screen lit up, a notification caught my eye- a text message from Nate. In an instant, the last vestiges of sleepiness vanished, replaced by a flutter of excitement. My heart quickened as I saw his name, a smile spreading across my face. Eagerly, I opened his message, anticipation buzzing through me.

Nate: Hey, I heard about your leave. I hope you're good.

I couldn't help but smile wider at his text. He was concerned about me. Quickly, I typed a reply.

Me: Yes, I'm fine. I wasn't feeling well for the past few days. Thought I could use a break.

I put aside the scattered work on my bed and was about to get up when my phone buzzed again. Nate had texted back almost immediately. This was the first time in months he had ever replied so quickly.

Nate: You didn't tell me about this. Never mind. I'm coming to see you.

A frown creased my forehead. The initial flutter of excitement I had felt quickly turned into a knot of anxiety. Butterflies that had been happily fluttering in my stomach now seemed unsettled. Nate has been my best friend since forever but I never invited him here or anyone. Most people don't even know where I live. But the question was... How is he coming? I mean, since the day he's come into a relationship with Norah, we barely spend time together or talk... Now, how does he have time for me?

Before I could dwell on it too long, another message from Nate appeared on my screen.

Nate: What's your address?

My fingers hovered over the keyboard, uncertain of how to respond. What should I say to him?

Nate: I'm already in my car. I just need to hit your address in my GPS.

I quickly typed back.

Me: It's okay, Nate. I'm fine. You don't have to come here.

Nate: I need to see you. I want to make sure you're fine.

My heart did a backflip at his words. A warm smile spread across my face, and my cheeks flushed a deep rose red. Hesitantly, I typed my address and sent it to him. Then, I fell back on my bed, closing my eyes.

Nate Wilson Anderson.

Images of him in the classroom flooded my mind. Those warm caramel eyes captivate me every time I look into them. His lips, perfectly shaped, often break into a lopsided, boyish grin that softens his otherwise serious expression. His broad shoulders carry the weight of his confidence effortlessly, and his strong, well-defined arms only add to his air of quiet strength. And his hands—veined, expressive, and graceful—seem made for more than just holding chalk or turning the pages of a math textbook.

He moves with easy grace, each step purposeful as he paces around the classroom, gesturing smoothly to emphasize key points. He explains even the driest mathematical theories in a way that makes them seem almost poetic. Something is mesmerizing about the way he leans forward, his voice steady and reassuring, drawing his students' attention with nothing but the depth of his understanding.

His habits are equally captivating. He's always adjusting his hair, fingers combing through the dark waves absentmindedly, as if unaware of how charming the gesture is. And his glasses—black-rimmed and refined—constantly slide down his nose. When he addresses the students, he slips them off, as though he wants to connect with them more personally, his gaze clear and focused. But the moment he turns to the board to illustrate a formula, he slides them back on, his attention shifting entirely to his work. It's such a small habit, but one that somehow makes him more magnetic.

He wears his style like a second skin—an "old money" look, always refined yet understated. Crisp button-down shirts, usually in soft shades of cream or muted blue, fit perfectly under a tailored blazer that seems made just for him. He often pairs it with pleated trousers, the fabric whispering with his movements, and leather loafers that add a subtle, classic touch. A gold watch glints on his wrist, a silent reminder of his attention to detail and preference for timeless things. Every part of his appearance speaks of effortless elegance like he belongs to a different era.

I opened my eyes, a smile spreading across my face, but the figure looming above me startled me. I screamed, my heart racing in my chest.

"My goodness woman. Why do you scream so much?" Adrian complains, his hands clamped over his ears. I sit up abruptly, shooting a fiery glare at him.

"Couldn't you knock?" I snap, my hand pressed against my racing heart. "Don't you know it's wrong to come into a girl's bedroom without her permission?"

"I did. Several times," he retorts, his voice sharp. "But you seemed lost somewhere because you didn't hear me calling your name."

I open my mouth to argue, but the realization hits me like a tidal wave, silencing me. My eyes widen in panic. "Oh, no."

"What? Why are you giving me that look? The same one you had when you first saw me in your house?" Adrian asks, his brows furrowing in confusion as he stares down at me.

"Nate is coming. You have to hide. I can't let him see you here with me," I blurted out in a single, frantic breath.

"Whoa, wait. First of all, who's Nate? And why do I have to hide?" Adrian's confusion was evident, his brows furrowed as he tried to grasp the situation.

"Because you're a man. I live alone. Everyone knows that. What am I going to tell him when he sees you? Who are you?"

"A friend of yours who's staying over for a few days?" he suggested matter-of-factly. I rolled my eyes, my panic mounting. "Okay, fine. Relax. I'll stay out of the house until your boyfriend is gone. Okay?"

I paused.

"Oh, he's-he's not my boyfriend," I stammered, feeling a flush of embarrassment at the admission.

"No? Then why are you worried if he finds me here?"

"I don't want him to see any man around me," I confessed, hoping he would understand. "I like him."

There was a moment of silence before he responded, "You're weird," His annoyance was evident, and I couldn't help but smile at his blunt honesty. Then, a notification from my phone demanded my attention once more. It was another text from Nate.

Nate - Oh, I forgot to mention. Norah is coming too.

My smile faltered, replaced by a surge of disappointment and a little anger as I clenched my jaw, gripping the phone with intensity.

"Miss Kirby?" His voice broke through my thoughts, over concern etched on his features. "You're close to cracking your phone's screen with that aggression."

I looked back at my phone, and let out a sigh. Upset.

"What?"

"His girlfriend is coming with him."

"Nate is in a relationship?" His surprise was evident in both his voice and eyes. I nodded, "Yet, you like him?"

"Why, is something wrong?"

Adrian chuckled, his chuckle almost lifting my spirits. There was a certain beauty to his smile that I couldn't help but admire. He looks beautiful when he smiles.

"You sound like one of those who wreck relationships," he said, his words provoking a gasp from me.

"What do you mean?" I snapped, feeling a pang of offense, "I'm not trying to steal him, and I never have."

He chuckled, clearly amused by my reaction. "It's okay," he said, meeting my gaze with a playful smile. "There's nothing wrong with falling for someone who's already taken."

"I haven't fallen for anyone taken," I replied firmly, earning a raised eyebrow from him. "I just realized my feelings a little late, that's all."

"Oh," he said, a brief pause settling between us. Then he added, "Alright. Since you're helping me find a way back, maybe I could return the favor."

I raised an eyebrow, intrigued by his offer. "Help me with what, exactly?"

"In getting Nate," he replied with a smirk, hands casually tucked into the pockets of his beige pants. My eyes sparkled at his offer. "Every goal has a goalkeeper, right? Let's see how strong his defense really is," He winked, his words laced with mischievous confidence. I grinned, "Ah, there it is," he teased, "That smile confirms it—you're definitely a homewrecker in the making, out to break that poor girl's heart."

I gasped in a mock offense.

Without hesitation, I grabbed a nearby pillow and struck him with it. His laughter filled the room, easing the tension between us and igniting a sense of camaraderie.

# Chapter 6

## The Looming Threat

*Adrian's POV*

I was in the kitchen, stirring the pot of white sauce pasta, the aroma filling the air. The rhythmic motion was calming, a brief respite from the whirlwind of thoughts in my mind. I heard footsteps and turned to see Liza walking towards me. She looked radiant, her hair falling in soft waves, her face glowing with a freshness that made my heart skip a beat. The subtle scent of her perfume reached me, a mix of floral and citrus, and I found myself taking a deep breath, savoring it.

There's something about her, something so inviting yet paradoxically repelling. I can't quite put my finger on it. We don't speak often, but whenever we do, I feel an unexpected sense of peace and calm wash over me. From the moment I met her, I haven't sensed any negativity or ill will emanating from her. Any bitterness I once felt has completely dissipated.

She exudes genuine goodness, making it impossible for me to be rude or arrogant towards her. What impresses me the most is her determination to rectify her mistakes, despite knowing that I am not an easy challenge to overcome. Her perseverance and sincerity make me reconsider my own approach, and I find myself increasingly drawn to her enigmatic presence.

Besides, if things can be done with a smile, what's the point of perfecting my scowl?

She stopped by the kitchen island, her eyes curious as she watched me cook, "What are you doing?" Her question was simple, almost childlike, and it made me smile.

"What does a person do in a kitchen, Liza?" My response was perfectly logical, highlighting the silliness of her question, but also masking the warmth I felt at her presence. I always feel this. Her aura is very positive and full of warmth.

She rolled her eyes, a small, endearing gesture that stirred something inside me.

"I'm making white sauce pasta."

She nodded, her gaze shifting to the pot with a look of fascination that made me smile. It was just pasta, but she looked at it like it was something special, something worth paying attention to.

I took a deep breath, "I never got to say this but thanks for the other night," Her eyes met mine, grey to green ones, "I woke up starving, and the food was right there in front of me. Thank you for not letting me sleep on an empty stomach.

She smiled warmly, "It's okay."

"Also, your architect came again," I mentioned casually, watching her reaction out of the corner of my eye. "I sent him back and told him to come back when you're back from your trip," She only nodded, her eyes glued to my hands as I moved around the kitchen, preparing our meal. "And, I booked the tickets to New Orleans. We're leaving in the evening. I hope you're packed?"

She froze for a second at the mention of New Orleans but regained her composure almost immediately.

"Yup. I'm done."

"Good," I smiled, but deep down, I wanted to know what caused her to freeze but I didn't bother much. I dished out generous portions of the white sauce pasta onto our plates, seeing her smiling wider, "I hope it tastes as good as it smells."

She took her plate with eagerness, her eyes lighting up. "I'm sure it will."

As we sat down at the table, the atmosphere was filled with pleasant anticipation. She twirled a forkful of pasta and took a bite, her eyes closing briefly in appreciation.

"This is amazing," she said, her voice full of genuine pleasure, "Delicious."

"I'm glad you like it," I replied, feeling a surge of pride. "I wasn't sure if I could cook well."

She nodded, taking another bite, a look of contentment spreading across her face.

I smiled, "Thank you."

We ate in comfortable silence for a few moments, the only sounds being the clinking of cutlery. I found myself watching her, appreciating the simple joy she took in the meal. Her enthusiasm was contagious, and I felt a warmth in my chest that went beyond the satisfaction of cooking a good meal.

"Can I ask you a question?"

I raised my brows at her, "Yes?"

She hesitated for a moment as if choosing her words carefully. "Is this the first time you're out in reality, or have you come out multiple times?"

"No. This is my first time," I answered, taking another bite.

"So, how did you learn that you're in reality?" she asked, her eyes searching for mine for an answer.

"I don't know," I admitted, a thoughtful frown creasing my forehead. "I just felt it. And I still feel that if I'm not sent back, it will be a catastrophe."

"Can you explain it?"

I set my fork down, the clink against the plate echoing in the sudden silence that enveloped us. Leaning back in my chair, I felt the weight of her words settle like a heavy fog between us. How could I articulate this sensation that had become my constant companion, this inexplicable dread that seemed to coil around my heart with each passing day?

"It's... it's hard to put into words," I began, my voice barely a whisper, as if I was afraid to disturb the fragile balance of the moment. "It's like... an instinct, you know? A deep-seated feeling that something terrible is looming just beyond the horizon. I don't fully understand it myself, but it's there, gnawing at me, eating away at any semblance of peace I try to hold onto."

Her expression shifted, a flicker of concern darkened her eyes like storm clouds rolling in. The sparkle that danced within them was extinguished, replaced by a raw, unfiltered worry.

I put my hand on hers, "We'll figure it out, okay?" I reassured her gently, my words a tentative attempt to soothe the unease that lingered between us.

She nodded, her expression softening.

The sudden ring of the doorbell broke the tension.

"I think Nate's here!" she exclaimed, a spark of excitement replacing the earlier worry.

I grinned, "Fantastic. Go answer the door. I'll take the dishes to the sink," I said, picking up the plates. Her quizzical look didn't go unnoticed, "What?"

"You haven't shared your plan with me," she remarked, curiosity tinging her voice.

A playful grin danced across my lips as I replied, "You'll find out soon enough. For now, just act normal."

She shot me a puzzled glance, her eyes searching mine for answers but found her own reflection only. With a sigh, she rose from her seat and headed towards the door.

While in the kitchen, I heard them coming in. Greeting Liza. My plan is simple but fun and I was already excited to execute it. I put the dishes in the sink and waited a minute before I finally made an entrance.

Emerging from the kitchen, I found myself bathed in a spotlight of attention, every eye fixed upon my entrance. Yet, as my gaze swept over Nate, I couldn't help but feel a twinge of disappointment. How could Liza have fallen for him, I wondered, when his allure seemed so ordinary? And to see him choose that woman over Liza, it struck a chord of disbelief within me. Had he never truly seen her? Liza, a vision of unparalleled beauty and kindness, her very presence a balm to the soul. The thought of her being overlooked, dismissed for someone so undeserving, ignited a fiery indignation within me. *What a fool!*

"Hello," I greeted enthusiastically, a fake gentle smile adorning my face as I joined the group.

Nate's expression darkened upon seeing me. "You didn't tell me you had company here, Liza," He sounded more disappointed than surprised as he asked her.

"Oh, yeah. I forgot to mention. Meet Adrian. My-"

"Boyfriend," I interjected swiftly, surprising not only them but also catching Liza off guard. She blinked in complete bewilderment. A quick wink from me reassured her that it was all part of the plan, and she quickly composed herself, understanding the situation.

Extending my hand for a friendly handshake, I introduced myself, "Adrian Scott."

"Nate Wilson," he responded with a not-really-friendly smile, "Nice to meet you " I saw a flicker of displeasure which caused me to frown a little, "And this is my girlfriend, Norah Kavanagh."

Turning my gaze to Norah, I gave her the most intense look I could pull to pretend to be captivated by her beauty, "Hi," I murmured, deliberately keeping my tone low to convey the impression of being struck by her beauty. My foot!

"Hello," Norah replied shyly, her shoulders tensing ever so slightly under my gaze, a subtle sign that my feigned captivation was beginning to take effect. With a silent smirk of satisfaction, I knew that my plan was off to a promising start.

I took my seat next to Nate on purpose and we began to talk.

"So, how are you?" Nate asked Liza, getting her attention. She replied, "Better."

"I was worried about you," As he said, Liza's eyes softened, "This has never happened before. You, getting a leave. Most students hate you because you never go on leave."

She smiled, "I know, but I really needed a break this time," He nodded with a soft smile, "Thanks for coming here. I appreciate it."

He placed his hand on hers and smiled, "Always."

*C'mon, Adrian. Let's get started...*

As they talked, I observed Norah. I couldn't help but notice the contrast between her appearance and Liza's. Norah seemed a bit too put together like she had spent hours perfecting her look, whereas Liza had a more effortless beauty, like she didn't even have to try. Liza's charm came from within, shining through in her genuine smile and easygoing demeanor. She didn't need fancy clothes or makeup to impress anyone; she was just naturally captivating. In comparison, Norah seemed a bit superficial, like she was trying too hard to be attractive. As I looked back and forth between them, I couldn't shake the feeling that Liza was the one who truly stood out. There was something authentic about her that drew me in, while Norah seemed a bit more manufactured.

Norah's jaw clenched, a subtle but telling sign of her inner turmoil. I followed her gaze and found Nate engaged in a soft conversation with Liza. As I observed him with more attention, an uneasy suspicion began to gnaw at me. His demeanor, the way he gazed at her, and the tone he used while speaking to her, the gentle smile, struck me as unusual. I glanced at Norah, catching a glimpse of her face contorted with displeasure. Her eyes, burning with irritation, betrayed a simmering jealousy that she could scarcely conceal.

I couldn't help but smirk at the unfolding drama. The tableau before me was more than enough to prove that Nate harboured feelings for Liza, and Norah was painfully aware of it. As I continued to observe, I noticed the subtle nuances in their interactions. Nate's lingering glances at Liza, the way his voice softened when he spoke to her, and the slight but telling nervousness in his demeanor were all clear indicators of his affection. Liza, seemingly oblivious, responded with her usual warmth and kindness, but the contrast in Nate's behavior when he addressed Norah was stark. Norah's jealousy was not unfounded. She sat rigid, her arms crossed tightly over her chest as if shielding herself from an emotional blow. Her gaze darted between Nate and Liza, and every now and then, she'd bite her lip in an effort to contain her growing frustration.

Everything was clear in front of my eyes but I still had to check. I have to be certain before I act on this newfound understanding.

"You could have called me, you know?" Nate says softly, "We've been friends for years, Liza. Next time you feel sick, just call me. Ok?"

Before Liza could respond, I interrupted.

"Well, there is really no need," I implored, gently taking her hand away from Nate's grasp, which didn't surprise Nate but Liza also, "Liza is not alone. I'm here now and I've been taking good care of her, am I not, my love?"

"Yes," she smiled, though a cloud of confusion lingered in her eyes, "Adrian is looking after me. With him by my side, I feel like I'm in good hands. I doubt I'll get sick again."

Nate's discontent was palpable, evident in the furrow of his brow and the subtle shift in his demeanor upon learning of my presence there. Jealousy!

I smirked inside, feeling totally vindicated. Bingo! Nate's all heart-eyes for Liza, just as I figured. And Norah? Her jealous glare? Couldn't be clearer if she had a neon sign over her head!

Way to go, Adrian! Your job just got upgraded to Easy Mode. The goalie's like a sieve, and scoring is a piece of cake!

"I'm happy you've finally found someone, Liza," Norah spoke, her tone didn't sound sincere but laced with jealousy, "Nate and I were very worried about you. We were worried that you might end up like your mother. Lonely and drug addicted."

*She did not just say that...*

*How dare she?*

Norah's words lingered in the air like a bad odor, and I could see Liza struggling to maintain her composure. Her forced smile faltered for a moment, and I could tell she was hurt by Norah's callousness. Nate's silence was telling, too. He seemed conflicted, caught between his feelings for Liza and his loyalty to Norah. I, on the other hand, couldn't suppress the flash of anger that made me squint my eyes at Norah.

Liza put on a gentle smile. "Thanks, Norah. I appreciate your concern," she said, her tone betraying the sting of Norah's words even as she kept her expression soft. She was clearly trying to steer the conversation to safer ground, hoping to avoid any further discomfort or awkwardness.

Nate's eyes followed her every move, his concern evident despite his silence. He seemed torn, wanting to comfort Liza but also wary of upsetting Norah. Norah, on the other hand, appeared oblivious to the discomfort she was causing, her smile fixed and unwavering.

"And I'm also relieved to know that Nate and I no longer have to ask you to join us for dinner to make you feel less lonely. It was so hurtful to watch you eat alone in the canteen. But now, you have a man to take you out," Liza's facade of composure wavered for a moment, a flicker of hurt crossing her features before she masked it with a forced smile.

I didn't know anything about her past but seeing her discomfort and pain in her eyes, I felt protective towards her. I felt a surge of indignation at Norah's callousness. How could she speak so casually about someone's past struggles and use them as a means to belittle them?

Now, I will not clear the path for Liza. I will destroy her relationship with Nate. You just watch me, Miss Norah Kavanagh. You are going to pay for this!

A few minutes later, while the chatter continued, I found myself subtly charming Norah, shooting her smirks and glances. She was confused at first but then became comfortable. Her positive reactions only fueled my confidence to keep at it. Meanwhile, Nate remained busy with Liza, utterly unfazed by the flirtatious banter happening right under his nose. He didn't give a damn about us.

*Nice.*

I must admit, I have a knack for seduction, and Norah seemed like an easy target. But my charm wasn't the only reason why she was that easy to seduce. It was her jealousy. For her, basking in the glow of attention from Liza's man is like scoring revenge points. If only she had a clue about the real game plan. Once I was certain she was captivated by my charm, I decided to elevate my game to a whole new level.

I surveyed the glasses of wine on the table and an idea formed in my mind. With a calculated 'accidental' kick, I sent the wine cascading onto Norah's beige dress. The timing couldn't have been more perfect.

"Fuck. I'm sorry!" I exclaimed, swiftly rising from my seat and moving to her side, taking her hand in mine to guide her away from the broken glass.

"Are you okay?" Nate's concerned voice cut through the chaos, drawing Norah's attention. She reassured him with a shake of her hand. "Yes, I'm fine. But it looks like my dress is ruined."

"Not at all. We have a stain remover in the bathroom. If we are quick, it'll wash off. Come with me," Liza, ever the compassionate soul, offered her assistance.

*How daftly kind of her!*

I moved Norah's arm away before she could reach me, earning myself a look of surprise and confusion from her, "No, you stay here. The doctor advised you to stay away from water. You guys continue. I'll help her," I interjected, leading Norah away before Nate could even respond. She silently complied, not even giving Nate a chance to speak.

It seemed like she was eager to have some privacy with me. *Oh, the games we play.*

As we entered the bathroom, I handed her the stain remover and stood by her side at the sink, watching her with keen interest.

"Wow, It's really working. The stain is coming off!" she exclaimed with a hint of relief in her voice.

"You're beautiful," I murmured, capturing her attention. Our eyes met in the mirror, and I could see a flicker of surprise and uncertainty in her gaze. Stepping closer, our bodies almost touching, I continued, "I can't stop thinking about the beauty you possess. You're absolutely stunning, and your eyes... they're mesmerizing."

She smiled, looking down before meeting my eyes again, "Thank you. You're handsome too."

"Handsome?" I raised an eyebrow incredulously, a smirk dancing on my lips. "You think I'm just... Handsome?"

She remained silent, her gaze locked with mine, and I could sense the intensity of her emotions in the way her breath quickened and her heart raced.

"I'm irresistible, love," I declared confidently, closing the distance between us as I leaned closer, the air between us thick with tension.

She gulped.

I gently took the piece of cloth from her hand, my movements deliberate as I began to dab at the stain on her blouse. My fingers traced delicate patterns across her abdomen, lingering momentarily just below her breast. She didn't flinch or pull away, allowing my touch to linger without protest. Honestly, I wasn't surprised by her reaction. I know my charm is deadly.

"I admit," she murmured, leaning into my touch, "You are indeed irresistible."

I smirked, meeting her desperate, lust-filled gaze, "You shouldn't be with someone who doesn't even care about you, Norah. He didn't spare you a glance while you were there. He was too busy talking about 'school'?" My words were a brick of realization for her.

The stain was gone. I set the cloth aside and caged her between my arms by placing them on the sink behind her. Leaning in slightly, I continued, "Who talks about school when someone as exquisite as you are present in the room?"

She took a deep breath in, letting my words sink in.

I glanced at her lips briefly before meeting her gaze again. "Make better choices, Norah. You still have time," she fell mute, just blinking.

I smirked inwardly. My task was done here; the seed of doubt had been planted. Now, she would inevitably confront her boyfriend, engage in a heated argument, and ultimately end their relationship, thus paving the way for Liza. And since Nate is already into Liza, he wouldn't even try to save this relationship.

Oh, dear Norah, all set to dump your man for me, but guess what? I'm just playing around. Should I feel sorry? Nah, can't seem to find it in me.

I began to step away, intending to leave, but she seized my wrist, causing me to turn back. My eyes widened as she pressed her lips against mine. It happened so unexpectedly that I was caught off guard. This wasn't part of my plan.

But, sometimes the unexpected is just better. Like when her lips met mine, Nate's voice decided to chime in. Talk about impeccable timing. Guess the universe is on my side!

Our eyes snapped open in unison, turning towards the source of the sound. There stood Nate, his expression unreadable. Beside him stood Liza, her own shock mirroring that of anyone in her position would have felt.

# Chapter 7

# The Turbulence of the Past

*Liza's POV*

"Out of everything I thought, this was not what I expected," I said, slamming the door behind me. My mind was racing as I turned to see Adrian, casually licking his fingers, savoring the last remnants of the pasta. "You kissed her?" I couldn't believe that.

He stopped mid-lick and looked at me as if I'd offended him to some level, "First of all, I didn't kiss her, she kissed me and I don't blame her," He smirked, "I'm tempting and irresistible," I threw him a tight smile which seemed to amuse him more.

Despite my facade, there was no denying the truth-he was indeed tempting.

"So, that wasn't your plan?"

"Nope. Kissing her was never my plan. But she got carried away. So weak."

I sighed, "They have been in a relationship since senior high school. I didn't think she would drift away that easily."

"Your path was always clear, dear. You just never noticed."

I frowned, "What do you mean?"

He placed the bowl on the table with deliberate care and turned to face me fully, his eyes locking onto mine with an intensity that made it impossible to look away. "This isn't just about a kiss. It's about revealing the cracks in their so-called perfect relationship. Norah kissed me, which means she wasn't as committed to Nate as you thought. And Nate, well, he didn't even care enough to notice what was going on under his nose," He paused, letting the weight of his words sink in before continuing. "My original plan was just to create a misunderstanding in their relationship. You know, a small rift, something that would make them argue and break up. But as I watched them, it became clear that neither of them is truly loyal or in love. They're just going through the motions, holding onto a history that doesn't mean anything anymore."

"So, you're saying that was all fake?" I asked, crossing my arms against my chest.

"You could say that. You see... when a woman is in love, she wouldn't spare you a glance, but with her, I didn't have to do much. I offered what she's been craving; attention and something more than what Nate has been giving her." He shrugged, a smug smile playing on his lips. "And then, she fell head over heels for me. And it's not her fault, really. She's just a victim of my undeniable charm." he winked.

I narrowed my eyes at him, "Right."

"And Nate likes you."

I blinked, taken aback. "What?" He nodded, his focus on his pasta, "And how can you say that?" I demanded.

He looks at me, "Have you ever paid attention to how he looks at you? The way his eyes light up when you walk into the room? Or how his voice softens and he listens more intently when he's talking to you? And come on, did you really not notice his expression when he found out I'm your boyfriend? Jealousy was written all over his face."

I thought back, replaying moments in my mind. Adrian's words started to align with things I had brushed off before. Nate's lingering glances, the way he'd always find excuses to be near me, his sudden mood shifts when someone else was around us. It all started to make a disturbing kind of sense.

"Nate's been harboring feelings for you for a long time," he reiterated, his tone grave yet earnest. "He's been trapped in this relationship with Norah, going through the motions out of habit rather than genuine love. That's why he didn't put up a fight when he found Norah with me. And Norah... well, now, she has a chance to find real happiness, because she was not at all happy with him."

"Nate likes me?" I repeated to myself, the words felt foreign on my lips as I struggled to process this revelation.

"Yes, dear Liza. Nate likes you," He affirmed, his voice gentle yet confident. "If he still had feelings for Norah, he would have punched me or put up a fight. But instead, he walked away. He's happy that Norah made such a move because now he has a valid reason to end things with her. Trust me, a day later or two, he will ask you out." He winked at last.

Butterflies stirred in the depths of my stomach, their delicate wings fluttering with a frenzy that mirrored the chaos in my mind. My heart, usually a steady rhythm in the background of my consciousness, suddenly took flight, performing an acrobatic backflip that left me breathless with anticipation.

Knowing that Nate also has feelings, that the connection between us was not one-sided but mutual sent waves of joy crashing over me. A grin, wide and irrepressible, spread across my face, illuminating the room with the sheer radiance of my happiness.

I screamed with joy, startling him with my sudden reaction.

"You scream a lot, Liza," He sighed, shaking his head.

I ignored him, lost in my excitement, and kept jumping happily, feeling completely overjoyed.

*But the universe can't see me happy, can it?*

It was past noon when we arrived at the Airport. I stood there, frozen. Adrian, fully absorbed in his online world, was glued to his phone, while I fought to keep my nerves in check. The tension was suffocating, constricting my throat and making it hard to breathe.

I never expected to be overwhelmed with such intense emotions at the thought of returning to my homeland.

*Keep it together, Liza. You can do this!*

As we made our way to the terminal, I couldn't help but gulp hard, feeling the weight of apprehension settle in my chest. The prospect of an eight-hour flight loomed before me, and the mere sight of the entrance had me on the brink of losing my cool. But I knew I had to keep it together. Summoning every ounce of courage, I forced myself to walk on, determined to face whatever lay ahead with resilience.

As we settled into our seats on the flight, I felt the familiar surge of anxiety creeping in. I started taking heavy breaths in an attempt to regain my composure. Adrian noticed my distress and turned to me with a concerned expression. "You alright?" he asked.

I offered him a reassuring smile, though my grip on the armrest tightened involuntarily. "Yup. Just get a bit nervous when the flight takes off. But don't worry, I'll be fine," I replied, trying to sound more confident than I felt.

"Hey," Adrian's voice softened, his hand reaching out to gently grasp mine, "Calm down. I'm here. You can hold onto me while it takes off, okay?"

I looked into his green eyes with my grey ones, feeling a sense of comfort washing over me. With a nod, I squeezed his hand, feeling much better.

*A sharp, relentless banging on the bedroom door, each thud reverberating through the fragile walls of the old house. Lisa, a frail thirteen-year-old girl, jolted upright in her bed, her heart pounding in her chest. The room was dimly lit by the moonlight seeping through the tattered curtains, casting eerie shadows that danced on the peeling wallpaper.*

*"Lisa!" Her mother's voice, thick with anger and resentment, pierced through the silence like a knife. "Open this door right now!"*

*Tears welled up in Lisa's eyes as she hesitated, her hands gripping the sheet in fear. She knew what awaited her on the other side - her mother's wrath, a storm of violence and abuse that she could never escape. But still, a glimmer of hope remained, a desperate longing for her mother's love, despite everything.*

*"Mom, please," She begged, hoping her mother would listen to her plea, "Please don't do this."*

*But her pleas fell on deaf ears as the banging grew louder, more insistent. Lisa's heart raced as she scrambled out of bed, hiding herself as far away from the door.*

*The banging became louder and more violent, each thunderous thud sending shockwaves of terror through Lisa's trembling frame. Her heart leaped to her mouth, and tears streamed down her cheeks in a relentless cascade. Curling into a tight ball, she pulled her knees to her chest, seeking refuge from the storm of anger that raged outside her door.*

*"LIZA, OPEN THE DOOR!!" her mother's voice thundered, echoing through the room with a chilling intensity.*

*A sob escaped Lisa's lips as she pressed her hands against her ears, trying to block out the deafening noise. Amid her fear and desperation, she longed for the comforting presence of her grandmother, wishing with all her heart that she was here to shield her from the terror that engulfed her.*

*The banging intensified, shaking Lisa to her core. With a final, forceful jerk, the door flew open, revealing her mother's menacing figure in the doorway. Liza's eyes brimmed with tears as she looked at her mother in pure terror.*

*"You worthless little brat," she spat, her voice dripping with venom. "You dare to defy me? HOW DARE YOU?!"*

*Lisa's throat constricted with fear as she struggled to her feet, her legs trembling beneath her. Her mother advanced menacingly, seizing Lisa's arm with a vice-like grip.*

*"You wanna hide from me, you brat? Fine. Let me hide you in a better place!"*

*Liza's eyes widened. With a cruel tug, she dragged Lisa towards the cupboard, her heart pounding with dread.*

*"Mom, please," Lisa begged, her voice trembling as she tried to free herself from her mother's grasp. "I'm your daughter. Please."*

*"You're not my daughter," she snarled, her grip tightening as she dragged Lisa towards the closet. "You're nothing but a burden, a curse that I can't get rid of."*

*Liza somehow removed her hand and backed away but with a violent motion, she lashed out, striking Lisa across the face. The force of the blow sent Lisa sprawling to the ground, her cheek stinging with pain. Her mother yanked her up and threw her into the closet, sealing her in darkness and despair.*

*"Mom, please! Please open the door. I promise I'll never do it again. Mom, please!"*
*"Please Mom, please. Open the door, Mom. Please. I am your daughter, mom!"*

"Liza?" A familiar voice rang in my ear but I couldn't recognize it, "Liza, wake up. Liza!"

*"Open the door, mom. Please. I am your daughter, mom!"*

"LIZA!!" A harsh shake pulled me abruptly from my dream.

I snapped my eyes open and found myself back in the dimly lit plane, Adrian's concerned face hovering inches from mine.

"Hey, you were dreaming."

I gulped hard, feeling the weight of his gaze and the curious eyes of fellow passengers on me. With a shaky hand, I wiped the sweat off my face, my mind still tangled in the remnants of the nightmare. Without uttering a word, I rose unsteadily from my seat, ignoring Adrian's persistent gaze, and made my way to the washroom, seeking solace in the privacy it offered.

I splashed water on my face again and again, desperately trying to wash away the remnants of the dream. But it clung to me, vivid and unyielding, flashing before my eyes with cruel persistence. Each splash only seemed to make the images clearer, sharper, and more painful. I couldn't escape it. My heart raced with a growing sense of dread as I realized that returning to my homeland after twelve long years was resurrecting ghosts I had thought long buried.

The nightmares had returned.

I gripped the edges of the sink, my knuckles turning white with tension. I forced myself to look up and meet my own gaze in the mirror. What I saw there made my heart ache. My face was a ghostly shade of pale, beads of water clinging to my skin like tiny, cold reminders of my futile efforts to find solace. My hair hung in disheveled strands around my face, and my eyes-those eyes-were wide with terror, glistening with unshed tears.

The confident Liza Kirby I had worked so hard to become was nowhere to be seen. In her place stood a frightened, vulnerable girl. The 14-year-old Liza, scared and innocent, helpless against the memories that now flooded back with brutal force.

A tear escaped, sliding down my cheek before dropping to the floor with a soft, forlorn splash. I squeezed my eyes shut, trying to summon the strength I had built over the years. I had endured endless therapy sessions, and swallowed countless pills, all in the hope of burying these nightmares for good. And for a while, it had worked. The dreams had stopped, and the nights had been peaceful. But now, the thought of returning to the place that had once been my home was undoing all of that.

"Liza?" A voice called from outside the bathroom door, startling me. "Liza, can you hear me?"

I quickly adjusted my hair and wiped my tears, "Yes?" My voice came out shaky and low. There was a brief pause before he spoke again, "Open the door," His voice was gentle, filled with concern and warmth.

I didn't respond.

"I know you need some privacy, but I can't just sit out here knowing you're... not okay," I bit my lower lip, struggling to hold back tears, "If you need peace, you can tell me to go and I will."

I took my time, breathing deeply and trying to compose myself before finally opening the door for him. As soon as our eyes met, his green to my grey, I saw a softness and understanding in his gaze that made my walls crumble. I couldn't hold it in any longer and burst into tears, my sobs echoing in the small space.

"Oh, Liza," Without hesitation, he grabbed my wrist and pulled me into a warm, comforting hug, "It's okay, it's okay," he murmured, his hand gently caressing my hair. I moved my hands to cover my face, feeling the weight of my emotions pour out. His embrace was steady and reassuring, a safe harbor in my storm, "I don't know anything about you or why you're crying, but I just want you to know that I'm here. Okay? And as long as I'm here, nobody will ever hurt you. I promise," he whispered, his voice filled with sincerity and compassion.

I pulled back and looked him in the eyes. His green eyes met my grey, tear-filled ones. No man had ever said anything like this to me before. Nobody had ever cared about me. Not a single person on this earth had ever looked at me the way he was looking at me right now. It seemed as though my tears were causing him pain.

I felt something shift inside me, something so unusual and unexpected. My heart, which had been in hurting, suddenly felt at peace. In his arms, it felt as if there was no safer place in the world.

I tried to make sense of this overwhelming feeling. My mind was a whirlwind of thoughts and emotions. How could someone I barely knew make me feel this way? It was absurd, yet undeniable. His touch, his words, his very presence seemed to wrap around me like a protective shield. Was this what it felt like to be genuinely cared for? Was this what I had been dying to feel all these years?

I never thought I would find solace in a stranger's embrace. The walls I had built around my heart, the defenses I had meticulously constructed, were crumbling. I felt exposed, vulnerable, yet oddly safe. It was a strange sensation. I had never felt so comfortable with someone I had only known for three days. What was happening to me?

I looked deeper into his eyes, searching for answers, for some reassurance that this wasn't a fleeting moment of kindness, but something real. His gaze was steady, unwavering, filled with a sincerity that was both comforting and terrifying.

Why did this man, who had no reason to, care so much about me? What had I done to deserve such attention, such compassion?

He smiled, "Wanna get back to your seat?" I nodded, and he guided me back to our seats. As we walked, I could feel the curious eyes of the other passengers on us, making me increasingly uncomfortable. "Ignore them, Liza," he whispered, sensing my unease. I didn't respond, quickly taking my seat next to the window to avoid their gazes.

Once we were settled, he turned to me, his expression gentle. "So, do you wanna talk about it?"

I took a deep breath, "No. But thank you."

"It's okay," he said softly, and then fell silent, turning his gaze away from me. I found myself unable to look away from him. There was something about his presence that was incredibly calming, "You're staring at me, Liza."

I looked away, "I'm sorry. I found myself lost again, marveling at how someone like you can seem so real, even though I know you're fictional," An excuse.

He chuckled, his eyes twinkling with amusement. "I take that as an offense. I am a real person. The only difference is that I live in a book," I smiled. His eyes softened as he looked at me, "Smile often, Liza. It suits you."

I grinned widely, exaggerating my smile just to tease him.

He made a disapproving face, shaking his head. "No. Not like this," I couldn't help but laugh. It felt good to laugh amidst all the chaos in my mind. "And honestly, you look so hideous when you cry. I bet that's why you covered your face " he teased, his tone light and playful.

"Shut up."

He laughed at my response. I rolled my eyes playfully and looked away, gazing out the window. The view outside was a blur of clouds and sky, but I felt a sense of clarity inside me. This man, who had been a stranger only days ago, had managed to break through my walls and bring a smile to my face.

"Would you like something, ma'am?" The flight attendant's voice grabbed our attention. I shook my head. "Okay, ma'am." Then she turned to Adrian with a different smile-the smile you put on when you want someone's attention, "How about you, sir?"

"Ah, show me the menu. I'll select and let you know."

"Sure, sir," She handed him the menu and left.

I rolled my eyes again. "Every person you interact with gets a crush on you. You're not that attractive."

"Excuse me?" We made eye contact. "I am capable of bringing any girl on this planet to her knees," I responded to him with a chuckle, mocking him. "Are you challenging me, Miss Kirby?" he asked, clearly offended.

"No, I'm not challenging you, but you're so delusional," He squinted his eyes at me with a tight smile and looked at the menu. He called the flight attendant and told her the meal he wanted. A few minutes later, a different woman returned with his meal and served him with politeness.

"By the way, ma'am. You're so lucky to find a husband like him," she said to me, and I frowned. "He really cares about you," And then, she walked away.

"When you were in the restroom," he spoke, knowing too well that I needed an explanation about this, "they wouldn't let me pass. So, I had to provide a convincing explanation."

I raised my brows, "And that was?"

"Trust me," A mischievous smile danced across his lips, "You don't wanna know."

I narrowed my eyes at him, a hint of curiosity lingering in my gaze. Despite my eagerness to know, his infectious smile dissuaded me from pressing further. With a resigned sigh, I relented. "I don't know what you said, but... Thank you."

He met my gaze for a fleeting moment before responding, "You're welcome."

I smiled.

## Author's POV

"You said what?" The man in his early sixties roared, his voice reverberating off the walls like a thunderclap, "You lost the book?!" His men stood rigid, faces expressionless, heads held high. Silence cloaked the room, thick and oppressive, for they knew the storm they had unleashed, "YOU LOST ONE OF THEM?!" he bellowed, the veins in his neck bulging with fury.

"We apologize for the mistake, sir," one of his henchmen spoke up, his voice steady. "I promise we'll find it along with the remaining two."

The old man's eyes flashed with an intensity that could burn through steel. In a swift, violent motion, he grabbed a cup from the table and hurled it at the henchman's face. The cup shattered on impact, shards slicing through the air as blood trickled down the man's forehead. His eyes closed briefly before he opened them again, unflinching.

"I apologize for disappointing you, sir," he said in a monotone, his voice betraying no emotion.

The man stalked towards him, fury blazing in his eyes. His henchman could see the depths of his anger, a rage more intense than he had ever witnessed. "Do you know my purpose, Miller?" the man demanded. Miller, who had served him faithfully for years, shook his head, eyes respectfully lowered.

"I have a monumental purpose, Miller. A destiny of immense importance. The eclipse is approaching, and I need you to use every resource at your disposal to find the book before it ends up in the wrong hands."

"I will, sir," Miller responded, his voice resolute. The blood now running down his face to his neck.

"I want all six of them in my hand by the end of this month. Am I clear?"

"Yes, sir," they all chorused.

He holds his arms and looks at him with desperation, "I can't wait any longer, Miller. Find them!"

"I will, sir," Miller repeated, his voice unwavering.

"Now go get to work!"

They bowed at him and left. As they dispersed, the air crackled with tension. The weight of their mission was a heavy shroud, pressing down on them with relentless force. A renewed determination took root in Miller's heart. He will find that book, along with the remaining three.

# Chapter 8

## *Absent*

### *Liza's POV*

After an exhausting 8-hour flight, we finally touched down in New Orleans, Louisiana. I didn't dare to sleep after that dream. Fear of confronting my past again kept my eyes wide open, and Adrian, steadfast and compassionate, stayed awake because of me. His unwavering presence and concern were baffling. We have known each other for a few days only, and yet, here he was, by my side, exhibiting a level of care I found difficult to comprehend. Is he truly that good of a person, or does he simply pity me?

Since yesterday morning, he's been so nice to me, and I can't help but feel a warmth spreading through me. Before today, he was almost a complete stranger. Our interactions were minimal and strained, confined to the bare necessities of our situation. His demeanor was often cold and distant, making it hard to gauge what kind of person he truly was. The silence between us was heavy, filled with unspoken words and a palpable tension. I often wondered what he was thinking, why he kept silent, and whether we would ever move beyond this awkward phase.

But this morning, something shifted. He joked with me and offered to help me get Nate. His smiles were genuine, his laughter infectious. He's showing care in ways I didn't expect. When he hugged me, it was like he understood exactly what I needed at that moment. The hug wasn't just a gesture; it was filled with warmth and reassurance, making me feel strong and supported. His kindness and comfort are a welcome surprise, especially after the tense silence we had before. It's as if he sensed my vulnerabilities and responded with compassion, something I hadn't anticipated from him.

He's not just a stranger anymore; he's becoming a friend, someone I can rely on. His transformation from a stranger to a friend is both unexpected and heartening. I find myself looking forward to our interactions, eager to learn more about him and to see where this newfound camaraderie will take us.

I smiled, but that didn't last long when I looked at the exit. My heart almost stopped, and my feet felt glued to the spot. The memories I dreaded seemed to loom in the air. It was as if the past had come to life, wrapping me in a suffocating grip. My mind raced, and I could feel the familiar panic rising within me, threatening to consume me entirely.

Then, I felt a gentle but firm grasp. Slightly startled, I looked down at my hand and then up at Adrian who had grabbed my hand. His touch was warm and reassuring.

Despite the significance of the gesture, he seemed oblivious to it, his focus solely on moving us forward.

A wave of peace and warmth coursed through me, melting the icy fear that had gripped my heart. My eyes were drawn to his face, and in that moment, everything else faded away. The world around us dissolved into a blur, leaving only Adrian and me standing there. His calm and determination seemed to seep into me, offering a solace I hadn't felt in a long time.

"What do you want?" he asked, his voice breaking through the fog of my thoughts. I blinked, struggling to process his words, "Tell me."

"What?"

"About what do you want to do?" he repeated, his tone patient yet firm. I was too lost in him to catch a word he said. My mouth opened, then closed again. Adrian let go of my hand, and I immediately missed the warmth of his touch.

"Did you listen to what I said?" he asked, his frustration evident. I shook my head, feeling a bit embarrassed. He scoffed, rolling his eyes in a way that was more amused than annoyed, "Fine. I'll repeat. I asked if you want to check in and rest for a while or go to Rachel's house first?"

I took a deep breath, trying to clear my mind. The idea of resting sounded appealing, but I knew I wouldn't be able to sleep with my thoughts in such disarray. Meeting Rachel seemed like a better option. I needed a distraction, something to focus on other than the turmoil inside me. Besides, I had a feeling that seeing her might provide some peace of mind.

"Let's go to Rachel's house," I finally said, my voice steadier than I felt. Adrian nodded, a small smile playing on his lips.

He hailed a cab with the confidence of someone who had done this a hundred times. As he loaded our luggage into the trunk, I couldn't help but steal glances at him. His movements were fluid, purposeful, and there was a quiet strength in the way he handled everything. Once the luggage was secure, he opened the door for me, our eyes meeting briefly before I looked away.

I sat inside and breathed out.

*What's wrong with me?*

The ride to our hotel was a blur of city lights and muted sounds. At the hotel, Adrian took charge again, checking us in and making sure everything was in order, "The luggage is safe. Now, let's meet Rachel," He said.

We booked another cab and headed to Rachel's house. During the ride, he didn't speak to me, engrossed in reading articles and information related to Rachel. I sat there silently, watching the city outside and trying to focus on the task ahead.

"Do you think she'll believe us?" I questioned, looking at busy Adrian.

"Let's see about it," he replied, his eyes still focused on his phone. I nodded and looked away, feeling a mixture of anticipation and uncertainty.

As we reached her house, I felt a wave of nervousness wash over me. The situation at hand was highly unusual, but there was also a sense of confidence growing within me. The quaint, cozy house ahead exuded a positive vibe, making me hopeful.

We walked towards the house, our eyes taking in its small, charming details. Despite her fame online, Rachel's modest home suggested she was genuinely a person dedicated to helping others. I knocked and waited. A few seconds later, an old man opened the door.

"Yes?" he asked. I glanced at Adrian as he replied, "We're here to meet Rachel Greene."

"Madam is not here. She went out of town early in the morning," the man informed us.

*Shit. No!*

"Oh, when will she return?" I asked, trying to mask my disappointment.

"Wednesday," he answered.

Today was Monday, which meant we have to wait for two days.

I forced a smile, "Thank you," He returned the smile kindly and closed the door. I turned to Adrian, feeling deflated. "What now?"

"We go to the hotel and sleep," he said curtly, turning on his heel and walking away. I stood there for a moment, confused and slightly hurt.

*Is he upset?*

*Of course, he is.*

Adrian had been so caring and attentive earlier, but now his abruptness left me feeling off balance. The ride back to the hotel was silent, the air thick with tension. He was upset by the news that Rachel was out of town.

"It's only for two days, Adrian. Try not to be upset," I attempted to console him, but he responded with silence. "If we see it positively, this gives us time to explore and-" My voice faltered when he snapped his head towards me, his expression sharp and his eyes piercing. I continued, "I mean I could show you around and-

"Liza," he said through clenched teeth, "Just stay quiet."

I blinked, taken aback by his sudden change in demeanour. I nodded subtly and turned away, gazing out of the window for the rest of the journey.

Throughout the ride, I didn't utter a word. I maintained a deliberate distance from him, trying not to intrude upon his space. I doubted if he even noticed my presence or heard my breath. When we arrived at the hotel, I swiftly exited the cab and walked inside, not bothering to wait for him to walk beside me. However, we ended up standing together outside the elevator as we waited for it to arrive. I kept my gaze fixed on the floor, the awkwardness between us palpable.

"I'm sorry," Adrian's voice broke the silence, causing me to look up at him. "I shouldn't have been rude to you. I'm sorry."

"Why were you rude?" I asked softly.

He hesitated, "Long story short, the longer I stay here, the greater the danger I feel looming over this realm. I have to be sent back soon, Liza. As soon as possible."

His revelation sent a chill down my spine, realizing there was more at stake than I had understood. "I will," I replied earnestly, though uncertainty gnawed at me. I had no idea how I was going to help him return, but I needed to reassure him of my support.

He nodded back. The weight of his words hung between us as the elevator doors opened, and we stepped out onto our floor. Adrian walked me to my room and bid me goodnight before leaving. I closed the door quietly behind me and made my way towards the bed. I lay back, my legs dangling above the ground as I stared up at the ceiling. Now, two reasons were keeping me from sleeping: my turbulent past and the looming danger that Adrian had spoken of.

I closed my eyes, attempting to block out the thoughts that plagued me. For a while, I focused on trying to envision a peaceful scenario, one that might lull me into sleep. But the memory came rushing back with vivid intensity. I could see it all so clearly as if it were happening before my eyes once more. The dimly lit room, my mother's figure, her face contorted with anger and disappointment. My eyes caught the sight of the knife she was holding at me and I screamed.

My eyes shot open and I sit up straight. My heart pounding irregularly in my chest. Beads of sweat formed on my forehead, and frustration clenched at my jaw. I gripped the sheets tightly, trying to anchor myself.

"That was your past, Liza," I muttered to myself, trying to rationalize away the fear that gripped me. "Leave it in the past," I told myself but the fear persisted, refusing to be rationalized away. I lay back and closed my eyes again, trying to distract myself by focusing on the positives of being here, but my efforts were futile. My palms balled into fists as frustration mounted within me.

"Sleep, Liza. Sleep! You're not a child anymore. You've become a strong independent woman. Don't be afraid of what happened in the past. Relax and sleep," I chanted, trying to encourage myself so I don't end up living on medication again.

*"I'm here, okay?"*

Adrian's voice cut through my thoughts like a lifeline. My grip on the sheets loosened slightly, and the furrow in my brow eased as I opened my eyes. Memories of Adrian's calming presence flashed before my eyes, along with his reassuring smile.

"Adrian," I whispered his name softly under my breath.

Without hesitating, I stood up and made my way to his door.

Knock! Knock!

A few seconds later, the door opened and revealed a tired and sleepy Adrian. "Liza?" He was surprised to see me and a shade of concern behind his beautiful green eyes didn't go unnoticed by me.

"I want you to tell me a story," I blurted out, pushing past him into his room. His dishevelled appearance caught me off guard and the fact that he was shirtless made my cheeks flush with embarrassment.

He frowned, "What story?"

"A story that will help me sleep," I replied, climbing under the sheets on his bed, "I just can't sleep."

He rolled his eyes, "What are you... four?" The concern was replaced with annoyance.

"Are you going to start the story, or should I tell you one instead?"

"Fine," he sighed, moving closer and settling into the bed beside me, much to my surprise. "Start."

"What? Adrian, get out of here. We're not sleeping in the same bed!" I retorted, feeling my heart race at the sudden proximity.

He raised an eyebrow at me, "Excuse me?" He looked so hot lying over his chest shirtless next to me.

I almost lost my voice at the sight, "Go sleep on the couch," I insisted, pointing towards the nearby couch next to the window.

"Miss Liza Kirby," he said with mock formality, "It's my room, you should be the one to adjust. You go there. I didn't book two rooms to share my bed or sleep on the couch."

I clenched my jaw in frustration, "Fine. I'll go back to my room then," To my surprise, Adrian didn't protest. His indifference stung, leaving me feeling disappointed and rejected. "Are you serious?"

"What?" He grumbled, burying his face in the pillow, his tone muffled.

"I thought..." I started, but stopped myself, feeling foolish for expecting more. "Never mind."

"I want you out of my bed," he stated plainly, his voice lacking its usual warmth. "So, no, I'm not going to stop you."

Feeling hurt and frustrated, I got out of bed and left his room without another word. I scoffed bitterly and collapsed onto my bed, staring up at the ceiling with crossed arms. "Mr. Rude and moody. I hate him."

Somebody knocked. I sit up abruptly, wondering who it could be. Without thinking much, I stood up and peeked through the peek hole. It was Adrian. A grin spread across my face seeing him, but I quickly suppressed it, not wanting to reveal how happy I was to see him.

With feigned nonchalance, I opened the door.

"Yes?" I asked, crossing my hands against my chest. Adrian lifted his hand with a poker face and pushed me aside before walking past me into the room without a word. He was holding his own duvet. "Hey, you don't just barge into a woman's room without her consent!" I yelled after I regained my balance after his 'gentle' push.

"The same goes for women as well," he replied casually, dropping himself onto the couch. "You don't enter a man's room without his consent either."

I closed the door behind him, "Are you sleeping?" I asked because I wasn't able to see his face from here.

"Nope. I'm waiting for your story to start." He grumbled, "It better be interesting."

A happy smile spread across my face and I climbed under my duvet. The warmth of the blanket enveloped me, a stark contrast to the earlier chill of loneliness. "Alright," I said eagerly, propping myself up on the pillows. "Let me tell you a real-life funny story. One day...

## Author's POV

A gothic mansion stands shrouded in darkness and fog, its towering spires and weathered stone walls partially obscured by the swirling mist. Ivy climbs the façade, and the tall, intact windows give an impression of haunting grandeur. The surrounding trees, with their twisted, gnarled branches, form a nearly impenetrable barrier, adding to the sense of isolation and mystery.

In front of the mansion, a man stands, his gaze fixed on the foreboding structure. He is impeccably dressed in a crisp white shirt and beige pants, exuding an air of old money and quiet confidence. His well-built frame is evident, even in the dim light. A cigarette smolders between his lips, the glowing ember casting fleeting shadows on his face. The man bore a scar that traced a jagged line from his eyebrow to his cheekbone, slashing through his eyelid and lending his face a permanently hardened, menacing expression.

Flanking him are four guards, each dressed in sharp three-piece suits. Black and white. They stand with a poised readiness, their eyes scanning the surroundings for any sign of danger. The fog curls around them, adding an ethereal quality to the scene as if the mansion itself is alive and watching.

The man takes a long drag from his cigarette, the tip flaring brightly for a moment. He exhales slowly, the smoke mingling with the fog and dissipating into the night. His eyes remain fixed on the mansion as if trying to unlock its secrets from a distance. The eerie silence is broken only by the occasional rustle of leaves and the distant call of an owl.

"Who in his right mind would like to live here?" He mutters to himself, narrowing his eyes as he watches the mansion before him. He drops the cigarette and stomps on it as he commands, "Unlock the gate," his voice cutting through the night like a blade. The tone was thick, authoritative, and brooked no argument.

His men, well-trained and efficient, nodded and moved swiftly. The clink of metal against metal rang out as they broke the lock chaining the iron gates together.

Zach took a measured step forward, his boots crunching on the gravel path as he walked through the entrance. Each step was deliberate, a study in control and purpose, as he approached the mansion that loomed before him, unyielding.

With the information he had gathered, the woman who lives here is Liza Kirby, an English teacher by profession. But there was more to her than met the eye. She is a loner, rarely seen outside the confines of this mansion except when absolutely necessary. Quiet and reserved, seldom seen in the company of others. No friends, no boyfriend, and no familial ties to speak of, she is the sole owner of this vast, eerie property.

Zach's presence here is due to a tip that Liza Kirby was seen near the spot where he lost one of the books his boss has been desperately seeking. CCTV footage from the area showed only a few individuals passing by, and Liza was one of them. Zach had personally interviewed the other people captured in the footage, but none of them had any knowledge of the book, leaving him frustrated and disappointed. His last hope is Liza. Unfortunately, she's out of town. However, Zach isn't one to wait. Determined to find the book, he decides to invade her privacy and gather as much information as possible.

Standing before the mansion's heavy wooden door, Zach paused, taking in the silence that seemed to press down from all sides. He glanced at one of his men, who quickly stepped forward and unlocked the door. The hinges groaned in protest as the door swung open, revealing a dark, cavernous interior.

"Seems like our Liza Kirby isn't quite right in the head," he mutters to himself before stepping inside.

Zach was immediately struck by the chill that permeated the air, a damp cold that seemed to seep into his bones. The mansion's interior was a testament to its age, with walls covered in cracks and the wooden floorboards creaking underfoot.

He moved around slowly, his eyes scanning every corner, every shadow, for any sign of hidden secrets but the only thing he received was silence. The hallway stretched out before him, lined with doors on either side, all closed and locked except for one - the room where Liza presumably stayed. He signalled his men to inspect each room methodically, while he made his way towards the only open door.

The bedroom was a stark contrast to the rest of the mansion. It was illuminated by a soft, warm light, and the walls were lined with shelves overflowing with books. The air here was different, less oppressive, almost inviting. It was the room of someone who found solace in words and stories.

Zach approached the large bookshelf that dominated one wall, his eyes narrowing as he scanned the spines of countless novels. He reached out, selecting a book at random, and flipped through its pages. The room, with its semblance of normalcy, only heightened his suspicions.

A woman who loved books would indeed be drawn to a mysterious one.

His lips curled into a smirk. His keen observation left him certain that Liza had found the book and that it was with her. He would find her and the book soon enough.

Content, as he replaced the novel on the shelf, his gaze fell upon a desk cluttered with scattered papers. He moved closer, his eyes picking out details, piecing together fragments of Liza's life.

The desk was reflecting a life dedicated to education and a whirlwind of responsibilities. Papers and folders are scattered across the surface, some stacked haphazardly, others fanned out in an attempt to find the most urgent ones. Post-it notes in various bright colors are stuck to the edges of the desk and computer monitor, each scribbled with quick reminders and to-dos.

A laptop sits in the middle, surrounded by a tangle of charging cables, flash drives, and a pair of reading glasses perched precariously on top. Nearby, a half-empty coffee mug leaves a faint ring on the wood, hinting at long hours and early mornings. Textbooks and reference materials are piled high on one side, while a grade book and a planner, filled with chaotic yet organized notes, lie open on the other.

Pens, pencils, and highlighters are scattered across the desk, with a few having rolled onto the floor. A small bulletin board behind the desk is pinned with important memos, a calendar, and student artwork, adding a touch of color and warmth to the clutter. Despite the apparent chaos, there's a sense of purpose and energy, a testament to the teacher's relentless dedication and hard work.

"Sir?" One of his men calls him out. As Zach looked at him, he said, "We found out where Miss Kirby is."

"Where?" Zach asked, his voice edged with impatience.

"New Orleans."

Taking a sharp breath, Zach issued orders to his men, "Good. Quit searching this place and prepare to head to New Orleans. Our quarry awaits," His guards nodded and scattered away.

Zach took one last look around the room. He could almost sense Liza's presence and sense how boring and barren her life was. He immediately figured out that she was just a common girl who hadn't meddled with them knowingly.

# Chapter 9

# A Night Out

*Liza's POV*

A serene and peaceful morning wakes me up. Slowly, I open my eyes to find my room still cloaked in darkness. I sit up and look around. The curtains are drawn, casting long shadows that blend into the stillness of the early hour. The couch is vacant, meaning Adrian must have gone back to his room during the night. Dragging myself out of bed, I shuffle over to the window and pull the curtains aside.

The sky surprises me with its delicate palette of pink and lavender, with the faintest whispers of light touching the earth. But something feels off. I sigh, taking in the tranquil beauty that seems to herald a new day. Despite the early hours, the street below is bustling with life. Cars zoom by, and people hurry along the sidewalks, lost in their morning routines. The contrast between my quiet room and the chaotic scene outside is almost surreal.

Turning around, I am startled to see Adrian standing in the doorway, a smile tugging at the corners of his mouth.

"Ah, you're finally up," he says, stepping closer to join me at the window. "I thought you wouldn't wake up today."

I stretch, trying to shake off the remnants of sleep. "What do you mean? I don't sleep for more than eight hours. It's been a rule since birth."

Adrian's eyebrows shoot up in surprise. "It's past 6 in the evening, darling."

I frowned, a yawn escaping my mouth. He nodded, a cute smile dancing on his lips as he showed me his watch. Stunned, I grabbed his wrist to confirm the impossible. My eyes grew even wider as I saw the time-it's indeed past 6. "I've been sleeping for 18 hours?!" I exclaimed.

Adrian's chuckle fills the room. "I think you needed the rest."

"But... the light... the sky..." I stammer, turning back to the window. "It looks like the dawn".

He smiles, shaking his head gently. "It's not morning, it's evening. You've slept through the entire day. The sun is setting, not rising."

I stare at the sky, my mind struggling to comprehend. The vibrant hues that I associate with the start of a new day are actually bidding it farewell.

"Eighteen hours... I must have broken some kind of record."

Adrian laughs again, his eyes twinkling with mirth, "Well, if you did, it's a personal best. Maybe you should try for twenty next time."

"Very funny. Next time, wake me up before I hibernate."

He grins, "Deal. But only if you promise not to grumble about it."

"Don't worry. I'm a morning person," I say, shrugging nonchalantly. He nods, "Now, can you order food while I'm bathing? I'm starving."

He chuckled, "Of course, you would be. Go freshen up. I'll be waiting in my room," he says with a smile. "And, wear something warm as it's chilly outside," I nodded and was about to turn around but didn't when he added, "And yeah, last night, you promised to give me a tour of the city, but since you've already slept away the day, you owe me a night out."

My heart skips a beat. "A night out?" I ask, my voice betraying a hint of uncertainty and anxiety.

His eyebrows shoot up, "What? You wanna sleep more?"

"No, I mean-" I started, my voice trailing off uncertainly.

"Liza," he interjected firmly, his expression serious now. "While you were sleeping, I was staring at the walls, and I'm not planning to do that again. I'm gonna spend the rest of the day, out, wandering with you," His sudden declaration caught me off guard.

I had always been an introvert, finding solace in quiet moments and familiar routines. The idea of venturing out into the unknown depths of New Orleans with him, even though I trusted him implicitly, stirred up a mix of uncertainty and anxiety within me.

I let out a sigh, "Okay," A smile graced his lips, "But," His smile dropped almost immediately, "The town shuts off after 10. There's nothing left to see. No jazz, no art, not even entries to the art galleries. What are we going to do?" I lied. It's a tourist place. The town never sleeps but I have to make an excuse to avoid this night out.

He blinked in disbelief. "What? Liza, you're born here and you don't know that New Orleans is known for its vibrant nightlife and cultural scene? Bars, jazz clubs, and some art galleries often remain open late-" He paused abruptly, his expression shifting to one of suspicion. "Did you just try to fool me?" His tone turned stern, eyes narrowing as he scrutinized me.

I felt a twinge of guilt but managed a weak smile, "I... That wasn't..." His jaw clenched, "I'll be there in fifteen minutes," Saying this, I turned on my heel and dashed into the bathroom, closing the door behind me with a sigh of relief.

I couldn't help but chuckle nervously at my failed attempt to deter him from dragging me out into the vibrant nightlife of New Orleans. Adrian's seriousness only made the situation more amusing, and I knew I would have some explaining to do once I emerged.

As we stepped out into the cold evening of New Orleans, Adrian's eyes darted around with a childlike curiosity. I couldn't help but smile at his eager demeanor as we strolled through the lively streets of the French Quarter. Neon signs flickered above us, casting surreal colors onto the cobblestone pathways. The air was thick with the scent of Cajun spices and the distant strains of jazz music.

"If I hadn't researched that this town never sleeps. I would be drinking coffee with you at that hotel."

"I'm sorry," I said, "I'm not a night-out person," He nodded understandingly as we passed by bustling bars and intimate cafes where locals and tourists mingled freely under the starry sky.

"Tell me about your place," he prompted, his eyes alight with curiosity as we stepped into a quieter street.

I glanced at him with a smile, ready to share what I knew. "Well, New Orleans is steeped in history. Each street has a story, and the architecture reflects its diverse past. Take that building over there," I said, pointing to a Creole cottage adorned with intricate ironwork. "It's a perfect example of our blend of French and Spanish influences."

He nodded, clearly intrigued. "And what about the music?" he asked, tilting his head towards the distant jazz melodies.

"Ah, jazz," I replied with a grin. "It's more than just music here; it's a way of life. Jazz was born in these streets, in the smoky clubs and lively parades. It's all about improvisation and expressing the soul of the city."

I pointed out architectural wonders and shared stories of the city's founding, its struggles, and its resilience. He listened intently, absorbing each detail as if trying to piece together the puzzle of New Orleans' rich tapestry.

"And here," I said, stopping in front of a mural depicting jazz legends, "is where you can feel the heartbeat of New Orleans. These musicians-they're not just names; they're the essence of our cultural identity."

Adrian nodded thoughtfully, clearly taking it all in. "It's incredible how much history and life are woven into every corner of this city," he remarked, his admiration palpable.

I nodded, "Yes."

We continued our journey through narrow streets and hidden alleys until we arrived at a small park illuminated by flickering lanterns. A jazz band played under the canopy of ancient oak trees, their music floating through the cold air.

"So much in love," He whispered, his eyes sparkling as he watched couples dance under the moonlit sky.

"Yes," I agreed, my gaze lingering on them with a wistful smile.

"How old were you when you left the city and decided to move to the UK?" His sudden question broke the serene moment, and I hesitated before responding.

"I was fourteen," I said softly, feeling a pang of nostalgia, "and it wasn't my decision. I was forced to move out."

"Who forced you?" He asked gently, he sounded more upset than curious.

I felt a twinge of discomfort at the probing question. "I think you're getting a bit too personal now, Mr. Scott," I cautioned sternly.

He raised his hands in surrender, his expression apologetic. "I'm sorry. I didn't mean to pry."

"It's alright," I reassured him with a small smile, though the memory lingered, casting a shadow over the romantic scene before us.

He started watching the couple, a soft, amused smile playing on his lips. As I observed him, it struck me just how breathtakingly gorgeous he was. Every detail about him seemed crafted to perfection—his tousled hair that caught the light just right, the dark sweep of his lashes framing eyes that seemed to hold their own secrets, the soft curve of his lips that could shift from a smirk to a heartfelt smile with ease.

His nose, straight and defined, gave him an effortless elegance, while the sharp angles of his jawline added a touch of strength to his beauty. His physique was equally captivating—the broad shoulders, the subtle strength in his arms, and the way he carried himself with a natural confidence that was impossible to ignore.

Lost in the details of his features, I didn't realize how openly I was staring until Adrian's gaze shifted to meet mine. His eyes sparkled with warmth, and that smile—so genuine and heartwarming—spread across his lips, leaving me momentarily breathless.

I smiled back.

"Okay, now what?" He raised his brows at me, "Are you contemplating the paradox of the non-existent existence in the mortal realm?"

"Nope. I have somewhere truly amazing to show you," Before he could reply, I grabbed his hand and dragged him through the crowd. We apologized and chuckled as we weaved our way out, bumping into people and stumbling along the way.

"Where are we going?" He asked, his curiosity piqued as I quickened my pace, still holding his hand.

"Shh," I hushed him with a grin, hearing his chuckle in response.

Leading him through several alleys and streets, we finally arrived. My eyes lit up at the sight, and I turned to see Adrian mirroring my expression of awe.

When I decided to come here, a thought popped that maybe it's been discovered and wouldn't be holding the peace it used to provide to me. But after all these years, this place remained hidden from locals and tourists alike. It retained its serene, unspoiled charm.

I glanced at Adrian from the corner of my eye. He stood quietly, captivated by the beauty of the small lake before us. The moonlight falls on the lake, giving it a diamond-like sparkle on its surface.

The lake was surrounded by trees and there was no place to sit except for the wooden dock where we had settled, our feet immersed in the cool water. A chilly fog was engulfing the trees and the water surface around the corner.

The moon, hanging gracefully in the night sky, was the most captivating sight from our vantage point. Its soft glow bathed the water, creating a serene and enchanting atmosphere. The silence around us was interrupted only by the rustling of leaves in the breeze and the gentle lapping of water against the dock. It was a moment of simple beauty and tranquility.

"What usually brought you to this haunted yet strangely serene place?" He asked me, his face looking a hundred times prettier under the moonlight. I didn't answer, I couldn't. He looked so pretty that I lost my voice, "Hm?" His raised brows urged me to speak and pay attention.

"I felt peace here," I replied softly. He nodded, his gaze drifting away. Silence enveloped us once more. "Do you want to stay here longer or head back to continue our night out?" I inquired.

He sighs, "Let's sit here for a while."

I smiled and gazed at the moon for a while before leaning back and stretching out on the dock, feeling the rough wood beneath me and the cool night air against my skin. Above me, the stars twinkled relentlessly, each one a tiny beacon of light millions of miles away. They seemed so close, yet impossibly distant, reminding me of the vastness of the universe and the wonders it held.

A moment later, Adrian joined me, lying down next to me.

"Watching stars now?" His voice, a soft murmur in the quiet of the night, pulled my attention away from the shimmering sky above.

"Stars, sky, and hoping to see an alien craft," I joked, making him chuckle softly. "Don't laugh. I'm sleeping with a man who doesn't exist in this world. I would believe in absolutely anything now."

"Did you just say 'sleeping'?" Caught off guard, I met his eyes and felt my cheeks warm with a blush. He raised his brows at me, a hint of amusement lingering in his expression, "Hm?"

I hesitated before saying, "Yes. I mean, aren't we sleeping here together right now?"

He bit his lower lip and left it almost immediately, "We're not *sleeping together*, Miss Kirby. We're lying here together on the dock, under the stars," He smirked, "Choose your words wisely next time."

Embarrassed, I looked away. I could feel his gaze on me as I stared up at the sky. "You're staring," I said without looking at him.

"You don't?" he remarked calmly.

I gulped, "Yes, but I don't make you feel nervous," I regretted it the moment these words slipped my mouth. I looked at him, meeting his intense gaze. His eyes narrowed slightly, a ghost of a smile dancing on his lips. Despite the cold water chilling my feet and the chilly night, his stare seemed to ignite a fire within me, heating my entire body.

"I'm making you nervous?" He asked, amused. My heart skipped a beat, "So," he continued, his voice soft, "What kind of discomfort am I causing you to make you nervous, Miss Kirby?" His gaze falls on my lips and my heart beats increase. Now I can hear it ring in my ears.

Silence.

The sound of the wind rustling through the trees and the gentle flow of the water seemed distant, drowned out by the relentless thudding of my heart. Each beat echoed in my ears, so loud I feared he might hear it too. I swallowed hard, my gaze slipping to his lips for just a second before I met his eyes again. There was a frown etched deeply into his features, and his eyes bore into mine, searching, questioning, but revealing nothing.

Before I could speak, his expression hardened, and without warning, he looked away and sat up abruptly. His movements stiff, his posture suddenly rigid as if putting up a wall between us. The warmth that had been there moments ago dissipated, replaced by an icy detachment that made my stomach knot with uncertainty.

I remained where I was, my eyes never leaving him, trying to decipher the reason for this sudden shift. Every fiber of my being urged me to reach out, to bridge the gap that had opened between us, but I was frozen by the unfamiliar coldness in his demeanour.

Finally, he rose to his feet, his expression unreadable, and extended his hand toward me. The gesture once filled with warmth and familiarity, now felt almost formal, obligatory rather than inviting. I hesitated, the weight of the unspoken words hanging heavy between us, but there was no choice but to take his hand, even as the distance between us felt more than just physical.

Without a word, I put my hand in his and let him pull me up.

I stood beside him awkwardly, the air thick with unspoken tension.

Leaving my hand he said, "Let's go back. It's getting late, and I don't think it's safe to stay here much longer," his tone is now urgent and devoid of the earlier softness.

Still perplexed by his sudden shift in demeanour, I refrained from questioning him and simply nodded in agreement.

Together, we retraced our steps through the quiet surroundings of the tranquil dock, leaving the starlit sky behind us. The distant strains of live jazz music grew louder with each step, guiding us back toward the bustle of city life.

We wandered around the town, barely speaking. I couldn't understand Adrian's sudden change in behaviour. Just a short while ago, he had been talking to me normally, laughing and engaging in our conversation. Flirting. But now, he seemed so distant, his mood as cold and uninviting as the evening air.

After we left the lakeside, where we had shared such a peaceful moment, we headed to a small, cozy restaurant. The warmth of the place contrasted sharply with the icy silence between us. We ate in an uncomfortable quiet, the clinking of cutlery and the murmur of other diners filling the space where our conversation should have been. The awkwardness was almost tangible, and I felt completely out of place, like an intruder in what should have been a pleasant meal.

As we finished our food and paid the bill, I hoped that stepping back outside into the fresh air might ease the tension. But as we resumed our aimless walk through the town, the silence persisted, growing heavier with each step. We moved through the streets like ghosts, our interactions reduced to watching the world around us and exchanging occasional, strained smiles.

"Do you want to go back to the hotel?" I suggested, my voice hesitant. I couldn't stand the oppressive quiet any longer. Adrian glanced at me briefly, his gaze unreadable, before he looked away again as if I was Medusa and looking at me would turn him into stone. He couldn't bear to look at me.

Frustration bubbled up inside me, and I felt a frown crease on my forehead. "What's wrong with you?" I finally blurted out, unable to keep my feelings bottled up any longer. "Why are you acting this way all of a sudden?"

He raised his eyebrows, "What?"

"Did I do something wrong?" I asked, my voice tinged with desperation. "Did I say something I shouldn't have?"

Now it was his turn to frown. "What are you talking about?"

"Adrian," I paused, "You're not normal."

"I am normal."

"No, you're not!" I almost yelled, the frustration and confusion getting the better of me. My outburst finally captured his full attention, widening his eyes a little, "If I've done something to upset you, I'm sorry. I didn't mean to," He stared at me, his gaze softening, and I thought I saw a hint of a smile playing at the corners of his mouth. "Say something."

"Have you ever been to an arcade?"

I blinked, taken aback by the unexpected question. "Huh?" Out of everything, that was not even last thing I expected him to say. The sudden shift in the conversation left me momentarily speechless, my mind scrambling to catch up.

His expression softened further, and for the first time in what felt like hours, I saw a glimmer of the Adrian I knew. "There's one just behind you," he said, his voice gentler now, "Maybe we could go there and have some fun. What do you think?"

I looked back. The neon lights of the arcade came into view, casting a colorful glow on the sidewalk. I looked back at him, the tension in my chest slowly easing. His suggestion, though unexpected, felt like an olive branch, a way to break the ice that had formed between us.

"Yeah," I said finally, "I'd like that."

And then he finally gave me the smile that can melt anyone or anything, "Let's go then," He grabs my hand and heads towards the entry.

Adrian's face lit up with a boyish grin as he took in the scene. The arcade was a vibrant contrast to the subdued atmosphere we had just left behind.

He turned to me, his eyes sparkling with excitement, "What do you want to play first?"

I looked around, my eyes settling on a classic claw machine filled with plush toys. "How about that?" I pointed, feeling a sudden surge of competitiveness. "Bet you can't win me one."

He laughed, a sound that instantly lifted my spirits. "You're on," he said, then hesitated. "But first, we need some coins." I nodded.

We made our way to the coin machine and exchanged our bills for a hefty stash of shiny tokens.

Armed with our coins, we headed over to the claw machine. Adrian inserted a coin and gripped the joystick with a determined look. I watched as he maneuvered the claw, his brow furrowed in concentration. The claw hovered over a cute, stuffed panda, and I held my breath as he pressed the button to lower it. The claw descended, grabbed the panda, and lifted it slightly before dropping it back into the pile.

He groaned dramatically, "You jinxed me,"

I laughed, "My turn."

"Best of luck."

I stepped up to the machine, inserted a coin, and took a deep breath, focusing on a bright blue teddy bear. Carefully, I maneuvered the claw, trying to position it just right. With a silent prayer, I pressed the button. The claw descended, closed around the teddy bear, and lifted it slightly-only to drop it back into the pile just like Adrian's attempt. I scoffed, and Adrian burst out laughing.

"Booohh," He teased me, "Loser."

"Says the one who couldn't win one himself?"

"Oh, let me show you how it's done," He said, stepping up to the machine and inserting a coin. He maneuvered the claw with precision, and I held my breath as it descended, grabbed a cute, stuffed panda, and lifted it steadily. The claw carried the panda over to the chute and dropped it in.

"No way," I exclaimed, half-genuinely upset, half-amused. Adrian picked up the panda and handed it to me with a triumphant smile. "Thank you."

"Told you I'd win." He said and I nodded, "Anyways, let's play something else!" He grabs my hand, leading me to a basketball hoop game. "How's your shooting arm?"

"Pretty good," I said confidently, "Watch and learn." I picked up a basketball and aimed for the hoop, feeling Adrian's eyes on me. With a deep breath, I threw the ball-and missed spectacularly, the ball bouncing off the rim and rolling back to me. Adrian's laughter filled the air, making me cross my arms against my chest.

"Nice try," he said, "My turn."

He took his shot, and of course, the ball went straight through the hoop. He gave me a smug look, and I stuck my tongue out at him.

He narrowed his eyes at me, "You did not just stick your tongue out at me."

"What? Am I not supposed to?" I challenged him, my palms on my waist now. He chuckled, shaking his head.

We moved from game to game, our initial tension melting away with each burst of laughter and playful banter. At the air hockey table, we faced off with intense determination. The puck zipped back and forth, and Adrian scored a goal with a triumphant cheer.

"You can't win them all," he teased, a smile tugging at his lips.

"Rematch," I demanded, trying to keep a straight face.

This time, the puck seemed to have a mind of its own, slipping past Adrian's defenses and into his goal. "Ha!" I exclaimed, pumping my fist in victory.

"Beginner's luck," he said with a wink, but his smile was warm. I flipped my hair back proudly.

Next, we tried a dance game, stepping onto the brightly lit platforms. The upbeat music blared as we struggled to keep up with the arrows on the screen. I stumbled more than a few times, but Adrian was surprisingly good, his feet moving in quick, precise steps. By the end of the song, we were both breathless and laughing, leaning on each other for support.

"You have hidden talents," I said between gasps of laughter.

"Years of practice," he replied, still catching his breath, "You're not too bad yourself."

We took a break at the skee-ball machines, rolling the wooden balls up the ramp and trying to land them in the highest-scoring holes. Adrian managed a perfect score on his third try, earning a handful of tickets that he proudly handed to me. "For our prize fund," he said with a grin.

As the night went on, we amassed a small mountain of tickets from various games. With our combined stash, we headed over to the prize counter. We debated over what to get, finally settling on a pair of matching friendship bracelets, a small stuffed rabbit for me, and a novelty keychain for Adrian.

"Here," he said, fastening the bracelet around my wrist with deliberate care. The cool metal felt both foreign and comforting against my skin, a tangible reminder of the night. "Now you can't forget this night out ever."

I smiled, "*As if I ever could*," My voice barely above a whisper. But as the words left my lips, an awkward silence enveloped us, thick and suffocating. The reality that Adrian would soon leave, turning this magical night into nothing more than a distant memory, weighed heavily on my heart.

I wasn't supposed to be his friend. We were from different worlds, our paths never meant to cross. Yet, against all odds, we had found each other. And now, faced with the impending separation, I couldn't help but feel a deep sense of loss and sadness.

"I will miss you, Adrian," I confessed, my voice trembling as I brought my gaze to meet his.

His eyes softened, and he smiled gently, a mixture of fondness and melancholy, "You're a good person, Liza," he said, his words filled with warmth and sincerity.

We stood there, the silence between us now filled with unspoken emotions. The bracelet on my wrist was more than just a piece of jewelry; it was a symbol of our unexpected friendship and the moments we had shared. I knew that no matter where life took us, I would always carry a piece of this night with me, forever etched in my memory.

With a warm smile, just as I was about to say something, someone collided with me from behind, causing me to stumble and twist my ankle. I almost fell, but Adrian was quick to grab me, his strong arms steadying me.

"Hey, are you okay?" he asked, his voice laced with concern. I clung to him, nodding, but the pain on my face betrayed my words. He looked over at the group of men who had bumped into me, his expression darkening with anger. "Hey, you!" he called out, his voice sharp and commanding.

My eyes widened with worry, "Adrian, it's okay. It's stupid to mess with people like them," I urged, trying to defuse the situation before it escalated.

"What do you mean? They should at least apologize," he retorted, his frustration evident.

"I don't want an apology. Forget them. We should go back to the hotel. The place is about to close, and I'm tired. I want to rest," I insisted, trying to steer his attention away from the men.

He sighed, the tension in his shoulders easing slightly. "Alright. Let's go back," he agreed, though his eyes still flickered with residual anger.

We began to walk out, but with each step, the pain in my ankle intensified. I couldn't suppress a wince, and Adrian immediately noticed.

"What happened?" he asked, his eyes scanning my face. I shook my head and tried to walk again, but the pain was too much. "Did you twist your ankle?" he inquired, his voice a mix of concern and irritation. I remained silent, not wanting to admit how much it hurt. His jaw clenched as he looked back, probably hoping to find those men again.

"It's okay, it's just a normal strain," I said, attempting to downplay the pain. I took another step, but my ankle gave way, and I stumbled. I heard a scoff before Adrian turned me around and, in one swift motion, lifted me into his arms. My eyes widened in surprise, and my heart skipped a beat.

"Oh my god, Adrian, you don't have to-" I started, but he cut me off.

"Shut up," he said firmly, his grip on me secure and reassuring. I could see the determination in his eyes, and I knew there was no point in arguing. I didn't say a word as he carried me to the hotel.

In his arms, I couldn't help but feel a rush of conflicting emotions swirling within me. His concern for my well-being was evident in the way he held me gently, as if afraid to cause me any more discomfort. No one had ever held me like this before-protectively, with genuine care-and it stirred something deep inside me.

Tears welled up in my eyes, blurring my vision.

For so long, I had grown accustomed to bearing my pain alone, both physical and emotional. I had become adept at masking my hurts, pushing through challenges without showing weakness, and often forgetting to acknowledge my own needs.
In his arms, I felt safe enough to let go of the facade of strength I so often wore.

For the first time in my entire life, I wasn't alone in facing my pain. Adrian was there, holding me close, and for that, I felt a profound sense of gratitude wash over me. I leaned my head against his shoulder and let the tear fall freely, it was a release of pent-up emotions.

# Chapter 10

# Whispers of Confessions

*Adrian's POV*

I was sitting on the couch near the window, the same couch I had slept on the other day. She was sleeping peacefully in bed. The doctor had told me she had twisted her ankle and prescribed painkillers, advising her to rest and warning her against putting any pressure on her injured foot. The pain must have been excruciating, which is why she was given painkillers to help her sleep.

I got up, retrieved the ice bag from the mini-refrigerator, and took a seat on the bed near her feet. As I placed the ice bag on her swollen ankle, she winced, causing me to halt. I placed my palm on her ankle and kept it there for a while. Then, I took the ice bag and began gently applying it to reduce the swelling.

The time I've spent with her has revealed so much about her character. She's a rare gem-free of grudges, devoid of malice, and utterly selfless. Her purity of heart and soul is a stark contrast to the world around us. And her strength is truly remarkable. Twisting an ankle can be agonizing, yet she bore it with such resilience. Many would have been in tears, overwhelmed by the pain, but not Liza. She remained strong-or at least, pretended to be strong.

She has no close friends, no family, and, as seen, no boyfriend. She isn't inherently strong but rather someone who has learned to handle hardship and pain alone, whether physical or emotional. It's a lonely strength, born out of necessity rather than choice, and it breaks my heart to see someone so vibrant be so isolated.

The time she cried in my arms on the plane, I wanted to tear the world apart. Her tears hurt me deeply, cutting through my own defences. I didn't know why I felt so close to her, so protective and caring. We barely knew each other, and our journey together might end tomorrow, yet I felt an inexplicable draw to her. The same happened the other night, when I slept beside her, she cried out in her sleep. She called for her mother, whimpering and shaking. It was heart-wrenching to witness. I had to hold her hand and caress her forehead to make her feel safe, to let her know she wasn't alone.

I wonder why she feels the need to pretend to be so strong. I want to know who hurt her so deeply that she has nightmares. Who caused her such pain that she had an anxiety attack at the mere thought of returning to her birthplace? What could have happened to make her so afraid of her birthplace, a place that should be a source of comfort and familiarity?

As these questions swirled in my mind, I felt a fierce determination to uncover the truth. To understand the source of her pain and, if possible, to help her heal from it. She deserved to be free from her fears, to live without the shadows of her past haunting her.

I want to stay by her side but I can't. My heart ached at the thought of leaving her, especially when she needed someone the most. The idea of abandoning her to face her demons alone was upsetting. Yet, staying too close might be even worse, complicating her already fragile state with the uncertainty of my existence.

She's drawing me in, breaking down my defences, and becoming entangled with me in ways that could only make things worse. I can't let myself get involved with her, nor can I afford for her to become entangled with me. Whatever I feel around her has to be put to rest because it's not good for either of us.

A soft grumble from Liza brought me back to the present. She turned over in her sleep, causing her injured ankle to shift. A wince of pain crossed her face, and without thinking, I moved to her side, sitting down gently. My hand reached out to her forehead, caressing it tenderly, hoping to soothe her in some small way.

Anger simmered within me as I thought about those men who had carelessly bumped into her. They didn't even have the decency to apologize. My fists clenched at the memory, and I had to fight the urge to find them and make them pay for their callousness. But I restrained myself.

Around 10 in the morning, Liza woke up and her first word was 'food'. One thing I admire about her is her unabashed love for food-she is a true foodie, ready to eat anytime, anywhere, under any circumstances.

"Showered?" I said as soon as I got in. Her hair was damped, the drops of water cascading down her back as she looked at herself in the mirror.

I decided to move into her room here as my room is not being used by me at all.

"Oh, thank goodness you're back," She exclaimed turning to me, "I was absolutely famished!"

"I know," Placing the food on the bed, I moved swiftly to her side, scooping her up into my arms. She gasped in surprise, clinging onto my shirt for support. "I told you not to leave the bed without my assistance. The doctor was quite clear-you need rest and should avoid putting any weight on your feet for a few days."

"But I feel fine," she protested softly. "It's like magic. There's no pain or swelling anymore. Look," I shot her a stern glance, silencing her objection.

Gently, I set her back down on the bed and began arranging the food, each dish selected with care, knowing her preferences and what would bring a smile to her face.

"The reason there's no swelling or pain is because of the strong medication you've been given. Don't take unnecessary risks by acting independently," I placed a plate of food in front of her, "Now, eat!"

"Aren't you hungry?" she asked me in her soft beautiful voice, her voice so gentle that it stirred something within me. God, what's wrong with me?

I took a breath in and shook my head, "Nope. I ate when you were sleeping," She nodded and continued eating quietly while I observed her, captivated by her presence. A minute later, her fork paused midway to her lips and she glanced at me through her lashes. I raised an eyebrow. "What is it?"

"Please, don't look at me like that," she murmured, her voice barely above a whisper.

I narrowed my eyes, "Like what?"

"Like... like you're looking at me right now," she stammered, cheeks flushing pink.

I hold back the smirk, "I don't know. You tell me," I leaned forward slightly, prompting her to instinctively lean back and blink at me, "How am I looking at you?"

Her cheeks turned red.

At that moment, it took everything in me to hold back my laugh. Liza looked so funny. Her fork hovered in the air as she stared back at me, her eyes wider than usual, lips slightly parted as she breathed nervously through her mouth. Her cheeks, nose, and ears tinged with a rosy hue. She was flushed, looking like she'd melt into water if I stared at her more. Honestly, I wanted to mess with her more, but seeing how nervous I was making her, I decided to stop.

"How's the food?" I asked, pulling myself back to make her feel less intimidated.

"It's... good."

"Then eat," I urged, gesturing at her spoon which was still hanging in the air.

"Right," Awkwardly, she finally took the spoon in her mouth, casting her eyes down to avoid mine. I smiled and looked away.

"I have a question," She looked at me with curiosity with those intoxicating grey eyes. I had fist my palms to not feel that jolt again but I failed to suppress it, "How did you know about the arcade when you've never come out of the book? I mean, you know a lot of stuff," I opened my mouth to answer, carefully considering my words, but she interrupted before I could speak. "Wait, why am I even asking? Of course, you'd know. You're written in today's setting, not some ancient jinn I accidentally unleashed from a dusty lamp."

I grinned. "Who knows? Maybe the book comes with a subscription to Modern Knowledge Monthly. Or perhaps there's a secret Wi-Fi connection between the pages. You'd be amazed at the download speed in there."

She laughed, shaking her head. "Right, and next you'll tell me there's a library in there with a helpful librarian who updates you on the latest trends."

"Exactly!" I fake shouted, leaning in conspiratorially. "Her name is Mrs. Fictionstein, and she's got a direct line to all the latest happenings. She's a bit strict about late returns, though."

She rolled her eyes, but I could see the amusement in her expression. "You know, for someone from a book, you have quite the imagination."

"Imagination?" I made my voice sound offended before I added with pride, "It's a superpower."

We chuckled, but then, her phone rang, grabbing both of our attention. I reached for it on the bedside table and saw Nate's name flashing on the screen. A strange sensation twisted in my chest at the sight of his name. I couldn't quite understand it; I had no problem with him, but now, all of a sudden, his call bothered me.

Shaking off the weird feeling, I turned to Liza, who was looking at me expectantly. "Who's it?" I turned the screen toward her, and her face lit up when she saw his name.

"Nate!" she exclaimed, her voice filled with unmistakable excitement. She reached for the phone, and I handed it to her, watching as she eagerly answered his call. The way her face brightened at the mere mention of his name made that strange sensation in my chest intensify. I tried to ignore it, but it lingered, gnawing at the edges of my thoughts as I watched her talk to him with a smile that I hadn't seen before.

## Chapter 11

# *Archon Astralis*

*Liza's POV*

The day had finally arrived. Today, we were going to meet Rachel and unravel the mystery that had consumed us for so long.

As I sat in the car, a whirlwind of thoughts and emotions swirled through me, making me scratch my jeans with my nails.

*Am I nervous?*

*No!*

*Am I scared?*

*Yes!*

*Why?*

I looked at Adrian next to me and sighed.

He was looking out the window, seemingly lost in his own thoughts, unaware of my silent scrutiny.

Today, Adrian could go back to where he came from. After today, I might never see him again. The thought was unbearable. This feeling was different, deeper, and more persistent than any anxiety I had experienced before. I would miss him-the fun we had, the time we spent together, even our little conversation and argument. Each memory we had created together felt precious and irreplaceable.

I wouldn't have felt this way if he hadn't shown me what it felt like to be genuinely cared for, something I had never experienced before. My ankle had healed, but he continued to look after me with a level of care and attention I had never known. The other night, when I woke up in the middle of my sleep, I found him sleeping near my feet, with an ice bag beside him. It was such a tender, selfless act. No one had ever taken care of me like that. I hate it that after he will be gone, I would long for that kind of attention and care again.

I took a deep breath, trying to steady myself, to calm the turmoil within.

In my entire life, I had never found it easy to make friends. Partly because I didn't know how, and partly because no one seemed interested in me. But Adrian had become my friend almost effortlessly, within just a week. He should have hated being thrust into a situation that wasn't his own, yet he had embraced it, looking after me with such generosity and kindness. It made me realize just how much I had been missing in my life.

Sensing that Adrian was about to turn and look at me, I quickly looked away, feeling a sudden rush of vulnerability. I could feel his gaze lingering on me for a moment before he turned his attention back to the window. The thought that he would soon be gone filled me with a profound sadness. He has to leave, but the emptiness he would leave behind felt almost unbearable.

I'm going to miss you so bad.

As the car continued its journey towards our destination, my mind raced with all the things I wanted to say but couldn't find the courage to. I wanted to thank him, to tell him how much his presence had meant to me, how deeply he had touched my heart. But the words stuck in my throat, and all I could do was sit there in silence, hoping that somehow, he already knew.

When the car arrived at our destination, my heart started pounding in my chest. I should feel a rush of joy, relief even, knowing that the mystery was about to unravel, the danger looming over us will die. But instead, a heavy dread settled over me, a sense of impending loss that I couldn't shake off.

With each step towards the door, it felt like my heart was getting daggered. My feet were momentarily halting but I kept pushing forward. I had no idea I'd feel this way when it's time for him to go.

Adrian, on the other hand, seemed oddly serene. There was a calmness about him, an almost palpable sense of relief, as if he was finally approaching a long-awaited resolution. His face was composed, his posture relaxed. He exuded a sense of peace that contrasted sharply with my inner chaos. It bothered me, this disparity between us.

*How could he be so at ease when everything feels so uncertain to me?*

We stood at the porch, in front of the door. Taking a deep breath, I raised my hand and rang the doorbell. The chime echoed in the stillness, each note amplifying my anxiety. We waited, the seconds dragging on interminably. Finally, the door creaked open, revealing the same man who had greeted us just days before. He raised an eyebrow, clearly not expecting us.

"Yes?" he inquired, his tone clipped.

"Uh, we came the other day to meet Mrs. Greene?" I stammered, surprised that he forgot us so quickly. His expression softened with recognition, "Is she back?" I asked, my voice a mix of hope and apprehension, a part of me wishing she wasn't.

He gave a nod, "Yes. Let me inform her about your arrival. Please wait here," Then he disappeared into the house.

Adrian and I stood in silence, an invisible wall between us. I shifted my weight from one foot to the other, trying to ground myself. The door loomed large before us, a barrier between the present confusion and the answers we sought.

"I have this feeling that she will have answers to all our questions," Adrian said suddenly, snapping me out of my reverie. His eyes locked onto mine, searching for my thoughts, "What do you think?"

I shrugged, trying to appear nonchalant. "Let's see. I'm hoping for the best," He nodded, his gaze drifting away, "You were right about, Nate," I continued, breaking the silence. His attention snapped back to me, "You said he'd ask me out soon. Last night, he called me again and asked me out."

Adrian smiled. "Congratulations."

I nodded, forcing a smile that didn't reach my eyes. I should have been ecstatic-this was the moment I'd dreamed of for years. Yet, as I stood there, I felt nothing. The joy I pretended to feel was hollow, a mask to hide the emptiness inside.

Maybe the fact that I was about to lose a friend was making me so upset that I couldn't even muster the energy to be happy for Nate finally asking me out. It felt like a cruel twist of fate, the timing of it all.

The door opened, drawing our attention back to the man who gestured for us to enter. "Please come in," he said with a gentle smile. We stepped inside, instantly enveloped by the warmth and elegance of the house. The aura was overwhelmingly positive, and I felt a wave of calm wash over me.

We followed the man inside and found Mrs. Greene seated on a plush sofa, a delicate teacup in hand. Seeing us, she set her cup down and rose to greet us.

"Hello, Mrs. Greene. I'm Adrian Scott, and this is my friend, Liza Kirby," Adrian introduced us, his voice steady.

She nodded, "Hello. Please, have a seat," her smile warm but her gaze piercing. I felt small under her scrutiny, as if she could see right through me. We took our seat and watched her as she sat down too before us, "Robert, please get something for our guests," The man nodded and returned with two glasses of water.

"Thank you," I took a glass with a warm smile but Adrian declined. Maybe he was not thirsty.

"So, how may I help you?" she asked, her tone polite. Despite her welcoming demeanour, a strange feeling gnawed at me. I felt a connection towards her and it was very awkward because I'm meeting her for the first time.

"Yes, but before I speak, I must warn you that what I'm about to say will sound ridiculous if you don't know about it already," Adrian began cautiously. She nodded, encouraging him to continue. "I'm not human."

Mrs. Greene's brow furrowed, and she glanced at me for confirmation. I nodded, my lips pressed tightly together.

"Anything non-human cannot enter this house. If you're here to play games, I suggest you don't. My time is valuable, and I won't have it wasted," she warned us, her voice firm.

"Mrs. Greene," I interjected, "He's telling the truth. I'm the one who has accidentally summoned him," She inhaled deeply, her expression a mix of anger and disbelief, "I swear, I freaked out myself when I realized."

"Alright. Who is he, then? Satan, demons, spirits, angels, and supernatural beings cannot cross this threshold. So, who have you summoned if not any of those?"

I fumbled in my purse and handed it to her the book, "A fictional character," I replied, my voice hesitant. Her eyes widened in shock. She examined it carefully before looking at Adrian, then back at me, "So, you know it's possible?"

"Where did you get it?" She demanded, ignoring my question.

"I-I found it."

"Where?"

"Next to a bus stand," I answered, "It caught my attention almost immediately and I couldn't leave it there. So, I brought it home."

"How did you do it? How did you summon him?" She asked, her voice demanding. I told her everything that happened that night and her dominating and scary composure relaxed and she put the book on the table, "How did you realize that you had actually summoned him out of the book?"

I looked at Adrian who was silently listening and observing us. *Why is he so chill?*

I replied, "He appeared in my house out of nowhere. I freaked out and had him jailed," I paused, "The next evening, I found a car in my backyard. I didn't recognize it at first, but then I remembered it from his story. It was the same car, with the number plate one zero one zero. I checked the book, and the number appeared the same. To recheck, I flipped the pages again and the car was gone. Then I realized Adrian wasn't in the pages anymore either."

"You never told me about this," Adrian's voice snapped me back to him, "Why didn't you tell me about it?"

I blinked, at a loss for words.

*Was I supposed to?*

"It's not a novel, Liza," Rachel's voice snaps both of our attention to her," Placing the book on the table ahead, she adds, "It's a tome."

"A tome?" I asked, frowning. She remained silent, her eyes narrowing as she studied me. I lifted my shoulders, "What?"

"Tell me about yourself, Liza," she demanded, her gaze never wavering. "And don't lie to me."

"Me?" I spoke hesitantly and looked at Adrian who was watching us silently. His expressions were calm, "Uh, but aren't you supposed to be more interested in Adrian here since he's the one who isn't from this realm?" I asked, bewildered by her sudden interest in me rather than Adrian, the supposed anomaly.

She took a deep breath and ran her hand over the book, murmuring something under her breath as she did. The once-beautiful cover now looked ancient, its surface weathered and worn. I gasped, my eyes widening in shock. The room spun around me as I struggled to comprehend the gravity of the situation.

"The tome you're seeing here isn't an ordinary book; it's a magical artifact created by ancient sorcerers. These sorcerers embedded the spell within the text, making the book a powerful conduit for bringing fictional entities to life. For the spell to work, a specific set of conditions must be met. The blood of the most powerful and the soul creator of this spell.

The blood of *Archon Astralis*. And from your reaction, it's clear you have no idea where your bloodline comes from."

"What-What do you mean?" I asked in a shaky voice. She replies, "The reason you managed to bring *him* into the real world is because you're the descendant of Archon Astralis, Liza. You're a witch."

# Chapter 12

# The Six Tomes

*18 years ago.*

The wind outside was slow and warm, a gentle caress that whispered through the night. It was the heart of summer, and the world outside the window was bathed in a serene, dark tranquillity. Only the symphony of night insects disturbed the silence, their chorus a soothing backdrop to the stillness. A seven-year-old girl lay in bed, her wide eyes fixed on the star-studded sky. There was something comforting about the quietude, a sense of peace that wrapped around her like a warm blanket. At this moment, free from the noise and bustle of the day, she found an odd solace, feeling a connection to the world that was deeper than usual.

"Lizzie?" The soft, affectionate call of her grandmother snapped her out of her reverie. She turned her head to see her grandmother approaching with a bowl of steaming soup.

The old woman smiled warmly, her eyes crinkling at the corners. Despite being in her early sixties, she bore few wrinkles and seemed much younger than her years, a testament to a life lived with grace and love.

"What are you looking at, honey?" she asked, her voice as gentle as the summer breeze.

Liza returned her smile, a light shining in her young eyes. "I was looking at this serene and beautiful night outside. It's so peaceful!"

Her grandmother nodded, placing the bowl of soup on her lap as she settled beside Liza. "You love nights," she said, her tone filled with understanding. "I love nights too. It's peaceful and quiet."

Liza's eyes lit up with excitement as she sniffed the aroma wafting from the bowl. "Is it tomato soup?" she exclaimed, her voice brimming with anticipation. Her grandmother nodded with a smile. "Thank you!" Happily, Liza reached for the bowl, but her grandmother gently slapped her hand away, surprising her.

"It's hot. Let me feed you!" With a tender smile, her grandmother picked up the spoon and blew on it to cool it down and began to feed her, each spoonful offered with love and care.

"Nana, why do you live here and not with us?" Liza asked between bites, her curiosity shining through her innocent eyes. Her grandmother paused, choosing her words with care.

"Because I like it here more, sweetheart."

Liza nodded, her voice dropping to a soft, contemplative tone. "Yeah, I like it here too."

Her grandmother smiled, knowing the child's heart, "I know, and that's why you're allowed to come here whenever you want to."

"But I'm only seven, Nana. I can't fly to you like a witch!" Liza's eyes had a shade of disappointment, and her grandmother laughed, a sound like the tinkling of wind chimes. "I wish I was. I would then summon you home whenever I want to!"

Her grandmother laughed again, shaking her head and putting the bowl on the bedside table.

"You can still do that by dialing my number. You memorized it, didn't you?"

"Yes. I do. I'd call you when I miss you and you'll pick. Alright?"

Her grandmother nodded, "I'd always pick my sweetheart. Always!" Liza's eyes shined as she grinned, "Okay, now it's time for you to sleep," her grandmother gently put Liza under the duvet and reached to turn off the light. But Liza grabbed her hand, snapping her grandmother's attention to her. "What happened, honey?" her grandmother asked, her brows knitting in concern.

"Can you tell me a story?" Liza's voice was soft, almost shy as if she feared her request would be denied. Her grandmother raised her eyebrows in surprise, frowning slightly. "A story?" Liza nodded, her eyes shining with expectation. Her grandmother's heart melted at the sight of her innocent granddaughter. She reached out, caressing Liza's hair with a touch so gentle it was almost like a whisper. She smiled, "Of course, darling," she said softly, taking a seat on the edge of the bed. Liza beamed, her face lighting up with pure joy as she snuggled deeper into the covers, her eyes never leaving her grandmother's face.

"Tonight, I'll tell you about the most wondrous, and dangerous, book ever created."

Liza's eyes widened with excitement as she settled closer to her grandmother. "What kind of book, Grandma?"

"A magical book," Grandmother began, her voice dropping to a dramatic whisper. "This was no ordinary tome, but a powerful artifact crafted by ancient sorcerers. Within its pages, they embedded a spell known as Reality-Binding."

"Reality-Binding?" Liza repeated, her curiosity piqued.

"Yes," Grandmother nodded. "This spell was the work of the Seven Covens of Witches: Sylvan Shadows - This coven is connected to the deep, mysterious forests and the magic that thrives within them. Witches here draw their power from nature and the ancient spirits of the woods. Lunar Veil - The Lunar Veil quarter is tied to the moon and its phases, harnessing lunar energy for their rituals and spells. Witches in this quarter are attuned to the cycles of the moon and use its power for divination and transformation. Mystic Flames - This quarter is associated with fire and the transformative power it holds. Witches here are masters of candle magic, pyromancy, and using the energy of flames for both creation and destruction.

"Ethereal Echoes - Linked to the element of air and the realms beyond the physical world, the Ethereal Echoes quarter focuses on communication with spirits, astral travel, and using the wind's energy in their magic. Aqueous Abyss - The Aqueous Abyss quarter draws its strength from water, the oceans, and the mysteries they hold. Witches in this quarter excel in water-based divination, healing, and connecting with the deep, hidden aspects of the psyche.

"Earthen Roots - Connected to the earth and its grounding energies, the Earthen Roots quarter focuses on herbalism, crystal magic, and using the earth's stability for protection and strength in their spells. Celestial Ascendants - This quarter is associated with the stars, planets, and the cosmic forces that influence life on Earth. Witches here are skilled in astrology, cosmic magic, and harnessing the power of the universe".

"Together, they assisted the most powerful sorcerer of them all, the Archon Astralis, in creating the Echo of Realms Spell. This spell allowed them to summon knowledgeable and powerful fictional characters during times of dire need. Imagine calling upon legendary heroes to save the day during natural disasters, wars, or when humanity faced existential threats!"

"Isn't it wrong to go against nature or the universe?" Liza asked, her brows furrowing in thought.

Her grandmother smiled, "It is, that's why they had to suffer! The spell was designed to bring forth characters from the most inspiring and powerful stories ever told. These characters would appear in the real world to aid in times of dire need, bringing their unique abilities and insights to bear against the threats at hand."

"But there was a crucial safeguard," The grandmother paused. "The summoned characters had to be returned to their fictional worlds after their task was complete. This was to maintain the delicate balance between reality and fiction. Without this balance, our world could unravel, blending with the realms of imagination in chaotic and uncontrollable ways."

Grandmother's voice grew somber as she went on, "Six tomes were created, each one holding a specific power. One book contained a character who could control fire; others could control water, wind, earth, and illusion. But one tome was different. This book contained the most powerful character of all-a being whose abilities were unmatched and whose wisdom was unparalleled. His name was Zephyr Valtor. When this character was summoned, he was so fascinated by our world that he insisted on staying."

"What happened then?" Liza asked, leaning forward in anticipation.

"The Echo of Realms Spell was designed with a strict rule: no character could stay in our world for too long. Prolonged disruption could weaken the barriers between worlds, leading to catastrophic consequences. Despite Zephyr's power and plea to remain, Archon Astralis knew the risks were too great. The sorcerer used his wit and immense power to send Zephyr back, but it was not easy. Zephyr's anger was like a storm, threatening to tear the very fabric of reality apart. In his wrath, he caused immense disruption and killed many people, especially the sorcerers. But in the end, he was sent back!"

"After this ordeal, the sorcerers realized the true peril of meddling with the universe. They understood that even the slightest imbalance could have disastrous effects. With heavy hearts, they decided to destroy all six books to prevent such danger from ever arising again."

Liza sat in silence, absorbing the thrilling tale. "So, no one can use the Echo of Realms Spell anymore?"

"That's right," Grandmother said with a nod. "The knowledge and power of those books are lost to time. It's a reminder, my dear Liza, that even the greatest magic must be wielded with caution and respect for the delicate balance of our world."

Present time.

## Liza's POV

I sat there, unresponsive, my eyes locked onto Rachel. The bed story I heard in my childhood is giving me a headspin. My grandmother's tales, the ones she spun with such vivid detail, were real. The books exist, and Adrian is living proof.

"Liza, what's wrong?" Rachel's voice pierced the haze clouding my thoughts. Her concern was palpable, her eyes a mix of worry and curiosity.

I swallowed hard, my throat dry. "I can't believe it," I murmured, more to myself than to her. "My grandmother used to tell me bedtime stories, one of them was about six magical books crafted to protect the world. She spoke of a name-Archon Astralis. I always thought they were just stories, fanciful tales to lull me to sleep. But now..."

"So you do know something about this?" Rachel interrupted, her tone sharper, demanding.

I shook my head slowly, the weight of disbelief pressing down on me. "No, not really. All I know is..." I took a deep breath, closing my eyes briefly to steady myself. "This is overwhelming. It's like everything I thought I knew has been a lie. My world seems to have turned upside down."

"It's okay. Drink some water." Rachel's voice softened, her hand extending a glass of water towards me. "I understand, Liza. This is a monumental revelation. It's normal to feel overwhelmed. You've lived your life under the assumption that these were mere stories, and now you find out you're a descendant of one of the most powerful sorcerers in history."

I nodded numbly, the water soothing my parched throat.

"What exactly did your grandmother tell you?" Rachel pressed gently, her eyes never leaving mine.

"She just told me about the books, why they were turned into magical artifacts, and why they were supposedly destroyed."

Rachel's expression hardened. "The tomes weren't destroyed," she stated firmly. "They were preserved. I wonder why your grandmother would lie to you."

"My grandmother wouldn't lie," I replied, my voice trembling with conviction. "She said the tomes were destroyed to prevent Zephyr from rising again."

Rachel's eyes widened with surprise. "You know about Zephyr, too? What else did she tell you about him?"

Before I could answer, Adrian's voice cut through the tension. "Wait, who's Zephyr?" He looked at me, his confusion evident. "I don't understand any of this. Fill me in," His bewilderment was almost palpable, and I stared at him, trying to fathom why he had kept his powers hidden from me all this time. He raised his brows, a defensive gesture. "What?"

"Why didn't you tell me you possess powers?" I demanded, feeling a surge of betrayal and hurt.

His expression softened, a hint of regret in his eyes. "I didn't think it was something you needed to know."

"What power do you have, Adrian?" Rachel asked him. Adrian sighed deeply, his shoulders sagging as if under an invisible burden. Keeping his gaze fixed on me, he snapped his fingers, and a flame ignited around his index finger, casting a flickering light on his face.

The sight was mesmerizing, the dancing fire reflecting in my eyes. It was oddly beautiful, and despite the turmoil within me, I couldn't tear my gaze away.

"Flame's Dominion," Said Rachel, staring at the fire.

# Chapter 13

# Flames and Taffeta

*Liza's POV*

I glared at him, arms tightly crossed against my chest, as I stood before the terrace railing. The cool night air did little to temper the fire within me. Adrian, on the other hand, kept attempting to make eye contact, only to glance away every time our eyes met. His inability to withstand the intensity of my gaze infuriated me.

Finally, he let out a frustrated sigh, his shoulders slumping slightly. "Stop staring at me, Liza," he pleaded, his voice tinged with weariness.

I clenched my jaw, feeling anger bubbling up inside me, threatening to spill over. "You lied to me, Adrian," I spat out, my words laced with betrayal and hurt.

His expression turned defensive, his brows knitting together in confusion and offense. "When did I lie to you?" he demanded.

"You lied about not knowing anything about yourself," I accused, my voice rising with each word. "You have powers, and you didn't think it necessary to let me know?"

He scoffed, a bitter sound that cut through the tension like a knife. "I still don't know anything about myself! All I know is I can do this." He snapped his fingers, and flames ignited on his four fingers, casting an eerie green glow in the dim light.

The sight of the dancing flames on his hand reminded me of how drastically my life had changed. Just that morning, I had been sipping coffee in my kitchen, dreaming of having my own family one day. By nightfall, I had met him, and my life had been irrevocably altered.

From that fateful night to this one, my understanding of the world had been turned upside down. First, I learned that Adrian was from a different realm. Second, I discovered that I was a witch. Third, Adrian possessed powers. Fourth, my ancestors had created a spell that brought fictional characters to life. Fifth, I could perform magic too. Sixth, the universe could collapse if Adrian wasn't sent back. Seventh, there were five more tomes scattered across the world, protected by other covens.

In a week, I had gone from drinking coffee in my kitchen to grappling with mind-bending revelations. It was almost too much to bear.

Adrian closed his fist, extinguishing the flames. I blinked and met his gaze. "But now you know," he said quietly, lowering his arm.

"Are you sure I know everything now?" I asked, my voice laced with skepticism.

There was a slight pause as he looked at me, his hard expression softening momentarily. "Everything is right in front of you, Liza," he finally said, his tone firm yet tinged with vulnerability. I pressed my lips together in a thin line, nodding slowly.

I was mad at him, but I could see that it wasn't as big of a deal as I had initially thought. Reluctantly, I decided to let it slide.

"I looked everywhere," a voice interrupted, drawing our attention to Rachel, who had just entered the balcony. After our talk in the hall, she had gone off in search of anything that might help us send Adrian back and had sent us to her guest room. "But I couldn't find anything. The grimoires I have don't contain any spells that can send him back either."

Strangely, the news didn't make me sad. Adrian, however, looked deeply disappointed.

"What do we do then?" I asked, trying to feign disappointment. I knew I should be worried because I knew the consequences, and Grandma had been very clear about not defying the universe when she told me the story. But a part of me wished to keep Adrian here, even though I knew I couldn't. He had to go.

"Where are your parents, Liza?" Rachel asked, her tone probing. My heart skipped a beat, and I raised my brows in confusion. "Your parents. If your grandma knew about your history, I'm sure your parents must have some idea about it too," Rachel explained.

I stood there like a statue, my mind reeling. I gulped, "My dad died when I was ten, and my mother and I barely talk," I finally said, feeling a heavy weight on my heart after speaking about my father.

"When was the last time you talked to her?" Adrian interjected, drawing my attention.

"Twelve years ago," I replied, my voice tight with suppressed emotion.

An awkward silence coated the atmosphere before Rachel decided to break it.

"Liza you have to try to talk to her about this," she said, "She's your mother. Plus, she would be happy to see you after all these years. Do you think you know where she might be?" I nodded, feeling a knot tightening in my stomach. "Where?"

"Here. In New Orleans."

"Liza," She held my arm and looked in my face, "I want you to go to your mother and ask her about this. Since you're her daughter, she must be a witch too and might have the answers we're seeking."

My heart stopped beating. The thought of going home and meeting her was almost too much to bear.

"G-Go home?" I stammered, my voice barely audible. She nodded. I fisted my palms to maintain a semblance of normalcy despite the emotional storm brewing inside me. Her expression turned into one of confusion as she watched my reaction. I gulped, clenching my fists so tightly that my nails dug into my skin, almost drawing blood.

"Is there a problem?" She asked, her tone concerned.

I nodded, feeling my heart race with anxiety. "Yes, there is. I spent fourteen years with her, and I can assure you, she knows nothing about it. Just like I didn't. And why do you need her help? You know everything. You can do magic. Why can't you do it?" Take any excuse but don't make me go there. Please!

"Archon created this spell, and he alone sent Zephyr back along with the other tome's characters. Only he knows how he did it. In fact, without his help, bringing them to life was impossible. You managed to do it because you're his descendant. I believe only you can send him back. We just have to figure out how."

I stood there, trying to process her words. How do I do it? The mere thought of going home terrified me. I tried to speak, but the words wouldn't come. My heart was racing, and my chest felt tight as if I couldn't breathe. I parted my lips slightly, struggling to draw in air. Panic rose within me, threatening to consume me entirely.

*No. Not now! Don't panic.*

The struggle to breathe normally intensified.

*No, no, no, no.*

I fisted my palms tighter, my shoulders moving transparently as I took a deep breath in. Then, a soft and warm palm gripped my wrist, snapping me out of my spiralling thoughts.

"We'll speak to her," Adrian said, holding my hand firmly. I looked at his face, his gaze fixed on Rachel. His lips were moving, but I couldn't hear anything. It felt as if the world had halted, and it was just the two of us. My racing heart began to calm. I wasn't shaking, nor was I struggling to breathe. I felt a sense of calm wash over me, the heavy weight on my chest lifting.

"You okay with it?" he asked, his voice gentle. I blinked, looking from Rachel to Adrian, and nodded absentmindedly. He grinned, a boyish excitement lighting up his face. "Cool."

"Okay, good. You bring your luggage here. In the meantime, I'll get you some clothes to wear for tonight's ball."

I frowned, my mind struggling to keep up. "A ball?" I whispered to myself, confused.

"Please make yourself at home. I'll ask Robert to get you something to eat. Goodbye," Then, she left us alone.

"Chocolate?" Adrian asked, holding out a packet. His eyes were soft and comforting. I nodded, taking it from him, and turned my gaze back to the scenery.

"Do you have your mother's number?" he asked, snapping me out of my thoughts, "You don't."

"I do," I turned my gaze back to the scenery and added, "But I haven't ever called her."

There was a brief pause before I felt his hand on mine again. I looked at him, his eyes filled with understanding and concern.

"I wouldn't ask you why you feel anxious at the mention of your home, but I promise, I won't leave you alone in any circumstances or let you feel even slightly uncomfortable. I'm with you," He squeezed my hand gently, his words comforting and sincere. I couldn't help but nod, earning myself a big smile from him. "Good, now let's go shopping."

I blinked in confusion, "Shopping?" He nodded enthusiastically, "Why? I've brought enough clothes."

"Did you bring gowns and corsets?"

I frowned, "No. Why on earth would I bring gowns here?"

"Rachel has invited us to a ball tonight," he said, his eyes sparkling with anticipation. "And I'm not waiting for her to bring some old clothes. So, we'll purchase."

"A ball? Seriously? How can she even think about going to a ball when we have this huge crisis on our hands?"

"She was invited, and she needs to go. Plus, she thinks someone there might have the answers we need. She asked us to join her so we don't sit around here, wasting the night while she's out there trying to find a solution."

Adrian's excitement was contagious, but I couldn't shake off the lingering anxiety about the prospect of going to that house and seeing my mother. As we walked through the bustling city streets, I tried to focus on the present, on the simple pleasure of being out with Adrian. The city was alive with people, the sidewalks crowded with shoppers, tourists, and street performers. The air was filled with the sounds of laughter, conversation, and the occasional street musician's melody.

Adrian, seemingly attuned to my every emotion, kept a firm yet gentle hold on my hand as we navigated the crowded streets. He talked animatedly about the shops we passed, pointing out interesting displays and quirky storefronts, his enthusiasm a welcome distraction from my worries.

"Look at that," he said, pointing to a boutique with an elegant window display featuring mannequins in stunning evening gowns. "I think we might find something perfect there."

I glanced at the boutique, its name-"Elysian Elegance"-emblazoned in gold lettering above the door. The gowns in the window were beautiful, their fabrics shimmering under the soft lights. I felt a mix of excitement and nervousness as we stepped inside.

The interior of the boutique was even more impressive, with racks of exquisite dresses in every colour imaginable. The air was filled with the subtle scent of lavender and vanilla, adding to the luxurious atmosphere. A saleswoman approached us with a warm smile, her eyes sparkling with professional curiosity.

"Welcome to Elysian Elegance. How can I assist you today?" she asked, her voice melodic and soothing.

Adrian took the lead, his confidence evident. "We're looking for a gown for the lady here. Something elegant, suitable for a ball tonight."

The saleswoman's eyes lit up with understanding. "Of course. We have a wonderful selection of evening gowns. What colour and style do you prefer, ma'am?"

"Uh, why don't you show me a few different styles and let me decide what I like the best?" I suggested.

The saleswoman nodded in agreement and led us to a section of the store where various gowns were displayed. She began pulling out dresses in a range of colors and styles, draping them over her arm as she spoke.

"We have classic ball gowns, modern sleek designs, and everything in between. Let's start with these and see what catches your eye."

I took a deep breath, feeling a bit overwhelmed but also excited. "Alright," I said, my voice steadier than I felt. "Let's see what we've got."

The first dress I tried on was a deep emerald green, its bodice adorned with intricate beadwork. As I stepped out of the dressing room, Adrian's eyes widened in appreciation. "You look amazing," he said, his voice filled with genuine admiration.

I smiled and turned to look at myself in the mirror, hardly recognizing the person staring back at me. The dress was beautiful, the colour complementing my skin tone perfectly. But as much as I liked it, I didn't feel like it was the one.

"What? You don't like it?" He asked me. I looked at him through the mirror and replied, "I do. I just want to try these on and decide."

He nodded.

Next, I tried on a soft lavender gown with delicate lace sleeves and a flowing skirt. The fabric felt like a dream against my skin, but when I stepped out to show Adrian, he tilted his head thoughtfully. "It's lovely, but I think we can find something even better," he said, his eyes meeting mine in the mirror.

I nodded and returned to the fitting room, determined to try on the remaining dresses. But as I reached for the zipper of the gown, I quickly realized that I couldn't pull it down. The zipper was stubborn, refusing to budge, and my arms were starting to ache from the effort. I let out a sigh, feeling a wave of frustration wash over me.

"Adrian?" I called out, hoping he was still nearby. His response was immediate, a concerned "Yes?" echoing through the fitting area.

"Can you send the saleswoman in? I need her help with this dress," I said, trying to keep my voice steady despite the growing irritation.

"Sure. Wait," he replied, and I heard him leave to find assistance.

As I stood there, I felt a surge of determination. I was a capable, independent woman. I didn't need to wait for help; I could handle this myself. But as I twisted and contorted, trying to wriggle out of the dress, I only managed to get myself even more stuck. The fabric bunched up around my shoulders and head, and I could feel the panic setting in as my breathing became shallow and laboured.

"Oh shit, I can't breathe," I muttered to myself, the realization of my predicament hitting me hard. The dress was now halfway over my head, the heavy fabric suffocating me. I began to sweat, my heart racing with anxiety.

"Uh, Adrian?" I called out again, my voice tinged with desperation. No response. I groaned and tried to get out of the suffocating dress.

*God, why do I always end up in such a horrible situation?*

*Now if I die this way? No one would pity me, they'd laugh at me!*

"Liza?" His voice came, and I felt a wave of relief wash over me.

"Send her in," I said, feeling more and more trapped with each passing second. My chest tightened, making it difficult to breathe normally.

"The staff isn't here," Adrian's voice was calm but urgent. "Maybe it's because it's lunchtime. Come out in the dress, and let's look around for more. I hope you remember I need a tuxedo too."

I paused, my eyes wide.

"Liza, did you hear me?" His concern was palpable, and I could imagine the furrow in his brow.

"Uh, yeah," I replied weakly, still trying to free myself. I don't want to tell him I'm stuck in this. That would be hell embarrassing! "Why don't you go look for a tuxedo while I stay here?" My voice wavered, betraying the discomfort and struggle I was in. There was no response, only silence, "Adrian?"

"Liza, are you stuck?" He asked. His voice was gentle but insistent.

I paused again, my eyes widening with embarrassment. The truth was undeniable, but admitting it felt like a blow to my pride.

"No-No. I'm not!" I lied, trying to sound confident, but I knew he wouldn't believe me.

"Then come out," His command was firm, leaving no room for argument. I squeezed my eyes shut, feeling like I was drowning in a sea of humiliation.

"Fine. I'm stuck," I finally admitted, my voice breaking. "Now, can you please get the saleswoman here to get me out of this? I can't breathe."

The moment those words left my mouth, I heard the curtains being drawn aside, the sound making me jump. My heart pounded in my chest as I stood there, trapped and vulnerable.

"Adrian?" I called out, my voice trembling with a mix of shame and anxiety. I needed to be sure it was him.

"I can't believe you," His voice was a blend of concern and exasperation, but it held a warmth that made my heart ache, "Turn around!"

"What do you mean turn around? You can't barge in here like this. Get out and send someone else!"

"Guess what? I'm already in. Now shut up and turn around before you die with suffocation."

Embarrassment flooded through me, but there was something about his commanding yet gentle tone that stirred something deep within me. Without a word, I turned around.

As much as I hate being in this embarrassing situation, I want to get out of it.

I slightly jumped when his cold fingers brushed against my warm skin, my breath got stuck in my throat and my heartbeats increased. His mere touch sent chills throughout my body as he tried to get me out of the gown.

"How did you end up in this situation?" He whispered to me, sounding a little irritated and I'm not sure but maybe I noticed amusemned too. I gulped and remained quiet, "Is it hurting?"

I shook my head, a little more than needed.

His fingers brushed my bare skin and made me curl my toes. I felt a current pass through me every moment his fingers brushed the exposed area of my body. But I stayed rigid as if his mere touch was not doing anything to me.

Carefully, he untangled the fabric and finally freed me from the suffocating gown.

It fell on my feet and I stood there, catching my breath, a wave of relief washing over me. But as I met his gaze, I slightly frowned. He was looking at me with... Infatuation?

My eyes widened in shock as the reality of my situation hit me: I was standing there in nothing but my undergarments.

# Chapter 14

# *Dazzling Desires*

*Adrian's POV*

I watched her, her face flushed with embarrassment, eyes wide as saucers. She stood there for a moment, frozen in shock, before quickly picking the fallen dress to cover herself. Her cheeks were a deep crimson, her eyes wide with a mix of embarrassment and indignation. The situation was far from appropriate, yet an inexplicable pull drew me toward her, and I felt my pulse quicken in response. "Get a grip," I fisted my palms and mentally scolded myself feeling things that I shouldn't. Again!

I blinked, tearing my gaze from her and turning my back, squeezing my eyes shut to block out the tantalizing image, "Put on your clothes and come out," My voice was firmer than I felt, reverberating with an authority I hoped would mask the turmoil inside me. I stepped out of the fitting room, releasing a breath I hadn't realized I was holding.

My heart was pounding furiously in my chest, each beat echoing the chaos of my thoughts. I licked my lips nervously, one hand resting on my waist, the other clutching the fabric of my shirt over my racing heart. The air felt thick, charged with a tension that was both electrifying and suffocating. I closed my eyes, taking several deep breaths to steady myself, feeling the weight of the moment pressing down on me.

A mischievous smile tugged at my lips as her startled expression replayed in my mind-those wide, shocked grey eyes, flushed cheeks, and heavy breaths. I had truly embarrassed her, and the memory of her surprise was too delightful to resist. I chuckled to myself the moment I saw her state, stuck in her dress. I wanted to laugh out loud but knowing that showing my amusement would only make things more awkward for her, I kept a poker face, maintaining an air of innocence, at least until the dress fell. The dress wasn't supposed to fall, but it did. I didn't realize she wouldn't hold it once the zipper was open.

*But oh well, accidents happen, don't they?*

The moment it hit the floor, time seemed to freeze. I watched her, standing in all her glory, a vision of effortless beauty. I had never seen such a stunning figure in my life. She doesn't go to the gym or follow a strict diet like so many people do. She is effortlessly beautiful, a natural goddess who made even the most meticulously groomed fitness enthusiasts look like amateurs. Her curves were perfectly proportioned, and her skin glowed with a radiance that seemed to come from within. Clad in those black undergarments, she looked so incredibly alluring that I had to force myself to look away. The worst part is, I didn't want to look away. *Damn it!*

The sound of the curtains opening snapped my attention back to the present. I straightened myself and faced her. She stood there looking... furious? I frowned, my eyes narrowing slightly. Shouldn't she be acting all awkward and embarrassed?

"You barged in?" she said, her jaw clenching as she glared at me. She crossed her arms against her chest and demanded, "Aren't you going to apologize to me?"

I shot my brows up and said, "Well," my index finger pointed at her, "Aren't you going to thank me for saving your life?" She tightened her jaw and advanced towards me. I quickly folded my finger into my fist and took a step back.

"You!" Now she raised her finger at me, making me lift my hands in surrender and tilt my head back as she stood close, too close, "How dare you get in without my consent."

I blinked twice, tilting my head sideways, "Wait, you're mad at me because I barged in without your consent?" her eyes slightly narrowed, "Ha! I thought you were angry because I saw something that I wasn't supposed to," she took a breath of fury in, her eyes shooting daggers at me, "Alright, I apologize for barging in and witnessing something that I wasn't supposed to," She shook her head in disbelief and I chuckled, "Next time, please wait for help," she rolled her eyes and walked away. I followed her, grinning.

After our shopping, we headed back to the hotel to retrieve our luggage before making our way to Rachel's place. It was 8 o'clock when we finally arrived, and without wasting a moment, we immediately began preparing for the evening. I had bought myself a stunning red and black royal outfit that hugged my body perfectly, emphasizing my curves in all the right places. The black gloves and bow added a classy yet sexy touch, elevating the ensemble to something truly special. As I gazed at my reflection in the mirror, I couldn't help but smile and sigh.

For the first time in a long while, I felt light-hearted, unburdened by worry. Since stepping out of the book, my days have been consumed with the quest. The stress, the irritation, and the impatience had weighed heavily on my shoulders, almost suffocating me. But today, for some inexplicable reason, I feel calm and at peace.

With a smile, I turned to the door where Liza was getting ready. The memory of her vulnerable, yet captivating, figure lingered in my mind, a dangerous distraction I couldn't afford. I clenched my fists, determined to push those thoughts aside, but the image of her standing there, so close and yet so far, refused to fade.

*Liza Kirby, what are you doing to me?*

A soft knock on my door pulled me from my thoughts. I opened it to find Rachel standing there, dressed impeccably in a purple corset dress that accentuated her graceful figure. A small, knowing smile played on her lips, and she held a black box in her hands, her fingers covered in elegant black net gloves. She was around fifty, but she carried herself with such poise and confidence that she hardly looked her age.

"Good evening, Rachel," I greeted her warmly, stepping aside to let her in.

"Good evening," she said, her eyes scanning the room, "Where's Liza?"

I glanced at the door of her dressing room and then back at her, "Uh, she's still getting ready."

Rachel chuckled softly, a sound full of warmth and understanding. "It's okay. A woman takes her time getting ready," I only smiled in response, "Anyway, this is for you two," she handed me a black box, "Put these on before entering the venue. Also, live this night without the burden of tomorrow. We have a hard journey ahead. Forget about the work at hand and enjoy the night. We don't know what's waiting for us. So, try to live the night freely," I nodded, feeling a sense of camaraderie with her, earning another warm smile. "Good. I'll meet you downstairs."

After she left, I waited another thirty minutes for Liza to emerge. Growing tired of sitting, I finally headed downstairs and took a seat on the plush sofa opposite Rachel, who had settled in with an air of serene patience.

"How long is she going to take?" Rachel asked, her tone light but with a hint of impatience.

"I don't know. She usually doesn't take this long to dress. I'll go check on her," I replied, starting to rise, but Rachel gently stopped me with a dismissive wave of her hand.

"It's okay," she said kindly. "I have guests waiting for me. I have to go. When she's ready, come join us. I'll leave my car for you."

I nodded and she left, leaving me alone in the house. Ten minutes later, with still no sign of Liza, I began to worry. What if she was stuck again? The thought worried me. I stood up, deciding it was time to check on her but just as I reached the foot of the stairs, I found Liza standing on the other end. As soon as I laid my eyes on her, my breath caught in my throat.

*Wow*

# Chapter 15

# Masquerade Ball

*Liza's POV*

I looked at him and felt my cheeks getting a natural blush under the blush I had put on. My hands held the hem of my gown and almost wrinkled it with how strongly I was holding it. Adrian's shoulders lifted and dropped by the intake of long breath he took. It made my heart run wildly. No man has ever looked at me the way he was looking at me right now. Completely mesmerized. But not as mesmerized as I am right now.

He looked absolutely stunning, every detail meticulously arranged to create an unforgettable impression. His hair was combed to perfection, each strand falling effortlessly into place, framing his striking features with an air of effortless charm. The deep red corset hugged his form, accentuating his figure while adding a touch of boldness. It was beautifully paired with a flowing black cape-styled coat, cascading down to just below his knees in waves. The rich red of the corset complemented the sleek black bow tied at his neck, which added a refined touch to his overall appearance. Black gloves adorned his hands, enhancing the sophistication of his look while creating an elegant contrast against the vibrant red. Completing the ensemble, his polished black shoes shone with a subtle gleam, every detail meticulously chosen to create a cohesive, striking appearance.

But what truly caught my eye, though, was the striking color scheme we both shared: a bold combination of red and black. It was as if we had unintentionally coordinated, our outfits reflecting a perfect harmony that seemed almost destined. I couldn't help but feel a flutter of excitement.

Slowly, I lifted the hem of my red corset dress, the fabric hugging my figure as I stepped down from the last stair. His gaze was intense, unwavering, and locked onto mine with an intensity that made my heart race. I took a deep breath, savouring the moment, and paused in front of him, fighting back a smile of pride. After hours spent perfecting this look, every brush and detail felt worth the effort. But-

"Shall we?" A frown crossed my brow; the words felt insufficient. No compliment, no acknowledgment of the transformation I had undergone.

*And here I though he was mesmerized?*

I placed my hand in his and stepped out of the house with a mix of excitement and unease.

As we settled into the car, a silence enveloped us, heavy with unspoken words. I stole glances at him, hoping for a glimpse of admiration or at least a casual comment. Yet, he remained quiet, his focus on the road ahead. Each passing second heightened my disappointment, turning my anticipation into a gnawing anxiety.

*Do I look horrible?*

*Is my makeup bad?*

*Is my hair not done well?*

*Is he upset because we're wearing the same colour?*

The question lingered in the air, thickening the tension.

Finally, as we pulled up to our destination, he spoke, "Liza?" His voice soft and as gentle as a breeze. I turned to him just as he reached for a box resting between us. He opened it, revealing two stunning black masks nestled inside, each one intricately designed. "Rachel asked me to put these on before entering," he said, picking up the delicate female mask.

My heart fluttered as he gestured for me to turn around. I complied, feeling the soft brush of his fingers as he gently put the mask on my face. When I turned back to face him, I caught him taking a deep breath, his jaw clenched, fists folding on his thighs. A flicker of concern crossed my mind-*is he alright?*

He quickly donned his own mask, and trust me, he looked incredibly sexy, the dark fabric accentuating his features and adding an air of mystery. The transformation was striking, and for a brief moment, the tension dissipated, replaced by an electric thrill.

"Let's go."

Hand in hand, we stepped out of the car, and my breath was instantly taken away by the sight of the ballroom before us.

It shimmered with an air of elegance that felt almost otherworldly. Crystal chandeliers hung from the ceiling, casting a warm, golden glow over the polished marble floor, reflecting like stars scattered across a night sky. Rich tapestries adorned the walls, each one telling a story of its own-some draped with regal patterns, others depicting scenes of grandeur from ages past.

The sweet scent of fresh flowers enveloped us, harmonizing with the soft melodies of the string quartet that floated through the air. Every note danced around us, adding to the enchanting atmosphere. My heart raced, not just from the beauty surrounding us but from the thrill of being by his side in this moment.

"Ah, looks like the night isn't going to be as exciting as I thought," he said, striding toward Rachel, who was busy chatting with a group of people. When she noticed us, her smile transformed into a warm, welcoming one. "Sorry we're late," he said. I noticed how all eyes snapped at him. Men included.

"It's okay. The party has just begun. Please make yourselves comfortable and enjoy the night," she said and we nodded, "And you both look absolutely stunning tonight."

I smiled. I needed this. But still deep down, I wanted him to say something but that mean guy still didn't say a word.

We talked a little about the decoration, people, and the one who had thrown this masquerade ball and then Rachel excused herself. I stood there quietly, hands resting on my belly like a lost little girl. Adrian glanced at me, raising his eyebrows, which earned him an eye roll from me.

"What?" he demanded, but I didn't respond, "Alright, what did I do now?"

"Do you have some kind of disorder?" I shot back, irritation bubbling beneath the surface. He frowned, clearly taken aback. "You didn't say a word during the ride, and now you expect me to act normal? Talk to you?"

"Don't blame me. You didn't say anything either."

I rolled my eyes again, "I was waiting for you to say something."

"I was waiting for you to say something too," I fell silent, frustration building. "Anyway, do you want to dance?" He held out his hand to me. I looked at his palm and then back at him, taking an angry breath. "Is that a no?"

I wanted to yell at him, to demand how I looked, but instead, I turned and walked away, battling my disappointment. I had invested two hours into this look, and all I wanted was at least a "pretty" to validate my effort.

I clenched my jaw, feeling angrier with every step I took away from him but all of a sudden, my wrist was grabbed and I was yanked back. The yank was gentle but strong enough to make me lose self-control and collide with his chest.

My grey eyes met his green ones. I held my breath and swallowed.

"Did I tell you how beautiful you look tonight?"

My heart fluttered, and a blush appearing on my face again. Glad, I was wearing a mask to hide it because there was no way he would not have seen it from standing this close. He snaked his arm around my waist, holding me securely, and gently tugged a strand of my hair, letting it fall across my face.

This mere touch sent a shiver throughout my body.

"Now you look extra gorgeous," He said, looking deeply into my eyes. The coldness of his glove left a heating sensation on the area it brushed.

I narrowed my eyes, "Stop pretending with me. You didn't say anything through the entire ride and now I look pretty? And that too with a mask on?"

"I was quiet because I couldn't find the words to truly appreciate the beauty you possess. Even with the mask on you exude an air of mystery-one I can't help but want to unravel."

My heart skipped a beat and I started struggling against his hold. Seeing my face, he understood that I wanted distance and freed me. My heart was racing, unsure if it was due to his touch or the compliment he had given me. I looked on the other side and smiled, realizing that this happiness stemmed more from the compliment than the touch itself.

"Tell me about yourself, Liza," His voice cut through the noise of the party, his green eyes now resembling dark emeralds under the dim lights. I noticed how every woman in the room was sneaking glances at him, their curiosity piqued despite the mask he wore. I scoffed inwardly.

*He has a mask on, for God's sake. How could they be so easily intrigued?*

"Liza, I've asked you something," he repeated, a touch of impatience creeping into his tone.

I blinked, "Yeah. Uh, what do you want to know about?"

He looked aside thoughtfully, then fixed his gaze back on me. A smile on his face, his dimple deepening as he spoke, "Tell me about your dating life."

My eyebrows shot up in surprise. "My dating life?" I repeated. He nodded, smirking as if he expected some juicy tidbit. "Sorry to disappoint you, but I've never had a dating life."

The smirk vanished instantly. "No dating life?" he asked, as though the concept was completely foreign to him. I shrugged nonchalantly. Even with the mask on, I could see his frown deepen, the confusion evident. "No boyfriend ever?" he asked, and I shook my head. "What about a teen romance or office affair?" Again, I shook my head, this time closing my eyes momentarily. He paused, staring at me like I was an alien from another planet.

I lifted my shoulders. "What?"

"You've never been in a relationship?"

I sighed. "No, Adrian."

"Why?" He sounded more shocked than curious. "Men must throw themselves at you," I pressed my lips together, staring at him in disbelief.

I chuckled, "Throw themselves? I used to be a nerd. Always studying and never making friends. No man ever found me interesting enough to even talk to. Plus, I don't have a pretty face to be approached."

"Excuse me, what?" He looked at me as if I had just told him the sky was green. "Not pretty face?" He repeated my words, emphasizing them with a hint of mockery. "Liza, have you ever looked at yourself?"

I exaggerated my smile, "I look at myself every day, and I know I'm just an average-looking girl."

"No. You're not an average-looking girl!" My eyes slightly widened at his tone. "You're gorgeous. People these days are more into superficial beauty, beauty that is bought. But you, you're effortlessly beautiful. Your eyes-they don't need mascara or eyeliner; they're naturally compelling. Your lips don't need shades; they're naturally pink and become a darker shade when you're emotional. Your hair is a hundred times better than those bought extensions. Thick and beautiful. Your face is flawless, and those freckles just add to your beauty. Your body is effortlessly stunning. I'm sure those who go to the gym and follow strict diets don't have a figure as perfect as yours. Your smile is the prettiest, and your voice is like a soft melody to the ears. You're absolutely gorgeous, Liza. I doubt there's any woman more attractive than you! And I think the reason you were called a nerd was because you didn't look like them-fake. You were naturally pretty and didn't require makeup or artificiality to attract."

By now, my heart was racing, as if it would leap out of my chest. In my entire life, no one had ever called me beautiful or even told me I was pretty. I'd been called names, labelled a nerd, and always felt out of place. His words sounded foreign but so honest. I'd never thought of myself as pretty, always seeing myself as just an average-looking girl.

"Thank you."

I didn't know what else to say. I felt a knot in my chest and something more that I couldn't explain. It was a foreign feeling. I'd never felt this way for anyone before. Never. There was this draw towards him that was so strong and so scary.

He smiled, lifting his palm forward to me once again, "Now, can we dance?" he asked again. I remained silent, "What?"

"I don't know how to dance." I finally confessed.

He chuckled, a warm sound that seemed to cut through my anxiety. "Don't worry, I'll lead. Just follow my steps."

With a deep breath, I placed my hand in his, feeling his fingers close around mine. As we stepped onto the dance floor, I stumbled slightly, trying to match his pace. His eyes twinkled with amusement as he guided me into position, my feet clumsy but determined.

"So, um, how do you keep from tripping over your own feet?"

He grinned, "It's all in the feet and the rhythm. Relax, just keep your steps close to mine and follow my lead."

I tried to follow his instructions, but my steps were more of a comical shuffle. I could feel myself turning red, but his laughter was warm and encouraging. "I'm going to step on your toes so many times, you'll have to get a new pair of shoes," I joked, hoping to ease the awkwardness.

"It's okay. I won't mind," he shrugged, his voice smooth and comforting. "Besides, your dance moves are uniquely yours."

As the music continued, I started to get the hang of it, though I still occasionally misstepped. He caught me each time with a steady hand, his presence both reassuring and captivating. I couldn't help but notice how his gaze lingered on me, his eyes softening with each shared glance. The dance, though filled with awkward moments and laughter, became a rhythm of its own—imperfect yet intimate.

I felt my heart quicken to an exhilarating pace, a fluttering sensation that made my cheeks flush with a warm, rosy glow.

Our dance slowed, and the space between us diminished as he took a step closer. His eyes, once warm and joyful, now bore an intense, almost tormented look. The playful smile was gone, replaced by a frown that suggested he was grappling with some internal struggle. We paused, our bodies nearly touching, as he stared into my eyes with a piercing intensity that made me feel small and vulnerable. His gaze narrowed slightly, and I swallowed hard, caught in the gravity of his unspoken turmoil.

"Have you ever been touched, Liza?" he asked, his voice dropping to a low, desperate tone.

I was taken aback, "W-What?"

He didn't respond. His jaw clenched and I noticed how his shoulders moved up and dropped by the intake of sharp breath. His hand, resting over my waist moved down and stopped over my hip, making my eyes go wide.

"Has anyone ever touched you here?"

My heart jumped. I inhaled a long breath, feeling a rush of heat passing through me. He looked into my eyes straight and I weakly shook my head. Slowly, his hand went lower, quickening my breath. It rested on my thigh, just below my hip.

"What about here, Liza?"

I bit my lower lip.

Every brush of his hand made that area heat up and caused a current to pass through me. I shook my hand again. Keeping his eyes on mine, he placed his hand on my abdomen. "Here?" I gulped and shook my head again. His hand continued its ascent, stopping just between my breasts. The coldness of his glove sent a chill on my open cleavage. "I bet nobody has ever touched you here," he murmured, his voice now husky and tinged with danger.

I curled my toes, trying to tear my gaze but held me captive under his gaze, not letting me look away. I wanted to run, to escape this intense scrutiny, but something kept me rooted to the spot. I didn't know what was wrong with me, nor did I want to know. I just liked whatever he was doing, and I hated to admit that I didn't want him to stop.

His hand slid up to my lips and he brushed my lower lips with his thumb while keeping his gaze on them, "What about here?" I closed my eyes and gulped, shaking my head again. Moving his hand up to my neck, he held it firmly from the side and yanked me closer. My eyes opened. The force he used made me clench my fists, trying to steady myself. "What are you doing to me, Liza?" He sounded desperate and it felt like the question was for himself, not me.

I couldn't say a word and stood there completely at his mercy. He glanced at my lips, his gaze lingering before he tore his eyes away and abruptly stormed off, leaving me standing there, trembling and breathless.

*What just happened?*

## Chapter 16

# Zephyr's Shadow

We left the party around 1 a.m. Adrian hasn't spoken to me since abandoning me on the dance floor. I had waited by the food court, expecting him to return, but he didn't show up until the party was nearly over. At least, it wasn't over for everyone else. Rachel, with her ingenuity, found a way to save the two worlds from falling apart. If I weren't so furious with Adrian for his behavior, I might have been sulking at the thought of him disappearing into thin air. Instead, I was elated and decided not to keep him here any longer. It was time to get rid of him.

We were heading back to Rachel's house, with Rachel sitting next to Adrian in the front seat and me in the back. I wasn't thrilled when he offered her the seat beside him instead of me, but I was glad in a way. If I had been sitting there, he would have seen the utter annoyance and displeasure on my face. He touched me in a way no one else ever had, only to leave me feeling like a dangerous creature that would burn him alive if he didn't back away. I will never forgive him for humiliating me that way.

Scowling, I turned my gaze away from him and sighed. I don't understand him. One moment he is warm and caring, and the next he is distant and cold. He makes me feel like he has a split personality. In fact, that's exactly how he appeared in his book before he jumped out of it. I looked at him again, seeing only his profile and his arm, his attention firmly on the road ahead.

I couldn't help but marvel at how he managed to navigate modern life so effortlessly, despite being from an era where even electric light wasn't invented. It was as if he had been born to this time, seamlessly blending into a world that should have been utterly foreign to him. How could he know so much about our world and handle everyday technology with such ease? I had asked him once, and he gave me a vague answer about being written into today's setting. But now that I knew the truth-that he belonged to an era a thousand years past-I was even more curious.

*How could he drive and interact with technology like someone from this era?*

The question gnawed at me constantly, and with it came other unsettling thoughts. Adrian, a creation of my ancestors, yanked out of a book to help humanity and save nature. He could control fire, drawing it from his bare fingers, a feat both awe-inspiring and terrifying. Sometimes, I feel like I have fallen into a coma and would wake up to find it all a dream. But other times, it feels like a terrifying reality. I, a witch, apparently the only person who could send him back. The weight of this responsibility hung over me like a dark cloud, obscuring my thoughts and filling my heart with dread. I don't know what is going to happen next, and I have no idea how long this ordeal will last. The uncertainty is a constant companion, an ever-present reminder of the chaos that has become my life. Yet, amidst all these uncertainties, there are moments of startling clarity. In the quiet spaces between panic and resolve, I find myself pondering the deeper mysteries of my existence. There is so much left for me to discover about myself, untapped reservoirs of power and understanding that I have barely begun to explore. And perhaps, even more, to learn about him.

"Do you know why you were taken out of the pages of the book?" Rachel's voice cut through the silence, pulling me from my thoughts. Adrian shook his head, his eyes fixed on the road ahead, his face an unreadable mask.

"Flames Dominion. That was the name of your book," Rachel continued, her tone measured but intense. "You were the third character we pulled from its pages to combat a universal threat. A malevolent entity, blinded by power, was draining the earth's core, siphoning its energy to fuel his dark magic. He sought unimaginable power, oblivious to the fact that he was on the brink of annihilating all life."

"We fought against him and defeated him," Rachel went on, "but none of us had the power to reignite the core. It was dying, drained of its life force, leading to catastrophic natural disasters and the collapse of magical systems. We turned to you, Adrian. Only your unique fire powers could rekindle the core, restoring balance and preventing the impending apocalypse."

I couldn't help but feel a surge of pride. Adrian had saved the world, like the hero he was. But his response was laced with bitterness.

"So, you yanked me out of the pages, used me, and then shoved me back into the book when I was no longer needed. Isn't that selfish, Rachel?"

I frowned but remained silent, understanding his perspective. It was selfish, but it was done for the greater good. He shouldn't be upset about it.

Rachel's voice softened, almost apologetic. "In some ways, yes. And we were punished by the universe for defying its natural order. We accidentally brought forth a very dangerous character, Zephyr Valtor. He was powerful, cunning, and heartless. Only someone as formidable as Archon Astralis could stand against him."

"What did he do?" I asked, my curiosity piqued.

"Zephyr killed sorcerers and witches, ravaging nature in his wake. His rejection of the universe's rules led to immense destruction," Rachel explained, her voice tinged with sorrow. "My mother told me stories of how he didn't even spare children, siphoning their power to become more powerful and then killing them."

"He's the worst. I hate him," I muttered, drawing Rachel's and Adrian's attention.

"You don't have to hate someone who's caged in the pages of a book, Liza," he said. I nodded, knowing he was right. But his next words sent a chill through me. "If you know so much, Rachel, do you think you know why I feel like someone is always watching me, lurking in the shadows, robbing me of my peace?"

Rachel sighed audibly, "The 'someone' you feel is magic. This was implanted to make you want to return to where you've come from. You're supposed to be sent back right after the task is over and this feeling of being under a rock is a way to make you hate reality so you don't insist on staying longer and attract destruction between the two realms."

The fact that Adrian is desperate to go back and feels danger breathing down his neck made me curious about Zephyr, who decided to stay longer despite feeling the same as Adrian. So, I questioned, "What about Zephyr then? Didn't he feel the same as Adrian when he was here?"

"He did. But he was very courageous. He feared nothing. The feeling that Adrian is telling us about was like fuel to him to find a way to get rid of it and he did. But before he could find a way to stay here, our saviour, Archon, sent him back." Rachel paused, looking relieved, "I'm glad that you didn't bring Zephyr to life, otherwise it would have been havoc."

I nodded but then a realization struck me like a tidal wave. "Oh my, God!" I exclaimed, my eyes wide. The car screeched to a halt in the middle of nowhere. Adrian snapped his head at me, not through the rear-view mirror this time, while Rachel also looked at me in shock and confusion.

"What?" He demanded. My sudden scream caused both of them to startle.

"The car... The car followed you out of the book, Adrian. What if...what if Zephyr follows too?"

The thought was sudden but concerning.

We all sat in stunned silence, the gravity of the situation sinking in. Seeing Rachel's expression, I realized that she didn't think it through either.

"You said you found a way to send me back?" His words cut through the tension, "Do it and get it over with."

The thought of him leaving made my heart ache.

"I never said I found a solution," Rachel corrected him. "I just think I know where to start," She looked at me and added, "We need to awaken Liza's powers. Only then can we do something."

Once again, a wave of silence enveloped us. The task ahead seemed monumental. My heart clenched at the thought of sending Adrian back. How ironic that the one who didn't want him to leave would be the one to send him off.

"How long will it take for me to gain my powers?" I asked, my voice tinged with worry and determination. Zephyr isn't supposed to get out, ever. He should remain in the book always.

"It depends entirely on you, Liza," Rachel replied. "Some witches gain their powers within a week, others take years."

"If that's the case, we should find a way to close the veil," I suggested, earning myself a frown from both of them, "What I mean is it might be easier to prevent the havoc than to send him back," I explained.

Rachel's response was immediate. "We can't do that."

"Why not?"

"Because it means going against nature once more, Liza. We cannot do that!" Rachel said, almost raising her voice for the first time since we met her.

"We're not defying the universe, Rachel. I just don't want Zephyr to rise. The only way to stop him is to close the veil," I paused, a shiver running down my spine, "And what if he has or about to?"

"No, he hasn't," Says Rachel confidently, "Because if he had, he wouldn't be keeping calm. By now, he must have unleashed chaos," Both Adrian and I nodded, "We'll try to find a way to close the veil. Before that, meet your mother and see if she knows anything. But remember this, Liza: you're treading a dangerous path. One wrong step, and it could cost us everything."

I nodded again, my resolve hardening. I would do whatever it took to keep Zephyr in his prison, even if it meant defying the universe itself.

After a long, utterly quiet ride, we finally reached Rachel's place. Rachel was convinced by me. We decided to make Adrian stay here longer and close the veil and only open it back after we've found a way to send him back. The task is tough but at least, it wouldn't be dangerous.

Our car stopped outside her house and I stepped out, letting out a moan of relief. I was utterly exhausted. The gown I was wearing was heavy and cumbersome, a stark contrast to my usual attire. It was my first time wearing a gown with a corset, which felt like it was squeezing the life out of me. My back ached, but my breasts hurt even more from the tightness of the dress. The saleswoman instructed me to make it as tight as possible by taking a deep breath in and holding it, explaining that this was how such gowns and corsets were traditionally worn. Initially, it was just uncomfortable because I couldn't breathe properly. But as the night wore on, the discomfort turned into excruciating pain.

Then the makeup on my face felt like a mask, heavy and suffocating, no matter how pretty it made me look, I was desperate to wash it off. And then there were the shoes. My god, the SHOES. The black high-heeled boots were undeniably stylish, but they were a torture device for my feet. My toes throbbed with pain, and I silently cursed whoever had invented such uncomfortable footwear. Yet, a part of me couldn't help but admire how they completed my look.

"You alright?" Adrian's voice cut through my stance, freezing me mid-step. I turned to face him, my anger simmering just below the surface. Sure, we had exchanged a few words in the car, but that didn't mean I had forgiven him for what he did to me. Without a word, I turned back around, gripping my gown tightly to avoid stumbling and making a fool of myself.

"Liza?" He called out again, but I didn't break the stride, my scowl deepening. Just as I was about to take another step, my foot caught on the hem of my dress. *Shit*. I stumbled, crashing to my knees with a dramatic flair, my palms smacking the floor. I grunted.

*Perfect. Just perfect.*

"Hey, you okay?" His voice, dripping with concern, grated on my nerves. He was suddenly by my side, hand extended like a knight in shining armor. "Get up."

I glared at him with all the fury I could muster. What does he think of himself? Being nice to me one second and then treating me as if I'm some kind of trash.

He sighed, a flicker of guilt passing through his eyes before they hardened. He leaned down, trying to help me up, but I slapped his hand away, offending him.

"Thank you, but I can manage," I snapped, hauling myself to my feet. My knees throbbed painfully, but I stood tall, locking eyes with him. I wanted to scream, to let out all the pent-up anger, but instead, I forced a sugary-sweet smile and swept past him towards the staircase.

I had barely set foot on the first step when I felt a firm tug on my shoulder. Before I could protest, I was swept off my feet and into his arms. My eyes widened in shock, and I gasped, clinging to him instinctively.

"Adrian, put me down!" I demanded, my voice rising in a mix of frustration and embarrassment.

"I don't want you to tumble down the stairs," he said, his tone unyielding. "So, hush up and let me carry you to your bedroom."

Speechless, I found myself mute, cradled in his arms as he ascended the stairs, a swirl of indignation and reluctant comfort washing over me.

*What the hell is he?*

When he reached my room, he threw me onto the bed, and I bounced twice before landing flat. The mattress creaked beneath me as I quickly sat up, throwing a glare his way. He rolled his eyes and took a seat at the edge of the bed, near my feet. Instinctively, I pulled them away, retreating as far as I could. Honestly, I didn't even know why I did it. Maybe I just wanted to maintain some distance from him. He noticed my movement and his expression softened, his body stiffening as he stood back up. His towering frame suddenly seemed even more intimidating.

"You hate me, don't you?" His voice was low, and he shoved his hands into his suit's pockets.

I frowned, "No. Why would you say that?" He didn't respond, just kept staring at me with that intense, unwavering gaze that made me feel small. I tilted my chin up defiantly, "What?"

"Did I upset you?" he asked, his tone softer but still probing. Yes, you did. But I wasn't about to admit it. I took a deep breath, trying to steady my racing heart, and shook my head, "Then why the cold shoulder?" he pressed.

"Cold shoulder?" I let out a hollow, bitter laugh. "I'm just returning what I've been receiving from you."

He frowned, confusion flashing in his eyes. He took a moment before he said, "What's wrong, Liza? You don't behave this way."

"I'm behaving just like you. Why, does it feel awful?" My voice dripped with sarcasm, each word laced with the hurt and frustration I had been holding back.

"I make you feel awful?" He looked genuinely taken aback, and for a moment, I saw a flicker of something like regret in his eyes. But I wouldn't let him off the hook that easily.

I clenched my jaw, fighting the urge to scream. "I need you out of my room." He stood there, silent, just watching me, "Adrian, get out."

"Liza, calm down," He said, his voice gentle and soft, almost calming enough but I was stubborn.

I rolled my eyes, "I am calm, just get out," For a moment, he just stared at me, his face an unreadable mask, "Adrian-

"I'm sorry for upsetting you, Liza," He cut me off, his voice as gentle as the breeze, "I shouldn't have left you alone. I just didn't want to hurt you."

"Hurt me?"

His silence stretched into an agonizing moment before he spoke again, each word twisting a knife in my heart.

"I'm destined to return, Liza. I should keep my distance," I stared at him, my mind reeling. The fact that he had left me to create distance made me feel a rush of anger I've never felt before, "I'm sorry," He sighed, his shoulders dropping.

"So, you want distance?" My voice was hollow, my eyes betraying no emotion.

"No, not distance. I'm just suggesting that we should stay within our limits. We have completely different paths to follow. I'm destined to return while you will be here."

"Limits?" I chuckled bitterly, mocking. My blood boiled as I continued, "You're the one to talk about limits? Adrian, you have been doing things I never asked for. I never asked you to hold my hand or hug me when I was crying, nor did I ever ask you to pick me up in your arms when I couldn't walk. You looked after me when I injured myself. You were the one who offered to get Nate. You showed me care, gave me attention, made me feel like I mattered, and called me pretty when I never asked you for it. You crossed the limits long before, Adrian, and I will not allow you to humiliate me again."

"When did I do that?" He demanded, looking genuinely surprised.

"When you left me after touching me in a way no one else has. You humiliated me. You made me feel awful and embarrassed by leaving me there as if you had made a mistake."

"It's not true. I was protecting you." His voice rising.

"Protecting me from what?"

"From myself, Liza Kirby! I was protecting you from MYSELF!!" His voice thundered and those calm and beautiful green eyes of his gleamed like the flash of lightning in a thunderstorm—brilliant, electric, and a vivid shade of green.

It startled me.

Realizing he had frightened me, his expression softened, and he sighed, closing his eyes for a moment, "I'm sorry for raising my voice at you. But stay away from me. I'm not good for you," Then he left the room, the door closing with a rough thud behind him.

A knot formed in my chest, and a lump rose in my throat. I stared at the door, a torrent of emotions crashing over me. My eyes watered, and I clutched my pyjamas tightly in my fists.

*What does he think of himself?*

**Next Day:**

It was around seven in the morning when I sat down for breakfast with Rachel. My cereal sat untouched, a silent testament to the restless night I had endured. Sleep had been a distant dream, replaced by a relentless torrent of thoughts and emotions that refused to let me rest. Adrian's suggestion and his *sweet* and *tender* reaction lingered in my thoughts like a haunting melody. Especially, those warm green eyes which sparked like a thunderstorm.

All night long, I was consumed by what might happen if Adrian got too close. How could it hurt me? Sure, he is destined to return to his world, and his absence would carve out a gaping hole in my life, a void that nothing could fill. But then again, wasn't that inevitable? His departure would leave me hollow regardless, so why did it matter how it happened?

I am not some desperate, love-struck fool, clinging to the hope of a doomed romance. I wasn't pining for him, not in the way one might expect. It was more complicated than that. It was about the way he made me feel-exposed, vulnerable, and inexplicably drawn to him then behaving in a way that left me tangled in a web of confusion and longing and frustration. It's annoying.

And then there was Nate's call. His timing was impeccable, as always. Last night, he mentioned his flight would land in the evening today, and he'd come directly to see me. Panic surged through me. I couldn't let him come here, where the lines between reality and fantasy were already dangerously blurred. I quickly concocted a story, telling him I was staying with my aunt, which was a complete lie. Nate, in his typical cool manner, suggested I be ready because he was taking me out. The implication was clear: I had a date. *Fantastic!*

The irony wasn't lost on me. Here I was, navigating a minefield of supernatural complications with Adrian, and now I had to put on a brave face for a date with Nate. The contrast was almost laughable if it weren't so tragically complicated. I couldn't help but wonder how I would juggle these two worlds without losing my sanity-or my heart-in the process.

I sighed audibly, a heavy, frustrated sound that seemed to fill the room.

"Is something wrong, Liza?" Rachel's voice, ever soft and soothing, pulled me from my thoughts. I forced a smile and nodded, trying to seem casual, and glanced back at the breakfast I had barely touched, "When are you going to see your mom?" Her question yanked me back to reality, and my heart almost stopped. In the current chaos, I had completely forgotten about my mother.

"Uh, maybe uhm... in an hour," I replied, my voice sounding distant even to my own ears. Rachel nodded and returned to her meal. I clutched the fork in my hand tightly, trying to calm the rising tide of anxiety.

"Good morning, ladies," *And there he is.* I looked up to see Adrian approaching, his usual warm smile plastered on his face. Despite everything, my wildly beating heart seemed to settle at the sight of him. *I hate this.*

Rachel smiled warmly at him, "Good morning, Adrian. Please sit," He took his seat next to me, smiling at me before serving himself some food. I sat there, quiet and anxious, my mind a whirl of confusion. How could he act so normal after our intense argument last night? Or am I just overthinking everything?

I stayed mute for a while and then dropped the cutlery, grabbing their attention, "I think I'm done," I abruptly stood up and looked at Adrian, "Have your breakfast and meet me outside. I'll be waiting in the car," He nodded without looking at me, his indifference stinging more than I wanted to admit.

I clenched my jaw and left.

My mind was a chaotic storm of anger and second-guessing, and my behaviour is only making things worse. But if he wants distance, so be it. I will grant him his wish with a vengeance. I won't speak a single word to him, not even in passing. I won't flash him a smile, not even the faintest flicker. I won't stand anywhere near him, not even if the room is empty. I will become a fortress of icy indifference, a master of emotional restraint. I'll show him what staying within limits really means. I'll build walls so high and so thick that even his warmest smile won't be able to penetrate them. No matter how much it tears me apart inside, no matter how deeply it cuts, I will maintain this distance.

# Chapter 17

# A Love Unspoken

### Nate's POV

I watched the flight attendant move gracefully down the aisle. Her sweet voice and kind smile made every passenger feel special. She reminded me of Liza Kirby. Pretty, kind, generous, and soft-spoken.

Liza had captivated me since high school. She was always quiet, studying silently in the corner of the classroom, avoiding people and me. I used to watch her silently, captivated by her every move, whether it was something as simple as tucking a strand of her hair behind her ear or frowning at her book when she didn't understand something. She was simple, easy, and quiet, always minding her own business, and never caught up in any drama.

I was inexplicably drawn to her, yearning to be close to her, wishing I could gently tuck those strands behind her ear when they irritated her. She was beautiful and attractive enough to make any guy fall to his knees. Girls disliked her because she had the power to attract without trying, and guys hated her because, no matter how handsome or popular they were, she never cared. I lost count of how many guys I beat up for daring to misbehave with her and how many girls I had to put in their place for bullying her. I made it my mission to ensure her comfort and safety, becoming a silent guardian, a shadow that protected her from harm.

It took me a year just to break through the barriers of her solitude and three more years to earn the title of her friend. Despite our closeness, she never gave me the attention I so desperately craved. She always kept me at a distance-a distance that only fuelled my desire for her. Everyone in college knew about my feelings for Liza and how protective I was of her. Everyone, that is, except Liza herself. She never seemed to notice how much I cared, how much I liked her, how much I loved being around her, how much I cherished our time together. I used to beg teachers to pair us up for projects just so I could sit next to her and hear her voice. I even gave up my dream of becoming a travel photographer and chose teaching just to be close to her. I did everything I could just to be near her.

Despite my efforts, I knew my feelings would never be returned. Liza wasn't interested in me the way I wanted her to be. She never looked at me the way I looked at her. It was disappointing and hurtful, but at least she didn't hate me like she hated everyone else. She wasn't uncomfortable around me. She enjoyed my company and was open with me. She told me almost everything about herself and felt safe with me. And that was enough. I didn't want to lose her by confessing my feelings. If keeping my feelings to myself meant I could have her in my life, then I would never let her know.

But everything changed when I announced my relationship with Norah. I saw the hurt in Liza's eyes and realized she did have feelings for me. Regret hit me hard. I decided to break up with Norah but couldn't because she truly loved me, and despite not having feelings for her anymore, I didn't have the courage to break her heart. Plus, the news of our relationship spread throughout the college, putting me under pressure not to ruin her reputation. I was stuck.

Then our relationship went on without love. It dragged on for two years because Norah wasn't ready to leave me at any cost. It was like she was willing to spend her entire life in this loveless relationship rather than let me go to Liza. She hated her because, like everyone else in college, she knew about my feelings for Liza. She hated it that I loved Liza and not her and despite that, she proposed to me, and I accepted because I thought Liza would never love me back, so I decided to accept the person who did. There's a very famous quote by French writer Delphine de Girardin's, "Love the one who loves you, not the one you long for."

We were the perfect couple everyone admired, not knowing it became a façade after I learned that Liza has feelings for me too. Our relationship doomed. There wasn't a day when I didn't regret not confessing my feelings for Liza, but what I hated more was being with Norah despite not having feelings for her. I tried to love her, to forget Liza and move on with Norah, but I couldn't. I just couldn't picture myself with her after knowing that Liza felt the same for me.

Now, I've finally gotten rid of Norah, thanks to that fucker Adrian. If he hadn't cheated on Liza with my girlfriend, I wouldn't have been able to end things with her. Despite the favor, I hate him. Not because he cheated on Liza but because he touched her. When he took her hand away from mine in front of my eyes, I wanted to rip his arm off and beat the crap out of him, but I had to hold back and be patient because Liza liked him.

*I wonder what she saw in him.*

He didn't seem like a nice guy. I saw him seducing Norah shamelessly, making inappropriate gestures at her, kicking the table to ruin her dress, and taking her upstairs. I saw everything but pretended not to notice because I didn't care. I wanted to be there for Liza. I went there to see her. I was going alone at first, but then Norah insisted on coming too.

I'm glad for what happened. And somewhere, I'm thankful too, because by pulling that stunt, Adrian didn't just do me a favor but on himself too. I would have beaten the shit out of him one day. But just like Norah is gone, he must be gone too. There's no way Liza would have forgiven him for doing that.

At last, everything is finally in place. It took years, but I will finally have my Liza. I will finally confess my love to her. Tonight, I'll take her out and tell her everything I've been holding in for years. I'll tell her how much I love her and what a fool I've been not to tell her sooner. I'll tell her everything.

I'm coming, baby, and I promise, this time, I won't make any mistakes.

# Chapter 18

# The Crucible of Truths

*Liza's POV*

I remained mute throughout the ride, the silence thick enough to choke on. I didn't utter a single word to him, making sure even my breaths were barely audible. It was as if I was trying to convince myself that if I were quiet enough, I might disappear entirely.

He'd occasionally glance my way, perhaps expecting some conversation or at least a hint of acknowledgment, but I denied him that satisfaction. When he asked me to navigate, I simply keyed the address into the GPS and let him drive, wrapped in the silence that settled between us like an unwelcome guest.

I could see the tension building in him, the way his muscles tightened, how his grip on the steering wheel turned knuckle-white, and how his breaths became sharp as if he was trying to calm a storm within himself. I was testing his patience, but wasn't that what he wanted? Wasn't it all about not pushing boundaries and finding limits?

"We're almost there," he announced, breaking the silence. My heart leaped into my throat as the surroundings became painfully familiar. I'd been too preoccupied with my silent rebellion, with making him simmer in the discomfort of my quiet resistance, to realize where we were headed. Now, as the memories flooded back, I felt a cold dread seep into my veins.

I clenched my fists, my nails digging into my palms, a futile attempt to anchor myself to the present.

"No, Mom! Please, MOM!" The echoes of my past screamed in my ears, pulling me into a vortex of memories I'd long tried to bury. The darkness of those days closed in around me, suffocating me.

I could see her, my mother's wild hair framing her face, her clothes drenched in blood-*my blood*. "Mom, no. Please," I begged, my voice small and broken. But she didn't listen. She never listened. Her fury crashed over me, a relentless wave of violence and pain.

I was on the brink of screaming, my mind teetering on the edge of that horrific memory, when a gentle grasp on my hand pulled me back. I blinked, disoriented, and looked down at the hand holding mine, then up into those green eyes. Adrian's eyes, steady and sure, grounded me.

"I'm here, Liza," he murmured, his voice a balm to my frayed nerves. "It's okay."

For a brief moment, I felt a flicker of relief. I almost nodded, but then the realization hit me: in mere moments, this man would transform. He would be just as cold, just as cruel, as the worst parts of my past. Anger flared up, a shield against my vulnerability, and I yanked my hand away, earning a deep frown from him.

"Don't touch me again," I snapped, my voice icy and sharp. His jaw tightened, and before I could react, he grabbed my hand again, pulling me closer.

"Adrian?" I gasped, struggling against his grip. The more I fought, the tighter he held on. His face was so close to mine that I could feel the warmth of his breath on my lips. He smelled intoxicating, a mix of something clean and masculine. For a moment, I was dizzy with it.

"I've had enough of this," he sneered, his voice low and edged with impatience. His eyes bore into mine, intense and unwavering. "I never asked you to be silent around me or to keep a distance. And I certainly don't recall asking you to treat me with such disdain."

"But you asked me to stay within our limits," I retorted, lifting my chin defiantly. "And let me remind you, you're crossing it again." His eyes searched mine, a storm brewing behind them. For a long, tense moment, we stood like that, locked in a silent battle. Finally, he let go of my hand and pulled back, the tension between us snapping like a rubber band. I rubbed my wrist, the skin tender where his fingers had gripped me.

My eyes darted around, and I realized we had arrived. To my surprise, I didn't feel the fear I expected. I was afraid of what might happen now but I wasn't as frightened as I would have been if I had come here alone. I glanced at Adrian, who was unbuckling his seatbelt. It struck me then-his presence is the reason that I feel no fear gripping me.

I stepped out of the car and looked at my dilapidated house.

"Wow, I wasn't expecting... THIS much charm and sophistication packed into one place." Adrian's voice reached me, tinged with disbelief and sarcasm. The house, old and worn, looked as if a strong gust of wind could topple it over.

"It hadn't always been this way, but time and neglect had taken their toll." That was all I said and moved closer to the house.

My heart, which had been pounding moments earlier, seemed oddly calm because I had Adrian just behind me, close enough that I could feel the warmth of his body. He followed me, his movements deliberate and protective. His hands rested casually in his jeans pockets, giving him an air of nonchalance, yet there was a certain alertness in his posture, a readiness to spring into action. He moved like a guardian, and I couldn't help but smile.

*Don't smile!*

I quickly removed the smile

Finally, we reached the door. As I stood before it, my breath hitched in my throat. Adrian beside me was a solid presence, a quiet strength that I couldn't ignore but as I stood so close to her, the panic gripped me, almost suffocating me in its intensity. My heart pounded so loudly I was sure he could hear it.

*Come on, Liza. Don't be weak. You can do this.*

I forced myself to lift my hand, every movement feeling like it was happening in slow motion. The moment my knuckles made contact with the door, the sound echoed through the silence, loud and jarring. The wait felt like an eternity, every second stretching longer than the last. Then, with a slow, agonizing creak, the door began to open.

*Clam down, calm down, calm down.*

My heart seemed to stop as the familiar face came into view.

There she stood-my mother. The woman who had haunted my nightmares, who was the embodiment of all my fears. Her grey eyes met mine, cold and piercing, and I felt a chill run down my spine. It was as if the years hadn't passed at all, and I was that frightened child again, trapped and helpless.

Every muscle in my body tensed, ready to bolt or fight. But there was no escape, no turning back. I have to face her, and the weight of that reality pressed down on me, nearly crushing. Adrian's presence was a distant comfort, overshadowed by the overwhelming presence of the woman before me.

My skin prickled, and I clenched my fists to stop them from shaking.

This was it-the moment I had dreaded and anticipated in equal measure. The past was staring me in the face, and I have no choice but to confront it.

She narrowed her eyes. Clearly surprised to see me.

I swallowed hard, my heart now pounding in my chest as I stared at the woman before me. Her eyes were hollow, her skin pallid, and a ghostly visage of hatred that hadn't faded. She looked more skeletal than I remembered, her hair now a stark white, damaged and hanging limply around her shoulders. The only undeniable link between us was our eyes, mirroring the same shape and color. But no motherly warmth, only disdain.

She took a long, deliberate drag of her cigarette, exhaling smoke that curled around her like a shroud before she smirked with a venomous edge. "Hello, daughter. To what do I owe the pleasure?" Her voice dripped with sarcasm and disdain.

I tried to open my mouth to respond, but no words came out. My voice was trapped, swallowed by the torrent of memories crashing over me. I had thought I could face her, but no. I was a fool to think I can.

The ground beneath me tilted and my surrounding blurred and I realized I wasn't breathing.

*I need to breathe. I need to breathe.*

My heart pounded erratically.

*Breathe Liza breath.*

Just as I teetered on the brink of breaking, a broad back stepped into my line of sight, blocking her from view. It was as if a dam had been erected, halting the flood and giving me a moment to breathe, to gather the shreds of my shattered composure.

"Hello, Mrs. Kirby," Adrian stepped in, "My name is Adrian Scott and we're here to talk to you. Do you have time?"

I let go of the breath I was holding the moment he stood between us. My legs are not keeping me steady as I arch a little with my palm on Adrian's back, breathing in and out quietly.

"No," Came her reply, "Both of you get off my porch and never turn back. Thank you."

I gathered myself, standing tall and drawing in steady breaths.

*It's okay, Liza. You can do this. You're not alone.*

"Hmm, you should watch your tone with me, Mrs. Kirby. I don't like it."

I took a step aside to see her face and her piercing gaze landed on me briefly before she looked at Adrian with an unwelcomed look.

"Get out," she snarled, slamming the door with all her might, but Adrian's hand caught it midway. I flinched as he shoved it open with a force that made her stagger back. She glared at him when he nonchalantly strode inside, my hand clasped tightly in his, his presence a shield to me.

"Sit," he commanded, his voice like steel, pinning her in place with his glare.

"How dare you?" she spat, her voice defiant. "If you don't leave now, I'll call the cops."

He rolled his eyes, "Alright, don't sit. We don't wish to sit anyways. The ride here was very long. My back aches," he retorted, his sarcasm cutting through the tension.

She clenched her jaw and her eyes darting to me, seeking some hint of the fear she had always inspired. But this time, I stood firm, my fear replaced by a newfound resolve. This strength and courage isn't natural, it's coming to me because I have Adrian by my side.

"Why are you here?" she demanded.

"I'm here to ask you something," I answered, my voice steady, meeting her glare with unflinching determination.

"What?"

"Archon Astralis," The name slipped from my lips, and her expression morphed from surprise to the same evil one-the one I fear. My grip on Adrian's hand tightened, and he gave a reassuring squeeze, silently promising he was by my side, "What do you know?" I asked, trying to keep my voice steady and expressions fearless.

She smirked, her eyes gleaming with a twisted satisfaction. "You've changed a lot. Speaking to me without stuttering and even demanding answers. I'm impressed." My heart thumped to see that same sinister look again.

"Just answer her question," Adrian spoke, his voice was calm, but the tension was evident in his clenched jaw, "What do you know?"

She tightened her jaw, shooting daggers at his way through her eyes, "Who the hell are you and how dare you demand answers from me!"

He rolled his eyes again.

I grabbed my courage and spoke up, "I need your help, Mom. I have a very unusual situation on my hands so if you know anything about it, please tell me."

She remained silent for a moment, contemplating, before finally responding. "What do I get in return?" Her gaze was now on Adrian.

"What do you want?" Adrian's smile was strained, a veneer over his mounting frustration.

Her smirk deepened, and she fixed her gaze on me. "Your mansion." My eyes widened in disbelief. She let out a sinister laugh. "What, can't trade your precious house for some crucial information?"

Tears welled up in my eyes as I choked out, "No. I will not give it to you."

She raised an eyebrow, a mocking glint in her eyes. "Oh, the young Liza has finally learned to say no to me. Very impressive," Her expression darkened as she took a step closer, her gaze piercing into mine. "But guess what, my dearest daughter? Even if you offered your life, I wouldn't help you. I despise you. Your very presence makes my skin crawl, and it will take me years to scrub the memory of you from my mind.

"Please, stop," My voice trembled with the weight of my emotions, and she relished very bit of it.

"Stop?" she scoffed, her eyes burning with disdain. "How can you possibly ask me to stop when I loathe you to the core of my soul? How can you stand there, pretending as if you haven't ruined everything?" she took a step forward to me and made me step back. My tears now falling inconsolably down my cheeks as she continued, "You're the cause of everything that happened to me, to my husband—our misery, our downfall. You were the mistake we never should have made. You're nothing but a curse, a poison in my life, a blight-

Her voice choked as Adrian lunged forward, grabbing her throat and pinning her against the wall with such force that the canvas on the wall rattled violently before crashing to the floor. Her eyes widened in terror, gasping for air as she clawed at his arm, desperately struggling for breath while I stood frozen in shock, unable to move.

"Say another word and I'll rip your tongue off!" he snarled, his muscles tensing as he increased the pressure on her neck.

Everything slowed as I stared at him, shocked.

He didn't look like the Adrian I knew. He looked dangerous and terrifying, his face twisted with a cold, ruthless fury that sent chills down my spine. He looked utterly different, almost unrecognizable in his rage.

I swallowed.

Until now, I had only been afraid of my mother, but in this moment, Adrian scared me far more than she ever had. The intensity in his eyes, the raw power radiating from him-it was like staring into the eyes of a predator.

I snapped my attention on my mother whose eyes began to roll back, her face turning a disturbing shade of crimson as she struggled for breath. The veins on her neck stood out as she clawed weakly at his arm, her fingers trembling with desperation. Her gasps for air became shallow, her body convulsing under his relentless grip.

She was on the brink of dying.

The gravity of the situation crashed over me like a tidal wave, jolting me into action. I couldn't let this continue. The fear that had paralyzed me moments before was now replaced with a desperate urgency. I have to do something before it is too late.

"Adrian, let her go," I said, my voice shaking and my legs trembling. When he didn't respond, I shouted, "Adrian, Let Her Go!"

Hearing my cry, he released her instantly, causing her to collapse to the ground, gasping for air and massaging her bruised neck. Her face was pale, tinged with red. Though he nearly killed her, I felt no pity for her, only a numb detachment. My mind was consumed by Adrian's actions-an aggression I never thought he was capable of.

But what could I expect? He was Adrian Scott, a fictional character pulled into reality out of sheer necessity. Of course, he could be unpredictable.

With a sigh, Adrian crouched down to her level, one knee on the ground, his elbow resting on the other knee as he lifted her chin with a firm hand. I never imagined I would see my mother so terrified. Her eyes, wide with dread, had lost their usual disdain. Now they had pure terror.

"Now, Mrs. Kirby, tell us what you know," He said, his voice menacing, "And if you dare lie to us, I will dig your grave with my own bare hands. Is that understood?" She nodded fearfully, glancing at me. This time, I didn't flinch. Adrian's presence gave me the strength to face her without fear, "Eyes on me," he commanded, and she quickly obeyed. "Speak."

"The only thing I know is the tomes Archon turned into magical artifact are distributed to different covens for preservation. And one of them is with Liza herself," I frowned and exchanged a look with Adrian. "You don't know about it. Only your grandmother did and I do."

"So, Nana was a witch too?" I asked, and she nodded. "Why didn't I know this?"

"Because my mother wanted you to have a normal life. Witches have responsibilities and duties, a very different path to follow. She wanted you to be normal, to be different from us... to be normal."

Hearing this, a deep, suffocating pain gripped my chest. My grandmother had hoped for a normal life for me, but after her passing, my world fell apart. My mother destroyed everything she intended for me. Her cruelty turned my life into a never-ending nightmare, filled with regrets and suffering. Nightmares and panic attacks plagued me for years, her actions leaving a lasting scar on my existence.

"I never saw you or Nana doing magic," I said, my voice sounding robotic. My chest tightened with every breath I took.

"She transferred her powers into something and put it away. She did it before I was even born. And I can't do magic because, regardless of coven or bloodline, we're chosen by the universe itself. I'm just an ordinary human, while you are a witch."

A heavy silence filled the room until Adrian broke it. "You said one book is with Liza. What do you mean by that?"

"The mansion where she lives. One of the tomes is hidden in its walls," Another pause followed. "My mother was safeguarding one tome. She gave you that mansion so you could continue to protect it, whether you knew it or not."

"If you know so much, tell me how one of the characters can be sent back into the book," I demanded. Her eyes widened with fear and shock as she glanced at Adrian, then back at me, realising that Adrian wasn't from this realm. She stayed mute, looking at me in shock and fear.

"Do you know or not?" Adrian demanded, snapping her attention to him, his tone sharp and holding no softness as usual. She shook her head, but Adrian's eyes narrowed, his glare a silent threat. "Think again."

"Archon didn't really win against Zephyr. He died in the process. The spell he used, or whatever way he found, died with him."

It was disappointing to know that no one knew how to send him back. The only person who knew died the same day.

"Do you think you know how to close the veil?" I asked, her answers and knowledge kindling a small flame of hope within me.

She frowned, confusion marring her features. "What veil?"

"The veil from which Adrian has come."

"There's no such thing as a veil. The wall that separates fiction and reality is the book itself. The novels are the doors. His way back is through his tome," Relief washed over me, and it took all my restraint not to smile. "He won't just disappear into thin air; his ashes will return to his realm through the tome."

"Does it also mean that Zephyr can't rise unless he's summoned?" I asked, hoping to hear a positive answer.

"No, he can't. But if he isn't sent back, he could cause a disaster. This spell has strict rules: no character can stay in our world longer than necessary. If he does, it will disturb reality, creating chaos in both realms. And if that happens, Zephyr will be the least of your problems!"

It was a glimmer of hope that Zephyr couldn't rise, but the stakes were even higher. If Adrian wasn't sent back, the consequences would be catastrophic. Not only would Zephyr become a looming threat, but the entire boundary between fiction and reality could collapse. Fictional worlds could invade ours, blending with reality, while our world might be swallowed into the pages of a story. The delicate balance that kept our worlds separate would be shattered, plunging everything into a chaotic whirlwind where nothing could be trusted or understood.

The only solution was to send Adrian back to his realm. The challenge now was figuring out how to achieve that. The weight of the task felt overwhelming, but it was clear that restoring the balance was the only way to prevent a complete unravelling of both our worlds.

*But...*

I looked at Adrian and felt like someone had jabbed a knife through my chest.

*But how do I do it when I don't want to?*

"Looks like our work here is done, Liza," Adrian announced, rising to his feet. "We should go." I nodded, my gaze lingering on my mother.

She remained frozen in place, her eyes glued to the floor, her fear palpable in every trembling line of her posture. I scoured her face for any hint of motherly affection or a spark of concern, but all I found was a stark, icy indifference. Detachment. My heart ached once again.

Adrian's grip tightened around my hand, prompting me to move. With one last, fleeting glance at the woman who had once been my mother, I turned away, letting him guide me out as we left her behind, a mere shadow in the distance.

He opened the car door for me and took his place behind the wheel. As the engine roared to life, an oppressive silence filled the air. A tear slipped down my cheek and I immediately wiped that off.

"You know, it's okay to cry sometimes," he said, bringing my gaze at him. His expression a mix of concern and something deeper that I couldn't quite decipher. "You can cry, Liza."

Tears welled up in my eyes before spilling over, streaming down my cheeks in steady trails. The dam of pent-up emotions shattered, and I broke into uncontrollable sobs. The weight of everything I'd learned, combined with the painful truth that Adrian had to leave—no matter what—cut through me deeply, leaving an ache I couldn't ignore.

I put my hands on my face and cried hard, not caring that he was looking at me.

I heard him sigh deeply before he reached for my wrist, pulling me toward him. My upper body pressed against his as he held me close, his hand gently caressing my hair, "It's alright. It's okay," I let out another sob and hugged him back while he continued to caress my head and soothe me.

# Chapter 19

# The Breaking Point

*Adrian's POV*

Liza's silence was killing me. Her ignorance was gnawing at my very core, driving me to the edge of my sanity. I knew it was my fault-I was the problem. My behaviour was indeed annoying, infuriating even. But what could I do? When I was dancing with her, I couldn't help but feel an overwhelming urge to kiss her. This forbidden attraction was growing inside me, making me feel things I shouldn't. I knew that if I crossed the remaining line between us, it would deeply hurt her, and that was the last thing I wanted. So, if staying within these boundaries was the only way, then fine. I wouldn't cross it.

But her silent treatment was unbearable. I asked for it-I yelled at her. I demanded distance. But I never said she should act as if I didn't exist. I didn't like it at all. I loved speaking to her and answering her questions. I adored the way she rolled her eyes, smiled, and blinked when something worried her. I cherished it all. But she decided to take that away from me with her silence. *Fantastic.*

When we reached the place, I saw her slipping into that catatonic state again, and I pulled her out, assuring her that I was there for her. For a moment, she smiled, trusting me, but then her ego took over. She jerked my hand away with such audacity. I was taken aback, but recalling that I had invited this rift, I decided to let it slide and wait for her to forgive me.

As we walked towards the door, she didn't seem as worried as she had been in the car. But as soon as the door opened and she greeted her mother-a mother who didn't look at her with warmth, but with disdain-Liza's face went pale. I could see the change in her demeanor, the shortage of breath. She was on the verge of an anxiety attack.

Quickly, I stepped in front of her, giving her a moment to calm herself. I know her. Liza needed a moment to compose herself. She wasn't some fragile girl; she had a strength within her that was undeniable. But the sight of her mother drained all the courage she had mustered to come here. And that woman seems to show no emotion for her, only loathing.

While Liza was grabbing confidence to face her mother, I spoke to that woman with as much civility as I could muster, hoping she'd extend the same courtesy. But oh, that wretched bitch-she had the audacity to try and shut the door in my face. If she weren't Liza's mother, I swear, I'd have killed her right then and there. Her smile, her voice, her very presence made my skin crawl. How could someone like her give birth to someone like Liza? They were complete opposites, save for the same haunted grey eyes.

All the while, I was struggling to remain calm but when she made Liza cry, *my* Liza cry, I lost all semblance of control and grabbed her throat. I had every intention of killing her, choking the life out of her. Watching Liza's tears fall because of that woman's cruel words ignited a fury within me that I could barely contain.

Her mother's terrified eyes locked onto mine, and her face went as white as a ghost. My eyes must have been blazing green, like a brewing thunderstorm. I wasn't going to let her go until she was dead. But I had to, not for Liza, but because she might have the information I needed. I released her, and she crumpled to the ground like the worthless creature she was. When I looked back at Liza, I realized my grave mistake. She wasn't supposed to see this side of me. The Adrian she believed in wasn't violent. But now, I couldn't undo what had been done.

Later, her mother spilled every bit of information like a talking bird. Nothing she said included the crucial information we desperately needed—*how to send me back*. But we learned other things that surprised and angered me. Apparently, her grandmother wanted Liza to have a happy, normal life, but who was she to decide that for her? Wasn't it supposed to be Liza's decision? Instead, they chose for her, making her the guardian of something she knew nothing about. *Wonderful.*

While her mother spoke, I ensured she didn't scare or further discomfort Liza. But what truly upset me was the hope in Liza's eyes, a hope to see some motherly love, despite everything. Her mother remained cold and distant. I had to hold back my urge to grab her by the hair and slam her head against the wall when she couldn't even look into Liza's hopeful eyes. *Damn, I hated this woman.*

Knowing too well that I could lose control again, I quickly made our exit. The information we had gathered wasn't enough to solve our problem, but it was enough to calm the chaos in Liza's mind. She didn't want the evil Zephyr to return, but as things stood, he could if I wasn't sent back. Yet, she didn't want me to go back either. I've seen it. In her eyes, her change of tone and body language whenever it is mentioned that I need to return. Although, I know that despite it, she would send me back because she isn't some fool; she is Liza Kirby.

In the car, when she cried, my heart ached. I knew she was hurt-hurt because her mother hadn't changed at all. I didn't know what to do except hugging her. So I did and when I felt, she was calm enough to let go, I pulled myself back. Her eyes were swollen and red. Seeing her like that made me want to go back inside and kill that woman. But I stayed, needing to ask Liza the question that had been tormenting me ever since I witnessed it-her panic attack. I needed to know what had happened, why her mother hates her, and why her home scared her so much.

I placed my hand on her cheek, my thumb gently brushing the skin below her eyes. "Why does she hate you?" I asked softly. She remained silent, her gaze fixed and unblinking. My eyes drifted to her lips, now a darker shade from crying, and I had to swallow hard to resist the urge to lean in and taste them.

I forced myself to look back into her wide, unseeing eyes. "It's okay. I won't ask you again." I removed my hand and started the car.

"I was ten years old," she began, grabbing my attention, "when Dad died. I was playing outside the house. Mom was sitting on the porch steps, and Dad was playing with me." She pointed to the window, where I could see cars passing by. "I accidentally threw the ball that way. When Dad ran to grab it, a car-" Her voice choked, and her eyes filled with tears again. "It hit him." I quickly grabbed her palm, caressing it gently. "She hates me because I killed her husband."

"He was your dad too, Liza. It wasn't your fault."

"Maybe. But after he died, Mom changed. She started drinking excessively and began abusing me, both verbally and..."

A searing heat spread through my chest, a fiery rage that could only be quenched by killing her.

"I was fourteen when she kicked me out of the house and locked the doors. That day, I was chased by some drunk men and almost kidnapped-" She took a breath, steadying her tone while I clenched my fists tightly to keep myself under control. "A cop saved me and brought me back home, returning me back to her. When the cop yelled at her and warned her never to do it again, she got mad and almost killed me."

I took a deep breath in an attempt to calm myself.

Hesitantly, she lifted her shirt, revealing a scar on her abdomen-a scar long enough to get attention if she doesn't cover it. It was a brutal testament to her suffering that struck me like a physical blow. I clenched my jaw so tightly it felt like it might shatter, my heart breaking for her. That moment, all I could feel was rage, pure rage.

"I'm so sorry for making you relive this," I said, my voice cracking with a deep, aching remorse. "I'm really, truly sorry, Liza."

"It's okay. I never forget it. This scar is a constant reminder of my past. I can never get rid of it."

I wanted to pour out a flood of comforting words, to soothe her shattered spirit, but they wouldn't come. The enormity of her pain left me speechless, a deep, helpless ache gnawing at me. She had endured so much suffering, and the last thing I wanted was to add to her wounds. My heart ached with the weight of my unspoken empathy, desperate to offer solace yet paralyzed by the fear of hurting her more by pushing too much.

"Wasn't she arrested?" I asked, trying to take the conversation to a different path, rather than digging more. She shook her head, igniting every cell in my body, "Why?" I questioned, more like releasing a breath of fury.

"I was in a coma for three days after that. She told the cops that some intruders broke in and did this to me. Plus, I didn't dare to speak against her. So, I admitted that it was true."

Good. Because now, I will unleash upon her a torrent of suffering that will eclipse anything she's ever inflicted on you. I swear, she will endure agony a hundred times more brutal and relentless than anything she has ever known. This is not merely vengeance-this is about delivering a reckoning so profound that it will haunt her soul.

"Where was your grandma during this time?"

"She knew what Mom had done to me. She came and took me away with her. Today is the first time I have seen her after that."

"If she knew your mother was abusive, why would she leave you with her in the first place?"

"Because I wanted to stay, Adrian," her voice chocked again, "I had hope. I thought once she'd forgiven me, everything would be good again. I believed I could be happy."

"Oh, Liza."

I couldn't help but feel more drawn to her. She's the epitome of innocence, pure and sweet.

"I wish Dad hadn't died that day. Maybe things would have been different," she managed a small, sorrowful smile. I smiled back, nodding, but the truth was more complex and painful.

Her mother didn't hate her just because her husband died while playing with her. It was because Liza was loved more and valued above her. Liza was seen as special by the universe, while her mother was left in the shadows. Her husband loved Liza more than he loved her, and even Liza's grandmother, her mother's own mother, adored Liza. The hatred came from being denied the love she felt she deserved and given to the person she gave birth to. Her husband, the only person who truly cared for her, died in an accident while playing with Liza.

It's no surprise she'd direct her anger and resentment toward Liza, who symbolized everything she had lost.

"What are you thinking?" She asked, pulling me from my thoughts.

"Nothing," I muttered, forcing a calm tone. "Just reminding myself to keep my anger in check next time. That was completely unacceptable and wrong of me."

"Yeah, you...you scared me."

My heart clenched painfully, that's what I fear. I never want her to be afraid of me, to see the darkness I kept hidden beneath my surface. She believes in a version of me that isn't real, a carefully constructed illusion. The truth is far more horrifying, and once she uncovers it, she will despise me with every fiber of her being. The mere thought of her eyes filled with disgust and betrayal is unbearable. I would rather face death than let her discover the monstrous truth lurking behind the mask I've so meticulously worn.

I chuckled, trying to lighten the mood. "You should remember that I'm not some soft romance book character."

"Right," She smiled and settled comfortably in her seat, looking straight ahead.

"Liza," I called, drawing her gaze back at me. "Thank you for sharing that with me."

She smiled, "I feel better talking about it."

I smiled back, "Good. And... I hope you're not mad at me anymore and the silence treatment is over?" I couldn't help but ask. She laughed and I didn't require an answer. I smiled happily and then we drove back to Rachel's place.

"Oh, I almost forgot!" she exclaimed suddenly, "It's about to turn four. Nate's flight must have landed."

I frowned, looking at her with utter confusion. "Nate's flight?"

"Yeah, he called me last night to tell me about his arrival. Head to the airport, please."

My grip tightened around the steering wheel, knuckles white with the strain. A deep, searing sensation flared in my chest, a twisted knot of discomfort. I stared at the road ahead, but all I could see was the image of Nate Wilson-his smug face, his easy confidence.

The thought of him arriving ignited a blaze of resentment. I was consumed by the dark, corrosive envy that twisted my thoughts and tightened my chest.

# Chapter 20

# *Caught in the Crossfire*

*Liza's POV*

"You alright?" I asked Adrian, noticing the strange silence that had fallen over him since we arrived. When he finally turned to look at me, he flashed a smile-one of those perfect, dazzling smiles that could light up a room. But there was something off about it, something that made me uneasy. It was a beautiful smile, but for some reason, it didn't seem real.

I told myself I was overthinking it, letting my imagination get the best of me. Adrian was probably just tired, or maybe the weight of everything we'd been through was finally catching up with him. Still, I couldn't shake the feeling that something was wrong.

Deciding to push my concerns aside, I tried to lighten the mood. "I wonder how he's going to react upon seeing you. I mean, your meeting wasn't... Epic," I spoke in an attempt to draw him out of whatever was troubling him.

"He'll be shocked," Came his reply, his voice flat, his eyes fixed on the gate of the airport. There was no humour in his tone, no trace of the usual spark that made him so magnetic. Just a simple, almost resigned statement.

I nodded, "Of course, he will be shocked," I wanted to press him, to ask him what was really going on in that head of his, but I didn't say anything and let the silence settle between us as we waited.

As we stood by our car, waiting, I glanced at him and smiled. After sharing my past with Adrian, I find myself feeling something I never expected-freedom. It's as if a weight I didn't even realize I was carrying has been lifted off my shoulders, and the sense of release is overwhelming. It's strange, almost surreal, that I could feel this way with someone I've known for just a few days. I've known Nate for years-he's been my rock, my closest friend-but even with him, I've always kept a part of myself locked away, hidden behind walls I never thought I'd let anyone see behind. Nate knows that my mother was a drug addict and that I grew up lonely, but he doesn't know the full story, the darkness that stained my childhood, the trauma that lingered long after the bruises faded.

He doesn't know about the scar on my belly, the one I've never spoken about, not to him, not to anyone. He doesn't know how that scar is more than just a mark on my skin-it's a constant reminder of everything I endured, of why I never went home for summer vacations, of why I couldn't talk about my mother the way others talked about theirs. He doesn't know how deeply her actions wounded me, how her neglect and cruelty turned me into a shell of the person I could have been. For years, I couldn't smile without feeling like a fraud, couldn't speak without stumbling over my words, as if the trauma had lodged itself in my throat, choking me whenever I tried to express myself. I felt trapped, suffocated by the memories, by the nightmares that plagued me every night, by the fear that I would never escape the shadow of my past.

But then Adrian came into my life, and everything changed. The one who never even by mistake thought about returning home, came back here and met her mother-the mother who shattered my soul in a way that I never found my lost pieces again. Now, standing next to Adrian, I feel like I've finally found those lost pieces, and I'm stepping into the light for the first time in what feels like forever. The fear that used to grip me so tightly, that used to wrap around my heart like a vise, squeezing the life out of me, is gone. The anxiety that kept me awake at night, the tightness in my chest, the lump in my throat-all of it had vanished. In its place is a feeling I barely recognize-freedom. I feel free in a way I never thought I could, free of the trauma that I've carried for so many years.

And it's all because of him. Because of Adrian Scott. If he hadn't come into my life, I know I'd still be hiding, still pretending that everything was fine, still trying to outrun a past that was always right behind me. In fact, I think if I had met Adrian sooner, maybe it wouldn't have taken me years to reclaim myself. Maybe I wouldn't have spent so long hiding in my room, burying myself in work, or losing myself in books that allowed me to escape my reality. But Adrian made me see the truth-that running away from my pain was never the option. He made me realize that by avoiding my past, I was letting it control me, letting it dictate my every move, my every thought. He showed me that the only way to truly move forward was to face it head-on, to acknowledge it, to own it.

I've realized that healing isn't about forgetting or escaping the past but about reclaiming power over the places that once held us captive. The thought of coming here returned my nightmares and I thought it would again take years to suppress them with pills but I didn't see any bad dreams after the one on plane, nor am I having any discomfort walking around here. I completely forgot that these streets don't just hold their history and their own stories. But mine too. The transformation was palpable - what once induced fear now offered solace, what once brought nightmares now allowed for dreams of a different kind.

I never thought I would ever be able to stand here and smile. What had happened to me, had happened. Nothing I do can change that. But I don't have to let it define me anymore. I don't have to let it keep me trapped in a cycle of fear and self-doubt. I can choose to move forward, to embrace my past as a part of who I am, but not the entirety of who I am. I can choose to live, really live, for the first time in my life.

"There he comes!" Adrian's voice snapped me out of my thoughts, pulling me back to the present. I followed his gaze toward the large glass gates of the airport.

Nate made his entrance with a flair that was almost theatrical, striding through the doors with a trolley suitcase trailing behind him. He had that familiar, wide grin on his face, the one that always made me feel like everything was going to be okay. But the moment his eyes landed on Adrian, the joy drained from his expression. The spark in his eyes flickered out, replaced by shock and confusion. His confident stride faltered, his pace slowing as if he was questioning whether he was really seeing Adrian standing there next to me, or was his mind playing tricks on him?

I glanced over at Adrian, expecting to see the same blank, emotionless mask he'd been wearing since we arrived. But to my surprise, he was grinning, a mischievous glint in his eyes as he waved his hand in a playful wave at Nate.

Was this the same man who had been standing next to me moments ago, lost in some unfathomable thoughts, his face void of any emotion?

I tried to make sense of the sudden change in him, but there was no time to dwell on it. Plus, I'm used to his roller-coaster mood swings.

Nate was close now, close enough that I could catch the scent of his cologne, rich and familiar. I looked back at him, but he didn't seem interested in me as much as he was interested in Adrian Scott. His attention was locked on Adrian, his eyes narrow with disbelief and questions. I forced a smile, trying to draw Nate's focus back to me, to break the tension that was thickening the air between us.

"Hey, Nate!" I greeted him, my voice cheerful, almost too cheerful, as I tried to cut through the awkwardness and grab his attention on me. But Nate barely glanced at me, his eyes quickly darting back to Adrian as if I were invisible.

"You patched up with this bastard?" Nate asked, his voice sharp and laced with bitterness.

I was highly offended to hear him cursing Adrian. But then I remembered the last time they had seen each other. For Nate, he cheated on me with his ex. Of course, he'd hate him because he hurt me. But we all know that isn't true, he actually helped me get Nate but we're not telling him the truth, are we?

The memory cooled my anger, and I forced myself to take a breath, to let it slide, even though my heart ached from the effort

"No, it's not true. We've become friends," I said, hoping my words would calm Nate down, and the tension in the air would ease. But instead of the relief I expected, Nate's expression remained as stormy as before. If anything, my response seemed to have the opposite effect-his anger grew, and I could almost see the fury radiating off him, like waves of heat in the summer.

"How could you let this piece of shit be friends with you, Liza? Where did your morals go?"

I blinked.

It was the first time I'd ever seen Nate so mad at me-more than mad, he looked disappointed, and that hurt me. I opened my mouth to respond, to try to explain, but before I could say a word, Adrian's low chuckle filled the space between us, silencing me.

"I suggest you watch your words, Mr. Wilson," he said, his tone light, almost playful, but with an underlying threat.

Nate's jaw tightened, his eyes locking onto Adrian's with a burning intensity. "Or what?" he challenged, his voice hard. It was almost unsettling to see the contrast between the two- Nate, seething with anger, and Adrian, smiling like he was enjoying every second of this, like he was some kind of twisted puppet master pulling the strings.

"Nate, stop it," I requested, trying to keep my voice firm without sounding like I was taking sides. I didn't want to offend any of them, but this was getting out of hand. "Why are you trying to start a fight here? You've just arrived."

"Why the hell is he here, Liza?" Nate shot back, his voice rising with frustration. "Isn't he supposed to be out of your life?"

"Yes," I admitted, trying to keep my tone calm and reasonable. "But he apologized to me, and I forgave him. We're friends now."

"I apologized?" Adrian interjected, feigning surprise. A playful smirk on his face, "When?" I turned to him, irritated. I'm trying to handle this and he's enjoying this.

I sighed, trying to push down my growing frustration.

"I apologize for his attitude," I said to Nate, "He just likes provoking people. Ignore him." But Adrian's soft chuckle beside me only added to my irritation.

*What is wrong with him?*

"Likes provoking or breaking trust like he broke yours? He cheated on you and you're calling him your friend?" Before I could respond in my defence, Nate rolled his eyes, letting out a scoff. "You know what? I don't care. It's your choice and you're mature enough to decide what's best for you. Plus, I didn't come here to waste my time on this friend of yours," he pulled out his phone to check something before looking back at us. "The cab I booked is here. Please, come with me."

My heart skipped a beat at his request. I knew Nate had planned to take me out, but I didn't expect him to ask so soon, right after landing. I felt a sudden wave of anxiety, unsure of what to do.

"Uh-" I glanced at Adrian, hoping to gauge his reaction, but his face remained the same, amused. For a moment, I thought I saw something in his eyes, a flicker of... something. But it was gone as quickly as it appeared. Confused, I turned back to Nate with a nervous smile. "I would, but I'm not exactly dressed for a date," I said, gesturing to my outfit-blue denim jeans, a fitted red top with a denim jacket, and sneakers. My hair was down, and the only jewellery I wore was a simple white stone pendant that was given to me by my grandmother before she died.

Nate looked me up and down, taking in my appearance. "You don't have to wear jewellery or fancy dresses, Liza," he said, his voice softening. "You look perfect in everything you wear. But if you feel like you need something more, we can buy you a dress on the way. Cool?"

I nodded, unsure of what else to say, when suddenly Adrian grabbed my hand and twirled me around. My hair whipped across my face, and I felt my heart race as blood rushed to my cheeks, turning them a bright shade of scarlet. It was so unexpected, so out of the blue, that I didn't know how to react.

"Nope. I don't think you need a dress," Adrian said, his tone teasing as he let go of my hand. "You look absolutely fine." I glanced at Nate, wide-eyed, and saw his jaw clench, his fists tightening until his knuckles turned white. Adrian noticed too, and with a smug grin, added, "Plus, don't you think she should feel comfortable?"

I could see the amusement dancing in Adrian's eyes—he was enjoying this, provoking Nate, and it made me want to scream. This wasn't funny. Not at all.

But I forced a smile and nodded, trying to keep the peace. "He's right. I'm comfortable in this." Nate didn't take his eyes off Adrian, and before I knew it, he grabbed my wrist and pulled me toward him. My eyes widened as I nearly stumbled into his chest, my heart pounding in my ears. Nate smirked, a triumphant gleam in his eyes before he put his gaze on me, "Your comfort matters more. Now, shall we? I have so much planned for you."

Awkwardly, I glanced at Adrian, expecting to see that familiar smirk, but it was gone. Instead, there was something darker—displeasure, maybe even anger—flickering in his eyes for just a second before he masked it.

My heart twisted uncomfortably.

The cab pulled up, and Nate, ignoring the tension, eagerly grabbed my arm, pulling me along with him. He was grinning, and I forced a smile in return, but it felt hollow, like a mask I couldn't hold up. As Nate opened the door of the car, I couldn't resist glancing back at Adrian. If I hadn't met him, I'd be screaming with joy—this was my dream, going out with Nate. But now, the thrill was gone, replaced by a heavy emptiness, a weight pressing down on me, as though I were being forced into something I no longer truly wanted.

I took a deep breath, shaking my head to clear it. This was what I wanted, right? Nate, my long-time crush, was finally taking me out. I should be focusing on that, on the realization of this dream I'd held for so long. I needed to forget about Adrian, forget about whatever pull he had on me. But even as I told myself that, a part of me knew I was just trying to convince myself—to silence the voice in my head that whispered how different things felt now. The voice that warned me Adrian had already changed something deep within me, something I couldn't ignore, no matter how hard I tried.

I looked away from him and got in.

# Chapter 21

# *Shadows of Impending Doom*

*Rachel's POV*

The tome in my hands felt heavier with each passing second as if the weight of the worlds—both real and imagined—rested upon it. My eyes remained glued to its blank pages, unblinking, refusing to look away from the void that offered no answers.

Panic gnawed at the edges of my resolve, an icy fear creeping through my veins. How could this be? How could there be no trace, no whisper of a solution to the nightmare that had clawed its way back into our lives? No one had ever anticipated that this catastrophe might resurface, that the fragile veil between fiction and reality would tear once more. It had seemed impossible, inconceivable. The calamity of the past had been enough to deter even the most reckless of minds, to ensure that no witch would ever dare attempt the ritual again. We all knew the cost. We all bore the scars of that knowledge—the loss, the devastation, the lives that had been ripped away when the boundaries between worlds blurred.

Now, here I was, clutching a tome that had once been filled with vibrant life but was now an empty shell, waiting, and needing its essence restored. The knowledge that it was blank, that it needed its belonging back, sent a wave of dread coursing through me. The evil, Zephyr, might have been sealed away within the pages of one of the tomes, trapped and powerless for now, but the real danger wasn't just him.

Adrian, standing here in the flesh, was a reminder of the precarious balance we were teetering on. He was just as dangerous as Zephyr, if not more so. He was a wild card, a force of nature pulled from the depths of fiction and set loose in a world that wasn't meant to contain him. I can't help but feel a gnawing worry deep in my gut. The tome is a ticking time bomb, and with every second that passed, the risk of something going terribly wrong increased. I knew what was at stake—what we all stood to lose if I failed to find a way to reverse what had been done. The burden of it all threatened to crush me. I have to find a way to restore balance, to put things back where they belonged before the line between fiction and reality shatters beyond repair.

I searched the library frantically, my eyes scanning over the endless rows of grimoires from every corner of the globe, each one steeped in ancient secrets and powerful witchcraft. Yet, despite the overwhelming amount of knowledge, none of it held the key to solving the crisis at hand. Frustration built within me, but I couldn't afford to let it consume me. I gathered the most crucial items—grimoires, arcane texts, and the tome. I hurried out of the library and into my study, placing them carefully on the table. My mind raced as I reached for my phone to call Liza. She hadn't returned yet, and I needed to check on her.

Liza Kirby. There is something about this girl—an aura of purity and power that set her apart from everyone else. The first time I laid my eyes on her, I knew she wasn't an ordinary mortal. When she confided in me, telling me what she had accidentally set in motion, I believed her instantly. What surprised me was that she didn't seem to know anything about her own potential, her heritage, or the immense power she carried within her. *How could she not know?* She was Archon's descendant, a being with extraordinary abilities, and yet, she was utterly unaware of what she was capable of.

The phone rang once before she picked up. "Hey, Rachel?"

"Were are you, Liza?" I asked, setting up the witchcraft materials on the table. The ritual I was about to perform was complex, ancient magic that could help me find the answers I sought.

"I'm... I'm quite far, aunty!" Her words made me pause, and I frowned at the term 'aunty.' It wasn't like her to address me so formally. "I know you must be mad at me for not keeping you updated about my... locations and plans. I'm really sorry. But I'll be back before you even realize it. I promise."

"What are you talking about, Liza?" I asked, confused by her cryptic tone. There was a brief pause on her end before she spoke again.

"I forgot to inform you but," Her words made me frown deeper. "I'm going on a date tonight."

Suddenly, everything clicked into place, and I clenched my jaw in disbelief. "Are you insane? You know the stakes, and you're out on a date?"

"I know, I know. Adrian must have reached by now. Try calling him; maybe he can help you with dinner tonight," she said, brushing off the seriousness of the situation.

"How can you be so irresponsible and careless? Do you realize that every second we're edging closer to disaster?" My voice was tinged with anger and frustration.

"Yes. I understand. I'll talk to you when I'm back. I'm really sorry. I won't be late," she said in a hurry, and before I could say another word, she hung up. I sit there, stunned.

*During all this chaos, she had gone out on a date?*

With a heavy sigh, I turned back to the task at hand, trying to push the irritation aside. I needed to focus. But just as I began to prepare for the ritual, a noise from behind startled me. I spun around, heart racing, only to find Robert standing there, looking completely unaware of the near heart attack he'd given me.

"Oh, Robert, you scared me," I said, letting out a shaky breath.

"I apologize. Do you want me to get you something?" he asked politely.

I nodded, trying to calm my nerves. "Yes, draw the curtains and light all the candles."

He stayed.

"You wanna say something, Robert?"

He nodded, "Yes. I want a leave. I need to go to the village for some reasons."

"Okay, you can leave."

He nodded and set to drop the curtains as I refocused on the table, taking a deep breath to steady myself. I had never attempted this kind of magic before—communing with ancestors who had been dead for centuries was no simple feat. I lit the candles on the table and closed my eyes, ready to begin, but just then, the shrill ring of the telephone shattered my concentration. With a sigh, I walked over and picked up the receiver.

"Greene, speaking. How may I help you?" I said, trying to keep my voice calm.

"Hello, Rachel. Oh my God, where is your phone?!" Sabrina's panicked voice came from the other end of the line.

A frown creased my brow at her tone. "With me. What happened? You alright?"

"The tomes are being stolen!!" she cried.

My heart stopped. "What?"

"Yes. Three of them have been stolen, and the witches who were safeguarding them are dead!"

"What are you saying?" The words barely escaped my lips as I glanced around my house, suddenly hyper-aware of the unnerving silence that had settled over everything.

"Rachel, three tomes are gone, and whoever is after them isn't leaving anyone alive," Sabrina's voice was filled with urgency and worry, "When you didn't pick I thought—

"I'm fine. Don't worry," I cut her off, though the news had shaken me to my core. Now I didn't just have one problem—I had two. The tomes are being stolen, and it is clear someone has a massive agenda. It all made sense now—the tome Liza had found so mysteriously must have been dropped while someone was trying to hide it or lost by those who were stealing them. This also means that whoever's stealing them has two, not three.

"Yes, I know, but... you have one, Rachel. Whoever's behind this must be coming for you or whoever has the other tome because they know who's safeguarding them."

I swallowed hard, trying to keep my composure. "You have one too, remember?"

"I do. And I'll do everything in my power to keep it safe. But this..." She took a deep breath, "What do we do now?"

"We will do what we were chosen for. We will protect the tomes, no matter what happens."

"Yes," Sabrina agreed, determination in her voice.

"We have to find the one who's behind this, but before all that, cloak the tomes. Bury them deep in the earth if you have to, but hide them. And do you have any idea who might be behind this?"

"I wish, but sadly, I have no idea. I'm just praying they never find the remaining tomes. But I have a feeling something beyond our comprehension is unfolding, Rachel."

"Of course," I murmured, my mind racing. "The tomes hold unimaginable power. If someone tries to siphon that power, they could—" I paused as a realization struck me. "They could drain it."

"What?" Sabrina's voice was sharp with confusion.

"The only way to neutralize the threat is to drain the tomes' power. Suck the magic out and turn them back into ordinary books."

"Rachel, what are you talking about? I don't understand." Sabrina sounded bewildered, but I barely heard her. My mind was already working on the next step. "Rachel?"

"I don't know if it will work, but I have to try. But where on earth am I going to find someone with siphoning power?"

"Rachel, what are you talking about?" Sabrina's concern was evident, but I was too focused to address it. "Can you hear me?"

"Do you think draining the tome's magic could send its character back?" My voice was tight, my urgency barely contained.

A beat of silence, and then she shouted, "A character got out?!!"

"Yes. But it's fine—he's one of the good ones."

"Good ones? Are you out of your mind? Why would you risk something like this? And how in the world did you even do it? Don't tell me you managed without Archon's blood?"

"I didn't," I admitted, my tone dropping. "It's... complicated. Look, I'll explain everything—just not now. Right now, I need to know if draining the magic could fix this."

Her breath hitched audibly on the other end. "I don't know. Rachel, this is too much—too dangerous. Why didn't you tell me sooner? How could you keep this from me?"

"Because there wasn't time!" I said, my voice breaking with frustration. "Please, just do what needs to be done. Hide the tome. Now."

A heavy pause, then her voice softened, tinged with fear. "Okay. But Rachel... be careful. Whatever this is, it's bigger than either of us. Stay safe."

"You too," I murmured, then hung up, the weight of the conversation sinking into my chest as I let out a shaky sigh.

Without wasting a moment, I rushed back to the library, my footsteps echoing off the ancient walls as I made my way to the shelves. I sifted through the dust-covered tomes and grimoires, desperate to find anything—*anything*—that could help me find the mortal who has siphoning power.

My mind was a whirlwind of questions as I looked through the shelves desperately, each one more terrifying than the last.

Will it work? Could draining the magic truly neutralize the tomes, and make them ordinary again? And who is stealing the tomes? What kind of person—or creature—has the power to hunt down witches, murder them in cold blood, and steal the tomes they've sworn to protect? What is their purpose? Is it power? Revenge? Or something far darker, something that I can't even begin to comprehend?

My thoughts spiralled, tangled in a web of fear and uncertainty. I had faced danger before, but this... this was different. This wasn't just about me. It was about the tomes—relics of unimaginable power. In the wrong hands, they could bring about a catastrophe beyond anything our world has ever seen. And now, two of them are gone. Stolen. The witches who protected them are dead—murdered. The thought sent a chill down my spine.

I could be next. They are coming for the tome I'm guarding. The one that's in my possession, hidden away for now. But for how long? How long before they find me? Before they tear down my defences and take it by force? I paused in my spot and clenched my fists, trying to push the fear aside. I had to stay strong. I had to think clearly. I can't let fear consume me.

"Rachel?"

The unexpected call from behind sent a jolt through me, my heart pounding wildly as I whipped around. For a split second, my mind raced with dread, but then I saw Adrian standing at the entrance, his figure bathed in the soft glow of the hallway light.

"Oh, Adrian," I let out a breath of relief, my hand on my heart. The relief was instant, my heartbeat slowing to something almost normal.

Adrian gave me an apologetic smile, "I'm sorry. I didn't mean to startle you."

"No, it's okay. You didn't," I assured him, even though the remnants of adrenaline still coursed through my veins. "So, you found her mother?" The question lingering between us like the next step in a long journey.

"Yes," he replied, his voice carrying the weight of what he'd uncovered. "And you were right. Her mother had a lot to tell."

"What did she tell you?"

Adrian took a deep, measured breath, his gaze shifting to the window as though searching for clarity in the open sky. "We should talk outside," he said finally. "It's too suffocating in here, don't you think?"

"Okay."

We left the library and sat down in the dimly lit hallway. The weight of the situation was suffocating, and I knew I wasn't hiding it well.

"Are you alright?" he asked, his eyes narrowing as he studied my face. His voice was gentle, but there was an edge to it, a demand for the truth that I couldn't ignore. I forced a smile and nodded, hoping it would suffice, but he wasn't having it.

"Don't lie to me, Rachel," he insisted, leaning closer. "Tell me what's wrong. I've never seen you so worried."

I hesitated, the words dancing on the tip of my tongue before I finally decided to let them spill out. "Tomes are being stolen," His eyes widened, a flicker of alarm breaking through his usually calm demeanour. "And the witches guarding them are being killed."

"I... I already have a situation on my hands, and now this. I'm—I'm in shock, and I'm trying to process it so I can think clearly."

"So, you have no idea who's behind it?"

"Trust me," I paused, my frustration bubbling to the surface. "If I knew, I'd have given you his name already. You could have dealt with him and ended this madness. You know what you're capable of, don't you?"

He nodded, his expression hardening with resolve. "Yes, I do. But don't worry. As long as I'm here, no one will touch you." I nodded, grateful for his assurance but still deeply unsettled. "Anyway, there's so much more I need to tell you."

"Yes, please."

Then he told me everything. Including Liza's date that she couldn't say no to because of being helpless. The information was shocking, but none of it pointed to how we could send him back.

"I'm very disappointed," he said, his voice heavy with defeat. "All this effort and no results," He chuckled, the sound bitter and sarcastic.

"I think I might have found a way."

His brows shot up in surprise. "You did?" I'm not sure but maybe I caught a glimmer in his eyes—something that didn't quite sit right with me, something that sent a shiver of unease down my spine.

"Yeah. I'm not sure it'll work, but it's worth a try."

He grinned, though the smile didn't quite reach his eyes. "Tell me."

"Drain the tomes' magic," I said, the words hanging in the air like a dark omen.

His expression shifted, a frown creasing his forehead. "You want to erase me?"

"No!" I quickly said, "I just want to send you back where you belong and destroy the way you came here. The spell, the magic—it has to be undone."

"Are you sure it will work?" he asked, his tone skeptical.

"I don't know," the weight of the uncertainty crushing me as I said, "But we have to take the risk. If we don't, both realms could collapse."

"Rachel, you're thinking irrationally. Don't you think if it were that simple, Archon wouldn't have lost his life?".His words hit me like a cold slap. He was right. If draining the tomes' magic had been the solution, Archon would not have died. "We need to find a way to keep me here longer," he continued, his voice firm. "We need more time. Wasting it on risky experiments will only bring us closer to destruction."

I nodded, feeling the sting of defeat but refusing to let go of the idea completely. "You're right. I won't waste time, but I'm not dropping this idea. We have to try."

He was silent for a moment, his gaze intense as he weighed my determination. Finally, he nodded. "Fine. If you find someone powerful enough to drain the tomes, then alright. But while you're looking, find a way to keep me here longer. We can't afford to have this threat hanging over our heads."

"I know. I already found something," I said, my voice filled with a newfound determination. He was taken back and before he could speak, I said, "Wait."

I rushed to my study and grabbed the ancient text I had found in the library. It held a spell that could keep Adrian here longer. I stumbled upon it by chance and was relieved to have found something that could at least delay the looming threat. Coming back, I handed it to him, but as our fingers brushed, a jolt like a lightning bolt shot through me, freezing me in place.

My vision blurred, and suddenly, I was plunged into a swirling abyss of darkness. Flames raged all around, consuming everything in their path. People were burning, their screams filling the air. Blood soaked the ground, mingling with the ash of charred corpses. Amidst the chaos, a massive shadow loomed, crackling with green lightning, his eyes blazing green and his hands soaked in blood and he was moving closer.

In an instant, the vision snapped away, leaving me gasping for breath. My heart thundered in my chest as a bone-deep chill crept through my veins. The room around me felt foreign, the walls closing in as if they too sensed the impending doom.

I looked at him, my eyes wide with terror.

# Chapter 22

# The Cost of Envy

*Nate's POV*

Liza and I stepped into the restaurant, immediately hit by the contrast between the quiet, dimly lit atmosphere and the lively chatter from the street outside. The place exuded a refined elegance—the kind of classy that made you sit up straighter and question whether your outfit was too casual. Maybe it was a little too fancy for what was supposed to be a laid-back evening, but I tried not to dwell on it. After all, this was our first real date, and I wasn't about to let anything ruin it.

I nudged her playfully, breaking her attention away from the polished décor. She blinked at me, a little startled but quickly recovering with a soft smile.

"So, where do you want to sit?" I asked, scanning the room. "Somewhere you can people-watch and critique their outfits?"

She let out a quiet laugh, glancing around. Her eyes settled on a cozy table near the glass window, where we could see the street outside. The city lights twinkled like scattered stars, creating the perfect backdrop.

"There," she said, pointing.

"Perfect choice," I smiled. "I'll get a front-row seat to your reaction when someone walks by wearing socks with sandals."

She chuckled as we made our way to the table. I pulled out her chair, earning a gentle smile as she slid into it, her movements graceful yet slightly tentative. Her eyes darted around the room, taking in the other diners, all of whom seemed effortlessly at ease in their sophisticated surroundings.

The waiter arrived, placed two glasses of water on the table, and handed us menus before retreating. I picked up mine, pretending to study it as I tried to calm the nervous excitement bubbling inside me.

"So," I asked, my voice lighter than I felt, "how are you?"

She smiled—that smile that had been living rent-free in my head for months. "I'm good. Absolutely fine. How are you?"

I glanced at her, letting the words tumble out before I could overthink them. "I'm happy."

Her gaze lowered, a faint smile on her face. She didn't respond immediately, and the air between us grew heavier, though I couldn't quite put my finger on why. I leaned back slightly, watching her as she traced her finger along the edge of her water glass.

I should have been ecstatic. I was finally here, sharing a meal with the woman I'd been dreaming about for what felt like forever. And yet, something nagged at the edges of my mind. She seemed distracted, her smile not quite reaching her eyes. It was as if part of her was somewhere else entirely. The thought sent a small ripple of doubt through me, a shadow creeping over what was supposed to be the perfect evening.

"Are you alright, Liza?" I asked gently. "You seem... distracted."

Her eyes snapped back to mine, and for a moment, she looked startled. Then she shook her head, her voice just a little too bright as she said, "No, no, I'm fine. Really. Just... a little out of sorts, I guess. It's strange being here with you and not talking about school stuff. I never thought we'd hang out outside of work."

Her words were light, but they felt hollow, like they were hiding something beneath the surface. I tilted my head, studying her face. She was always so hard to read—one of the things that had drawn me to her in the first place. But tonight, it wasn't the usual mystery that intrigued me. It was the wall she seemed to be putting up between us.

"It is a little weird," I admitted, trying to match her tone. "But weird isn't bad, right?"

She smiled again, but it didn't quite reach her eyes. "No, not bad at all."

We fell into a silence that wasn't exactly uncomfortable but wasn't quite easy either. I sipped my water, glancing out the window as a couple strolled past, their laughter carrying faintly through the glass. I wanted to ask her what was on her mind, to press her until she let me in. But I held back, afraid of pushing too hard and ruining the fragile balance we were teetering on.

I reached across the table and gently tapped her hand. "Hey," I said softly, waiting until her eyes met mine. "Whatever it is, you can tell me. I'm here. I'm not going anywhere."

Her lips parted as if she was about to say something, but then she closed them again, her gaze dropping to the table.

"What happened, Liza? What's bothering you?"

She looks at me, "Nothing. I just feel a little... occupied. Mentally occupied."

"With what?"

"Stuff." She shrugged, offering a faint, almost apologetic smile. "Forget it. Let's just order something."

I wanted to press her, to find out what was weighing on her mind, but I didn't. If she wasn't ready to talk, I wasn't going to push her. Her comfort mattered more.

"Alright," I said with a gentle smile. "Let's focus on food, then."

She picked up the menu, her eyes scanning it as if it held all the answers she was looking for. But even after a few minutes, her gaze hadn't moved, her mind clearly elsewhere. Finally, she looked up and said, "I think I'll have soup. And maybe the seafood platter."

"Good choice," I replied, signalling the waiter.

As we sat waiting for the food, I couldn't stop my thoughts from circling back to him, her, and them. How could she forgive him after what he did? The lies, the betrayal—he was a cheater, through and through.

I tried to push the thoughts away, but the words slipped out before I could stop them. "Tell me about him," I said, my tone as casual as I could make it.

Her head snapped up, her brows knitting together in confusion. "Who? Adrian?"

I nodded, keeping my expression light, a soft smile carefully plastered on my face even as my chest tightened.

She took a sip from the soup served to her a minute ago. My eyes narrowed slightly, the curiosity in my gaze mingled with something more guarded.

I wasn't interested in hearing about Adrian—at least, not the way Liza might think. But there was a part of me, a small, persistent part that wanted to know what this guy had done to hold her attention, to make her keep him around even after everything that had happened. He cheated on her but still in her life. How?

She bit the corner of her cheek, her fingers fidgeting with the edge of her soup cup, "Well," she started, not meeting my gaze, "I don't really know where to start," her voice so faint it barely made it across the table, "He's... different."

"Different how?" I prompted, my curiosity piqued.

"He's not like everyone else, Nate," she said, her gaze drifting past me, as if Adrian's face was etched somewhere only she could see. Her voice softened, almost wistful, and I hated the way it sounded.

"He's selfless," she continued, her lips curving into a faint smile. "Kind, supportive, funny... though he can be so formal sometimes, like he's afraid of letting his guard down."

She paused, a flicker of something unreadable passing through her eyes. "And yeah, there are times he's arrogant, rude, even distant. But at the end of the day, he always apologizes. He makes it right."

Jealousy gnawed at me, a bitter emotion I couldn't ignore. The truth was painfully clear—Liza adored him deeply, perhaps more than she ever adored me, and it ate away at me. I despise the way her eyes softened when she spoke about him, how she smiled, and how her shoulders relaxed. It was as if his topic alone was calming her. I hate it. I hate it so much that it hurt, a sharp, twisting pain in my chest that refuse to go away.

"Sounds like quite the guy," I said, my voice tight, almost forced, "Where'd you meet him again?"

She hesitated, "Tinder. We met on Tinder."

My eyebrows shot up in surprise, and for a moment, I just stared at her. "Tinder?" she nodded, tugging her free strands behind her ear, "Didn't think you were the type."

"Yeah, well... desperate times, right?" She mumbled, a tiny smile on her face.

I stayed silent, biting back the words that clawed at the back of my throat. But the restraint didn't last.

"How can you forgive him after what he did to you?" The question slipped out, sharper than I intended.

"Like I said, Nate. He apologized, and I forgave him." Her voice was calm, but there was a sharp edge to it, a quiet firmness I couldn't ignore. After a pause, she added, "But I'm not back with him."

I clenched my jaw, trying to rein in the frustration bubbling up. "But you're still talking to him," I said, the words sharper than I intended. "I get that he's done some good things, but that doesn't erase what he did. He doesn't deserve you."

Her eyes narrowed, her gaze locking onto mine like steel. "You don't get to decide who deserves me, Nate. You don't know him the way I do."

"Maybe I don't know him," I countered, my voice firm, "but I know you, Liza. I know you deserve better. He hurt you in ways no one should, and you can't just sweep that under the rug."

Her expression faltered for a moment before her defenses shot back up. "You're not being fair," she said, her tone rising. "People make mistakes. He made one—just one—and he's been trying to make up for it ever since. But you? You're judging him without even understanding the full story."

I leaned forward, my voice low but intense. "I don't need the full story to see what's in front of me. People like him— they know how to play the part. They know how to make you forget the pain, only to hurt you again. And let's not forget, Liza—he kissed Norah. That's not a mistake. That's betrayal."

She scoffed, her laugh bitter and full of disbelief. "You're projecting. You've decided he's the villain because of your own issues, not because of who he is. That's not fair to him—or to me."

"Fair?" I said, my voice rising. "Was it fair when he shattered your trust? When he broke you, Liza? How can you sit here and defend him?"

Her eyes blazed, and she straightened in her seat, her words cutting like a blade. "I'm not defending what he did. But I'm not going to cling to anger and let it poison me. I've moved forward, Nate. I forgave him because I want peace, not because I'm excusing his actions. And you don't get to tell me how to feel about it."

"You're so focused on peace that you're blind to what's right in front of you," I said, my voice quieter now, but no less forceful. "He's manipulating you. He's wrapping you up in sweet words and apologies, and you're letting him."

Her face flushed with anger, and her voice trembled with frustration. "Do you think I'm some kind of fool? That I can't see things for what they are? You don't trust him—I get it. But don't you dare question my ability to make my own decisions. I'm not some helpless girl who needs saving, Nate. I've been through enough to know what's good for me."

The weight of her words hit me, and silence fell over the table, heavy and suffocating.

The waiter arrived, setting down our food and a bottle of wine. Neither of us acknowledged him, our gazes locked in an uneasy standoff. The air between us felt charged, thick with everything left unsaid.

I stared at the untouched plate in front of me, the weight of my own words crashing down on me like a relentless wave. What had I done? Bringing him into this—dragging his name into our evening—had been a colossal mistake. I could see it now, clear as day, how my jealousy had unraveled the night I had been dreaming of for years. I had built this date up in my head, imagining laughter, connection, and moments we'd both remember forever. Instead, I'd let my insecurities taint everything. Why couldn't I just let it go? Why couldn't I trust her judgment? Talking about him, questioning her, letting my frustration boil over—it was all wrong, every bit of it. This wasn't how tonight was supposed to go. And now, the perfect evening I'd envisioned felt like it was slipping through my fingers.

No. Fix this, Nate.

Don't ruin this.

Fix it!

I reached across the table, my hand brushing against hers. She didn't pull away, though she didn't look up either.

"Lizzie," I said softly, my voice barely above a whisper. Her gaze lifted reluctantly, meeting mine. Her eyes—stormy, unyielding—were rimmed with the shine of unshed tears. "I'm sorry. I let my frustration get the better of me. I didn't mean to question your choices. You're smart, strong, and capable. I should trust you to know what's best for yourself. I just..." I hesitated, my voice breaking slightly. "I worry about you. I don't want to see you hurt again."

Her expression softened, the fire in her eyes dimming slightly, though her shoulders remained stiff. After a moment, she nodded, her gaze dropping to the table. "I know you mean well," she murmured, her voice quieter now. "But this is my decision to make, Nate. And if I'm wrong, I'll live with it."

I gave her hand a gentle squeeze. "Okay. No more arguments. Let's eat before the food gets cold. I'm starving."

She let out a small laugh, the tension breaking ever so slightly. "That depends on who starts the next argument," she teased, a faint smile tugging at the corners of her lips.

I smiled back, grateful for the crack in the tension. "Mocking me, Lizzie? That's bold."

She laughed again, and just like that, the storm between us began to settle, leaving behind a fragile but hopeful calm.

# Chapter 23

# In the Wake of Flames

*Liza's POV*

Guilt gnawed at me, a relentless beast that refused to let go. I wasn't just guilty—I was drowning in it. I had wasted his time, trampled on his feelings, shattered the night he must have carefully crafted. He deserved so much more than the disappointment I delivered. Even if I spent a lifetime making amends, I knew deep down that his forgiveness was something I could never truly earn.

When I first moved to the UK and saw Nate at the same school, I was floored. He wasn't just some familiar face from my past—he was a living, breathing reminder of everything I tried to bury. Back in New Orleans, he had been my neighbor, the one who stood beside me at my father's funeral, his presence a fleeting comfort before he too disappeared a week later. His family moved, and with them went the last connection to a life I was desperate to forget. So, when fate cruelly placed him in my path again, I did what I had to—I built walls, thick and high, distancing myself at every turn, inventing excuses to avoid him. But Nate... he was persistent, and patient, chiseling away at my defenses until, slowly, he carved out a place in my heart.

It took over a year to let him in, to feel something other than fear. I started to admire him, then more than admire—I began to fall. He became my secret, silent crush, the one I rooted for in every small way, though he never seemed to notice that. For a while, I convinced myself that just having him close was enough, but then Norah came.

I never despised her, but her presence tore at something deep inside me. She took him—or at least, she took the version of him that I had built up in my mind, the one I foolishly believed was mine alone. It hurt, more than I wanted to admit. Still, I accepted it, though a part of me never stopped longing for him. And now, he's here beside me, and I can't help but feel like a completely different person—someone far removed from the one who used to be so crazy about him.

Is this new change truly the result of the stress and torrent of revelations that have overwhelmed me, or is something else shifting within me?

"I have a question," Nate's voice cut through my reverie, snapping me back to the present. His eyes were curious, maybe even a little concerned. "Of all the places, why your hometown for your trip? I thought you hated this place," His words hung in the air, and I could feel the weight of them pressing down on me.

Hated this place? He wasn't wrong. The town was a patchwork of painful memories, a place I had spent years trying to escape, both physically and emotionally. But here I was, choosing to face it to save both worlds. But I can't tell him that, can I?

I replied, "I just wanted to relive my childhood again."

Nate nodded, understanding without pressing further. We continued down the street, the soft glow of streetlights casting long shadows in our path and the quiet between us stretching out comfortably. The cab we'd booked must be close by, but for now, the walk felt right, grounding us in the moment.

"I hated it when Dad told me we were moving from here," Nate said, his voice tinged with a wistful nostalgia. "New Orleans is my favorite place. I loved everything about it—the air, the atmosphere, the people, the history in every wall, the mysteries that seemed to seep into your soul. But then again, you can't change what's written for you, right?"

"Right," I agreed, the words came out almost too quickly. "You never really know where life is going to take you. It could lead you to peace or... an agonizing torture."

A heavy silence settled between us after that, it wasn't uncomfortable, but it carried the weight of unspoken thoughts, the kind that linger just beneath the surface. The breeze tugged at my hair, and for a moment, I felt the chill of more than just the night—there was something else, a sense that both of us were teetering on the edge of saying something important, but neither knew quite how to begin.

"Will you join me if I tell you that I want to see my home?" he asked, his voice careful, as if he knew the weight of his request.

I froze, the world around me narrowing to that single question. His house was near mine, and if I went with him, it meant seeing it again—the house I had visited earlier, where my mother lives.

Why wasn't I afraid? Why wasn't my heart hammering in my chest, my breath shallow, or my thoughts spiraling into panic at the thought of returning there? How was I standing here, so remarkably calm, when just thinking of that place once sent me into a frenzy?

He noticed my hesitation, his eyes softening with concern as he raised an eyebrow. "You can say no if you don't want to," he said, his voice gentle, offering me a way out, a chance to retreat from the discomfort of it all.

To my own surprise, the words that followed were steady, without the tremor I expected. "It's alright. I haven't seen my house either. With you, I'll get to see it too."

A grin spread across his face, relief mixing with excitement. "But where's our cab?" he glanced around as if suddenly realizing we were still stranded on the street.

I couldn't help but smile back, a small, tentative curve of my lips. At that moment, the fear I expected never came. All thanks to the one person... Adrian Scott.

Five minutes later, the cab pulled up, and we slipped into the backseat. The city unfurled before me as I gazed out the window, a soft smile tugging at my mouth. The wind whispered through the slightly open glass, cool and soothing, carrying the quiet hum of the city night. It was... peaceful. The kind of peace that wraps around you and makes you feel like everything, for just a moment, is going to be okay.

"What are you thinking?" Nate asked me, his tone just as gentle as the breeze.

I kept my eyes on the sprawling cityscape, the lights twinkling like scattered stars as I replied, "That... it's beautiful. This place."

He sighed, "I know. I've been thinking about buying a place here. I don't want my kids to grow up not knowing their roots. This is home. Every vacation, every holiday—this is where they'll come. No Russia, no Los Angeles. New Orleans. Just here," His words pulled a genuine laugh from me, "C'mon, I'm being serious."

I shook my head, laughing. But as my eyes swept over the view outside, I froze. The smile vanished, replaced by a cold, creeping dread that crawled up my spine. My eyes widened, the world outside twisting into something unrecognizable, something terrifying. When Nate sensed the shift in me, he followed my gaze and his sharp intake of breath confirmed it—he saw it too.

"Stop the car!" I screamed, the words ripping from my throat with a force I barely recognized. The cab screeched to a halt, the tires skidding against the pavement as we lurched forward. But I couldn't wait—I was already out the door before the car fully stopped, my knees hitting the ground in a frantic rush.

"Liza?" Nate quickly grabbed my arm and helped me up. But I couldn't respond. I stood there, watching the scene in front of me with wide eyes.

My home, the place that held every memory, every piece of my life, was engulfed in flames. The fire raged with a ferocity that seemed almost alive, its greedy fingers clawing at the night sky, casting an eerie, hellish glow over everything.

Rescue teams swarmed the scene, their efforts futile against the relentless inferno. Water arced through the air, hissing as it met the flames, but it was like trying to extinguish a volcano with a bucket of water.

I sprinted toward the inferno, Nate close behind, my breath ragged and desperate. The world blurred around me, nothing but flames and smoke and chaos filling my vision. The roar of the fire was deafening, a monstrous, crackling growl that drowned out all other sounds. The heat hit me like a physical blow, searing my skin even from a distance, but I couldn't stop. I kept running towards the frames, my mind struggling to process the nightmare before me.

A firefighter grabbed my arm and pulled me away from the heat. I barely registered the firefighters and police swarming the scene, their shouts a distant hum against the roaring blaze.

"Ma'am, stay back!!" He yelled at me. But I grabbed his arm, clinging to him as if he were a lifeline, and asked, "A woman lives here—where-where is she?" My voice was raw, the words torn from me, frantic and trembling.

"Please, ma'am, stay back!" he urged, his tone firm, "It's dangerous!" He warned me but I couldn't stop. My mind was a storm of panic, my thoughts spinning out of control.

"The woman who lived here is my mother!" I cried out, my voice breaking as the tears welled up, blurring my vision. "Please, tell me, where is she?!"

The firefighter fell silent, his expression turning grim, and for a moment, the world seemed to hold its breath. He didn't have to say a word. I saw it in his eyes, in the way he glanced to the side, unable to meet my gaze.

My heart slammed against my ribs, each beat more painful than the last, as I turned to follow his line of sight. My stomach lurched violently when I saw it—a stretcher, covered in a white sheet, the outline of a body beneath it still and lifeless. My eyes caught the sight of her hand, hanging out of the sheet. It was completely burnt and bleeding. A sound I didn't recognize escaped from me, a strangled gasp that was somewhere between a sob and a scream. My legs buckled as if they no longer knew how to hold me up, and the ground seemed to rush up to meet me. But before I could fall, Nate's arms were around me, strong and steady, holding me up as my world collapsed around me.

"Liza?" Nate called me. My chest heaved, desperate for air that wouldn't come, and a tear slipped free, carving a cold path down my cheek. I felt my lips part, trying to form words, to breathe, but nothing came out. "Liza, breath?" Nate's voice cut through the fog, but it sounded distant, distorted, as though he was calling to me from miles away. "Oh, my god! Breathe, Liza!"

But the world was already slipping away, the edges darkening as the weight of it all crushed me. I felt myself falling, surrendering to the darkness, Nate's voice fading as everything went black.

"Liza?!!"

# Chapter 24

# *Irrevocably Mine*

*Zephyr's POV*

I watched her, her breath coming in shallow gasps, her body shivering uncontrollably, and her eyes wide, filled with pure, unadulterated horror. I smirked, reveling in the way it only heightened her anxiety, watching as the fear in her eyes shattered the last fragile shard of bravery she was clinging to.

"Zephyr," she managed to whisper, her lips trembling as she spoke my name. The shock had stripped away her ability to speak, to think, to comprehend the full weight of what was happening. The strongest witch, the one they all looked up to, was trembling like a leaf in a storm. Oh, how much I enjoyed this moment.

"Ah, finally someone knows," I said, stretching myself as if how tired I was. When I met her gaze, locking my blazing green eyes onto her blue ones, the intensity of it made her jump slightly in her spot, a pathetic attempt at courage that only amused me further. "Good for me," I added, a sinister smile spreading across my face. "I would no longer have to manipulate you to work for me. I was tired of being the nice guy."

"I will never work for you!" she sneered, though I could see the effort it took for her to muster that defiance. Her fists clenched tight, as if holding onto whatever courage she could scrape together.

I smirked, letting the silence between us stretch out, savoring the fear that still lingered in her trembling form before I leisurely stood up.

She inhaled deeply, trying to steady herself, but I could see the struggle behind her eyes. I tilted my head slightly, studying her with a mix of amusement and menace.

"Are you sure?" I asked, my voice was low and dangerous. "Think again. Are you sure you want to defy me?" My gaze locked onto hers, daring her to move, to speak, to even breathe without my permission.

"I would rather die than do anything for you, you bastard!"

I chuckled, shaking my head slowly, almost pitying her naivety. "Careful how you talk to me, Rachel," I mused, my voice dripping with condescension. "You seemed to know a lot about me when you warned Liza, but the way you're speaking to me now makes me believe you have no idea of the lengths I can go to, or what I'm truly capable of." I leaned closer, lowering my voice to a menacing whisper. "Your defiance, Rachel, won't end in your death because that would be too merciful. No, you will live, and you will suffer. And when you realize that your only escape is through me, you'll beg for the chance to serve."

"I will kill you!"

I laughed, a deep, mocking sound. "See, you lack so much knowledge about me."

She muttered a spell, clenching her fist as she tried to gain control over me. But I was far too powerful for her feeble attempts. She strained, pouring all her energy into caging me, but it was futile.

"Kneel," I commanded, my voice like steel. Instantly, she dropped to her knees, her terror palpable, though she still tried to maintain an air of defiance. I leaned down on one knee, bringing my face close to hers, our gazes locked. "How did I do that? Well, I told you, Rachel, I can do things far beyond your comprehension. So don't make this hard for yourself. Surrender to me."

"Never!" she spat, her voice quaking with the last remnants of her courage. "Kill me in the cruellest way possible, but I will never surrender to you."

I chuckled darkly. "Ah, I like this," I said, almost amused by her stubbornness. Without breaking the eye contact, I lifted my hand, closing my palm into a fist. Her eyes widened in horror as she began to choke, her airways constricting without me even touching her.

I threw her a fake concerned look, "What happened, Rachel? Can't breathe?" She clawed at the ground, her throat, desperate for air, her body convulsing as I held her life in my hand. I smirked sinisterly and took away the small gasps of air she was taking. . She gasped for breath, her eyes turning bloodshot, her face flushed as she struggled against the invisible force cutting off her oxygen.

Just when she was on the brink of death, I unfisted my palm, letting her collapse, gasping, her breaths ragged and frantic.

"So," I asked, tilting my head slightly, "have you changed your mind?" She glared up at me, defiant even in her near-death state, and shook her head. I tightened my jaw, the barest flicker of annoyance crossing my face. "Should I call you brave or stupid?"

"Wait until Liza finds out the truth," she rasped, her voice hoarse but filled with conviction. "She will kill you. If you think you're strong, she's stronger. Don't forget she's the descendant of Archon, the most powerful sorcerer."

I knew this was about to come. I had seen everything coming from a mile away and I was ready with the answers.

"Ah, Liza," I said, standing up and leisurely taking my seat back on the sofa. "Such a nice girl. She'll be my only victim for whom I might feel an ounce of guilt when I kill her," A visible shiver ran throughout her body, and I smiled, savouring her horror.

"You see," I continued, my tone deceptively casual, "I've come to realize that the only person who can send me back is Liza. If I get rid of her, no spell will be able to return me to my world. Which means, both worlds will fall apart," I watched as the full weight of my words settled on her, the terror in her eyes deepening. It was a beautiful sight, the strongest witch, crumbling in fear before me.

"You will not do this," she said, her voice a mix of defiance and desperation.

"I can do anything to stay here. If it means killing Liza, then I'll kill her," Her heart was pounding so loudly I could almost hear it. "But if you help me find a way to remain here without causing this world to fall apart, I'll let you both go."

She was silent, and I could almost see the wheels turning in her mind. An alliance with me meant a chance to betray me later, to use Liza against me. She knew Liza could potentially send me back, but I was always several steps ahead, always prepared.

"Don't think too much about it, Rachel," I said, my voice dripping with impatience. "I have far more important matters to attend to than waiting for your internal struggle to resolve. So, tick-tock."

"Fine," she said, her voice resigned. "I will help you. But you must give me your word that you will not harm her."

I stayed silent for a moment, contemplating her request.

Harm her? The mere thought of causing her harm sent a shiver through me, a visceral recoil deep in my soul. The idea of laying even a finger on her was not just repulsive was anathema, something so vile that I'd sooner embrace death than bring any form of suffering to her.

She had become more than just a fleeting fascination or a mere presence in my life. She had transformed into my obsession, the very embodiment of my desires, my most prized possession. She was no longer just a woman; she was the air I breathed, the essence that sustained me. Without her, it felt as though the world would close in on me, the walls constricting, leaving me gasping for breath, struggling against an inevitable drowning in a sea of emptiness.

I tried, I truly tried to keep my focus on my goal and distract myself from her. But from the moment I saw Nate taking her away from me, I realized just how deeply obsessed I've become. It's not just a desire anymore—it's an all-consuming need to possess her completely, to ensure that she belongs to me and me alone.

My mind drifted back to that first fateful moment when I laid eyes on her. She was standing there, by the window, her delicate fingers drawing the curtains, utterly oblivious to the cataclysmic event she had just set in motion. She had summoned me, pulled me from the confines of ink and paper, and thrust me into a world I had never known. As I leaped from the pages, there was a brief moment of disorientation, a fragmented awareness that left me scrambling for context. The century was a mystery to me, an unfamiliar landscape. But the reality-binding spell, that ancient and powerful enchantment, swiftly wove its magic. Within seconds, I was no longer a stranger to this era. I absorbed every nuance, every detail, the rapid-fire influx of knowledge flooding my mind until I was as much a part of this world as she was.

The next thing I remember is I was about to end her life before she even had the chance to comprehend the danger. My hand itched with the desire to kill her, to crush the fragile flame of her existence. But then, the knowledge settled in-a bitter, iron-clad truth that froze me in place. Only the blood of Archon could accomplish such a deed, only that cursed lineage had the power to end what she had begun. And so, I restrained myself, held back the darkness that threatened to consume me, and instead, I made a choice. I would become Adrian Scott-a role, a mask, a façade of kindness and nobility. I would weave a tale of a man desperate to return to his world, a man of goodwill and innocent intent.

Through this charade, I would earn her trust, insinuate myself into her life until she believed, with every fiber of her being, that I meant her no harm and when she embarked on her quest to send me back, to sever the ties that bound me to this reality, I would be the hidden saboteur, the unseen hand that manipulated every step she took. I would undermine her efforts, and twist her path until it led nowhere, all while secretly pursuing my true goal-to remain here, permanently anchored in this world. And to do so, I would have to destroy the one rule that dictated my existence: the law that condemned all fiction to return to its origin, to the pages from which it was born. That rule, that cursed decree, would be shattered, and I would stand victorious, a free being in a world that had no place for the likes of me.

But as my journey unfolded, something unexpected happened-I began to lose focus, and distracted from my original goal. Her smile and kindness were having an effect on me I hadn't anticipated. I found myself doing things I never thought I was capable of. I smiled with her, joked, laughed, and felt at ease around her, comfortable. This wasn't part of the plan. I had set out to manipulate her, to use her, to betray her without a second thought. Yet, the day Norah hurt her, something shifted deep inside me. I felt a surge of protectiveness, a fierce responsibility I hadn't anticipated. The sight of her discomfort, the tears brimming in her eyes, the way her hands trembled and her lips quivered-it all sparked a fury in me that only subsided when Norah's relationship with Nate ended. If it weren't for the role I was playing, I might have ended Norah's life instead.

That day, I questioned everything. Why did I care? I was supposed to deceive her, to lie and manipulate without remorse. But why, then, did I feel this urge to protect her? I told myself to refocus on my mission, to remember why I was here. Yet, when she cried in that plane, weeping in my arms, I wanted to burn the entire world to ashes for causing her pain. I thought I was getting too deep into the character I was playing, so I tried to distance myself. But no matter what I did, the pull towards her only grew stronger with every second I spent with her, a magnetic force that drew me closer and closer until it became an obsession, unhealthy for both of us.

I tried to protect her, to shield her from the darkness within me, to guard her from the monster I knew I was, but it was futile. No matter how hard I fought against it, the truth remained—I wanted her. I would have still pushed her away and kept my distance to preserve her innocence and safety, but when Nate took her away from me, I realized how pointless my efforts had been.

Liza is mine. She belongs to me in ways that transcend reason or logic, and I would do anything for her. Anything. The plan was simple: deceive her, use her, and ultimately kill her. But now, as my obsession with her has consumed every part of me, I've abandoned that plan entirely.

I don't just want to stay-I need to make her mine. Not just in the casual, fleeting sense, but wholly, utterly, *irrevocably mine*. She will be bound to me, caught in a web of desire and possession so strong that there will be no escape. I want to own every breath she takes, every thought that crosses her mind, her very soul. She will be utterly bound to me, with every single aspect of her life under my unyielding control. She will be trapped in my world, completely consumed by my obsession, until there is no part of her left untouched by my desire. And nothing, no force in this world or any other, will stand in my way.

"Tell me, Zephyr," Rachel's voice snapped me back to the moment, "Will you give me your word that you will never harm that child?"

I smiled, "I promise, Rachel. I will never hurt her."

*Or let anyone else hurt her.*

# Chapter 25

# Maybe Not

*Liza's POV*

I woke up to a blinding assault of light, the harsh brightness searing into my eyes like daggers. The walls of my room, a suffocating blue, seemed to close in on me as I struggled to bring the world into focus. I blinked rapidly, my vision swimming with spots, and finally, the room sharpened into view. I was in a hospital room. A cannula drip on my arm. The first figure I saw was Nate, his face a mixture of relief and exhaustion as he sat by my side, a magazine discarded in his lap as his eyes locked onto mine.

He exhaled a deep breath, as if he had been holding it for hours, and rushed to my side. "Liza, thank God," His voice trembled, thick with emotion. "How are you feeling? Are you okay? Do you need anything?" His concern poured over me like a wave, but all I could do was stare blankly, my mind reeling as memories crashed over me with the force of a tidal wave.

The fire. The acrid stench of smoke. My home reduced to ash. And my mother-my mother's lifeless body on the stretcher. A sob caught in my throat as the full weight of the loss settled into my bones, heavy and cold. She never loved me, never cared about me, never showed the warmth a mother should provide. Our relationship was a twisted tangle of pain and disappointment. Yet, seeing her like that-gone, forever-ripped something raw and vulnerable inside me.

My heart clenched with a grief so profound it felt like it might tear me apart. She didn't love me, but I did. After all the abuse and loathing, I always had a hope that maybe one day she would change, that she would see me, love me, but that hope was gone now, consumed in the flames.

"Liza," Nate's voice cut through the fog of my despair, pulling me back to the present. His hand clasped mine tightly, an anchor in the storm of my emotions. "Please, don't do this to yourself. Calm down." His eyes were filled with a feeling of deep sorrow, reflecting the pain he saw in mine. He wasn't just concerned but was devastated for me, sharing in my loss as if it were his own.

But all I could think about was... *Adrian*. I needed him, needed to see him, to hear his voice, to feel his presence beside me. My heart ached with a desperate longing, and I barely registered my own voice as I whispered, "Where's Adrian?"

Nate's expression flickered, surprise mingling with something darker-something that looked like hurt. He hesitated, the pause stretching unbearably long before he finally answered, "I called him. He's on his way." His voice was strained like he was forcing the words out. "Good thing you don't keep a password on your phone," He tried to smile, but it didn't reach his eyes.

Just then, the door to the room flung open, instantly pulling our attention. My heart skipped a beat as my eyes locked with his piercing green ones. His presence filled the room, and for a moment, it felt like there was no one else but the two of us. The intensity in his gaze was overwhelming, and I had to summon every ounce of strength to keep myself from collapsing into the storm of emotions threatening to consume me.

Adrian's eyes flicked to Nate, and I saw a flash of raw anger in them. But just as quickly, he dismissed Nate as if he were nothing more than a nuisance, shifting his focus entirely onto me. He moved to my side in a fluid motion, his hand reaching for mine, and the instant our skin touched, a sense of calm washed over me. The turmoil in my chest eased, and for the first time since waking up, I felt a small measure of peace. His smile was gentle, yet tinged with worry. "Didn't you eat anything, Liza? You fainted like that?" His tone was light, but the concern was unmistakable.

I couldn't find the words to respond. The horror of what I had seen, my burning house, my mother's death left me speechless, unable to articulate the depth of my pain.

Before I could find my voice, Nate interjected, his tone sharp with irritation. "She fainted in shock," The words hung in the air, heavy and cutting. Adrian's attention snapped to him, confusion briefly clouding his features. Nate didn't miss a beat, continuing, "Her house... it exploded due to a gas leak, and her mother-" He stopped short as Adrian's gaze shifted back to me, the reality of the situation settling in.

His grip on my hand tightened, grounding me as the memory of my mother's lifeless body flashed through my mind again, bringing with it a wave of grief so intense it threatened to pull me under.

He took a breath in, "What did the doctor say?" Adrian's question was calm, measured.

Nate, still unsettled, replied, "She can be discharged after the drip is finished."

Adrian didn't say a word in response and without hesitation, he gently but firmly removed the cannula drip from my arm, and before I could comprehend what was happening, he scooped me into his arms. A gasp escaped me, and from the corner of my eye, I saw Nate's expression-a mix of shock and disbelief that mirrored my own.

"What the hell, Adrian?" Nate's voice was a thunderous roar, vibrating with confusion and fury. "You could have hurt her! Where do you think you're taking her?"

Adrian didn't even glance at him as he strode towards the door, carrying me as if I weighed nothing. His voice was calm, but there was an underlying edge to it, sharp as a knife. "I would never hurt her. And this drip, lifeless room wouldn't help her recover." He paused at the doorway, then added, "And please do take care of the paperwork and the bill."

And with that, he walked out of the room, leaving Nate behind.

"Where are we going?" I asked, my voice trembling slightly as I turned to him. My heart was still a tangled mess of emotions, but being beside him brought a strange sense of comfort. He glanced at me briefly, his hand firm on the steering wheel, guiding the car down the quiet road.

"Nowhere in particular," came his reply, a soft smile tugging at the corners of his mouth. "I'm just taking you for a long drive, so you can breathe normally," His tone was light, almost as if trying to ease the heaviness in the air, but I couldn't bring myself to respond. I looked away, my thoughts spiraling back to the painful reality I was struggling to accept.

My mother is dead. I have no family left. How am I supposed to move past that?

"She doesn't deserve it, Liza," his voice cut through the silence, startling me. My head snapped towards him, confusion and anger flaring up inside me as he continued with his gaze fixed on the road ahead. "This mourning, this heavy heart, those tears that refuse to fall-she doesn't deserve any of it."

"She was my mother, Adrian," I choked out, my words barely coherent as the flood of emotions threatened to drown me, "My only family. How can you say that?"

Adrian's grip on the steering wheel tightened, "Don't forget she's the same woman who nearly killed you. Who tortured and abused you. The same woman who, even after years of you being away, had no warmth for you when you finally returned. You need to stop grieving for someone who was only a mother in name, not in action."

His words hit me like a tidal wave, crashing over me with a force that left me breathless. I wanted to deny it, to fight against the harsh truth he was laying before me. But the pain in my chest was real, a throbbing ache that I couldn't ignore. Sure, she never loved me, but she was still my mother. She gave birth to me. How can I just let go of that?

"I'm going to sound mean here, but honestly Liza... you're not mourning your mother," he continued, his voice softening, yet still holding that unyielding edge. "You're mourning the loss of a woman you knew. You're kind, Liza. You're selfless and sensitive. Of course, it's going to shock you that someone you knew died in such a horrifying way. And I'm sorry, I truly am. No matter how much I hate her for ruining your childhood, I never wanted her to die like this. I didn't want her to die at all."

His words hung in the air, heavy with the weight of painful truths and unresolved emotions. I couldn't respond, my throat was too tight with grief. But deep down, I knew he was right but partly. I wasn't just mourning the loss of someone who was my mother-I was mourning the loss of what could have been, the love I never received, the closure I would never get. And that was a pain I wasn't sure I could ever escape.

"You can take your time to get over it. I can drive through the entire night if you want me to but once we're out of this car. I don't wanna see a single drop of tear from your eyes. Is that understood?"

I frowned, "Don't be an asshole, Adrian. A long drive can't be enough to get over someone's death," I muttered, unable to hide my frustration. He can't expect me to deal with my pain like this. I'm not a robot-I'm a person with a heart.

He didn't flinch. "I'd act differently if I didn't know what she did to you, what kind of person she was." He turned to me, his eyes locking onto mine with an intensity that made my breath catch. "So, yeah, I'm being an asshole because I'd rather show you the truth than let you waste your tears on someone who doesn't even deserve your sympathy."

His words hung in the air, and for a moment, I was silent, lost in the turmoil of my thoughts. "But it hurts, Adrian. It hurts," I finally whispered, the pain in my chest tightening with every word, "It hurts deeply to know that my only family is gone."

He nodded, his expression softening just a fraction. "I get it. But don't say she was your only family. Am I not your family?"

My heart melted at his words, and I found myself staring at him, speechless. The streetlights flickered across his face as we drove, casting shadows that made him look even more striking, more unreal. I felt like I was drowning in the depth of his gaze, the weight of what he said settling into my heart.

He called himself my family. It was a huge statement, one that carried more weight than he probably realized. He could have said it just to soothe the chaos inside me, or maybe he meant it. But as much as those words comforted me, they also terrified me. Because deep down, I knew the truth: one day, he would be gone too. Maybe not today, not tomorrow, but eventually, he would become nothing more than a distant memory, a gaping hole in my heart that would never truly heal.

"But you will be gone too," I said, my voice barely above a whisper, "And when that day comes, it will hurt me more than it hurts now."

The words tasted bitter on my tongue, a painful truth I had been trying to avoid. The thought of losing him-of him becoming just another painful memory was unbearable.

Adrian's eyes locked onto mine, a strange intensity burning in their depths. "Maybe I will be gone. Or maybe not," he said, his voice laced with a quiet certainty that only stirred something uneasy inside me. There was something in his tone, something that felt like a promise, though I wasn't entirely sure I understood it. "You don't need to worry about tomorrow. We'll deal with it when it comes."

A part of me wanted to press him, to dig deeper, to uncover the truth behind his cryptic words, but another part of me-the part that was exhausted from all the pain and loss-couldn't bring itself to question him. Maybe he was just trying to comfort me, to say whatever it took to keep me from falling apart.

And so, I found myself nodding, accepting his words for what they were, even as a flicker of doubt lingered in the back of my mind.

*Maybe not...*

# Chapter 26

# Beneath the Veil of Fear

*Sabrina's POV*

I stood at the threshold of my home, my eyes fixed on the distant taillights of the car carrying away my beloved grandchildren. The night had fallen, casting a deep, foreboding shadow over my heart. Since the time I had learned that the tomes were being stolen and the witches who were safeguarding them were being murdered, fear had taken root in my soul, twisting its tendrils around every thought. To protect my family from this threat, I made the agonizing decision to keep them away until the storm passed, even if it meant enduring the unbearable loneliness that now seeped into every corner of my home.

As the car disappeared into the darkness, a solitary tear escaped down my cheek, a silent testament to the agony tearing at my heart. The ache in my chest tightened as if a vice had clamped down on my soul, squeezing until it hurt to breathe. I had hidden the tome, fortified my home with every protection spell I knew, and steeled myself for the coming battle. But no amount of preparation could quell the dread gnawing at my insides, the creeping fear that I might not be ready for the horrors to come.

With a heavy heart, I turned away from the door and trudged back into the house, my steps echoing through the eerily silent rooms. I made my way to the kitchen, my hands trembling as I reached for a glass of water. The walls seemed to close in on me, suffocating me with the weight of the unknown. Worry surged within me, cold and relentless, as I grappled with the realization that I had never faced anything as dangerous as this in all my years. What kind of being could be responsible for such atrocities? A sorcerer with unimaginable power? A creature of nightmares? Or something far beyond my comprehension?

As these terrifying questions swirled in my mind, another unsettling thought crept in. I wondered about Rachel, my friend who had done the unthinkable—pulled a character from the confines of a book and brought them into this world. But why? What had driven Rachel to take such a reckless step? And more importantly, how had she managed to succeed in such an impossible? The questions tumbled over each other, relentless and unanswerable, feeding the growing sense of dread that clawed at my heart.

Just then, a cold shiver ran down my spine. My breath caught in my throat as I felt an unfamiliar presence in the house. My heart pounded in my chest, each beat echoing like a drum of impending doom. I wasn't alone. Clearly. The realization struck me like a lightning bolt, freezing me in place as the air around me grew heavy with unseen menace.

I put the glass of water on the kitchen counter and with a long, shaky breath, I stepped out of the kitchen, my pulse quickening as I moved forward cautiously. My breath hitched in my throat and I froze to my spot as I saw a stranger in my hall, standing casually like he owned the place. The man was tall and imposing, his presence suffocating the room. His hands were casually dipped in his pockets, yet everything about him screamed dominance and control.

"Good evening, Mrs. Cabello. I'm Zach Miller," he introduced himself, his voice cutting through the air like a blade. There was no warmth, no emotion—just cold, hard steel. His face was a mask, devoid of any readable expression, and I felt a chill crawl up my spine. His calm demeanor was terrifying as if he knew—beyond a shadow of a doubt—that he was unstoppable, that nothing and no one could challenge him.

I raised my chin higher to show defiance and bravery. My fists clenched to my sides as I asked, "How did you get in?" I couldn't help but wonder how because I have cast spells over this threshold which can't let anyone in without invitation.

"I'm here to get something. You probably know what," he ignored my question, his tone unwavering. "You either hand it to me kindly, or I will have to be the bad guy and snatch it from you."

My heart pounded in my chest, but I remained silent, watching him, observing him. He seemed more machine than man, with his rigid posture, emotionless voice, and the way he moved, precise and calculated, like a robot programmed for a single purpose.

His eyes narrowed, his head tilting slightly as he watched me. "Choose wisely, Mrs. Cabello," he urged, his voice as cold as ever.

I took a deep breath, steeling myself for what I was about to say. "No!" The room fell silent and turn cold, "Be kind or violent, but I'm not giving you the tome. You wouldn't even get it after my death," My voice shook slightly, but I stood my ground, my gaze locked on his.

For a moment, he said nothing, just continued to study me with those piercing, unreadable eyes. Then, almost lazily, he tilted his head the other way. "61-10-TMD," he said, the words rolling off his tongue like a death sentence. "Ring any bells?" My blood ran cold, my eyes widening in horror as I understood what he was implying. It was my children's car number—the one which had just left.

I clenched my jaw, "Don't you dare hurt them!!"

"I won't," he said, his voice icy and devoid of emotion. "But if you keep wasting my time, I can't promise I'll remain so... civil." His words were a chilling threat, a warning of the violence that might come if I didn't comply.

Tears welled up in my eyes, and a feeling of helplessness washed over her. The weight of the impossible choice pressed down on my chest like a crushing burden. Should I give up the tome to save my children, or should I uphold the sacred promise I made to protect it at all costs? I was chosen by the universe to guard the tomes, bound by a duty greater than myself. But my children—my family—were in immediate, mortal danger. I couldn't let them die. How could I choose between my sacred duty and my flesh and blood?

"What's there to think about?" His words cut through her thoughts like a knife, each one twisting the blade deeper, "Save your family, Sabrina!"

"What do you plan to do with it? And who's behind this?" I asked. My voice was barely a whisper, trembling with sadness, uncertainty, and anger.

He closed his eyes momentarily, taking a breath in, "Where's the tome?" He ignored my question entirely, his patience clearly running thin.

My heart pounded so loudly I could barely hear myself think. "Do you promise not to hurt my family?" I asked, my voice breaking with the weight of fear—fear of losing them.

"The tome, Sabrina," He repeated, his tone final and unforgiving. His gaze bored into mine, unrelenting, making it clear that this was my last chance to comply before he took matters into his own hands.

I inhaled deeply, drawing in all the courage I could muster to defy him. "Sternere eum!" As soon as the words left my mouth, a powerful gust of wind erupted, hurling Zach across the room. He crashed into the wall with a resounding thud, the force so strong that it rattled the windows and caused the paintings and frames to crash to the ground. For a fleeting moment, I felt a surge of triumph, but it was quickly overshadowed by the cold reality of what I had just done. I defied him, it could cost me everything—my family, my life. But despite the fear gnawing at me, I knew I couldn't back down now. I love my family more than anything, and though

I had put them in danger, I couldn't let the tome fall into the wrong hands. Its power could unleash death on countless innocents. If there was even a sliver of hope that fighting back could protect both my family and the tome, then I would fight—fight until my last breath.

Zach rose from the floor with a calmness that sent chills through me. He got up with unsettling grace, his body showing no signs of struggle. Blood trickled down his cheekbone from a fresh cut, his hair disheveled from the impact, yet his face remained an emotionless mask. His eyes, cold and lifeless, betrayed nothing. He stood there, as composed as ever, as though the force of her attack had been nothing more than a gentle breeze. My triumph evaporated, replaced by a rising dread. This man, this creature, was unlike anyone I had ever faced. He was beyond pain, beyond fear—perhaps even beyond humanity.

Panic clawed at me as I opened my mouth to cast another spell, but before I could utter a single word, I felt an invisible force grip me like an iron vice. In a blink, I was yanked off my feet, my body hurtling through the air as if I were weightless. The force slammed me into a wall with bone-crushing speed, the impact sending shockwaves of pain through my back. My vision blurred, stars dancing before my eyes as I struggled to regain my consciousness. When I finally managed to focus, I saw him—Zach, standing mere inches away, his cold eyes boring into mine.

I gulped.

His proximity was suffocating, a physical presence that pressed down on me, paralyzing me with fear. "You chose the hard way," He whispered, his voice low and devoid of emotion. "Now, suffer."

His words were a spell of their own, dark and binding, sealing my fate. My heart raced, adrenaline flooding my veins as I realized that after the blow, he was far from defeated. If anything, he seemed to draw strength from my defiance, his power looming like a storm about to break.

But I can't let him win. I have to fight.

With a surge of desperation, I summoned another spell. The air around me shimmered, and with a flick of my wrist, a sharp knife that had been lying innocuously in the fruit basket flew across the room, embedding itself into Zach's back. I held my breath, waiting for a reaction—a cry of pain, a stagger—but all he did was narrow his eyes, the blade protruding from his body as if it were nothing more than a splinter. A cold wave of fear washed over me, the realization sinking in that my attacks were as futile as striking a shadow.

Then, with terrifying precision, Zach's power surged. My breath caught in my throat as every object in the house, from the smallest trinket to the heaviest piece of furniture, lifted into the air. The very ground beneath me seemed to shift, tilting as if the foundations of reality were being undone. Dark magic swirled around me, thick and suffocating, making it hard to breathe. My heart pounded in my chest, my mind racing as I tried to comprehend this.

Zach's voice cut through the chaos, cold and unyielding. "The tome, Sabrina. Where. Is. The. Tome?" I gulped hard, my eyes wide and fearful.

# Chapter 27

## Wicked Justice

*Zephyr's POV*

I looked at her, her small frame curled up in the shawl, her breathing soft and steady as she slept silently beside me. There was something almost fragile about the way she lay there as if the weight of everything she had endured could crush her in her sleep. A pang of emotion surged through me, one I couldn't quite suppress, one I wasn't sure I wanted to. I inhaled deeply, letting the cool, early morning air fill my lungs as I forced myself to look back at the road ahead.

The sky was beginning to lighten, the deep indigo of night giving way to a pale shade of blue, a prelude to the sunrise that would soon follow. But the beauty of it was lost on me; all I could see was the road stretching out before us, winding endlessly into the unknown. I tightened my grip on the steering wheel until my knuckles turned white, trying to anchor myself to the present, but my mind kept drifting back to the events of the past few hours.

The anger-the searing, blinding rage that had surged through me when I had walked into that hospital room and seen her lying there, pale and fragile, with Nate hovering over her like some goddamn saviour. I had almost lost it. I was this close to beating him to a pulp. Killing him. I had only left her with him for a few hours, and now she was lying in a hospital bed because of it. The rage boiled inside me, every muscle in my body tensed, ready to explode. But then he told me why she was there-why she had fainted. It wasn't just his incompetence. No, it was worse. She had found out about her mother's death. The actual reason doused my anger, leaving only a deep, unsettling ache in its place.

She's always been the purest soul, wearing her heart on her sleeve, sensitive, kind, and soft and I knew when she'll learn about her mother, it would hurt her. That's why I never wanted her to know. But some stupid bastard took her to the scene and forced her to witness the horror firsthand. *Brilliant move.* I knew she wouldn't take the news well, but I didn't expect this. I didn't think she would faint, didn't think the grief would consume her so completely. But it did, and now I was left with this responsibility to make her feel better. So, I took her away-away from that lifeless room and Nate's sight.

In the car, I talked to her, tried to make her see that her grief was misplaced, that she was mourning someone who didn't deserve it. True. But who was I kidding? This was Liza Kirby-someone who, despite all the torture and abuse, still longed for her so-called mother to look at her with warmth, to show her the love she had been deprived of for so long. I said everything that needed to be said, every harsh truth, and I could see in her eyes that she understood me, realizing that I was right. That was a good thing, a necessary thing actually. But understanding doesn't make the pain go away. But it will... Eventually.

I looked at her once again and my heart raced, pounding harder than ever before. My gaze wandered over her form before resting on her beautiful lips. Every ounce of my willpower was strained, fighting the urge to lean in and kiss her, or to obliterate every fragile boundary between us. My grip on the steering wheel tightened, my knuckles white with the strain. I looked away. These feelings, these desires, were alien to me—an ache so deep I hadn't known was possible, a hunger to consume her completely, to obliterate her innocence until there was nothing left. I wanted to claim every part of her, to own her entirely, and only I knew how I wrestled with myself to maintain control. But amidst this tempest of emotions, one force stood paramount: protectiveness. Every fiber of my being roared to shield her, to ensure her safety, no matter the cost.

I risked another glance at her, cocooned in the shawl, so vulnerable, so fragile, yet exuding an inner strength that defied everything she had endured. Everything she went through made me angry again. The abuse, the torture, and then nightmares and panic attacks. The fury I felt was almost uncontrollable, a seething hatred that burned hotter with every passing second.

I could barely suppress the urge to bring that woman back to life just to kill her all over again, to make her suffer a thousand fold for every ounce of pain she caused to my Liza.

While cursing that damn woman, my mind drifted to the time I went to her house to make her pay for every ounce of pain she had inflicted on my Liza.

I knocked on the door twice before it swung open, revealing the woman I despise with every ounce of my being. I smiled, a slow, deliberate curl of my lips, "Hello, Violet." I said, my voice cold and cutting.

Seeing me, the color drained from her face in an instant. I had traumatized her before, and now I was here to offer her freedom-from the trauma I inflicted. Her heartbeat was so loud, I could practically hear it echoing in the silent hallway. Her eyes, wide with dread, desperately searched for Liza.

"She's not here," I told her, bringing her gaze back to me. My palms itched to choke her again, to watch the life drain from her eyes, but I restrained myself. She doesn't deserve such a merciful death.

Her grip on the doorframe tightened, and I watched with satisfaction as she visibly gulped, her terror plain to see. Without waiting for an invitation, I stepped inside, forcing her to stumble back weakly. The mark of my hand was still visible around her neck, a dark reminder of our last encounter, and I could see her touching it in horror as if reliving the moment.

My eyes sparked with a dangerous gleam, and she began trembling uncontrollably, the fear in her eyes nearly palpable. I stepped closer, lowering my voice to a menacing whisper, "Didn't expect me to see me again?"

"Why are you here?" She asked, her voice trembling, "I have told you everything I knew and everything was true. I know nothing now."

I remained silent, refusing to dignify her with a response. Instead, my eyes swept over the house, taking in every detail with a sigh. My heart clenched, a surge of fury rushing through me as my mind painted a vivid, tormenting picture of what must have happened here.

I could almost see Liza, her small frame trembling as tears streamed down her face. I could almost hear the sound of her ragged breaths, the soft thud as she tried to find an escape. In my mind's eye, she's running, frantic and desperate, her steps faltering as she trips over the stairs, hitting the ground hard.

Blood. I could see it now-her blood, pooling beneath her as she clutched her stomach, her small hands soaked in crimson as she tried to stem the flow. She whimpered and got up, taking the help of the nearby surface for support, leaving a blooded handprint behind.

Clutching her abdomen, she dragged herself, colliding with furniture, leaving trails of blood behind her, each droplet marking her path like a twisted breadcrumb trail of suffering. My eyes flicked to the wall, and in my mind's eye, I could almost see it-her hand, smeared with blood, leaving a desperate, fading print on the wall. The sight of that imagined handprint-a silent, heart-wrenching cry for help-gripped my heart with an unbearable sorrow and rage.

The horror of what she must have gone through clawed at my insides, leaving me hollowed out and filled with a fury that begged for release. My fists clenched so tightly that my nails bit into my skin, drawing my own blood, but it was nothing compared to the pain I felt imagining what she endured.

I closed my eyes and took a long breath in before turning back to face her mother. The very sight of her ignited a firestorm of rage within me. Without hesitation, I swung my arm, the back of my hand connecting with her face in a brutal slap. The impact was so forceful it sent her reeling, her body crumpling to the ground with a sickening thud. She looked up at me, her lip split and bleeding, a deep red mark forming at the corner of her mouth.

Horror. All I could see was pure horror in her eyes.

"Now," I said, my voice low and menacing, "I'm going to ask you some questions, and you're going to answer me honestly. Understood?"

Her entire body trembled, her eyes wide with terror. I almost struck her again, the urge was so strong, but I forced myself to hold back.

"The first question," I continued, my voice laced with venom as I gestured toward her bleeding cheek, "How much did it hurt?"

She didn't respond, too consumed by fear to even breathe properly. She started to crawl backward, pathetically trying to distance herself from me as if that would protect her.

"Do not move," I snarled, causing her to stop immediately, "Now, answer me."

"It did. It did hurt!" she stammered out, her voice shaking with panic. But her answer didn't satisfy me. I grabbed a fistful of her hair, yanking her head back before slamming it into the glass table beside us.

The table shattered on impact, the jagged pieces digging into her skin as blood started to pour from a gash on her forehead. She let out a pained cry, but I wasn't about to give her the satisfaction of expressing her pain. With a flick of my wrist, I took away her voice, silencing her completely.

The realization hit her immediately, and her panic reached a fever pitch. She clawed at her throat, trying to scream, trying to make any sound at all, but nothing came. Her eyes were wild with terror, her blood-smeared face contorted in agony. She was shaking uncontrollably now, like a leaf caught in a violent storm. I grabbed her by the throat, lifting her off the ground as I brought her face close to mine.

"Tell me, Violet," I whispered, "how much does it hurt now?"

Tears streamed down her face, her entire body wracked with silent sobs. She clasped her hands together, pleading for mercy, but her desperation only fueled my anger.

"Oh, right," I mocked, tightening my grip on her throat. "You can't speak, can you?" Then, I restored her voice, and her choked cries immediately filled the room. "Now, answer my question. How much does it hurt?"

"I'm sorry!" she wailed, her voice cracking under the weight of her fear. "Please, don't do this to me. Please, I beg you."

Her pitiful cries only stoked the flames of my rage. With a snarl, I hurled her across the room, her body slamming into the wall with a strong thud before crumpling to the floor. She lay there, whimpering, broken and bleeding. Her cries filled the room, a twisted symphony of suffering that was music to my ears.

I raised my hand, and with a decisive flick, lifted her into the air. She was teetering on the brink of death, but I wasn't about to grant her that mercy. I dragged her to me, forcing her to collapse onto her knees before me. Her disheveled state, her face streaked with crimson and her body a mangled mess, might have elicited pity from anyone else, but not from me. My purpose was far from complete; I needed her to suffer further.

I approached her with deliberate slowness, my hand sweeping over her forehead. A sickly green light emanated from my touch, healing her wounds just enough to keep her breathing. The only injury I've healed after coming out in reality is Liza's ankle. The medication didn't heal her ankle, the magic was done by me. I was happy to see her smile the next day, not realizing that there's a part of her that can't be healed by magic.

Her mother's eyes widened in shock, disbelief etched across her face as she struggled to understand why I would heal her. She clasped her hands together, perhaps in a futile gesture of gratitude or surrender.

I seated myself on the couch, a picture of calm cruelty. "Get up, Violet," I commanded. Her body, no longer under her control, responded to my will. "Go get a sharp knife sharp enough to match the one you used on your daughter."

Tears streamed down her cheeks as she stumbled towards the kitchen, her hands shaking uncontrollably. She returned with a knife, her entire body trembling in fear as she sobbed in front of me. I regarded the knife with cold detachment. Memories of Liza's suffering surged in my mind-the searing pain, the betrayal she must have felt, the mental pain she must have gone through to become a victim of such evilness.

"Please, don't do this to me. I beg you."

I clenched my jaw, refocusing on Violet. Her plea was doing nothing to me. The sight almost drove me to the edge, the fury within me bubbling just beneath the surface.

"I'm-I'm her mother."

My eyes narrowed dangerously as she dared to identify herself as a mother now as if that pathetic claim could ever make me reconsider what I was about to do. "Stab yourself," I ordered, my voice dripping with cold malice. Her eyes widened, and then without hesitation, she drove the knife into her flesh. Screaming. Blood gushed from the wound, mingling with her anguished cries. The sound was almost symphonic in its brutality, a chilling melody of retribution.

"How much does it hurt now, Violet?" I asked, my voice icy and relentless as her pleas for mercy mixed with her sobs. "Is it unbearable?"

"P-please, st-top. I b...b-beg you."

I stood before her, gripping her jaw with an ironclad hold, forcing her to meet my blazing green eyes. The green spark in them was proof of how angry I was, "Think about the suffering you inflicted on that little girl," I hissed, my voice a venomous whisper. "She was your daughter, and you subjected her to this horror when she was only fourteen. She was just a child. You didn't pity her. Why are you expecting mercy from me?" I twisted the knife in her wound, drawing out another scream of agony, more guttural and desperate.

"Is this pain more than you ever gave her? Or is it just a taste?!" I wrenched the knife out, letting her collapse to the floor, a crumpled and broken heap. Her cries filled the room, a harrowing symphony of despair that meant nothing to me but served as a grim satisfaction for my warped sense of justice.

Turning my attention to the kitchen, I unhooked the gas pipe without moving a muscle. The gas hissed and began to seep into the air, a silent harbinger of the devastation to come. I looked back at her, "I hope that in your next life, you learn to cherish your child," I said coldly, as I healed her wound once more. I didn't want to leave behind any evidence that could trace back to me.

I stepped out of the house, casting one last, lingering glance at the dwelling that had tormented my Liza for years. The memories of her suffering, the pain inflicted by this very place, burned in my mind. With a deep, steadying breath, I raised my hand and snapped my fingers. The explosion that erupted was a cataclysmic end to the suffering I had inflicted, a final act of retribution that left only ashes and ruin in its wake.

The house and the woman who I burnt alive are proof that I could go to unimaginable extremes for her. If the world dares to hurt my Liza, it will face the same fiery end, or maybe worse. I would turn the entire world to ash if it dared to stand between us. I'm not some benevolent figure bound by morals.

I'm a twisted soul with no sense of right or wrong, and my brand of justice is as sickening as it is unforgiving.

I know what I did is unforgiving and insane but there's a twisted comfort in knowing I protected her in the only way I knew how. It's cruel, it's deranged, but what else could anyone expect from me? I'm not some hero, and calling me a villain doesn't even scratch the surface. I'm Zephyr Valtor, a force of chaos and destruction, and I will do anything-burn, break, or annihilate-to keep my Liza Kirby safe.

She stirred in her sleep, drawing my gaze to her. Her eyes fluttered open and met mine. Grey to green. I smiled softly, "Morning, beautiful."

# Chapter 28

# *Ceremonial Reckoning*

*Liza's POV*

I woke up when I felt someone carefully lift me into his arms. My head rested against a firm, warm chest, and the familiar, intoxicating scent of Adrian filled my senses. Without even opening my eyes, I recognized his protective hold. I couldn't help but smile. "You don't have to carry me, Adrian," I murmured, my voice still thick with sleep. "I can walk."

His heartbeat was steady, a soft and calming rhythm against my ear. He took a quiet breath in. "I didn't want to disturb you," he said, his voice gentle, almost a whisper. It wrapped around me like a soft breeze, lulling me back into comfort. Instinctively, I snuggled closer, my chin finding the crook of his neck. His scent was warm, grounding, and it stirred something deep within me.

I breathed him in again, feeling an unexpected lightness in my chest. "I always thought if you were ink on paper, you'd smell like ink or paper," I looked him in his face and added, "But you smell like human. I'm highly disappointed."

A smirk tugged at the corner of his lips as he looked down at me. His gaze was captivating, those green eyes holding a mix of mischief and warmth. "Oh, don't be sad, love," he said, his tone laced with amusement. "I may not smell like ink or paper, but I'm certain I taste like them. If you don't believe me..." He paused in his tracks, his face leaning slightly closer to mine, "Kiss me."

In an instant, the drowsiness vanished, replaced by a sharp jolt of awareness. His words echoed in my head, leaving me wide awake and breathless. Heat rushed to my cheeks, the blush spreading like wildfire as I stared at him, utterly shocked. My body tensed, every nerve on the edge, and I felt a flush creeping up my neck, burning under my skin. I couldn't speak, couldn't move—too stunned by what he'd just said, the teasing smirk still playing on his lips as if he hadn't just turned my world upside down.

*Did he really say that?*

Adrian didn't say anything more. He simply started walking again, carrying me as though nothing out of the ordinary had been said. But I was frozen, my mind still reeling from his bold words.

"Tell me you were joking!" I demanded, my voice a little too high-pitched for my liking. The smirk on his face grew wider, amusement dancing in his eyes. "Adrian?" I pressed, bringing his eyes back to me.

One.

Two.

Three.

And then he laughed—an easy, deep laugh that made my stomach flip. It was contagious, even if it made my state worse. My body was still tense in his arms, my cheeks flushed, while he laughed on, completely unbothered by the chaos he'd just caused in my mind.

"Put me down," I ordered, my voice firm, though my lips twitched in betrayal.

"Why?" His smirk remained, teasing, playful.

"Because your jokes are terrible! You can't just say things like that!" I glared at him, though my lips betrayed me with a small smile. "That was so inappropriate."

He chuckled, and every fiber of my being felt offended. I wasn't angry—at least, not really. It wasn't even that his joke had crossed a line. It was something deeper, a disappointment I couldn't quite put into words. Maybe his teasing had hit too close to home, or maybe I was embarrassed that I reacted like a blush-monster. Or perhaps I actually believed he wanted me to kiss him for real.

"I hate you," I muttered, half-heartedly.

But he only laughed harder, shaking his head in disbelief. And despite myself, despite the embarrassment and the frustration, I smiled too.

He may have offended me, disappointed me even, but there was something about his laughter—about the lightness in his eyes and the ease with which he carried me—that made it impossible to stay upset. No matter how hard I tried.

Smiling, he carried me inside with such ease that it felt as if I weighed nothing. I was wide awake now, my head resting against his chest as I listened to the steady rhythm of his heartbeat. My eyes closed and a small smile on my lips. His warmth enveloped me, the intoxicating scent of him filling my senses, pulling me back into a hazy state between sleep and wakefulness. Just as he stepped onto the stairs, I heard a voice call out from behind us.

"Liza?"

I opened my eyes, the sound dragging me out of my sleepy fog. I recognized the voice instantly—Rachel. I glanced up at Adrian, then gestured for him to put me down. He complied without hesitation, gently lowering me to my feet. His hands lingered at my waist for a brief moment, steadying me as I found my footing. I gave him a small nod before turning to Rachel, who stood across me, her expression filled with concern.

"I thought you must have gone to bed by now," I said, walking towards her. She was wearing a simple nightgown, and the soft moonlight spilling through the windows highlighted how pale and tired she looked.

Rachel smiled, but it was a weak, tired smile. "I couldn't sleep until I knew you were alright." She stepped closer, her eyes scanning my face with a mixture of worry and warmth. Without warning, she reached out, taking my hands in hers. "How are you, Liza?" Her voice was gentle, filled with an almost maternal concern.

I tried to smile, though guilt twisted in my chest. "I'm fine. Really. I'm sorry for disappointing you like that. I didn't mean to worry you. I just got caught up in—"

She interrupted me before I could finish. "It's okay," Her hand moved to my cheek, cupping it gently as her thumb brushed against my skin. Her eyes held a deep sadness as she spoke again, "Adrian told me about your mother. I'm so sorry for what happened. No one should have to go through that."

Her words hit me like a punch to the gut, and for a moment, I felt my chest tighten. The grief, the loss I had buried deep inside, began to stir again, threatening to break free. And before I could respond, Adrian stepped forward, his voice cutting through the air.

"I think we should talk tomorrow. She needs rest."

There was a firmness to his tone, a quiet protectiveness that I hadn't expected. He stood just behind me, his presence solid and unwavering. But when I glanced back at Rachel, I noticed the subtle change in her expression. Her eyes flickered toward Adrian, and for a split second, there was something in her gaze—something cold, almost disapproving. It was as if she didn't like the fact that he was speaking to her.

"No, it's fine," I said quickly, not wanting to cause any tension. "I had a long day, but I'm alright. I can talk," I forced a smile, trying to reassure them both. "Besides, every second is precious."

Rachel's smile returned, though it was tinged with sadness, "It's okay. Adrian is right. You should rest." Her fingers brushed a strand of hair from my face before she leaned in to place a gentle kiss on my forehead. The gesture caught me off guard, and for a moment, I stood there frozen, my heart aching in a way that I hadn't felt in years, "Goodnight, honey," She whispered, her voice soft and full of affection.

I swallowed hard, blinking back the tears that threatened to spill over. "Goodnight," I murmured, watching as she turned and walked away, her figure disappearing down the hallway.

I stood there for a moment, my heart feeling heavy yet light at the same time. It was such a simple gesture, but it had stirred up so many memories—memories of my nana, of the nights she used to tuck me in and kiss me goodnight. The ache in my chest grew, and I suddenly felt like I was a child again, longing for that same comfort and warmth.

"What's wrong?" Adrian's voice broke through my thoughts. His tone was gentle but filled with concern.

I turned to look at him, blinking rapidly to clear the moisture from my eyes. "She kissed my forehead," I said, my voice barely above a whisper. "Just like my nana used to do." I swallowed, trying to keep my voice steady, but the emotion were too strong. "It's been so long since anyone did that."

Adrian's expression softened, his green eyes reflecting an understanding I hadn't expected. He sighed, gently took my hand, and before I realized it, he pulled me into a hug. His arms wrapped around me, holding me close against his chest. For a moment, I was stiff, surprised by the sudden gesture.

But then I relaxed, realizing all this care was his response to everything that had unfolded today. His warmth, his steady heartbeat—it was a quiet comfort in the middle of the chaos.

### Next Day

We were seated in the grand hall, a place that now felt more like a sacred altar than a home. The air hung thick with the scent of burning herbs and wax, and the moon, obscured by clouds, loomed behind the towering windows. In front of me, a large, deep bowl filled with blood sat at the centre of the room. Its dark, almost black liquid catching the flicker of candlelight. Surrounding it were a variety of eerie, ancient-looking tools and ingredients—crystals that pulsed faintly, bundles of dried herbs tied with twine, and a jagged silver blade that glinted ominously under the pale light. Besides the blood, strange totems carved from bone lay scattered, along with symbols etched into the floor in what looked like ash. All this arrangement to perform a ritual.

In the morning, Rachel dropped a bombshell: she had discovered a spell that could extend Adrian's stay. The news was a glimmer of hope, but my heart sank when she revealed the catch—this spell could only be used once. Of course, Archon had cunningly embedded a drawback.

Rachel's face grew somber as she detailed the ritual's requirements. The spell had to be performed during the full moon, which, fortuitously, was very night. Her eyes darkened with worry as she spoke of the spell's immense power, revealing that its potency could very well cost her life. Despite my faith in her formidable skills as a witch, a gnawing sense of dread took hold. This wasn't just any spell; it was a high-stakes gamble with the very boundaries of fiction and reality.

As if the spell wasn't enough to process, Rachel hit me with even more startling news. Tomes were being stolen, and the witches protecting them are being murdered. Her friend Sabrina Cabello had been the latest victim. The weight of everything—the tomes being stolen, the witches being killed, Rachel's friend Sabrina, the dangerous spell, the looming threat over us—It was an avalanche of shocking revelations to absorb all at once.

"You need to gain your powers, Liza. Only then we can do something," She said, looking at me with hope. I didn't know what to say. "I have given you enough time to handle yourself. I understand you must not be in the right state of mind after your mother's death, but Liza, if we don't fix this, we could get into huge trouble," I took a deep breath in and nodded. Sure, it's becoming tough and tough and time is slipping away like a bullet train.

I glanced at Adrian who was carrying an unreadable expression until his gaze landed on me. A soft smile made its way to his lips and I couldn't help but smile back, a small comfort amidst the tension swirling around us.

It was nearly time. Rachel had told us that the moon's shadow must fall on Adrian for the spell to take hold. The very idea seemed otherworldly, as though we were standing on the precipice of two realities, ready to merge them with a single act.

"Can I ask you something, Rachel?" I spoke, bringing her attention to me. She gave a subtle nod, signalling me to go on while her hands moved with precision as she arranged the items on the floor. There was no hesitation in her movements, only purpose and focus. "I've heard that rituals involving blood are... dark magic. Is that true?"

Rachel paused, her entire attention on me, "Yes, it's true," she said, her voice grave. A cold shiver ran down my spine. I glanced at Adrian, who stood with an unsettling calmness as if he was already familiar with the darkness of this magic. "This spell, everything we're about to do—it's dark. The kind of magic that can kill."

"So, the spell which brings fiction to life—it's dark magic too?"

"Yes. And the consequence of wielding it is right next to us." She gestured towards Adrian with bitterness. Adrian only threw her a tight-lipped smile. Since morning, I've been noticing tension between them. A cold war of eyes.

*Had they had a fight or something?*

"Alright, we should begin now," She announced, gesturing for Adrian to stand in the centre of the witchy art she had made.

I had no real part to play in the ritual itself, not beyond the blood I had already given. My only task now was to watch.

Rachel closed her eyes, her lips moving in a silent incantation. The candles flickered wildly, casting long, shifting shadows across the walls. The air crackled with energy, thick and electric, as though the very space around us was reacting to the power she was calling forth. I could feel it—an ancient force stirring from the depths, rising from the earth to meet her summons.

The temperature in the room seemed to drop, a bone-chilling cold seeping into my skin. I gripped my skirt tighter, trying to focus on the rhythm of Rachel's voice. But my eyes kept drifting to Adrian. He stood in the centre of the circle, his face bathed in the flickering glow. He looked calm and composed, yet there was something about him that seemed almost... vulnerable. As if the power around us could affect him in ways none of us fully understood.

Rachel opened her eyes and dipped her hands in the blood, gesturing Adrian to do the same. The sight of the blood made my stomach churn, its metallic scent filling the room. I fought the nausea creeping up my throat, knowing full well that this was only the beginning. One day, I too would have to take part in rituals like this. One day, I would have to embrace this dark, unknown side of me—this magic that was both my heritage and my curse. But that day was not today. Today was a training day, a glimpse of what-my-future-is-going-to-look-like day.

They joined hands, their eyes closing as Rachel began to chant. Her voice was low, almost a whisper, sending chills down my spine. The room grew quiet, too quiet, with only the sound of her words and my breath breaking the stillness. Then, without warning, a cold gust of wind swept through the hall, snuffing out the candles in one breath.

My heart lurched, and the room was plunged into complete darkness, the only light now coming from the faint glow of the moon as it struggled to pierce through the clouds.

"Rachel?" I whispered, my voice trembling slightly.

"Stay calm," she murmured, though I could hear the strain in her voice. "This is normal."

But it didn't feel normal. The air was thick with tension, as though we were waiting for something—or someone—to strike. I clenched my fists, my knuckles white. My eyes strained against the darkness, trying to make sense of the air around us. Adrian's figure was barely visible now, swallowed by the shadows.

The silence was deafening, broken only by the occasional creak of the old house settling. I could feel my pulse in my throat, each beat hammering against my skin. And then, from the corner of my eye, I saw it—a faint glimmer. The clouds had parted just enough for the moonlight to slip through, casting a pale glow directly onto Adrian.

It was time.

Rachel's voice rose, louder now, more urgent. She began to chant, her hands no longer joined with Adrian who stood motionless beneath the moon's light. The bowl of blood began to bubble, the liquid swirling unnaturally as though pulled by some unseen force. The symbols on the floor began to glow faintly, the ash lifting into the air as if alive, swirling around Adrian in a slow, deliberate dance.

I held my breath, watching as the energy in the room intensified, growing stronger with each passing second. The candles reignited spontaneously, their flames burning a deep, eerie blue. It looked too unnatural to witness.

But then, out of nowhere, Rachel's nose started bleeding. A thin stream of blood slipped down her face, and her body began to convulse violently. Her head snapped back, eyes rolling until only the whites showed. Panic surged through me, and I looked at Adrian, desperate for any sign of help—but what I saw terrified me even more.

Adrian stood rigid in the circle, his body eerily still and slightly above the ground. His usually vibrant green eyes had turned completely white, glowing with an unnatural light. It was as if his spirit had been snatched away, leaving behind only an empty vessel. The ash that once circled him lazily had shifted to a soft, shimmering blue, its light casting an eerie glow across the room.

"Oh my God! Guys?" I called out, my voice cracking with fear, but none of them responded. Rachel's body shook harder, and the blood flowed faster from her nose, dripping steadily onto the floor. My heart pounded in my chest, and a suffocating fear wrapped around me. Rachel had warned me—this spell was dangerously powerful, and it could kill her.

I looked back and forth between Adrian and Rachel, my mind spinning in frantic circles. I didn't know what to do, didn't even know where to begin. Rachel's condition was worsening by the second, and Adrian... I couldn't tell if he was even still in there. He looked as if he was trapped somewhere between life and death.

The blood from Rachel's nose began to pool at her feet, and the sight of it sent a jolt of terror through me. I couldn't just sit here and do nothing. My hands trembled as I reached for her, gripping her hand tightly in mine, hoping—praying—that it would somehow help. But the moment our hands connected, I felt it—an overwhelming surge of energy, raw and wild, tearing through me like lightning. The wind outside grew fiercer, howling through the open windows and rattling the glass in their panes. The entire room seemed to tremble under the weight of the spell, the walls groaning as if they were about to collapse under the force of the magic being unleashed. For a split second, I thought I'd made things worse.

But then I heard it—a gasp, sharp and breathless.

I whipped my head around just in time to see Adrian, his chest heaving as though he'd been pulled from the brink of death. His muscles tensed, every inch of him vibrating with the raw magic that was now binding him to this world.

Then, just as suddenly as it had begun, everything stopped. The wind fell silent, the windows ceased their rattling, and the candles flickered weakly before their eerie blue flames faded back to a warm yellow. Adrian's eyes, no longer glowing, found mine, and in that moment, I felt a rush of relief wash over me, loosening the tightness in my chest. The eerie feeling that had filled the room slowly disappeared, leaving only the quiet aftermath of what had just happened.

I thought it was over until I heard a soft thud from beside me. I whipped my head around to find Rachel crumpled on the floor, her body limp and lifeless. My eyes widened, "Rachel?!"

# Chapter 29

## *Petals of Despair*

### *Liza's POV*

These three days have passed in a haze, each day blending into the next as I desperately try to breathe life into this dead rose. For three days straight, I've been consumed by this impossible task. I was in an indoor botanical garden, surrounded by many kinds of flowers that are meant to bring me peace, but as I stood here, it felt like every petal, every bloom, was mocking me, laughing at me with their vibrant colours as I try to revive a lifeless rose. It's absurd, yet here I am, lost in this madness.

Rachel said this is the first step to unlocking my powers. She told me I needed to understand my connection to nature, to the universe itself. But no matter how many hours I pour into this, I can't seem to make it work. Maybe, mother earth doesn't like me.

I draw in a shaky breath and close my eyes, my hands hovering over the wilted flower on the centre table, hoping—almost foolishly—that some spark of life will flow from my palms, that somehow, I can bring it back to life but as I opened my eyes again, it remained the same.

"You're distracted," a voice from the doorway jolted me from my thoughts. I jumped, startled by the sudden interruption. He stood at the doorway, leaning casually against the frame, dressed head to toe in black. A pack of chips was in his hand, and that all-too-familiar smirk danced on his lips, amusement clear in his eyes.

As I looked at him, my mind went to the events of a few days ago. Rachel discovered a spell—a spell to extend the days of fictional characters in our world. It was Archon's creation, an ancient and immensely powerful incantation. But when Rachel began the ritual, things spiralled out of control faster than either of us anticipated. The energy that poured from the spell was overwhelming, and Rachel was caught in its grip. I watched, helpless, as her nose started to bleed, and she grew deathly pale. In that horrifying moment, it looked like the very essence of her being was slipping away, her soul unravelling.

Then, something unexpected happened. The moment our hands touched, it felt like the world shifted. Suddenly, I wasn't just holding Rachel—I had become something else, something more. Like I was her anchor, pulling her back from the brink. I could feel it, the raw power of the spell clashing with something deep inside me, something I didn't even know was there.

It wasn't just about holding her hand—there was more to it, something beyond my understanding. The spell, which had nearly swallowed Rachel whole, suddenly recoiled, as if it had hit a force it couldn't overpower. And the strangest part? The ritual, which had spiralled out of control, somehow completed itself, giving Adrian more time in this world—all because I had held onto Rachel. It was like my presence alone was enough to bring everything back from the brink.

After it was over, Rachel collapsed, and for a split second, I thought I'd lost her. Panic shot through me. But no—it wasn't death. It was the sheer energy she had poured into the ritual. It drained her, weakened her, leaving her unconscious but alive.

Even now, I struggle to understand it. How could something so simple—just holding onto me—make such a monumental difference? The spell that nearly destroyed Rachel seemed insignificant against whatever force lay within me, and the realization of that was... terrifying.

"May I help you?" His voice cut through the fog of my thoughts, pulling me back to the present. I blinked, shaking my head slightly and putting my focus back on the withered rose in front of me. It lay there, lifeless, mocking my efforts to breathe life back into it. I heard him sigh, then the soft sound of his footsteps as he approached. "You need to focus, Miss Kirby."

I let out an audible sigh, "I'm trying. But it seems like the universe is either playing with me or testing my patience."

"Nope. The reason you're not able to put life into this dead rose is because your head is fogged. You have to focus. Feel the connection. Let it sink in."

I stared at him, and for a moment, I was lost. His smile was so disarmingly beautiful that it felt like I might melt on the spot. This week has been tough, stressing with the task at hand but Adrian's change in behaviour has just made it easy to handle. It's baffling because it's like a switch had flipped. The sharp mood swings, the silent response, arrogance—they were gone. In their place was this man, all smiles, sarcasm, warmth, cuteness, and something more that I can't name. The cold distance he usually kept was gone, replaced with a warmth that made me question everything I thought I knew about him. Every word he spoke seemed to be laced with something deeper, something that made my heart race and my mind stutter. It was like he was peeling back layers, showing me a side of himself I'd never seen before, and I didn't know how to react.

All I knew was that, whenever he looked at me like that, with that soft smile and those eyes that seemed to see right through me, it took every ounce of willpower not to lose myself completely. And by that I mean...

"How can you focus on this when you can't even focus on my words?" His voice broke through my thoughts again, a playful edge to his tone. I blinked, realizing I'd drifted off once more. He shook his head, a small smile playing on his lips.

"You need to get out of here, Adrian. I need to focus," I said, trying to dismiss him, hoping he'd take the hint. But the playful smile he wore moments ago faded, replaced by a look of intensity that sent a shiver down my spine. His expression was so different, so serious, that I couldn't help but ask, "What?"

He didn't answer. Instead, he took a step closer to me, closing the distance between us in a way that made my heart leap into my throat. He was close enough that I could feel the heat radiating off his skin, his presence overwhelming. My gaze flickered to his lips, just for a second, before I forced myself to look back into his eyes—those green eyes that seemed to hold back a storm of emotions I wasn't ready to confront.

"Let me help you focus," he whispered, his voice low and almost hypnotic as he stepped back, setting the packet of chips aside. "Turn around."

I blinked, taken aback. "What?"

"Turn yourself toward the flower," he instructed, his voice gentle but firm.

I hesitated, glancing over my shoulder at the wilted rose on the table before turning my attention back to him. His expression hadn't softened, and there was an undeniable command in his gaze that compelled me to comply. Reluctantly, I turned around, facing the flower, my heart pounding in my chest.

He moved silently, taking his place behind me, so close that I could feel the warmth of his breath against my ear.

"Close your eyes," he murmured, his voice sending another wave of shivers down my spine. My heart rate spiked, and I had to clench my fists to keep myself steady. The air between us felt charged, alive with an energy that made every nerve in my body buzz with anticipation.

"What are you planning to do?" I asked, closing my eyes.

He didn't answer right away. Instead, his fingers traced a slow, deliberate path along my arm, starting at my shoulder and moving down to my wrist, his touch light but electrifying. I shivered involuntarily as he paused on my palms. "Help you," he whispered, his breath warm and tantalizing against the sensitive skin of my neck. I bit down on my lower lip, trying to ground myself.

"Now, keep your eyes closed and focus on my voice," he murmured, his tone slipping into something almost hypnotic. I nodded, though my mind was drifting to his voice, his touch, his breath, his scent, the way his proximity was making me feel.

"Try to focus. Let the world dissolve into darkness, Liza." His words were soft, but they held an authority that I found impossible to resist. I swallowed hard, forcing myself to concentrate solely on the sound of his voice. It was low, soothing, and carried a gentle command that wrapped around my thoughts like a velvet rope. "Forget everything and put your entire attention on my voice."

His hands, still holding mine, lifted them slightly, almost as if preparing me for something more. I took a breath in and tried to erase every sound, every feeling, every emotion, every thought.

"Focus on the sound of our breath, Liza. Block out everything else. Just listen to the rhythm of our breathing."

I did as he said, willing myself to follow his instructions. It took a moment—longer than I'd expected—but gradually, the world around us began to fade. The distant sounds of the outside world, the hum of life itself—it all melted away until the only thing left was the soft rise and fall of our breaths, perfectly synchronized.

"Let the peace of isolation consume you. Let it envelop you, wrapping you in the darkness of peace."

A strange calm settled over me, washing away the chaotic thoughts that had been swirling in my mind. My heart, which had been racing like a wild horse, began to slow, each beat steady and sure. The emotions that had surged with his simple proximity started to fade, replaced by a tranquil stillness I hadn't felt before.

"Now, feel your connection with the universe. Look for its beauty. Picture nature—waterfalls, the sky, everything in its purest form," Adrian's voice was smooth, calm, and wrapped in that magnetic pull that always unsettled me.

I took a deep breath. His words echoed in my mind, letting my thoughts conjure up serene images. The mist from a waterfall, the warmth of the sun over an endless horizon, the soft rustle of leaves carried by a gentle breeze. It was beautiful, vivid, almost real. The scene brought a small, fleeting smile to my lips.

"Liza," his voice interrupted my thoughts, piercing through the quiet. "Focus on the sound of your breath. Nothing else. When all you can hear is your breathing, search for a light. Let it guide you. Let it consume you."

I tried—God, I tried. The light he spoke of flickered at the edges of my mind, almost in reach. But just when I thought I could grab hold of it, memories of the other night, of blood and fear, came crashing down. My eyes snapped open.

"I can't!" I blurted out, turning sharply to face Adrian. I hadn't realized how close he was until I turned. Our faces were mere inches apart, his warm breath brushing my skin. Our lips were so close they could've touched, and instinctively, I leaned back against the table, desperate to create distance between us. But that space—God, I regretted it instantly.

"Why?" His voice was soft, questioning, but there was something else beneath it. Something more than curiosity—something darker. I swallowed hard, trying to find the words, but my mind was a chaotic mess, scrambling for answers. I gripped the edge of the table, knuckles turning white, feeling the tension coil tighter in my chest. It was like two forces were battling inside me—the need to keep him away and the overwhelming desire to pull him closer.

"What's wrong, Liza?" he asked, his eyes were intense, concerned. I wanted to answer, but nothing came out. How could I explain that the very presence of him was unraveling me? I wanted to push him away but, at the same time, the thought of him not being near suffocated me. I was drowning in the storm of feelings I didn't know how to navigate.

I felt my pulse quicken, heat spreading through me like wildfire. From the moment he joked about kissing me, that thought had been a relentless, maddening echo in my head. What would it feel like? His lips on mine, consuming me... How would it taste, how would it change everything between us? The idea of it drove me to the edge of reason. Yes, I had grown attached to him, but more than that—I had started to want him in a way I hadn't dared to admit. And I was terrified. Because I knew that once I crossed that line, there would be no turning back. My growing feelings for him are the biggest reason I don't want to send him back.

He sighed softly, shoulders dropping as his hand moved to cup my face, his fingers warm against my skin. The simple touch sent a wave of heat through me, and I froze, helpless under his gaze. His eyes locked onto mine, forcing me to stay in that moment as if he could see straight into the chaos inside me.

"I know the events of that night terrified you, Liza," he murmured, his voice low, his thumb brushing gently against my cheek. "But you need to stop running from what you are. Your identity isn't something you can hide from. It's your fate. You have to embrace it."

I gulped.

His words were logical, even comforting, but I barely registered them. All I could think about was his mouth—how close it was to mine, how his lips would feel pressed against mine. My heart hammered in my chest, my skin tingling with a hunger I didn't know how to control.

"Embrace who you are," he whispered, his breath fanning against my lips, so close I could feel the warmth of him. "You're the most powerful witch alive, and the only one who can undo the chaos that's been unleashed. You have to—"

"Can you kiss me?" The words slipped out of my mouth before I could stop them, hanging in the air between us. His eyes widened in shock, and for a brief moment, neither of us moved. I could see him processing what I had just said, disbelief flickering in his eyes.

"You shouldn't have joked about it," I continued, the words tumbling out uncontrollably. "Since you did, I can't stop thinking about how—" I didn't get to finish my sentence when his hand slid to the back of my neck, fingers tangling in my hair, and before I could take another breath, his lips crashed into mine with a force that stole the air from my lungs.

The kiss was not soft, not gentle—it was raw, desperate, like a dam had broken, and everything we had been holding back came pouring out in a torrent of need. His lips were hungry and demanding, and I felt my body react instinctively, pulling him closer. My hands found the fabric of his shirt, fisting it as if I could drag him even nearer, the space between us unbearable. His tongue parted my lips, tasting me, teasing me, and it felt like fire was spreading through my veins, my whole body trembling under the intensity of it.

It wasn't enough. I needed more. I wanted to drown in him, lose myself completely. I could feel his hands roaming, sliding down my back, gripping my waist, pulling me closer until our bodies were flush against each other. The kiss deepened, became more frantic, more out of control, and I let out a soft, involuntary moan, every nerve in my body alight with sensation.

It was intoxicating, exhilarating, and terrifying all at once. I had never felt so out of control, so consumed by another person, and I knew—deep down—I was crossing a line I couldn't come back from.

But just as the kiss spiralled deeper, a cold wave of reality crashed into me. What was I doing? Liza, no! Get away from him! Don't fall!!

I snapped my eyes open and broke away from him, breathless, my chest heaving, my lips swollen from the kiss, and my palms resting over his heaving chest. He stared at me, his eyes dark with lust, but there was a flicker of something else there, something I couldn't quite place.

I staggered back, putting space between us, but the regret lingered. I had wanted the kiss so badly, but now that it had happened, I didn't know how to deal with the consequences.

"Ink or paper?" he asked, still catching his breath, a smirk playing on his lips. His chest rose and fell, that teasing glint never leaving his eyes. I opened my mouth to reply, but the words caught in my throat. My voice—my entire ability to speak—seemed to abandon me when I saw the flowers around me.

Adrian followed my line of sight, his smirk faltering as his expression turned grim.

Every single flower, every plant in the botanical garden had withered away. Their once vibrant colors had drained to a sickly grey, their petals curling in on themselves, shriveled and lifeless. What had been full of life just moments before now looked like it had been touched by death. It was as if the very essence of life had been sucked out of them, leaving nothing but a haunting stillness.

*What did I do?*

## Chapter 30

# Rookie Blunder

*Zephyr's POV*

We stood there in the garden with Rachel in front of us. She stared at the dead flowers in utter disbelief. They lay before her, once vibrant, now withered and lifeless, as if some unseen force had sucked the vitality from them. Beside me, Liza stood, flushed, still, her chest rising and falling with shallow, uneven breaths. Her eyes flickered with confusion and concern as they darted from the flowers to Rachel, her mind clearly searching for an explanation. It wasn't long before she called out to Rachel, her voice trembling, desperate for answers. Liza needed to know what had happened, what had caused the flowers to decay so suddenly, so violently.

And to be honest, I wanted to know too because I hadn't done this. I have absolute control over my powers. They don't spiral out of control, not even in my most vulnerable state, not even in the moments when my mind is overwhelmed by desire, need, and craving. No, that wasn't it. The kiss hadn't done this.

But that kiss... God, that kiss!

It felt as though I had been craving it for an eternity, yearning for it like a man lost in the desert craves water, like a dying star longs for one last moment to shine. When her lips touched mine, it wasn't just a kiss. It was a release, an explosion as if a dam had burst inside me, unleashing all the emotions I'd kept bottled up for so long. Every suppressed thought, every hidden desire, every forbidden wish had come rushing to the surface. It was more than just a moment of passion. It was a culmination of every glance, every touch, every time our eyes had met and I had wanted nothing more than to close the distance between us.

I had been waiting for her to make the first move. I had been waiting for Liza to take the initiative because she's *Liza*—sweet, innocent Liza. I couldn't just take what I wanted from her, not unless she asked for it. She had to want it too, and I had to be sure of that. When she kissed me, it wasn't just her lips on mine. It was her heart, her soul, pouring into me, telling me without words that she needed this as much as I did. Her lips tasted like redemption, like everything I had been searching for but never knew I needed.

I could have taken more. I could have let myself drown in her, surrendering to the relentless urge to claim her wholly, to bind her to me in every conceivable way. The primal hunger inside me yearned to seize every moment with her, to engulf her completely in the fire that burned within me.

But I didn't. I held back. I held back because it's Liza, Liza Kirby. I want to go slow with her, savor every second, every heartbeat, every breath that passes between us.

I had planned to kiss her slowly too, slowly and passionately. But something happened. Something broke inside us both, and neither of us could stop it. The kiss wasn't just a kiss. It was hunger, raw and insatiable. It was like we'd both been holding back for so long, denying what we truly wanted. And when the dam broke, when that first kiss happened, all that restraint, all that careful consideration just disappeared. It melted away into nothingness, leaving only the two of us, tangled in a desperate, frantic embrace.

The sensation of her lips on mine was an intoxicating reminder of what I had, and what I needed more of. It was far from enough. I craved more intensely, completely. And I would claim it all, savouring every moment, until every last fragment of her innocence was devoured.

"You gained your powers but lost control over them," Rachel's voice pierced the silence, her gaze fixed on Liza. My eyes followed hers. Liza's face was pale, wide-eyed with shock and terror. She looked as if the world had just tilted on its axis, and I couldn't blame her.

Rachel's smile softened, almost comforting, "Relax, losing control like this is... normal, especially when you're just starting. You don't know how to harness them yet. You were trying to breathe life into that single rose, but instead, you drained the life from every single flower here," her tone matter-of-fact, as though it was the most natural thing in the world.

"She did this?" I asked, my voice slicing through the room. The eyes locked onto mine—one pair brimming with warmth and barely concealed anxiety, the other glinting with cold, unrestrained loathing.

Rachel's jaw tightened as she glared at me. "Yes. This demonstrates her power," she said, the words almost a veiled threat as I squinted at her. "And the good news?" Rachel turned to Liza, a flicker of something like triumph in her eyes. "Your powers have been awakened. All you need to do is embrace them."

Liza blinked in disbelief. "What?"

Rachel sighed, her hand sweeping through the air as she murmured a silent incantation. The flowers sprang back to life, their colors vibrant and full of life as if time itself had been undone. It was a breath-taking transformation as if nature itself was celebrating a miracle.

"When you saved my life the other day, Liza. I *felt* it. Your powers surged through you, not only saving me but finishing the ritual I had started. This was a test-a task-to see if I was right. You only needed to *feel* your own magic and let it flood through you. And it did. That's why I gave you the rose, to see if you could sense it. Sure, you made a rookie blunder with your magic, but it proves you can do magic now."

Liza looked at Rachel, then at the relived flowers, and back again, her shock transforming into a mix of disbelief and pride. "I can do magic now?" she whispered, her voice trembling.

"Yes. You can," Rachel said, her voice carrying both pride and warning. "But here's what you need to understand... you're not just a witch, Liza." Rachel's gaze bore into her. "You're special. That means you don't need to rely on spells for everything like we do. You have something much stronger inside you. You only need focus and you can perform magic beyond anything you can imagine."

I stole a sidelong glance at Liza, struggling to contain a smirk. Naturally, she had to be the strongest—after all, she was Zephyr Voltar's woman, and such a title demanded nothing less than extraordinary strength. Yet, a nagging feeling whispered that the truth was more complex. This wasn't some rookie blunder with her magic—it was something beyond.

"So, what now?" Liza asked, sounding nervous. Her eyes landed on me before she put her attention back on Rachel.

I smirked.

*So now we avoiding eye contact?*

Rachel turned toward me, her smile sharp, venomous. "Now," her gaze held mine in a challenge, "We find a way to send your friend back to his realm," I smirked, challenging her right back. There was no way I was leaving now. But Rachel ignored me and looked back at Liza, her voice softening but still laced with authority. "You are far more powerful than you ever imagined, Liza. But with that power comes responsibility. You need to learn control, and fast, because if you don't... well, let's just say draining a few flowers will be the least of your worries."

Liza swallowed hard, her wide eyes a mix of fear and excitement. I could see the battle raging inside her, "So, when do I start practicing?" she asked, her voice stronger now, more determined. I could see her slipping into that role Rachel wanted her to play, the powerful sorceress who needed to master her abilities.

*God, damnit. I wanna kiss her again.*

Rachel's smile widened. "From today," she replied firmly, leaving no room for hesitation.

Liza nodded, but before we could delve into the practice, the shrill sound of a phone ringing cut through the air. Liza's phone. I watched her pick it up, her expression turning softer. I could tell from her expression exactly who it was. Nate *Fucking* Wilson. That idiot couldn't leave her alone, could he?

As Liza answered, my eyes wandered for a moment, lingering on her plump lips, her sexy curves, and those breasts before I forced them back to her face. I clenched my jaw, forcing myself to remain cool.

Nate's voice echoed faintly through the phone. She smiled, and that little smile provoked me to snatch the phone from her hand and throw it across the room. But more than that, I wished to bring that dipshit here and kiss Liza again and show that she's mine and mine alone.

Soon, Liza hung up the phone and looked at Rachel, "Would you be mad if I tell you that I called someone over, Rachel?" she asked, her voice a little too casual, her eyes darting toward me like she was trying to gauge my reaction.

My reaction was crystal clear. Displeasure.

Every muscle in my body tensed at her words. *Called someone?* I could feel my pulse quicken, my blood heating as if the fire was racing through my veins.

Rachel raised an eyebrow, curious but amused. "Sure, you can. Who's someone if I may ask?"

Liza hesitated. *Hesitated?* My eyes narrowed at that slight pause. What the hell is she battling with herself about? He's just a "*friend*," right? What is the hesitation for?

"A friend of mine." She finally spoke, her voice tight,

Rachel's smirk widened, teasing. "A *friend*, huh? Nice. Please let me know if he's going to stay because then I'll make sure the room next to yours is vacant." Rachel's grin grew wicked. "Or... will you be sharing with him?"

The words hit me like a punch to the gut. Red. Heat. Discomfort. Fury. That's all I felt at that moment. My vision blurred as the rage boiled up inside me. Rachel's teasing smirk was like a knife twisting in my chest. How could she talk like that? How could she be so damn casual about someone she didn't even know? But then again, how could I blame her? Liza was acting as if she *liked* him like she was still wrapped up in this ridiculous idea of Nate.

But no-*no*. She couldn't still have feelings for him. Not after what happened between us. We kissed. *We kissed*. She couldn't possibly still care about that pathetic man. Could she?

I felt my jaw clenching so tight it ached, and my fists rolled even tighter until I nearly drew blood.

"Oh, my god, Rachel?" Liza's eyes widened as they flitted towards me for a brief, electric moment before she quickly averted her gaze. Her voice trembled as she stammered, "We're just f-friends."

*Hesitation. Again!*

Rachel's laughter spilled out, a sound both dismissive and caustic. I couldn't help but roll my eyes, my temper barely restrained. The temptation to make Rachel slip and fracture her bones was almost unbearable.

"It's okay, sweetheart," Rachel said, her tone syrupy sweet but edged with a dangerous undertone. "You can invite your friends here. Just remember that every second counts. Adrian's extended stay doesn't mean the threat has magically disappeared."

Liza nodded, her expression a mix of relief and apprehension. "Yes. Now, if you don't mind, I'd like to go answer the door," she said, my gaze shifting from her face to the phone she held up, Nate's name flashing on the screen.

Fire.

"Sure, go ahead," Rachel replied, a hint of amusement barely concealed in my voice.

Liza smiled and walked out the door. I stood there for a moment, my eyes following her retreating figure, and then a grin spread across my face as the memory of moments ago flashed in front of my eyes.

"Why are you smiling?" Rachel's voice snapped me out of my thoughts. Her eyes were a blend of suspicion, curiosity, and a simmering loathing that was as palpable as ever.

I rolled my eyes, giving her my most insouciant look. "You don't need to scowl at me all the time, Rachel. It's not good for your complexion. Relax a little," I said, but her expression remained as icy and hostile as ever. "Yes, I know I'm the villain in your story. But believe it or not, I'm not always scheming something diabolical. Sometimes, I'm just indulging in a little... You know, personal satisfaction."

Rachel narrowed her eyes, her gaze intense as she tried to decipher my cryptic statement. "Relax. I'm not planning to kill anyone. At least, not today," I added with a smile that was more unsettling than reassuring. With that, I turned on my heel and made my way toward the door.

Yes, I'm jealous. But insecure? Absolutely not. Liza is mine. Every time Nate's name comes up, it claws at my patience, but I hold back. He's just a friend—a friend she was once drawn to, nothing more. But still, the idea that she was ever attracted to him ignites something dangerous inside me. He had her attention, her curiosity, even if for a fleeting moment. But now, it's me who holds her soul, her mind, her heart, and her body. Every part of her belongs to me, and there's no one—*no one*—who can take that from me. Nate can try all he wants, but it's pointless. She's already mine, and that will never change.

I stepped into the hallway, frowning when I found it empty. My eyes darted around, searching every corner. Then, I heard it—a soft chuckle, unmistakably Liza's. My head whipped in the direction of the sound, and I followed it with quick steps. In the backyard, I saw them walking side by side, and there she was, holding a bouquet, her smile bright.

*Flowers? Did he buy her flowers?*

*That bastard.*

My hands clenched, and I wanted nothing more than to march over and rip them from her hands and throw them to the ground. But that smile on her face... damn it. If they made her happy, I could let it slide. But still, the thought of him buying them gnawed at me.

*Calm down, Zephyr. They're just flowers. He's nothing.*

I forced myself to take a deep breath, letting the anger coil tightly in my chest before finally turning my back on them. I couldn't stand the sight anymore, but walking away without causing a scene took every ounce of restraint.

"Zephyr?"

The sound of my true name slashed through my thoughts like a blade. I whipped my head around, irritation flashing in my eyes as I met Rachel's cold, unwavering stare.

"I'd suggest you stick to Adrian," I said, the smirk on my lips barely masking my annoyance. "We wouldn't want dear Liza stumbling onto the truth, would we?."

Rachel didn't even blink. Her expression was stone-cold, her hatred for me obvious. "We're heading to the UK—Liza's house," she said, completely ignoring my suggestion, "Her mother mentioned the tome. There's a chance the mansion holds more secrets, something buried deep in the walls that we haven't uncovered yet."

I nodded, thoughts racing. Her logic was sound, but that didn't make it any less irritating to hear from those expressions. "We leave tomorrow. Book the tickets."

I scoffed, crossing my arms. "You don't get to order me around, Rachel."

Her expression remained frigid, a glint of arrogance in her eyes. "I'm not ordering you. I'm keeping you informed and giving you tasks. You're supposed to handle things, aren't you?"

I narrowed my eyes, my voice dripping with sarcasm. "That sounds a lot like an order."

"Are you booking them or not?" she shot back, her tone sharp, clearly unimpressed by my attitude.

I tilted my head slowly, a smirk creeping back onto my lips, dangerous and mocking. "Have you forgotten who you're speaking to, Rachel? Or perhaps it's slipped your mind that I'm... *Dangerous?*" I could see the frustration growing behind her cold stare, but she masked it well, rolling her eyes in irritation. I rolled my eyes. "Fine, I'll book them. But a word of advice—don't be so bold in front of me. Bruising my ego might just be the last thing you do. You should be showing me a little fear, darling."

She shook her head, clearly done with me, and turned on her heel to walk away.

But before she could get far, we both stopped, a sudden presence drawing our attention. Both of us turned, and there he was—a man stepping through the doorway. His presence was a shadow stretching over the room, tall and broad-shouldered, his suit immaculate and tailored to perfection. But it was his face that commanded attention—a long, jagged scar slicing from his eyebrow to his cheekbone, marking his skin with the evidence of some violent past. His expression was a frozen mask—cold, calculating, devoid of warmth or humanity.

He didn't smile. He didn't smirk. There was no arrogance in his stance, only a steely resolve. His eyes, sharp and dead like shards of ice, swept over the room, landing on me and Rachel with an intensity that spoke of authority.

Rachel stiffened, her usual composure cracking just a little as her eyes flickered with confusion. Despite her attempt to maintain control, it was clear she was unsettled by the man's presence.

As for me, I wasn't worried. Not even close. Instead, a slow, predatory smile curved my lips. I was genuinely intrigued. This man, scarred and silent, was clearly here for something, and I knew exactly what.

I folded my arms and tilted my head towards Rachel, my eyes locked on the man before us. "I'd bet he's here for the tome," I whispered. Her eyes widened, and shock seeped through her usually calm demeanor. "Relax. I've got this."

"You think you can handle him?" she asked, her voice edged with concern. I snapped my head towards her, deeply offended. "He's been killing powerful witches and alone here for the tome, no guards," She tried to justify her statement.

"Have you really forgotten what I'm capable of?" I asked her, offended, "I'm Zephyr, Rachel. What is wrong with you?"

Before Rachel could respond, the man spoke, drawing all attention to him, "Good morning. I'm Zach Miller and I'm here to take something."

I raised an eyebrow, "Take what?"

His gaze was unblinking, his voice flat and chilling. "The tome," The weight of his words seemed to make the air grow colder.

A smile stretched across my face, satisfied that I'd guessed his purpose correctly. Rachel's frown deepened, her anxiety evident, especially with the recent murders of witches. But with me standing beside her, she managed to hold her composure, though the worry was clear.

"Hand it over now, and I assure you, no harm will come to any of you."

I chuckled, finding his bluntness entertaining. "Hurt us? Do you even know who you're dealing with?" My tone was casual, but it carried an undercurrent of menace.

Zach didn't flinch. His gaze remained cold and steady. "Don't test my patience, sir. Hand me the tome."

"Sir? Interesting," I murmured, stepping forward slightly, my gaze never leaving his. "Tell me, who are you working for?"

He didn't respond. His expressions and composure were still the same. I signed, "Fine," I lifted my hand and was about to compel him, but before I could, the door of the backyard swung open with a loud creak. Nate and Liza stepped in, their faces alight with smiles that instantly vanished as they took in the scene. The man's imposing presence was impossible to ignore, and their expressions shifted to immediate concern.

Zach's eyes flicked towards them briefly, acknowledging their presence with a cold stare before turning his attention back to me. The tension in the room spiked, the atmosphere thick with anticipation.

*Shit!*

# Chapter 31

# The Price of Pretence

*Author's POV*

Zephyr stood perfectly still, yet a storm churned within him, his chest coiling with tension like a serpent about to strike. Worry-an emotion as foreign as it was unwelcome-had taken root inside him, and it gnawed at him like a festering wound. It wasn't for Nate, the clueless bystander caught in the swirling chaos, but for Liza. If he used his powers now, if even a sliver of Zephyr slipped through the carefully crafted facade of Adrian, everything would come crashing down. Liza couldn't see the truth. She wasn't ready. She couldn't know the monster lurking behind the mask-the cruelty, the ruthlessness, the willingness to cross any line for what he wanted. And if she did, if she saw the real him, her world would shatter into pieces she couldn't put back together. And with it, the fragile bond he had so painstakingly cultivated would be ripped apart. And he can't let that happen.

Beside him, Rachel stood tense, her expression a mask of barely concealed fear. She knew the truth, knew the horrors that would unfold if Zephyr let himself loose. If Liza saw what lay beneath. She had witnessed the way Liza's eyes lit up whenever she looked at Adrian-the admiration, the trust, maybe even the spark of love she dared not speak aloud. But Liza didn't know the man behind the mask, didn't know the monster that wore his face. Not yet. And if that truth surfaced now, if Liza saw Zephyr for who he really was, it would break her. Break her in a way no one could fix. Rachel knew Liza couldn't survive that kind of betrayal. The truth was too heavy, too dark. Liza would crumble beneath its weight, and Zephyr's plans would turn to ash and then he'd hurt her for his selfishness which would break Liza entirely.

Liza shifted uncomfortably, her eyes flicking between Zephyr, Rachel Nate, and the newest threat: Zach. The atmosphere in the room was suffocating, thick with unspoken danger. She could feel it, the electric crackle of tension that made the hair on the back of her neck stand on end. And then there was Nate- her heart twisted at the sight of him, standing at her side, oblivious to the depth of the danger surrounding them. He was the only one who didn't know, the only one who hadn't been dragged into this dark, twisted world. He was... normal. And that made him vulnerable.

Meanwhile, Nate remained unnervingly composed. Though he didn't understand the full extent of the threat, he could feel it. Zach's presence was like a dark cloud looming overhead, and it clawed at Nate's nerves with every passing second. His muscles were tense, his jaw set in quiet determination, but he stayed close to Liza as if sensing that something was wrong.

And then there was Zach. Cold, detached, unmoved by the flurry of emotions swirling around him. His eyes were dark and calculating as they swept over the room, assessing everything, taking in every weakness, every possible threat. He wasn't here to negotiate. He wasn't here to make deals. His goal was simple, and his patience had run thin. The tome was all that mattered. Anyone who stood in his way would be nothing more than collateral damage.

"I'll say this once." Zach's voice cut through the room like a blade, low and sharp, yet carrying a weight that made everyone freeze. "Give me the tome."

The command rippled through the air, thick with the promise of violence. The tension in the room spiked, suffocating them all in its grip. Liza's breath hitched, panic clawing at her chest as her eyes darted to Zephyr, then back to Zach. *He's the killer.* The realization hit her like a punch to the gut, knocking the breath from her lungs. Zach wasn't just any threat. He was the one behind the murders, the one stealing the tomes. And now he was here, standing in front of them, demanding the tome.

She gulped. The weight of the revelation threatened to crush her. Nate, still clueless, took a small step forward, his hand brushing Liza's arm in a silent gesture of support. He didn't know. He couldn't know the danger they were in. The kind of man Zach was. The kind of monster Zephyr could become. But the tension that swirled around him was enough for him to know that he was a threat and his only instinct was, to protect Liza.

Rachel's hands twitched at her sides, her magic bubbling beneath the surface, but she hesitated. She knew better than anyone what would happen if Zephyr revealed himself here. She shot him a glance, a warning. She was pleading with him to hold back, to keep his true nature hidden for just a little longer. Zephyr's fists clenched, as much as he wanted to turn this man into ashes, he held back. Because he cared, he cared about Liza, and standing there he realized how scared he was to lose her.

Zach was done waiting. His eyes narrowed, dark and dangerous. "Don't make me ask again."

"Alright, Liza. Please take your friend upstairs with you?" Zephyr said, his voice calm but laced with something darker, his gaze locking onto hers. Something was unsettling in the way he held her gaze, as if trying to offer comfort, while an invisible storm raged beneath his skin.

Liza swallowed hard, nodding. Her fingers gripped Nate's wrist tightly, trying to pull him towards the stairs. But just as they took a step, a heavy rumble shook the floor. The sofa in the hallway screeched across the ground as if possessed, slamming into place right in front of the staircase, blocking their way.

"What the hell?" Nate's voice cracked with disbelief. His eyes widened, shock etched on his face as he tried to make sense of what just happened. His breath quickened, panic setting in.

Liza's heart pounded so fiercely in her chest that it drowned out everything else. Fear crawled up her spine, turning her blood cold. Without thinking, she moved in front of Nate, her body acting on instinct to shield him from whatever danger was brewing. Her eyes darted to Zephyr-no, Adrian. Was it still Adrian? His gaze was fixed on Zach. His jaw clenched and chest heaving.

The mask- Adrian's charming, playful mask was slipping, unraveling before her. Liza felt her breath catch in her throat. She sensed it from far away that this wasn't going to end well.

Rachel's face paled as she stood frozen near the wall, eyes darting between Zephyr and Liza. She knew what Zephyr was capable of, she'd seen his cruelty firsthand. If anything happened to Liza, he wouldn't care because he only wants to use her for his selfishness. Or at least, that's what Rachel believed. She didn't know that behind that twisted mask, Zephyr had already thought of a hundred ways to make Zach suffer. The image of Liza hurt-No, *his* Liza hurt was driving him to the brink of madness.

And Nate? Nate stood like a statue, completely stunned, unable to comprehend what was happening. His world, everything he knew, was shattering before his eyes.

"No one's going anywhere until you hand me the tome!" Zach's voice cut through the tension.

Zephyr's jaw clenched, his fists balling at his sides. He could end this right now. With a flick of his wrist, he could make the ground beneath Zach's feet split open, bury him so deep in the earth that no one would ever find him. The thought danced tantalizingly at the edge of his mind, and for a brief moment, he wanted it more than anything. The hunger to make Zach pay was nearly irresistible.

But he couldn't. Not yet.

Zach, impatient, took another step forward, his eyes burning with rage, hand outstretched as if ready to strike. A black smoke of dark magic swirled around him as he walked near them. Nate's eyes widened as he witnessed this while all three tried their best to think of the least destructive way to defeat him.

Zephyr spread his hands, flames erupting from his fingertips, as he stood with a steely resolve. The fire danced around him, casting ominous shadows on the walls.

"No fire!" Rachel's command cut through the chaos, her voice sharp and commanding. Before Adrian could react, she chanted an incantation with unwavering confidence, "Ventus Imperium!" The words hung in the air, and in an instant, Zach was lifted off his feet and hurled against the wall with a thunderous crash. Nate's eyes widened in shock, his jaw hanging open as he watched the scene unfold in stunned silence.

"Shall we run?" Liza's voice trembled, her grip on Nate's hand tightening as if to anchor herself amidst the chaos.

"This house is made of wood. One spark, and we're all done for. Besides, I don't think fire will stop him," Rachel said urgently, her eyes darting between Zach and the encroaching danger.

Zach, shaken but unbowed, got up, extending his hands. A powerful force erupted from his palms, slamming everyone to the ground. Liza, however, was gently lowered onto the sofa by an invisible force, courtesy of Zephyr's unseen hand.

Zephyr stood to his feet and conjured flames and directed them at Zach. But Zach stood firm, his own force pushing the fire away, even though the intensity of it left him feeling strangely weak and disoriented. The energy was overwhelming, baffling him with its raw power.

"Adrian, no fire!" Rachel shouted again, her tone desperate. Zephyr glanced her way, momentarily distracted, only to be thrown backward by an invisible force wielded by Zach. He crashed into the wall with a grunt, pain evident in his grimace.

"Adrian?" Liza screamed, her eyes locked on Adrian. She began to move towards him, but Nate, still reeling from the intensity of the moment, grabbed her wrists with a firm grip.

"Stay back. It's too dangerous!" Nate's voice was urgent, filled with a mix of fear and determination. As Liza looked at Nate, Zephyr seized the opportunity to strike. With a wave of his hand, he used an invisible force to drag Zach towards him and delivered a brutal blow across his face. The force was so intense that it sent Zach crashing to the other side of the room.

Liza's head was snapped towards the noise and her eyes widened. She thought Rachel had done this.

Zach lay on the floor, stunned by the sheer strength of his opponent. He had never faced someone with such raw power before. Yet, instead of fear, he felt a deep curiosity and intrigue. Determined to end the confrontation, Zach stood and lifted a wooden table with his power, shattering it into a myriad of sharp fragments. He aimed the shards at Zephyr with precision. "Let's see if you can handle this!" he declared fiercely. The deadly projectiles hurtled towards Zephyr, but he deftly avoided them and when Rachel distracted Liza again, Zephyr changed the direction of those fragments towards Zach. Zach managed to deflect most of the shards, but some struck him, causing cuts and bruises.

He fell to the ground. The room was filled with a tense silence as Zach's wounds began to heal instantly, the gashes closing up and the blood vanishing. The sight left everyone in stunned disbelief.

"He can heal himself?" they all thought simultaneously, astonished by his regenerative abilities.

Zach's eyes burned with malice as he looked at Zephyr. "You're impressive," he said, his voice dripping with contempt. With a snap of his fingers, he unleashed chaos. Every object in the room, the chairs, lamps, and books, whizzed through the air, aiming straight at Zephyr.

Zephyr moved with lightning speed, dodging and weaving through the barrage. His agility was incredible, but Zach's power was relentless. The room darkened with swirling smoke as Zach hurled Zephyr against the wall with a forceful slam. The impact rattled the room's very bones. Zach didn't stop there. He yanked Zephyr across the hallway with an invisible force, his face twisted in satisfaction. Without warning, he sent Zephyr crashing through the window, shattering it into a deadly shower of glass.

The shards embedded themselves into Zephyr's skin, and blood streamed down his body. He tried to stand, but before he could fully recover, a table was hurled at him with brutal force. It exploded on impact, and though Zephyr raised an arm to shield himself, the blow left him gasping in pain.

Liza's heart pounded as she watched in horror. She felt paralyzed, unable to help as the brutal scene unfolded. Rachel, who had always hated Zephyr, found herself torn. The urgency of their situation-preventing Zach from taking the tomes-made her desperate for Zephyr to fight back.

Zach's face was a mask of fury as he grabbed Zephyr by the collar. He was about to deliver a crushing blow when, in a flash of lightning, both Zach and Zephyr were thrown apart. Rachel had intervened, her face set in a grim line. The lightning strike was her last-ditch effort to turn the tide.

Zephyr struggled to his feet, wincing as he pulled a jagged piece of glass from his arm. The wound was deep, and he could heal himself but that would make Liza question him or worse, know the truth. He hated the situation he was in.

Zach struggled to his feet too, frustration etched deeply into his features. His anger was palpable; no matter how much he assaulted Zephyr, it felt like his blows were merely brushing against a stone wall. Every attack seemed ineffective as if Zephyr's resilience turned his most ferocious efforts into mere breezes. He was hurting him but not as much as he wanted and that drove him mad.

With a snarl, Zach seized Zephyr by the collar once more. For the first time, raw frustration painted his face. "What are you?" he demanded, his voice a dangerous growl as he tightened his grip.

Zephyr's eyes blazed with an ominous green light. Despite the pain, a dark, twisted smirk crossed his face. "I will kill you," he said coldly, "but not before you beg me."

Zach's jaw clenched in a mix of rage and determination. In one swift, brutal motion, he seized Zephyr by the throat, lifting him effortlessly off the ground. With a roar of sheer power, Zach slammed Zephyr down with such devastating force that the very floor beneath them cracked. The impact sent a tremor through the air, and Zephyr's body hit the ground with a sickening thud, pain exploding through him as cracks spider-webbed across the floor. It was as if the world itself buckled under the sheer weight of Zach's wrath.

Zach then raised his arm, encircled by swirling black smoke-*dark magic*-preparing to deliver a crushing blow. But just as his fist was about to connect with Zephyr's face, a sudden, invisible force halted his arm mid-air. Shocked, Zach stared at his frozen limb, confusion flashing across his features. Before he could react, an overwhelming force lifted him off the ground, dragging him violently across the room, and then he was unceremoniously thrown into an adjacent room, the door slamming shut behind him. Red lightning crackled around the door, forming an unyielding barrier that sealed him inside.

Zephyr, bewildered by the sudden turn of events, turned his gaze towards Liza. There she stood, her breath heavy and her hand outstretched towards the door. The intensity in her eyes was unmistakable, she had intervened. The realization that she had used her power to confine Zach left everyone stunned, especially, Nate. She possessed such formidable abilities was a jarring shock to him, reshaping his perception of her entirely.

## Chapter 32

## Run Run Run

*Liza's POV*

The memory of Adrian's words crashed into me with the force of a tidal wave: "I'm sure by the end of this, you'll also learn about yourself because you certainly don't know what you're capable of yet."

I had not believed him then, convinced he was wrong, that it was just some fluke. Me, and magic? It seemed impossible. It had to be. Even after that accident with the flowers, when they withered around me, I couldn't accept it. But now... standing here, my hand outstretched, shaking, pointing toward the door where I'd trapped Zach-the killer-it was undeniable.

I was a witch. Not just any witch, but a powerful one. The truth hit me like a freight train, stealing my breath and tightening my chest. No one could ever make me believe I was ordinary again. I had power-real power. But the most terrifying part was the sheer weight of it. This wasn't a game. It wasn't some childhood fantasy brought to life. I was in control of something ancient, something bigger than myself, and that scared me more than anything Zach could have done.

Now I know I can do magic but I have no idea about how I can control it.

"What do I do now?" I screamed, the panic rising in my throat, my voice high-pitched and trembling. My eyes were locked on the door, the red lightning wrapping around it like chains, pulsing and sparking with a life of its own. My hand, still stretched toward the door, was shaking uncontrollably. I could feel the energy flowing out of me, wild and untamed, and no matter how hard I tried, I couldn't stop it.

Rachel rushed toward me, her hand landed on my shoulder, meant to comfort me, but instead, it sent a jolt of fear through me.

"Don't touch me!" I shrieked, recoiling from her. "I'll get distracted!"

I didn't know what would happen if I lost focus, but I wasn't about to find out. Not now. Not when everything was on the line.

"Liza?" Adrian's voice cut through the haze of panic, but I couldn't look at him. I was too afraid to turn my head, too scared that even a second of distraction would cause the killer to break free. "Liza, look at me," he said again, his voice softer this time, but still, I didn't. I couldn't.

The fear was paralyzing. I could feel it in every inch of my body, cold and heavy like chains wrapped around my limbs. I couldn't look away. I wouldn't look away. If I did, I'd lose control, and Zach would escape. He would kill us all. He'd kill Adrian. My Adrian.

"Oh my god, Liza," Adrian's voice grew sharper, more urgent. I could hear the worry in it now, the disbelief, and something else-a tremor of fear. "Liza, you have to control yourself," he urged, and for the first time, I dared to look away from the door. My eyes flicked to the walls, and a gasp tore from my throat.

The red lightning, the energy that had only been around the door, was spreading fast. It had climbed up the walls, licking at the corners of the ceiling like fire, and it was growing. Expanding. Consuming.

"Oh my god!" I cried out, my heart pounding wildly as the red light began to cover every inch of the room, spreading faster than I could comprehend. It was like the walls were bleeding, and I was powerless to stop it.

"Liza," Rachel's voice tried to reach me, but it was distant, like she was speaking through water. I couldn't hear her. I couldn't focus on her. The red was everywhere now, the walls, the ceiling, and moving toward the floor. "Alright, Liza, you're sealing us all in! You have to stop it! Control it!" Rachel's voice was urgent, frantic now, but I couldn't do anything. The power was too much, too wild, and it was consuming everything.

I started to shake, my breath coming in short, panicked gasps. My throat was dry, my chest constricted, and my vision blurred as the tears welled up. I didn't know how to stop it. I didn't even know where to begin. The energy wasn't mine anymore-it had taken on a life of its own.

"Liza!" Adrian's voice snapped through the chaos, loud and commanding, but I was too far gone. I couldn't hear him. I couldn't think. I couldn't breathe. I was gone, consumed in fear. "Liza, look at me!" Adrian shouted, his voice piercing through the thick fog of panic that had clouded my mind. But I still couldn't. I was trapped in my own fear, my gaze glued to the red lightning as it wrapped around us like a tightening noose.

Then his voice cut through again, sharper, more intense. "Liza Kirby, LOOK AT ME!" he barked, the authority in his voice pulling me back, snapping my attention to him.

My eyes finally met his, and the tears spilled over, blurring my vision. Adrian stood there, bloodied and bruised, his body battered from the fight. His face was pale, his jaw clenched in pain, but his eyes-those dark, familiar eyes-held me.

"Adrian?" I whispered, my voice barely audible, but the second I spoke his name, something inside me broke. His breath was heavy as he extended his hands forward to me. I turned toward him, taking shaky steps as the red lightning crackled and hissed above us. The power was still there, but it was fading, retracting like a wave pulling back from the shore. When I reached him, I threw myself into his arms, holding him tight. He winced, a sharp hiss of pain escaping his lips, but he didn't pull away.

"Hey, witch," he murmured, his voice low, his usual teasing edge softening the chaos around us.

The moment I touched him, everything stopped. The red lightning, the power that had threatened to tear the house apart, retreated, shrinking back until it was contained to the door where Zach was trapped. It was over, the chaos I had unleashed was finally contained, but I could still feel it.

The power hummed beneath my skin, dangerous, unpredictable. It hadn't gone away. It had just been controlled. For now.

But as I stood there, wrapped in Adrian's arms, his blood staining my hands, I realized something that chilled me to my core:

I was no longer just Liza Kirby.

I was a witch-a powerful one. And nothing, not even myself, would ever be the same again.

"He hurt you," I breathed, my voice trembling as I clung to Adrian, holding him tightly like I was afraid to let go.

"With this grip, you're hurting me more," he responded with a weak chuckle, his usual teasing tone trying to mask the pain. I pulled away just enough to look at him, and the sight of him made my heart clench.

His lip was split, the blood drying into a dark red line. A bruise was already forming on his cheek, a faint pink mark that would no doubt turn purple soon. His neck had tiny cuts, likely from shattered glass, and his shirt-his once black shirt-was soaked with blood. His own blood.

"I hate him," I whispered, my hand trembling as I gently touched his face, my fingers brushing over the bruise.

"Me too," he said, but his eyes weren't on me anymore. They were focused over my shoulder, and I followed his gaze, remembering that we weren't alone. "We need to get out of here," he added, his tone shifting, more urgent, more like an order than a suggestion.

"I feel the same. We need to run now," Rachel cut in, her voice tight with tension as she turned to Nate. Her gaze was hard, her body on high alert, as if waiting for Zach to break free at any moment. "Your friend has a lot to tell you, but this isn't the time. You saw it for yourself. I'm really sorry-"

"Please, spare me the apology," Nate cut her off sharply, his voice cold and detached. "Just drop me back at my hotel." His eyes found mine, and when they did, the pain in them was unmistakable. They flickered to Adrian's hand on my waist, and then back to my face, and I felt my stomach drop. His words were distant, but his expression... it was personal. "I wanna go home."

My heart broke at the look in his eyes-disappointment, hurt, betrayal. He was hurting, and it was my fault. I opened my mouth, wanting to say something, anything to make it better, but before I could, a loud, blood-curdling yell echoed through the hall.

Zach.

The sound was primal, filled with rage, and it made my blood run cold. I froze, my body instinctively tensing as I realized just how furious he was.

"I believe you've caged him, but he seems quite powerful," Adrian said, his voice calm but firm, though his hand was gripping my waist tighter now. "So let's leave the apologies and explanations for later. We need to leave. Now."

There was no room for argument. We all nodded, too shaken to protest.

"I have to get the tomes, wait," Says Rachel frantically before she rushes to her study. Nate stood there, his eyes lingering on me, and I could see it in his face, the frustration, confusion, pain, and hurt.

"Nate-" I started, taking a step toward him, but I stopped in my tracks when Rachel returned and walked past me towards the exit.

"Let's go," Says Adrian as he pulled me with him, ushering me toward the exit. I glanced back at Nate, my heart aching, but I knew he was right. There wasn't time. The air around us felt heavy like it was charged with electricity, and the red lightning around the door crackled and hissed, threatening to give out.

Zach's yell turned into a roar, shaking the walls. The ground beneath us seemed to vibrate with the force of it as if the entire house was responding to his fury. He was pushing against it, and I didn't know how much longer my magic could hold him.

Adrian yanked the door open, but immediately slammed it shut, his face pale and tense. His eyes, wide and alert, darted to Rachel as his grip on the doorknob tightened.

"What?" we all asked, breathless and un easy.

"His guards," Adrian said, his voice low and sharp. "They're outside. Guarding the place."

A wave of dread swept over us as we all exchanged worried glances. I stared at the closed door, my mind racing. We were trapped. The realization sank in like lead, the urgency in the air thickening.

Adrian's jaw clenched, his lips pressed into a thin line as he thought, his eyes darting around as though trying to find an escape. Then his gaze snapped to Rachel. "You know that magic that can knock people unconscious, right? You can do that."

Rachel's brow furrowed in confusion, shaking her head. "No, Adrian, I don't know that magic. I-" Suddenly, her eyes widened with realization, her frown shifting into one of knowing expressions. "Wait. I do know something like that."

"Good." Adrian's voice was quick and firm. "Cast it. Now," Rachel hesitated. Adrian raised an eyebrow as if he were talking to her with his eyes, "Rachel, we don't have time for this. Do it!"

She nodded. Her hand trembled slightly as she raised it toward the door. "Uh-ibilituto cecero!" she chanted, her voice shaky but steadying as the spell took form.

I frowned, confused. That didn't sound like any spell. The words were different and unfamiliar, and they didn't carry the usual weight of her incantations. Something felt off. She wasn't her usual confident self, but given the circumstances, I shouldn't be surprised.

Adrian threw open the door again, and to our shock, every single one of Zach's guards was lying unconscious on the floor, their bodies slumped like rag dolls.

"Why didn't I do this before?" Adrian muttered under his breath, his frustration clear. It was barely audible, but I was close enough to hear him.

"Done what?" I asked, my eyes snapping to his. There was something about the way he said it like he was keeping something from me.

He met my gaze, a flicker of something unreadable in his eyes before he quickly looked away. "Nothing," he said, brushing it off before stepping outside. He opened the car door for me, gesturing for me to sit next to him, but I hesitated.

I glanced toward Nate, who had been quiet and withdrawn ever since we left the house. I couldn't ignore the weight between us, the tension that had settled like a stone. Without saying a word to Adrian, I climbed into the back seat beside Nate. As soon as I sat down, Nate shifted uncomfortably, as though my presence was a burden, and that small movement felt like a knife to the chest.

Rachel took the passenger seat beside Adrian, and in a flash, we were speeding away from the house. I stole one last glance behind me, watching as the walls trembled and shuddered from the force of the magic holding Zach inside. The barrier was still there, still holding him, but I could feel it. Deep down, I knew.

It wouldn't last.

The car was silent as we drove, but it wasn't a peaceful silence. It was thick, weighed down by everything unsaid. My heart raced as I sat beside Nate, the awkwardness between us suffocating. I wanted to say something, to explain everything, but every time I opened my mouth, the words died on my tongue. I couldn't find the right thing to say, and the fear that I'd lost him-truly lost him-kept me frozen.

I glanced at Adrian and slightly frowned when I noticed his expression. He was trying to keep his eyes open. Taking a large breath in and holding tightly on the steering wheel.

"You okay, Adrian?" I asked. His eyes briefly flicked to the rearview mirror, catching mine for a second.

"Yeah," He replied, giving me a small smile. I nodded and looked back at Nate.

He stayed silent, his arms crossed over his chest as he stared out the window, his profile hard and distant. The distance between us was more than just physical. It felt like an ocean, and I wasn't sure if I could cross it.

"Nate?" I called softly, unsure if he'd even acknowledge me. For a moment, he didn't move, didn't react, and I braced myself for more silence. But then he turned, his eyes meeting mine, heavy with disappointment and confusion. It was as if he wanted me to speak, but I suddenly couldn't find the right words. I swallowed hard. "I'm sorry," I finally managed.

"For what?" His voice came out sharp, cutting through the tension between us like a knife. I flinched but didn't respond right away. His eyes bore into me, waiting for an answer I didn't know how to give.

"I thought I knew you, Liza," he continued, his tone growing harsher. "But as I sit here, next to you, I realize I don't. I don't know you at all. You, him, this woman, all of you can do things that are beyond anything I've ever seen, things that are... unbelievable. And I keep asking myself how the hell am I still sane? How haven't I lost my mind after everything I've witnessed today?" His voice grew louder, each word thick with anger, disbelief, and something else... hurt.

My heart clenched at his words, at the pain in his eyes. "I'm sorry," I whispered again, but it felt hollow. My apology wasn't enough. "I never wanted to involve you in any of this. I regret calling you over tonight more than anything."

"We've known each other since we were kids, Liza," he spat, his voice cold. "How is it possible that you never told me? All those years, you never let me in, not the way I wanted. Is this why? Is this why you always kept me at arm's length? Because I'm different than you?"

"No," I shook my head desperately, my voice trembling. "That's not it. I didn't know, Nate. I didn't know anything about this until Adrian came into my life. I only discovered this about myself recently. Tonight was the first time I ever did real magic. I mean, yes, I've done magic before, but it was... accidental."

His gaze hardened. "So who are you, Liza? Who is he? Who are you all?"

Before I could respond, Rachel chimed in, her voice oddly casual given the gravity of the situation. "I'm a witch, Rachel Green. Nice to meet you, by the way. And I have to say, I'm quite impressed by how well you're holding up. Most people would've cracked by now."

Adrian, ever the charmer, gave a small, sarcastic nod in Nate's direction. "And I'm Adrian Scott. Fictional character, thanks to Liza over there. Oh, and I can summon fire. Neat, right? Also pretty impressed you haven't lost your mind after all that chaos."

Nate's eyes darted from Rachel to Adrian, then back to me, his expression a storm of confusion and disbelief. "Wait," he said slowly, "he's a fictional character?" Of all the revelations we'd thrown at him, this one seemed to rattle him the most. The absurdity of it almost made me laugh if I weren't so utterly exhausted. Of course, witches and magic were one thing, those legends were as old as time. But pulling a man from the pages of a book? That was something new.

I nodded, confirming the impossible truth. "Yes."

Nate's brow furrowed deeper as he tried to make sense of it. "And you brought him out? How?"

"It was an accident," I admitted, my voice barely above a whisper. He didn't respond right away, his mind working furiously to process everything. "I promise, Nate. I'll explain everything-"

Before I could finish, the car jolted violently to a stop, throwing us all forward in our seats. Panic surged through me as my heart raced, my breath catching in my throat.

"What happened?" I asked, my voice shaky as I turned toward the front of the car. Adrian was slumped over the steering wheel, his breath shallow, his eyelids drooping. "Adrian?"

Rachel put her hand on his shoulder, her brow furrowed in concern. "Hey, you alright?" she asked, but he barely managed to lift his head before going limp, collapsing against the wheel.

My eyes widened and fear gripped my heart.

# Chapter 33

## Cooking Together

*Liza's POV*

When my grandma was in the hospital, the doctor's words felt like a punch to the gut: she might not survive for tomorrow. In that instant, my world collapsed. Time seemed to slow, each second ticking by with unbearable weight, pressing down on me, suffocating me. I couldn't breathe, couldn't think, couldn't process the thought of losing her. I was paralyzed with fear—terrified of a world without her in it. My grandma was more than just family; she was my anchor, my safe place, the one person whose presence made everything okay, no matter how bad life got.

The thought of never seeing her smile again, never hearing her laugh, never feeling the warmth of her embrace shattered my heart into a thousand pieces. I remember holding her hand so tightly, as if somehow, by sheer force of will, I could keep her tethered to this world. I begged her—through my tears, through the sobs that wracked my body—to stay. I wasn't ready. I couldn't let go. But she did. And when she died, something in me died too.

For days, I cried like I had never cried before, feeling an emptiness so profound it felt like the ground had fallen out from beneath me. I shut myself off from the world, locking myself away in my room, refusing to let anyone in. I couldn't face the reality that she was gone. I couldn't bear to walk out into a world that no longer had her in it. Life without her was terrifying. The thought of being truly alone haunted me, gnawing away at the edges of my mind, leaving me in a constant state of dread.

It took me years—years—to pull myself out of that dark place. Years to learn how to smile again, to laugh, to live on my own without her. And even then, the pain of her loss never truly went away; I just learned how to carry it.

Now, as I sit here, staring at Adrian asleep on the bed in front of me, I feel that same fear rising in me again—the fear of losing someone who means so much. The fear of being left alone all over again. But this time, it's worse. Because this time, I'm not sure I'll be able to pull myself back up if he's gone.

When Adrian fainted, I felt my heart stop. For a moment, it was like the world tilted on its axis, and everything went cold and dark. I was terrified—terrified in a way that I hadn't been since my grandma's death. But this fear...it's different. It's deeper, more raw. The fear I felt when I lost my grandma was crippling, but this...this feels like it could break me completely.

This isn't to say my grandma mattered less—she was my whole world once. But Adrian...Adrian has become something else entirely. He matters in a way I never expected, in a way I never allowed myself to admit. And now that I've let him in, now that he's become such an important part of my life, the idea of losing him isn't just terrifying—it's unbearable. It's not just fear I'm feeling; it's pain. The thought of him leaving, of him not being here tomorrow, feels like someone is ripping my heart out.

I've grown attached to him in a way that's dangerous, in a way that makes me vulnerable. And now, as I sit here watching him sleep, I realize just how deeply he's embedded himself into my life. Into me. The thought of waking up tomorrow without him here—it's not just a fear. It's a wound, a deep, aching wound that I'm not sure I'll be able to heal from.

And that terrifies me more than anything.

Adrian grumbled softly, and in that moment, it felt like the world had snapped back into place. I sat up straighter, my entire focus on him, my hand holding his with a tenderness I hadn't realized I was capable of. Slowly, his eyes fluttered open and found mine. A wave of relief washed over me, and I couldn't help but smile.

"Hey," I said softly.

"Hey," he replied, his voice deep and raspy, sending a shiver down my spine. It was too sexy for my own good. He raised a hand to his forehead and groaned, glancing around the room with a deep frown. "Where are we?"

I followed his gaze around the room dimly lit before looking back at him. "Rachel's husband's house," I answered quietly. His eyebrows shot up in surprise, his eyes wide.

"Rachel has a husband?" he asked, clearly just as shocked as I had been.

I chuckled, "Yup. News to me too. I thought she had no family, but... surprise, surprise."

He huffed out a laugh, the corner of his lips lifting briefly before his expression sobered again. His eyes drifted down to his body, his fingers brushing over his skin as if noticing for the first time that his wounds had disappeared. The frown returned, deeper this time.

"Rachel healed you," I added, watching him carefully. "I'm not sure when, but... I'm glad she did."

He nodded slowly, though his gaze stayed on me, his uncertainty clear. There was a tension between us, something unspoken lingering in the air, thick and heavy.

"Where's your friend?" he questioned, his voice quiet but firm.

"In the other guest room."

He nodded again, and without warning, he pulled his hand out of mine. He tossed the sheet off, sitting up abruptly. I blinked in confusion as he swung his legs over the side of the bed. "I feel like I'm lying on my deathbed," he muttered under his breath, the irritation in his tone undeniable.

Before I could respond, his hand shot out, wrapping around my wrist. With a gentle but firm tug, he pulled me toward him, catching me off guard. I gasped as I found myself on his lap in a blink. The heat of his body seeped into mine, and my heart thudded wildly in my chest.

"Now, I feel alive," he murmured, his voice low, almost teasing.

My mind raced, my body tense as I shifted slightly in his lap, trying to regain some control. His arms, however, held me in place, not forcefully but with an undeniable firmness that sent a strange thrill through me.

His brow arched, his lips twitching into a slow, deliberate smirk. "What?" he whispered, his voice like velvet. "Did I do something wrong?" His eyes drifted to my lips, and he licked his own, the movement slow, deliberate, making my pulse race.

Heat rose in my cheeks, spreading through my entire body like wildfire. I felt an unfamiliar ache settle deep within me, a warmth pooling between my legs that I couldn't ignore. My thighs pressed together involuntarily, and I held my breath, willing myself to stay calm. His eyes flickered up to meet mine, catching every subtle movement, and I could see the spark of amusement and desire in his gaze.

"Are you uncomfortable?" he asked, his breath warm against my skin. His voice was soft and intimate, pulling me deeper into the moment. His eyes, so intense, held mine captive, waiting for my response.

I opened my mouth to speak, but no words came. Instead, I shook my head slowly, the movement barely noticeable. A small, knowing smile tugged at his lips, and his hand came up to cup my jaw, his thumb brushing ever so lightly over my bottom lip. The touch was electric, sending a shiver down my spine, and I couldn't help but lean into it, my eyes fluttering shut.

"Did I scare you, Miss Kirby?" he murmured, his voice a low, sultry whisper, teasing yet tender.

My heart pounded so hard I was certain he could hear it, feel it. The tension between us was palpable, thick enough to drown in. Every beat of my heart seemed to echo louder in the silence, and I couldn't bring myself to pull away from him.

"Tell me," he urged softly, his thumb still caressing my lip. "Did I?"

I opened my eyes slowly, feeling the weight of his gaze. I hesitated for a moment before nodding, my breath coming out shakily. His eyes narrowed slightly, and he tilted his head, studying me, his grip on me not loosening.

"Careful, baby," he said, his voice barely audible, "You shouldn't care about me so much. Remember, I'm destined to vanish."

What I said next surprised me.

"Destined?" I echoed softly, my voice steady yet brimming with something unfamiliar. "Isn't your destiny written in my hands?"

His eyebrows shot up, and a smirk curled on his lips. I had no idea where that came from. The reminder of his inevitable departure stirred something dark inside me—something I wasn't ready to confront. Something I shouldn't even feel.

"Get off," Adrian said suddenly.

I frowned in confusion, "What?"

"Liza, get off me," he repeated, still smiling, but the command behind his words was unmistakable. Before I could make sense of it, he rolled his eyes and gently lifted me off his lap, setting me on the bed beside him. His casualness was disarming, leaving me speechless.

I opened my mouth to respond, but the door creaked open and Rachel walked in, holding a plate of fruit. *Oh, that's why.* Her expression was as detached as ever, not even a flicker of relief at seeing Adrian awake.

"You're up," she remarked, approaching the bed, her voice devoid of emotion.

Adrian shot her a grin. "What, did you think I wouldn't?"

Rachel's lips barely twitched. "No, you just fainted. How could I possibly think that?" She placed the plate on the bedside table with the same indifferent grace and glanced at me. "Now that he's awake, you should rest, Liza. It's 3 in the morning."

I nodded, though sleep was the last thing on my mind.

Adrian picked up a slice of apple and shoved it in his mouth with little regard for the situation, "Offering me fruits and not handing me in the hands, rude," he said, reaching for more.

Rachel's eyes narrowed. "Those were for Liza, not you." He paused, then continued chewing with an almost smug smile.

I frowned, sensing the tension between them. "Did you two have some sort of fight? You've been giving each other the cold shoulder for days." Neither of them responded, the silence hanging in the room like a thick fog

"We have an early flight tomorrow, Liza," She said, "Get some rest," And then she left.

I sighed as the door closed behind her. I then glanced at Adrian, who was still making his way through the fruit.

"I can cook something for you if you're hungry," I offered, trying to steer the mood in a lighter direction.

He looked at me, his gaze softening. "Aren't you tired?"

I shook my head. "It's fine. Fruits aren't much of a meal. What do you want to eat?"

"What can you make?" he asked, a spark of interest lighting his eyes.

A smile tugged at my lips. "Well, it depends on what's in the kitchen. But I can whip up Italian, Chinese, Japanese, Indian—take your pick."

His brows lifted, clearly impressed. "You know India has a huge variety of foods, right?"

I chuckled. "I do, and I can cook almost everything on the list."

"Impressive," he mused, his smile growing wider. "I don't know what you're going to make, but now I want Indian food."

"Alright," I said, excitement fluttering in my chest. It had been weeks since I last cooked. "Let's see what we've got, and I'll whip something up."

He raised a hand, standing up. "Hold on. You're not cooking alone. I'll help." He moved closer, a little too close.

"Indian food needs four hands anyway," I teased, grinning. We both headed to the kitchen, and he took a seat at the island, still nibbling on fruit from earlier. I opened the fridge, scanning the shelves and hoping for something useful. Bread, cream, dry noodles, and rice stared back at me.

"Alright, I give up. There's nothing here," I admitted, turning back to him.

He pouted, clearly disappointed. "There's rice here, though. You could've made something with that—mixed veg rice or biryani. Both are popular in India. But without spices, they'd be...very bland."

Adrian tilted his head thoughtfully. "Mixed veg rice sounds tangy and finger-licking good."

I smiled, nodding. "It is. Way better than plain boiled rice."

"Wouldn't know," he said with a shrug, casually popping a strawberry slice into his mouth. "I've never had rice before."

I blinked in surprise. "Never? Not even once?"

He shook his head, completely unfazed. "Nope. Had whatever was given to me—burgers, pizza, and that amazing thing you left for me the other day. What was it again?"

I chuckled softly, feeling warmth spread at the memory. "Pancakes," I reminded him, watching his grin stretch wide, dimples and all.

"Pancakes! Yes. I'd love more of those," he said, almost giddy.

I chuckled softly, my heart warming at his sight, "Pancakes," I said, watching as his grin spread wide. Dimples. "I could make those again if you want?" I offered.

He gasped, "I'd love that!"

I laughed at his happiness. He almost looked like a child, a side of him I'd never witnessed before.

"Let me make you a promise. From today on, I'll cook for you every day and introduce you to all kinds of different foods. How does that sound?"

He looked genuinely touched, his eyes brightening. "That sounds fantastic. Thank you."

"You're welcome."

I felt a soft warmth in my chest as I grabbed a few ingredients and started on his pancakes. I also set a pot to boil for spaghetti on the other burner. Adrian's gaze followed my movements, an intent look on his face. There was a quiet comfort in his watchful presence, in the easy focus we shared as I cooked and he watched.

"You look cute when you're focused," he said out of nowhere, admiration lacing his tone.

I nearly dropped the knife. "Adrian," I muttered, blushing. "You're distracting me."

"Am I?" He leaned in, feigning innocence. "I thought I was helping."

"Then help," I replied, handing him a bowl and some flour. "Mix this with sugar, baking powder, milk, and an egg. Think you can handle that?"

He nodded with mock seriousness. "Challenge accepted."

I watched him crack the egg, a little too forcefully, splattering some on the counter.

"Nice move, Gordon Ramsay," I teased.

"Hey, I'm just warming up," he replied, wiping his hands and whisking the ingredients a bit too enthusiastically. A puff of flour rose from the bowl like smoke.

"Adrian, you're making more of a mess than pancakes," I laughed.

"Details," he grinned, whisking harder. "It's coming together."

I leaned over, trying not to laugh as he finally got the batter smooth. "Good enough. Now, let's see if you can handle the pan without burning down the kitchen."

Adrian eyed the stove as if it were his enemy. "Don't worry, I've got this."

I poured a bit of the batter into the hot pan, and it started to bubble. "This is where the magic happens. Now, when it bubbles, you flip it gently. Not too aggressive, or you'll send it flying." I offered him the spatula but he refused to take it.

"Watch and learn," He grabbed the pan and flipped the pancake with way too much enthusiasm, sending it flipping straight onto the counter.

We both stared at it for a moment in utter silence then I burst into laughter.

"Impressive," I teased, nudging him. "That counter-flipping technique is next level."

"I'll have you know, that was intentional," he said, grabbing the pancake and tossing it back in the pan with a grin. "Adds flavor."

"Sure, it does." I handed him the spatula, "Now, I insist, use it."

"Yes, ma'am," He grinned, his hand brushing against mine as he took the spatula from me. The brief contact sent a shiver down my spine, but I quickly masked it, pretending to focus on the pan beside me.

He slid the spatula under the pancake batter, but his flip was way too enthusiastic, and the pancake almost catapulted out of the pan. We both gasped as he fumbled, barely managing to catch it before it hit the ground.

"Hey, I saved it," he said triumphantly, flashing me a grin.

"You know what? Hand it over before you drop the next ones... or the entire bowl," I said with mock seriousness.

"No way, I've got this," he insisted, like a determined kid not ready to surrender.

I scoffed, shaking my head. "Alright. I'll finish up with the spaghetti while you try not to destroy the kitchen."

"Rude," he muttered under his breath, though his smile remained intact.

After a while, when I was done with Spaghetti, I glanced over at Adrian, who was standing there looking irritated, scratching the back of his head. I looked at the pancakes and gasped audibly, my eyes wide.

He looked at me, "Uh... wanna take over? I, uh... overcooked them," he admitted sheepishly.

The sight was hilarious—burnt pancakes piled up, some torn apart, and others in strange, misshapen forms. I couldn't help it—I burst into laughter. His adorable, guilty expression made it impossible to be mad.

I snatched the spatula from his hands. "I shouldn't have let you do this in the first place. Move."

"Sorry," he said, hopping up to sit on the counter, watching me with fascination as I expertly flipped the next pancake. "You're too good at this."

"Experience, my friend," I replied, carefully pouring more batter into the pan. I heard him sigh and then silence coated the atmosphere. It was just me, him, and utter peace.

"You've got flour on your face," he pointed out, suddenly grabbing my full attention.

I blinked, confused, as he reached out and brushed his fingers against my cheek in an attempt to wipe off some flour. His fingers lingered a second too long, his eyes meeting mine in a silent, unreadable look. I felt a warmth rise on my cheeks and was about to brush it off with a joke when I noticed his hand was covered in flour.

I narrowed my eyes. "Did you just...?"

"Did I just paint your face?" He finished, looking sheepishly amused. I glared, and he stifled a laugh, finally letting it out.

I rolled my eyes, wiping the flour off with my apron before I continued my work while he silently watched me. Soon enough, we had everything ready—the golden-brown pancakes and spaghetti.

We sat down together, and Adrian wasted no time, slicing a piece of pancake and eating it. His eyes widened in delight. "Wow, this is really good! You sure you're not a professional chef?"

I chuckled, taking a bite. The blueberry flavor danced on my tongue, and I let out a small moan of satisfaction. "Nope, just a girl who knows her way around the kitchen."

Adrian, clearly amused, took a spoonful of the spaghetti and moaned loudly, mimicking me.

I couldn't help but laugh at his theatrics.

As we ate, the moment felt surreal, almost like a dream. After everything we had been through lately—the chaos, the danger, the tension—this peaceful moment felt like a rare gift. Sitting here with Adrian, laughing and enjoying the simple act of sharing a meal, I found myself wishing that this moment could stretch on forever, untouched by the worries that always seemed to be lurking just beyond the horizon.

For once, I didn't want to think about what came next. Just for tonight, I wanted to hold onto this feeling and forget about the threats that loomed over us. If only it were that simple...

Suddenly, an idea popped into my head and I glanced around the kitchen, my eyes landing on a cabinet near the far end of the kitchen. I stood up, pushing my chair back quietly.

Adrian gave me a curious look. "Where are you going?"

"Stay right here."

I moved toward the cabinet, tiptoeing as if sneaking through enemy territory, my movements exaggerated. The kitchen wasn't even mine, but it felt like it was forbidden to go rummaging through someone else's things—especially for what I was about to grab. I slipped out a bottle of wine from the bottom shelf, quietly placing it on the counter before rummaging through the drawers for glasses. My heart raced a little, even though it was a simple thing. It felt like I was breaking some unwritten rule. But that's just wine. The thrill of it made me chuckle softly to myself.

"What're you doing?" Adrian asked, his curiosity now full-blown as he leaned forward on his seat, watching me with a grin.

I held up the wine bottle, wiggling it slightly. "I bet you haven't tasted this either."

He watched it, "Wine? Nope. Never."

I pulled two glasses from the drawer and placed them on the counter. "Well, there's a first time for everything," I said with a grin, feeling almost giddy with the secretive air we'd created.

"I don't know... Is it even allowed? I mean, food is okay but wine?" Adrian asked, narrowing slightly.

I pressed a finger to my lips, shushing him with an exaggerated whisper. "We're borrowing it. It's fine. Totally fine," I whispered, my eyes dancing with mischief. "We'll put it back if there's anything left."

Adrian shook his head, a soft laugh escaping him. "You're terrible, you know that?"

I shrugged, popping the cork out of the bottle with a quiet pop that somehow seemed louder in the quiet kitchen. "Terrible? Maybe. Fun? Definitely."

I poured the wine into two glasses, the deep red liquid swirling as I handed him his and placed mine on the table. He looked down at the glass like it held some sort of mystery, turning it slightly before raising it to his lips.

I took my seat and lifted the glass of wine in the air, "Cheers," he looked at me and clinked it against mine with a smile.

"Cheers."

# Chapter 34

## The Sacrifice

*Author's POV*

793 AD. (8th century)

Thick smoke choked the air, swallowing the sky in swirling shadows. Fires crackled, but their light felt cold, their heat consumed by the darkness that spread like a plague. Homes—once safe, filled with laughter—were nothing but blackened ruins now, reduced to smoldering skeletons of what had been. The screams came in waves, piercing and raw, carrying the weight of despair. Each cry was a life snatched away, another name lost in the wind.

Blood soaked into the earth, pooling around broken bodies, turning the dirt into a sticky red mire. It spread slowly, like the pain in the hearts of the few who were still alive. The village was no longer a place of life—it had become a graveyard. People stumbled through the chaos, disoriented, their faces streaked with ash and tears, eyes hollow from the horrors they had seen.

In the midst of this carnage, the dark sorcerers moved like shadows, unhurried and deliberate. Their cloaks—blacker than the smoke that filled the air—swept along the cobblestones, trailing behind them like the specters of death they had become. They were calm in their destruction, indifferent to the screams, the blood, the pleading. Their faces were obscured beneath deep hoods, but their eyes—those glowing, empty eyes—pierced through the chaos like the eyes of a predator surveying its kill.

One of them raised a hand, pale and cold as if beckoning something unseen. The air shuddered, and from the tips of his fingers, tendrils of dark energy unfurled, crawling across the ground like serpents. They twisted and writhed, searching, seeking. And when they found their mark, they struck.

A man, running for his life, froze in his tracks as the tendrils coiled around him. His body convulsed, his scream cut short as the darkness swallowed him whole, leaving nothing but an empty shell where he once stood. The sorcerer's lips curled in a slight, cruel smile, but he did not linger on the man's lifeless body. There was no need. There were so many more to kill.

At the edge of the square, a young witch stood trembling, her eyes wide with terror as the nightmare unfolded before her. She was barely more than a child, her hands shaking as she tried to form a spell, her voice cracking as she muttered the incantation. She had practiced these words a hundred times, had learned them in the safety of the coven's halls, but here—now—they felt weak, meaningless.

The spell fizzled in the air, nothing more than a flicker of light, and her heart sank. She was alone. And there was no one coming to save her.

One of the sorcerers, taller than the rest, turned toward her, his gaze locking onto hers with a cold, calculating precision. He did not rush. He didn't need to. His eyes burned with dark, twisted power, and with a simple gesture, a wave of energy shot from his hand. It snaked toward her, faster than she could react, wrapping around her like a noose.

She gasped, her small hands clawing at the invisible grip tightening around her throat. Her feet lifted off the ground as the force pulled her higher, her breath stolen from her lungs. She kicked, she struggled, but it was futile. Slowly, her body grew limp, her wide, terrified eyes staring blankly into the sky. The sorcerer dropped her like a discarded rag doll, her body hitting the ground with a hollow thud, her life extinguished before she even had the chance to fight back.

The sorcerer didn't even look back. He simply moved on, his attention already shifting to the next innocent soul, the next life to extinguish.

The scent of burning wood mingled with the sharp, metallic tang of blood in the air. Screams of the dying still echoed, carried by the wind, though fewer and fewer now. The devastation was nearly complete.

At the center of it all stood the dark sorcerers. Their black cloaks swirled like living shadows, their faces obscured beneath deep hoods. But their eyes—glowing a cold, unnatural light—betrayed their nature. They moved with deliberate calm, with the assuredness of those who knew their power was unchallenged.

The leader of these dark mages, tall and imposing, stepped forward and took off the hood from his head, revealing his face.

"People of Armon!" His cold voice cut through the air like a knife, "You stand on the edge of oblivion. Surrender, and you may yet live to serve your new masters. Defy us, and this land—your homes, your families—shall burn until nothing remains but ash and bone. We come not for wealth, nor petty conquest. We come to rule."

His voice was deep, unhurried, as though he had all the time in the world to deliver his ultimatum. His words hung in the thick air, and the few survivors still huddled in the dark corners of the square dared not speak. Fear had taken them, and hope was a memory too distant to grasp.

Archon stood near the flames, his body shaking not from fear, but from the sheer intensity of his fury. He watched the sorcerers with eyes burning as bright as the flames that licked at the remnants of his village. He had fought with all he had—magic coursing through his veins, lashing out at these invaders—but it wasn't enough. They were stronger, their dark magic deeper, older, and more ruthless than anything he had faced before.

But he was not done yet.

Archon stepped forward, his robes tattered, the blood of both allies and enemies marking his hands. His heart hammered in his chest, but his mind was clear. His power—

though not what it once was—still surged within him. He raised his voice, cutting through the stillness.

"I shall never yield to you, nor see my people bow before your kind!" His voice rang out, strong despite his exhaustion. "You think yourself rulers? You are but thieves, stealing life and land with the foul magic that poisons your very souls."

The leader of the sorcerers turned his head slightly, his glowing eyes narrowing in disdain. "You speak of power as though you understand it, Archon. But your strength has failed you. You are but a remnant of what once was."

Archon's lips curled into a snarl. He extended his hands, fingers crackling with the remnants of his magic. The air around him hummed with energy as he drew on every last reserve of power within him.

"I understand enough," he growled, "to know that no conqueror wins without a fight."

He thrust his hands forward, unleashing a torrent of energy that spiraled into the sky before crashing down toward the dark sorcerer with blinding speed.

But the leader of the sorcerers did not flinch. With a flick of his wrist, a wave of black energy surged from his body, colliding with Archon's attack. The force of it shook the ground, but Archon's magic was absorbed into the darkness, disappearing as if it had never existed.

The dark sorcerer smiled, though his face remained hidden. "Is this all that remains of the great Archon? A flicker of light that dies in the shadow?"

Before Archon could react, the sorcerer raised his hand and clenched his fist. The air around Archon seemed to freeze, and in the next moment, he was thrown backward by an unseen force. His body slammed into the cobblestones with a sickening crack, pain exploding through him.

Coughing, he struggled to rise, but his limbs felt heavy, weighed down by exhaustion and despair. Still, he forced himself to his knees, refusing to give in.

The leader approached slowly, each step echoing in the hollow silence that had fallen over the ruined village. "You cannot win, Archon. Your magic is weak. Your people are broken. You are a sorcerer, yes, but you lack the resolve to truly claim what is yours. Yield, and perhaps I will spare you long enough to see the world we create."

Archon, blood dripping from his mouth, glared up at the sorcerer. "You shall never have my surrender."

The leader's smile faded. "Then you will watch everything you hold dear turn to dust."

He raised his hand, dark energy swirling once more, ready to strike the final blow. Archon closed his eyes, preparing himself for the end. He had failed—failed his people, failed his land. But he would not give these monsters the satisfaction of seeing his fear.

The energy struck, wrapping around him like iron chains. Pain ripped through his body, but the sorcerer stopped short of killing him. The dark magic constricted around him, holding him in place, every muscle screaming in agony, but not enough to grant him release.

The leader leaned close, his voice low and filled with cold malice. "Surrender, or next time, I will not be so merciful. This land will belong to us, whether you live to see it or not."

With that, the sorcerer released him, letting Archon collapse to the ground, his body trembling from the pain and the weight of his failure. The sorcerers turned and walked away, their dark forms fading into the smoke and shadows, leaving Archon broken in the center of his ruined village.

Hours passed, or perhaps it was only moments—Archon could not tell. Time had blurred in his pain and despair. The fires had begun to die down, and the silence that followed was worse than the chaos. He staggered to his feet, his heart heavy, his mind swirling with thoughts of vengeance.

He needed more power. He had to fight back.

Archon staggered through the ruins of his village, his body battered and weak, but his resolve unbroken. His heart pounded in his chest, not from fear, but from the fury that now consumed him. He had failed—failed to protect the people who had entrusted their lives to him. And now, as the dark sorcerers faded into the distance, Archon knew there was only one option left.

He stumbled toward what remained of his home—a crumbling hut that had once been a sanctuary of peace. The walls were blackened by fire and the roof partially collapsed, but inside, hidden away beneath the floorboards, lay the tomes. Powerful, and dangerous, they held the key to magic so dark that even he had been afraid to wield it again. But now, with his village destroyed and his people slaughtered, fear no longer held any meaning.

His fingers trembled as he pried open the hidden compartment, revealing the heavy, leather-bound books within. The tomes radiated an energy that made the air hum with power. He had sealed them away long ago, after the last time he'd used them. He and the seven covens of witches had come together, pooling their strength to bring forth five characters to fight against unimaginable threats. The ritual had nearly destroyed him then—ripped apart his soul and left him teetering on the edge of madness.

And now, he would do it again.

His breath came in ragged gasps as he pulled the tomes out, their weight heavy in his hands, not just physically but with the burden of what he was about to do. The ritual he had performed before had been dark, forbidden by the laws of magic. To summon characters from the pages of the tomes meant defying the natural order, bending reality itself.

Archon's fingers brushed over the ancient symbols etched into the leather, and a surge of energy shot through him, reminding him of the power within these pages. He knew that by using them again, he risked losing himself to the very darkness he sought to destroy. But the faces of the villagers—of the innocent people who had been mercilessly slaughtered—flashed through his mind. He couldn't let their deaths be in vain. He couldn't let those monsters win.

The full moon hung heavy in the sky, casting an eerie silver light over the devastation. The time was right. The magic that bound the tomes to the earth was strongest under the light of the full moon, and Archon knew he had no time to waste. He set the books down on the cold stone floor, arranging them in a circle as he prepared to begin the ritual once more.

He picked up the knife to draw blood from his palm but before he could start, the sound of footsteps approached from behind. Archon turned, his hand instinctively reaching for the dagger at his side, but his grip relaxed when he saw who it was. Two witches stood before him, both cloaked in black, their faces shadowed by the hoods they wore. One was old—her hair silver, her face lined with the wisdom of centuries. The other was young, her eyes blazing with a fire that Archon knew all too well: the fire of vengeance.

The older witch stepped forward first, her voice soft but firm. "Archon?!" she called, her gaze heavy with the weight of her warning. "What on earth do you think you are doing? You know what this magic does. It nearly consumed you before."

Archon's jaw clenched as he looked at her. He knew she was right—knew the danger that lay ahead if he continued down this path. But the memory of the slaughtered villagers, of their screams, of the blood that soaked the earth, was stronger than his fear.

"I do not have a choice," he said, his voice low and filled with the weight of his decision. "They are taking everything from us. If I do not fight back with everything I have, they will destroy the rest of the land and kill our people. Our children. I would not let that happen."

The younger witch stepped forward now, her eyes burning with a passion that seemed to light up the darkness around them. "He's right," she said, her voice sharp. "We cannot let them win. They took everything from us—our homes, our families. They need to pay, and we have the power to make them."

The older witch's eyes narrowed as she looked at the younger one, her expression full of concern. "This is madness," Sorcha muttered, her voice shaking. "Archon, you know what this will cost. You know what summoning these characters will do. The magic—it demands a price. If you do this again, there will be nothing left of you. The darkness will take hold, and you will become no different than those sorcerers you seek to destroy."

Archon's gaze flickered between the two witches, torn between their words. He knew the risks—knew that the magic in those tomes wasn't something to be used lightly. But the devastation around him, the destruction of everything he had ever known, weighed heavily on him. He couldn't let the sorcerers win. He couldn't let them claim his land without a fight.

The younger witch stepped forward again, this time pulling a small, weathered book from beneath her cloak. She handed it to Archon, her eyes glinting with a dark determination. "This is Arcane Flame," she said, her eyes gleaming under the light of the full moon. "We do not need those characters. Not when we can bring forth someone far more powerful." She thrust The Arcane Flame toward Archon. "This—this is who we need."

Archon stared at the book in Alina's hands, his brow furrowed, "What is this?" He asked.

"This is a book which has a character whose powers are unimaginable. We want you to summon him."

Archon was shocked to hear her.

"Have you gone mad, Alina?" Sorcha yells, grabbing Alina's arm and making her look at her, "You are asking to make another book a tome, a magical artifact. Do you have any idea about what you are asking for?"

"These tomes won't be enough!" Alina snapped, yanking her hand out of Sorcha's grip, her voice sharp, cutting through the air like a blade. "You think those characters will stand a chance against the sorcerers? We need more than just soldiers, Archon. We need someone undefeatable—someone with unimaginable powers." She thrust the book toward him again, her eyes alight with a feverish intensity. "We need *Zephyr Valtor*. He's in here. His wisdom is unmatchable, his power unimaginable. If we summon him, we will have someone they can't defeat."

Archon hesitated, glancing between Alina and the tomes. Zephyr Valtor—the name sent a chill down his spine. The stories spoke of him as being God, even immortals fear him.

"Alina! You are letting vengeance cloud your judgment," Sorcha's voice broke through the tension again, "This magic is not a tool for revenge—it's dangerous. It corrupts. If you push Archon to do this, he will not just be fighting them—he will be fighting himself. And how exactly do you plan to control him? If his powers are unmatched, do you think he will obey your command?"

Alina's lips twisted into a sneer. "Maybe you are too old to see it, Sorcha. Maybe your fear is what blinds you. We have already lost everything—our homes, our people. What more do we have to lose?" She turned to Archon, her voice softening, dripping with desperation. "You know this is the only way. The tomes—they are not enough. Zephyr is the answer. He will bring us the revenge we need, and with him, we can save our land."

Archon's hands clenched into fists. He could feel the weight of the decision bearing down on him. He knew the magic required more than just blood. He can't do it without the help of other witches either.

"We are going against the law of nature again, Archon. Playing with reality and fiction again. It's dangerous. You know that too well," Sorcha said, her voice sharp as steel, "Our ancestors will never forgive us, or save us from the danger that will come along with the character. And you know the price of this dark magic, Archon. What it demands!"

"We know the price," A voice grabs her attention to the door along with Alina and Archon. A group of witches stood there, their expressions grim, "The cost is nothing compared to what we have lost. We will make them pay for it. Whatever it takes, we will not spare them. We are here to do anything for our land and avenge the death of our family. And you, Sorcha... will NOT Interfere." Sorcha tried to see sense in them, a small piece of sanity but they had seen their homes burned and their loved ones slaughtered, and they were willing to do whatever it took to stop the sorcerers from claiming any more lives.

Archon looked at Scorcha and said, "For our home, Scorcha," But she said nothing and walked away. She knew their madness was going to end in ruin and she was not going to stand there and watch.

At midnight, the ritual begins.

The full moon hung heavy in the sky, casting an eerie glow over the clearing where seven witches stood, their faces shadowed by flickering candlelight. The air was thick with the smell of burning incense, smoke curling into the night sky, and dark, oppressive energy pressed down on everything in the clearing. They stood in a perfect circle, silent but determined, their eyes fixed on the book laid upon the stone altar at the centre. The Arcane Flame—a simple book, but soon, it will become something far more dangerous.

Black candles surrounded them, the flames dancing as though they too were part of the ritual. Dark symbols, drawn in ash and blood, marked the earth beneath their feet, twisting and warping with every gust of wind that blew through the clearing. The witches—draped in black robes—were motionless, their expressions hard and unyielding. Each of them had suffered, each had lost, and tonight, they would take their vengeance.

At the head of the circle stood Archon, his breath steady but his heart pounding with the weight of what was about to happen. He had led them here—he had pushed for this. There was no turning back now. They would finish what they had begun, no matter the cost.

The air grew colder, biting at their skin, but none of them wavered. They all knew what was required of them.

"Repeat after me," Says Archon, "Sangui- nem virtutis tibi offero omnibus malis."

Alina, her voice low and resonant, spoke the first words of the ritual, her eyes glowing with dark fire, "Sangui- nem virtutis tibi offero omnibus malis." The others joined her, their voices merging into a single, haunting chant. The words were ancient, twisted with dark magic, rising like smoke into the cold night air.

They all used their knives and slit their palms, chanting the spell aloud. Their eyes flickered with an unnatural light as the power began to build, coiling through the air, wrapping itself around their bodies like invisible chains.

"Sanguini, carni, tibi offerimus animam nostram ad consumendum," Archon chanted aloud and the witches followed.

The tome began to hum, its pages trembling, reacting to the energy surrounding it. Archon could feel the pull of the magic—deep, ancient, malevolent. It clawed at his insides, reaching for his very soul, demanding more.

Alina stepped forward first, raising a ceremonial dagger to her throat. Her face was emotionless, but there was a glint of something deeper—something dark, savage—in her eyes. The ritual required more than words. It required blood.

"omnibus iniquis, accipe animam meam et da potestatem ad vitam vocandi non existentem!"

Alina didn't hesitate. The sharp blade cut deep, and her blood flowed freely, dripping down her neck and onto the earth below. She staggered but remained standing, her body trembling as the magic took hold of her. Her lips still moved, chanting through the pain, calling to the dark forces that lingered just beyond the veil.

One by one, the other witches followed her lead. Each slit their throats, their blood spilling into the dirt, mixing with the symbols drawn on the ground. The earth seemed to drink it in, hungry for their sacrifice, as though it, too, was part of the dark ritual.

The air crackled with power, the magic now palpable, swirling around them in a chaotic storm of energy. Their voices grew louder and stronger, as the magic fed on their sacrifice, devouring their life force with ravenous hunger. The blood ran thick, soaking into the soil, pooling around the altar where the tome now glowed with an unnatural light.

Archon stood at the center, his eyes wide, his body shaking with the force of the power coursing through him. The dark magic slithered into his veins, winding through his bones, binding him to the ritual. He could feel it—the raw, untamed power—growing stronger with every drop of blood spilled, with every breath they took.

The candles around them flickered wildly, the flames twisting into strange shapes, the shadows they cast seeming to writhe like living things. The earth beneath their feet trembled, as though the very ground was trying to escape the dark magic rising from below.

Archon's breath grew ragged, his vision blurring as the power consumed him, pulling him deeper into the ritual. He could hear the whispers—voices not of this world—urging him forward, promising vengeance, promising destruction.

He raised his hands, palms outstretched, and felt the magic surge through him like a torrent. His veins burned with it, his skin prickling as if thousands of needles pierced him at once.

He welcomed the pain, the darkness. He had brought them here for this, to call upon the one being who could bring them victory.

Zephyr.

He began to chant louder, more frenzied, as the witches' bodies began to falter, their sacrifices nearly complete. Their blood soaked the ground, and the tome on the altar burned with a blinding light, its pages turning of their own accord, glowing with eerie, otherworldly energy.

The ground beneath them shook, threatening to split open as dark tendrils of magic clawed their way up from the earth. Archon gasped, stumbling back as the power surged around him. His vision darkened, and for a moment, he thought he would be consumed by it—devoured by the very magic he had summoned. The wind began to swirl and twist, forming a dark vortex that drew everything into its eye. It howled and raged, but as if at a silent command, it suddenly calmed. The furious winds eased, and the trees, which had been shaking violently, froze in place. The air grew still, thick with an unsettling silence as if the world was holding its breath.

Archon stood at a distance, watching with a mix of dread and anticipation. His heart raced as he took in the sight. The storm had stilled, and in the centre, a figure began to emerge from the shadows, untouched by the chaos around him.

It was him.

He had come.

Zephyr Valtor had come.

He stood tall, impossibly tall, his long white hair flowing down his back like molten silver. His armor—black as the void, ancient and inscribed with runes of power—gleamed faintly in the flickering light. His eyes... those blazing green eyes... burned with an intensity that sent shivers down Archon's spine.

But it wasn't his appearance that struck worry into Archon's heart. It was his aura—the sheer, overwhelming force of his presence. It was as if the very air recoiled from him, the earth beneath his feet trembling in his wake. The darkness that radiated from him was palpable, twisting and warping reality, bending the world to his will.

Zephyr's gaze swept over the witches' lifeless bodies, their blood still pooling at his feet, but there was no emotion in his eyes—no recognition, no gratitude for the sacrifices made in his name. He was above them, beyond them, untouchable and terrifying.

His eyes locked onto Archon, and for a moment, the world seemed to freeze. Archon could feel his heart pounding in his chest, his breath caught in his throat. The magic inside him—the dark, corrupting force—was nothing compared to the overwhelming power that radiated from Zephyr.

And in that moment, Archon knew that they hadn't summoned a weapon or even a savior.

They had summoned his end.

## Chapter 35

## He's Alive

*Zephyr's POV*

Desire. Need. Lust. They burn inside me, an all-consuming fire that ignites within me.

Desire. It's a relentless, pounding ache deep within me, an instinctual drive that compels me to keep her safe and happy. Every moment spent with her heightens that need—a fierce urgency to protect her, to wrap her in a cocoon of warmth and security where nothing can reach her. I will move mountains if I have to, navigate any perilous path, all for the sake of her happiness. I'll face any threat, endure any hardship, just to see her happy and thriving, far removed from any pain.

Need. A relentless, aching need to be close to her, to share the same space, to breathe the same air—as if my very existence depends on it. This need to be around her is maddening, a magnetic pull that draws me closer, compelling me to lock my gaze onto hers, paralyzing me with the fear that she might vanish the moment I look away. The need to see her smile, that radiant curve of her lips brightens even my darkest days, a beacon of light I can't resist.

Lust. Raw and primal lust surges through my veins like a hunger that can never be satisfied. It beckons me, urging me to pull her close, rip her clothes off, and run my fingers along the curves of her body, to memorize every inch of her skin with my lips. I crave the heat of her against me, the way her breath quickens in response to my touch. I want to see just how wet I make her with my mere glance. It's an insatiable need, a burning desire to explore her, to kiss every curve, to taste every inch of her, to lose myself in the sensation of her body entwined with mine.

The mere thought of being with her, of finally crossing that line, sends electric currents through me, heightening every sense and leaving me utterly consumed by the possibilities.

When we cooked together, I was trying my best not to ruin that cute moment. Every stir, every playful nudge, every laugh made me feel this ache that only wanted to be calm by claiming those lips. Every time our fingers brushed or our gaze met, my desire to cross the remaining boundary between us increased. The need to close the space between us was almost unbearable. I could feel it building in me, a storm I've been trying to hold back for so long, one that's been brewing beneath the surface, ready to break.

But I held back, trying to control the hunger that clawed at me.

I sighed, forcing the wave of lust down, trying to steady my breathing as I reached out, brushing a thumb against the cheek of fast asleep, Liza. She didn't stir—she was drunk, two glasses of wine and she was done for the night. She was peaceful, completely unaware of the battle raging inside me, unaware of how much I was holding back. When she collapsed on the table, I had to carry her to bed, and there was something both painful and perfect about that. Feeling her weight in my arms, the way her body molded to mine, the soft hum of her breath against my chest—it was almost too much to bear. Every instinct screamed at me to stay close, to never let her go.

But it wasn't just the physical closeness that drove me wild—it was something deeper. The way she trusted me, how she looked so vulnerable, so at peace in my arms. I felt my chest tightened. The weight of my deception pressed heavily on me, suffocating in its intensity. Each lie I told her twisted like a knife, disturbing me in ways I hated to admit. She remained blissfully unaware of the shadows lurking beneath my facade, and the thought of her discovering the truth—the darkness I carried—made my stomach churn. I knew that revealing who I truly was would shatter her trust and plunge her into pain. I wanted to protect her from harm, yet I was the very danger she didn't know existed.

I closed my eyes and inhaled deeply to calm the storm inside me. I looked at her, her chest rose and fell with each breath, the way her lips curled into the faintest smile even in sleep. Slowly, I leaned down, my lips just inches away from hers. I wanted to go nearer, to taste them again, to feel them against mine again. But I couldn't. I wouldn't. Not when she's asleep. I dragged a deep breath in and pressed a kiss to her forehead, and my lips lingered there longer than they should have. Her skin was soft, warm, and I couldn't help but inhale her scent one last time before I pulled away.

As I walked out of the room, my heart was pounding in my chest, my mind racing with everything I was trying so hard to suppress. The wine I'd had was beginning to catch up with me, making the world spin slightly, but it wasn't the alcohol that had me off balance—it was her. Always her. The way she invaded my thoughts, my senses, my very being. She was under my skin, and no matter what I did, I couldn't shake her. I didn't want to.

The door closed behind me with a soft click. I made my way down the hall, arriving at Rachel's bedroom door. I knocked, waiting for a moment until it creaked open. To my surprise, it wasn't Rachel who answered—it was her husband. The man's face was set in a hard frown, his eyes narrowing as he looked me up and down with clear disdain.

"Yes?" he asked, his tone clipped, making no effort to hide his irritation. I raised a brow, catching a glimpse of Rachel behind him, hurriedly fixing her hair. My lips curled into an involuntary smirk, and the man's voice snapped me back.

"Eyes here, young man!" His sharp command cut through my amusement, and I cleared my throat, adjusting my stance.

"I need to talk to Rachel. I'm sorry for disturbing you both, but it's urgent," I said, attempting to sound apologetic, though the smirk tugging at my lips probably gave me away. His jaw clenched, his eyes narrowing even further.

Rachel stepped beside him, her expression a mixture of frustration and something else. "Let me handle this," she said to her husband, her voice soft but firm. He shot me one last look before retreating inside, and Rachel closed the door behind her, crossing her arms as she faced me.

"Having fun, Rachel?" I teased, the smirk returning to my face. Her eyes flared with irritation, and I couldn't help but roll my eyes in response. "Can you stop hating me for just one minute? I'm not that evil, you know," I said, throwing my hands up in mock surrender.

Her sigh was loud and exasperated. "You said this was urgent. What is it?"

"Right. Well, for starters, Liza and I left our passports and important IDs at your place, and as much as I'd love to fly without them, we both know that's impossible."

"So, why are you informing me?" She asked, rudely.

"Well, I'm informing you because there are chances that I might be late for the flight. So, while I'm at your place, I want you to handle Liza. Also, we need to figure out who's stealing the tomes. Because while I might be a problem, the people behind this are a much bigger threat. I'm going to get those documents back and make sure I get answers about who's pulling the strings here from Mr. Miller."

Rachel nodded, her demeanor serious now. "Alright," she said quietly, turning her back to me as though the conversation was over.

But I wasn't done. "Hey!" I called after her, my voice louder than intended. She stopped, turning back to me, her eyes wide with surprise. "I'm not finished." My tone was sharp, and I could see her taken aback by the sudden shift in my attitude. "We used your kitchen to cook earlier. We might have also polished off one of your wine bottles."

She frowned, a crease forming between her brows. "You're drunk?" she asked, her surprise evident. I nodded, though I wasn't as drunk as she probably thought. "Where's Liza?" Her voice softened, the concern for Liza clear. As much as I hated to admit it, I liked that Rachel cared about her.

"She's asleep. Peacefully," I reassured her, though I didn't mention the part where I had carried her to bed and how I controlled myself back from not kissing her.

Rachel let out a relieved sigh, her shoulders relaxing slightly. "Alright."

"Yes. Now, you may go," I ordered, my tone dripping with finality. Her eyes narrowed, burning with silent fury. The indignation radiating from her amused me. I let out a soft laugh, the sound cold and dismissive, before turning my back on her and walking away.

I hate to admit it, but I like her.

By the time I arrived at Rachel's house, the sun had already risen, painting the sky in pale shades of dawn. I parked outside the gate and stepped out, surveying the scene as if it were another Tuesday. The bodies of the men who had dared to stand in our way still lay strewn across the yard, lifeless. How unnecessary. I could've ended Zach with a simple snap, the same way I stopped their hearts by making it look like Rachel did it. Instead, I let him beat me into unconsciousness, all because I had to play the role of the wounded mortal for Liza.

I let out a low chuckle at my absurdity. What a joke. A god pretending to be weak. The strain of keeping those wounds open, the constant drain of power—it was enough to make even me lose consciousness.

I'm a god. But even gods have their limits.

The door swung open as I approached, the air inside heavy with magic. My steps were slow and deliberate, each one calculated. I could feel the residual energy humming in the walls, an echo of the spell Liza had cast to contain Zach. It was strong—much stronger than I had anticipated. Her power was remarkable, more than I'd realized.

When I reached the sealed door, I raised my hand and let my fingers brush against the wood. The magic pulsed beneath my touch, defiant but vulnerable. It took only moments for me to siphon it away, unraveling the spell with ease. Liza's magic dissolved in my grasp, and as soon as it did, the doors burst open with a violent crack.

A sharp piece of wood shot toward my chest, but I caught it just inches away from my heart. I smirked, watching as Zach Miller's face twisted into a mask of unrestrained fury. His eyes were wild, but he still managed to maintain his composure, a mildly impressive feat.

I glanced at the splintered wood in my hand before turning it to ash with a mere glance, "Really? I freed you and that's what I got?" I mocked, letting the ash fall to the floor as I met his gaze. His silence was heavy, filled with anger and disbelief.

"What are you?" he finally growled, his jaw clenched tightly, the words barely forced through his teeth.

I let the question hang in the air, deliberately ignoring it as I dusted the ash from my hands. He didn't wait for an answer. With a roar, Zach lunged, his fist glowing with a sickly, pulsating energy. His power surged toward me, a dark wave of smoke and magic that tore through the air.

I sidestepped, barely moving, letting his punch sail harmlessly past me. He whirled around, frustration contorting his face as he threw another punch, this one laced with deadly energy. I leaned back, his fist missing me by inches.

"Come on, Zach," I taunted, hands still in my pockets. "You're not even trying. Or is this really the best you've got? I expected more from a lapdog of... I don't know, someone."

Zach's eyes flared with renewed anger. His hands sparked with a dark light, the smoke wrapping tighter around his form as he unleashed a barrage of attacks—punches, kicks, wild bursts of magic, all aimed at me with deadly precision. But I was faster. Each blow he threw was effortlessly dodged, my body moving with a calm, almost bored ease.

"Stay still, damn you!" he roared, slamming his fist toward my face. I tilted my head, feeling the gust of wind from his strike, but nothing more.

"Oh, I'm sorry," I replied, smiling. "Were you trying to hit me?"

He let out a furious cry, and this time, his hands ignited in flames. He swung wildly, but again, I wasn't there. His fiery fist met only empty air as I stepped aside, casually brushing some dirt off my sleeve.

"You know," I said, still smiling, "you're really wasting your energy here. All this magic, all this rage—yet you haven't landed a single hit. Maybe you should reconsider your career choices. Have you tried knitting? I hear it's very calming."

Zach's face turned crimson, veins bulging in his neck. His attacks became more frantic, more desperate. He lashed out with a blade of dark energy, aimed directly at my chest. I caught it mid-air with two fingers, watching his eyes widen as I crushed it like a twig.

"Impossible!" he growled, his voice a mixture of disbelief and frustration. His breathing grew heavy, and beads of sweat began to form on his forehead.

"Oh, it's very possible," I corrected, stepping closer, my smile turning wicked. "You see, Zach, this is the part where I break your spirit. Slowly. Methodically. You're already sweating, and you've been throwing your best at me. But look at me. Not a scratch. Not even a wrinkle in my shirt."

Zach growled in fury, summoning more power. He launched himself at me again, swinging with everything he had. His fists crackled with raw energy, but every blow missed. I moved like a shadow, too quick for him, dodging every strike without breaking a sweat. His fists hit the air, over and over, until finally, I caught one of his punches mid-swing.

His eyes widened in shock as my grip tightened around his fist. I could feel his bones shift under my hand, the magic flickering from his skin like a candle in the wind.

"Getting tired, Zach?" I asked softly, my voice dripping with amusement. "You've been at this for, what, five minutes? And you're already winded. That's disappointing." I twisted his arm painfully. He gasped, stumbling backward as I released him, but he wasn't done yet.

He roared again, summoning a final burst of energy. His hands blazed with dark fire, and the ground beneath us trembled as he poured every ounce of his remaining strength into one last, desperate attack. The smoke swirled around him, forming a massive, writhing serpent of energy that lunged at me with terrifying speed.

I smiled, "On your knees," I commanded, my voice barely above a whisper, but the power in it was undeniable.

Zach dropped instantly, the smoke dissipating as if it had never existed. His body trembled as he fought against me, but it was futile. "No words," I added, sealing his lips with nothing more than my will. His mouth snapped shut, and I watched with pleasure as his veins bulged, the strain of resisting me nearly tearing him apart.

I crouched down in front of him, meeting his exhausted gaze with a smile. "That was fun," I said casually. "But I'm afraid playtime is over. It's time for a chat. So, who do you work for?"

Zach's eyes flared with defiance, his body shaking with the effort to resist me. But he couldn't. He was under my control. His veins bulged against his skin as he fought to keep his silence, but the magic I held over him was too strong. "Archon Astralis," he finally spoke.

My smirk dropped. *Archon Astralis?* A surge of energy exploded within me, rage spilling over as my eyes ignited with a fierce green light. It flickered and sparked, illuminating the room with a menacing glow.

He's alive.

I narrowed my eyes, disbelief clashing with the boiling anger building in my veins, "Archon Astralis died years ago. Centuries," I growled, my voice tight as my blood began to simmer beneath my skin.

"Magic can make anything possible."

Those words were a match to the gasoline of my rage. Alive. The bastard was alive.

The air crackled as if charged with electricity, waves of raging power radiating from my body and sending shivers down the walls. My fists clenched tightly at my sides, muscles taut with the effort to contain the storm brewing inside me.

Memories of betrayal and pain tore through my mind, each one more vicious than the last, feeding the storm inside me. Archon. The traitor. The thief. He's alive.

Zach's eyes widened, fear finally creeping into his expression as he witnessed the green electric waves swirling violently around me, scorching the ground beneath my feet.

I took a slow step forward, my heart pounding in sync with the storm raging inside. "Where is he?" I asked, my voice was low, menacing

The defiance in Zach's eyes crumbled. "Italy," he stammered, the answer wasn't given by my control anymore.

Without a word, I lifted my hand, and Zach's body was lifted clean off the ground as if he weighed nothing. He gasped, his eyes wide in terror as I dragged him closer, my power crushing the air from his lungs.

I leaned in, my face inches from his, and through clenched teeth, I hissed, "When you meet your master, let him know..." The air crackled dangerously as my power flared. "Zephyr Valtor is back. And he's going to kill Archon again. This time, without a shred of mercy."

His breath quickened and eyes widened upon bearing my name. Terror. I could see it in his eyes. Terror mixed with realization. He struggled against my hold. Good. Let him understand the weight of what he was caught in.

"Archon wants the tomes," I continued, letting each word drip with malice, savoring the taste of revenge that lingered on my tongue. "Tell him I have them. Let him come for them. I'll be waiting. We have some old matters to settle."

With a sharp gesture, I released him, his body collapsing to the floor like a rag doll, a futile gasp escaping his lips as he struggled to regain his composure.

I turned away, letting the anger simmer just beneath the surface, ready to explode at the slightest provocation. The room felt charged, electric with the remnants of my fury, my heart pounding in time with the echoes of my thoughts.

Let him warn Archon. Let him tell him that the past is coming back to haunt him. Let him make Archon regret being alive. He will pay for every betrayal, every moment of pain he inflicted upon me. The memories of his treachery burned hot in my mind, fueling the storm within.

I will kill him. Again.

# Chapter 36

## Confession

*Liza's POV*

I checked my watch for what felt like the hundredth time, sighing in frustration, and then glanced back at the door.

"You seem stressed," Nate's voice broke through, snapping me back to reality. I blinked and forced a smile in his direction, though it barely reached my eyes. "What's going on?" he asked.

"Uh... Adrian isn't answering his phone, and because of him, we missed our flight." I was fidgeting, unable to sit still, "Rachel told me he left without telling her where he was going and warned her not to wait for him if he got delayed. I wonder where's he and what's taking him so long?"

Nate sighed and sat next to me, his presence grounding, though it did little to soothe the anxiety that had been gnawing at me all morning. "Relax. He must be on his way," he said gently.

I nodded absently, still lost in my own swirling thoughts, irritated by Adrian's disappearance. "Anyway, how are you?" he asked, a kind smile tugging at the corners of his lips.

I hesitated, then smiled nervously. "Ah, I don't know what to say here. I'm... surprised. I've just learned to do magic, and I feel... oddly content." My voice was soft, but it held the weight of everything I hadn't said yet. "I mean, considering everything that's happening, I should be terrified. What started as a mistake has now turned into a game where I have to survive... making sure I don't lose to the threat or... myself." I muttered the last part, almost hoping he wouldn't catch it, but Nate frowned, his concern visible.

I quickly forced a brighter, albeit fake, smile. "Anyway, how are you?"

He paused, his eyes searching mine as if trying to understand the whirlwind of emotions behind my facade. "Surprisingly, sane," he finally said with a chuckle, though it was clear there was more he wanted to say.

I couldn't hold back the guilt anymore. My smile faltered, turning guilty. "I'm sorry, Nate. You didn't sign up for this."

He shrugged, attempting to appear nonchalant, "I could let it slide... if you tell me everything. Now that I know about all this witchy woo, I think I deserve to hear more. Especially about you, you witch."

I chuckled half-heartedly, appreciating Nate's attempt to lighten the mood. It was a relief that he wasn't mad or upset, considering everything I'd thrown his way. His calm acceptance of this surreal, magical mess was unexpected. Most people would have lost their minds, but Nate had taken it in stride as if all of this—witches, spells, and Adrian's bizarre presence—was just another part of life.

"It's funny," I said, glancing at him, "You're handling this better than anyone else would. I think most people would've freaked out by now. I did."

He smiled, leaning back in his chair. "What can I say? I've seen weirder things in life. Not magic though but... I'm holding up. But, if you start turning me into a frog, we might have a problem."

I laughed, this time more genuinely, the tension loosening. "I'll try to keep that in mind."

But beneath the humor, I couldn't shake the feeling of guilt. He didn't deserve to be dragged into this chaos, and yet here he was, still by my side. It was something I couldn't take for granted.

"I have a question, by the way," He said, sounding serious all of a sudden. I nodded. He cleared his throat, his voice more serious than I'd ever heard it. "If you brought Adrian out of a book, does that mean..." He paused, his gaze narrowing. "He was never your boyfriend?"

I froze. The blood drained from my face, my cheeks flushing deep red as panic clawed its way into my chest. This was not the conversation I wanted to have right now.

Nate's words hung in the air like a weight pressing down on me. I opened my mouth, but nothing came out. His eyes were fixed on me, waiting for my answer but I didn't know how to explain everything, how to admit the truth.

"I—" I paused when the door creaked open, breaking the moment. My gaze snapped toward the entrance, and there he was—Adrian—finally. He looked utterly worn out, pale as if he hadn't slept in days. His hair was tousled, his shirt wrinkled, and there was a tension in his movements that sent a ripple of unease through me.

Our eyes locked—green to gray—and for a brief second, the hardness on his face softened. But my frustration, my worry, had built up too much to let him off so easily.

"Where have you been?" I demanded, stepping towards him with all the pent-up anger from the morning. "And where the hell is your phone? I've been calling you nonstop! Did you not see any of my messages?"

Adrian lifted a small stack of passports and IDs, his expression still unreadable. "I went to Rachel's place to get these," he said, holding the documents up as if they were some kind of peace offering. "I forgot my phone here... otherwise, I wouldn't have ignored you."

I blinked, momentarily taken aback by the passports, but that didn't lessen the irritation swirling inside me. "You went to Rachel's house?" My voice shot up, disbelief and anger mixing. "Rachel's? The same house where Zach is trapped? You could've been killed, Adrian! What were you thinking?!"

He stayed silent for a beat too long, and the lack of an immediate answer only fanned the flames of my frustration. Without thinking, I punched on his arm—hard. Adrian's eyes widened, surprised like he couldn't believe I'd hit him.

"You idiot!" I yelled, anger and relief stinging at my chest. "Zach almost killed you the last time, and you still went back there? Are you insane?"

I punched him again, even harder this time, but Adrian caught my wrist before I could hit him a third time. His grip was firm but not rough, and for a moment, we were locked in place, the tension palpable.

"Hey!" he protested, though there was no malice in his tone—just a weariness I hadn't noticed before. "I got beaten up because Rachel restricted me from using my powers, Liza. I could've turned Zach to ash if I wanted to. You know that.

"Oh, shut up!" I said and yanked my wrist free, stepping back, my chest heaving with the rush of emotions.

Learning that he went there almost stopped my heart. How could he go to someone who nearly killed him?

Adrian took a deep breath, his expression softening again as he tried to ease the tension. "I didn't go there to fight, Liza. Zach is still locked in that room. I just grabbed our things and came straight back. I'm fine." He gestured to himself, spreading his arms wide as if to show me there wasn't a single mark on him. "See? Not a scratch."

I clenched my fists, the anger still simmering beneath the surface. Why did he always act so casual? I had watched him nearly die at Zach's hands and the memory of his state still burned into my mind. How could he be so casual about it?

Before I could respond, Rachel's voice cut through the tension. "What's going on here?"

I looked up sharply, startled by her sudden arrival. She was walking toward us, her husband right beside her. And wow—that man was undeniably hot. He had that tall, dark, and fit vibe going for him, with a rugged charm that screamed power. The silver streaks in his dark hair only added to the allure, his piercing blue eyes catching the light as they landed on us. There was a definite "Daddy vibes" quality about him—strong, composed, and dangerously attractive.

"Uh, nothing," I blurted, trying to compose myself, acting as if I hadn't just been yelling at Adrian seconds ago. "When's the flight?"

Rachel's eyes flicked between Adrian and me, clearly sensing the lingering tension but choosing to let it slide. "In three hours. Lucas and I need to head out for some work. We'll meet you at the airport directly. My luggage is already in the car. Just get there and wait for us, alright?"

We all nodded.

Rachel glanced at her husband. "Shall we, honey?"

Lucas, silent and commanding as ever, gave a brief nod and took her hand. They walked past us, his presence lingering like a shadow as they disappeared through the door.

The second the door clicked shut, I turned to Adrian, who dared to smile. I rolled my eyes, the anger fading but not completely gone. I was still upset that he had gone there, risking everything. Last time, I'd saved him—it had been shocking, but I had done it. Who would have saved him if Zach had escaped his cage?

"You were asking Liza about something, Nate," Adrian said, his smile cold, almost taunting.

I immediately remembered the question and felt a surge of panic. I didn't want Nate to bring it up again. I glanced at Nate, noticing how his eyes narrowed at Adrian, the tension in the room thickening with each passing second.

"I asked Liza about you," Nate said, his voice hard. "How could you become her boyfriend when you've recently jumped out of a book?"

Adrian's smile didn't waver. "I wasn't her boyfriend."

Nate's frown deepened as he turned to me. "Why would you lie to me?"

Before I could respond, Adrian's voice sliced through the air, sharp and biting. "Don't act like you don't understand, Nate." His words made me tense, and Nate's expression darkened further. But he stayed quiet, watching Adrian warily. "Liza used to like you. A lot. But she was too scared to tell you, especially while you were with Norah. So, I removed the obstacle for her. Norah Kavanagh."

What?!

My heart sank as the embarrassment rushed through me, spreading like wildfire. How could he say that out loud?! I wanted to crawl into a hole, anything to escape this nightmare.

Adrain went on, "Although, I wouldn't have continued on it if Norah was actually in love with you or you were. But you both had fallen out of love for each other and were just dragging that relationship to torture yourselves. I pretended to be Liza's boyfriend because, Liza never even invited you to her house, I had to be someone special enough to be there." His words were a taunt, daring Nate to respond. "All clear now, Mr. Wilson?"

I wanted to disappear, please, let the ground open and swallow me whole. My face burned with shame, and I couldn't even look at Nate. How could Adrian just lay it all out like that?

Nate's gaze finally shifted to me, his eyes softening, though there was a mix of hurt, confusion, and guilt behind them. "Why didn't you ever tell me, Liza?" His voice was quiet, almost gentle, but there was a deep sadness in it. "If you had feelings for me, why didn't you just say something? Things could've been different."

I opened my mouth to say something, anything but before I could respond, Adrian's voice cut through again. "Don't put this on her," he said with a cold edge, stepping forward as if defending me from Nate's words. "Blame yourself only. You didn't confess to her because you're a coward. You were too afraid of ruining your friendship with her. Now you're standing here, trying to figure out why you're heartbroken? You did this to yourself."

"Adrian!" I gasped, shooting him a glare. But he ignored me completely.

*Why is he being too harsh, too blunt?*

Nate's face tightened, the muscles in his jaw visibly working as he struggled to hold back his emotions. His voice came out strained, filled with raw vulnerability as he finally addressed Adrian. "I don't owe you any explanations, Adrian

Scott," he started, his voice rough around the edges, but there was more to it now—a deep, unspoken pain that had been building for far too long. He took a step closer, his body tense with frustration, but his eyes—his eyes revealed a world of hurt. "But you know what? I'll say this. Yeah, I was scared of losing Liza. More than scared. Terrified. She meant everything to me. She still does."

"But it wasn't just fear that held me back. I didn't want to push for more because... because I thought I could protect what we had by leaving things the way they were. I thought if I didn't try to change it, I wouldn't risk losing her altogether. Maybe it was stupid, maybe it was cowardly, but I didn't need more. I was happy just... seeing her every day. Hearing her voice. Watching her laugh. Even if I could never have more than that, I thought, at least I still had her in some way. I didn't need anything else. She was enough for me."

His voice lowered, trembling with emotion. "Do you know what that feels like? To love someone so much that just being near them is enough? Epic. I was happy with the small moments, the conversations, the smiles, the quiet moments where I thought, 'Maybe this is enough.' I didn't need grand gestures or confessions. I didn't need her to love me back, Adrian. I didn't need anything more than the way she looked at me when we talked or the way she smiled when I said something dumb. That was enough for me, even if it sounds pathetic."

His voice broke on the last word, and he swallowed hard, trying to hold back the emotions that were spiraling out. "But that's the problem, isn't it? I convinced myself that just being in her life, in whatever capacity she'd let me, was better than risking everything by telling her how I felt. But now... Now, I realize that maybe I was just fooling myself. Maybe I should've been braver, I should've told her about what I felt before it was too late. But I didn't, because I thought I was protecting what we had. And now it's gone. All of it."

Nate's chest heaved as he fought to keep his voice steady. "So yeah, I was afraid. Fucking terrified! But more than that, I was content—no, I was grateful. Grateful just to be in her life, even if I wasn't the one holding her hand or the one she'd call late at night. It didn't matter, because I thought I was doing the right thing by staying silent. I thought I was being selfless. But you're right... maybe I was just a coward."

I bit my lip, a wave of guilt crashing over me, tightening in my chest. I had once cared about Nate, deeply, and there was no denying that. There was a time when I would've given anything to hear him say the words he was saying now. If he had confessed back then—back when I used to watch him from the corner of my eye, hoping for some sign that he felt the same—maybe things would've been different. Maybe I would've kissed him, maybe I would've taken that chance and told him everything I had buried inside my heart.

But now? Now, standing here with Adrian just a few feet away, I realized how much had changed. The feelings I'd once had for Nate had dulled over time, like a memory that had slowly faded with every passing day. I still cared about him, but the intensity, the longing I once felt—it was all gone. And the worst part was, I regretted that. I regretted that I couldn't feel the same way for him anymore. All I could feel was... sorry.

Adrian stepped forward, his voice darkening with a new level of contempt. "And what about Norah? You dragged that hollow relationship on for how long? You claim you were in love with Liza this whole time, but you couldn't break it off with Norah? What was that about, Nate? Keeping one foot in each world, too scared to make a real decision?"

Nate's jaw clenched, his fists curling at his sides as he fought to maintain his composure. "It wasn't that simple," he said, voice low and strained. "I cared about Norah. I didn't want to hurt her. She loved me, and I... I didn't want to be the one to break her heart. So, yeah, I waited for her to end things. I wanted her to walk away."

Adrian snorted. "How noble of you," he mocked, shaking his head. "Too cowardly to end things, but not above stringing her along while pining for someone else. And why are you confessing all this? I mean, why now, Nate? No longer satisfied with what you have with her?"

Nate's expression hardened, his jaw tightening, but there was a flicker of pain in his eyes. "I'm confessing because I saw it, Adrian. I saw it in her eyes the day I told her about Norah. The feelings were there, clear as day. I wasn't imagining it."

Adrian's jaw clenched, "What about now?" he asked, stepping closer. "Can't you see it in her eyes anymore that she doesn't feel the same for you now?"

"Adrian, enough!" I intervened, stepping between them, my voice firmer than I intended. The tension in the air was suffocating, and I couldn't bear to see Adrian pushing Nate like this. Yes, Nate had made mistakes, but he didn't deserve this. I glanced at Adrian, his jaw clenched tightly, and I could see the anger simmering beneath the surface. "You need to go," I said quietly but firmly.

He stared at me, almost incredulous, like he couldn't believe I was taking Nate's side. "Adrian, leave," I repeated, my voice steady. His eyes flicked to Nate, cold and venomous, before he finally stormed out, slamming the door behind him.

Silence settled between us. Nate's shoulders slumped, the weight of everything crashing down on him. "I'm stupid," he muttered, his voice barely audible, as if he were speaking more to himself than to me.

I sighed, walking closer to him.

He ran a hand through his hair, his gaze fixed on the floor, "I've been a fool, Liza. I should've ended things with Norah the moment I realized you felt the same. But I didn't. I kept waiting for things to change, for her to let me go first. And in doing so, I hurt everyone."

His words hung heavy in the air, thick with remorse. Without thinking, I stepped forward and pulled him into a hug. He stiffened at first, caught off guard, but after a moment, he relaxed into it, his arms wrapping around me as if he was holding onto the last piece of something he'd lost.

I hugged him because it felt like the right thing to do. I never realized Nate had feelings for me, and now I feel terrible. If I had been braver back then, maybe he wouldn't have had to keep his feelings hidden for so long. His confession made me see that I'd always had the kind of love I wanted—pure and selfless—but I was too blind to notice.

If Adrian hadn't come into my life, maybe Nate would have kept silent still. But the truth was, I didn't feel the same way anymore. I wasn't sorry I didn't love Nate now—I was sorry I never told him how I felt back when it mattered. And the worst part? I knew I could never feel that kind of feeling again.

What I feel for Adrian now is different, something I can't explain. And even though I care for Nate, I have already moved on from what could have been.

I sighed, "We all make mistakes and our mistake was not confessing our feelings. You did it because you didn't want to ruin our friendship. I did it, because... I wasn't brave enough to confess," I pulled back and smiled at him, "But I assure you, our friendship will never change, Nate. This will always remain the same. No matter what."

He smiled softly, "Thank you. I feel much better now."

"I do too."

"Just stay happy, Liza. All I want for you is to be happy. Really happy." I could see the concern in his eyes—he was worried about me. Of course, with Adrian in the picture, there was plenty to be worried about.

"Trust me," I said, feeling a warmth inside me, "I've never been happier."

He nodded again, looking relieved, as if the weight of his unspoken feelings had finally been lifted. Maybe, for the first time, he felt free.

"You should go to him," he said gently, letting me go completely and stepping back, "He's probably boiling right now. You know, with his firepower, he could set the house on fire."

I chuckled at his comment. For a moment, I just stood there, looking at him, and without hesitation, I wrapped my arms around him again. "I'm sorry," I whispered, feeling the weight of everything between us pressing down, feeling the need to apologize.

He took a shaky breath and hugged me back, letting out a deep sigh. "I love you, Liza," he confessed softly, the raw honesty in his voice hitting me harder than I expected.

I nodded, my heart heavy, "I know." There wasn't anything more to say—his love was something I couldn't return, but I felt it deeply.

# Chapter 37

# Did I scare you, Miss Kirby?

*Liza's POV*

I opened the door to the balcony and stepped inside, feeling a gentle breeze brush against my skin. Adrian stood by the railing, staring out at the vast expanse of nature. It was a stunning view—trees swaying softly in the wind, flowers blooming in vibrant colors, and the lake shimmering under the soft glow of the sun. But none of that seemed to matter right now.

I could see it immediately—the tension in his body, the way his breath came in sharp, measured intakes. His fingers clenched tightly around the railing, knuckles pale. And though he knew I was there, he didn't turn to acknowledge me. The silence between us was thick, charged with an energy that made my chest tighten. He was upset, no doubt about that, and the subtle anger radiating from him was impossible to ignore.

I hesitated for a moment before stepping closer, standing next to him, and taking in the view. I took a deep breath, trying to ground myself. "It's a beautiful view," I said, hoping to break the tension, even if just a little.

I half-expected him to ignore me, to brush off my attempt at conversation with the cold silence he'd been maintaining. But to my surprise, he answered, his voice low and controlled.

"It's breathtaking at night. The lake shines brightly under the moonlight."

I glanced at him, his face still set in that hard, unyielding expression as he gazed out into the distance. There was something in his voice that felt distant like he was holding back more than he was letting on.

I nodded, turning back to the view, though I could hardly focus on it. "You were too blunt out there," I said after a moment, my voice quiet but firm. "Nate didn't deserve that."

The air between us shifted with those words, but Adrian remained silent, his grip on the railing tightening ever so slightly. I waited, but he said nothing, the silence growing heavier with each passing second. I couldn't tell if he was thinking about what I'd said, or if he was simply choosing to ignore it. Either way, I knew I had struck a nerve.

"Adrian, I'm talking to you," I pressed, keeping my voice gentle. His eyes snapped to mine, sharp and cold, sparking the same way they had when he'd yelled at me last time. But I wasn't scared this time. "You were arrogant," I added, my voice firm.

His eyes narrowed, the spark flaring dangerously. "Arrogant?" The word rolled off his tongue, his voice cold and measured. "You think I'm arrogant for telling him the truth?"

"Don't give me that look—you were. You can't talk to him like that. And why did you have to tell him the truth?"

"You wanted me to lie?" His voice was low but biting.

I hesitated, then said, "No, but it could've been avoided."

"Why?" His voice grew sharper, more controlled. "When I told him you'd pulled me out of a book, he got to know. He was curious about why you'd lie, so I did him a favor and told him everything. What did you want me to do?"

"Stop yelling at me," I snapped, feeling the tension between us deepen.

He paused, "My voice is barely reaching my own ears, Liza, and you think I'm yelling?"

I rolled my eyes, exasperated. "You were rude to him. Harsh. Unnecessarily blunt. You can't be rude to him. Don't forget that he matters to me."

He snorted and without warning, he grabbed my wrist and yanked me toward him. I gasped as my chest collided with his, my heart racing as our proximity intensified.

"What about me, Liza Kirby?" he asked, his voice dangerously low. "Do I not matter to you?"

"Adrain, let go," I whispered, trying to pull away, but he only drew me closer, crushing me against him.

"Answer me, Liza. What about me? Where do I stand in your life? Who am I to you?"

I met his gaze, my breath catching in my throat. The intensity in his eyes, the raw emotion—anger, and something darker—sent a chill through me. And yet, it was impossible to look away.

"Tell me, who am I to you?"

"Everything," I finally confessed, "You're my everything, Adrain Scott," His gaze softened. "You matter to me more than you could ever realize."

Silence. He stared into my eyes. I shivered under his gaze inwardly but kept a poker face.

"Just because you matter doesn't mean you get to say whatever and do whatever. Your behavior was wrong and you should apologize to him."

He raised his brows, "Excuse me?" He was literally taken aback.

"Yes. I want you to apologize to him for being unnecessarily arrogant."

"And what if I don't?" He challenged me. I inhaled a large breath in, my jaw clenching. He lifts his hand and touches my cheek with the back of his hand. "Tell me, baby. What if I... don't?"

I swallowed hard, feeling the heat between us.

He smirked, moving his hand to my lips and brushing his thumb gently across my lower lip. I parted my lips involuntarily, closing my eyes as I leaned into the touch, "I'm your everything, huh?" he whispered, his voice thick with restrained desire, "I hope you do realize that you're breaking the rules of the universe. You're going against its law."

I opened my eyes slowly, biting my lower lip, my mind clouded with the intensity of the moment. That simple action of mine made him draw in a long, ragged breath. His gaze flicked to my lips, lingering there before meeting my eyes again.

"Are you ever going to regret your decision, Liza?" he asked, his voice a rough whisper now, filled with heat, "Regret us?"

"What are you talking about?" I whispered, the fog of desire clouding my thoughts. His nearness, the heat of his body pressed against mine, made it impossible to think clearly.

He smirked again, a dangerous gleam in his eyes. "You'll understand soon enough."

And before I could protest, before I could even comprehend his words, his hand tightened behind my neck, and his lips crashed down on mine.

My hands instinctively found their way to his shirt, gripping the fabric tightly, as if holding on to him would steady the storm of emotions surging through me. Adrian's hand slid to my waist, pulling me even closer until there was no space left between us. His fingers threaded into my hair as he deepened the kiss, his lips moving over mine with an intensity that made my knees weak.

I gasped against his mouth when his cold hand slipped under my shirt, brushing against my heated skin. The sensation sent a shockwave through me, making my pulse quicken. He took the opportunity, his tongue slipping past my lips, teasing mine in a way that made heat pool low in my belly. His kiss was commanding, consuming, as though he was claiming me, every part of me, in that single moment.

A moan escaped my lips as his teeth gently tugged at my lower lip, a mix of pleasure and need swirling inside me. He took a step forward, guiding me backward until my back collided with the wall. His hand cradled the back of my head, protecting me as he pinned me there, the solid pressure of his body making me gasp again. Breathless, he left my lips, gripping a fistful of my hair and gently pulling my head back, exposing my neck to his burning kisses.

His lips traveled down my jawline, sucking and biting at the sensitive skin of my neck, and I shuddered, my breath coming faster, eyes rolling back in pleasure. The sensation of his lips, hot and insistent, sent a flood of desire crashing through me.

He pulled back just long enough to meet my gaze, raw desire burning in his eyes before he ripped my shirt open with one swift movement. The buttons scattered, and my breath hitched in shock.

"Adrian!" I gasped, eyes wide, but before I could process it, his mouth was back on mine, fierce and demanding. I pushed lightly against his chest, needing a moment to breathe, to think, but he wasn't letting me go. He seized my wrists with one hand, pinning them above my head and crushing his body against mine. I gasped again when his hardness pressed against my belly, giving him another opportunity to slip his tongue inside.

He leaves my lips and goes to the exposed skin of my neck and collarbone.

My breaths came out ragged as he bit and kissed my neck, each sensation more intoxicating than the last, "Oh my God..." The sting of his teeth against my skin sent a jolt of pleasure through me, and I couldn't hold back the moan that slipped from my lips.

"Yes, baby. Call out to me," He whispered against my neck before biting on it.

"Adrian..." I gasped, breathless, but he wasn't stopping. His hand slid down, roughly grabbing my ass, pulling me harder against him. My eyes fluttered shut as his hand moved back up, slipping beneath my torn shirt. His touch was fire against my skin, his fingers grazing my ribs before cupping my breast. His thumb flicked over the sensitive peak, sending waves of pleasure through me, and when he squeezed roughly, a shameless moan escaped me.

He growled softly in response, kissing along the curve of my neck, his grip on my wrists still firm as I tried to wiggle free. Desperate. His lips found the spot below my ear. He licked me there and the sensation made my toes curl, my body arching toward him, craving more.

With a swift movement, he unhooked my bra, and my eyes snapped open, heart racing. He hovered at my ear, his breath hot against my skin, his voice low and rough, filled with barely restrained desire.

"Please tell me to stop," he whispered, his hand moving back to my breast, his thumb brushing over my now bare skin.

I didn't want him to stop. Every part of me ached for him, the intensity of his touch, the fire in his eyes—but I couldn't do this. Not now. Not like this.

"Stop... stop, please," I breathed, my voice trembling, fists clenching as I forced the words out. "Not now... not here."

He stilled, his grip loosening as he stepped back slightly, his eyes searching mine, filled with the same desire, but now tempered with restraint. He freed my hands, letting them fall over his shoulders. My cheeks flushed crimson. His eyes, once filled with desire, now sparkled with a hint of mischief.

"Did I scare you, Miss Kirby?" he chuckled, the teasing lilt in his voice igniting my indignation. "Good thing you stopped me," his eyes fell to my lips for a moment before he finally brought them back to my face, "I wasn't planning to stop," The heat rushed back, and before I could think, he leaned in and kissed my lips again. My hands instinctively gripped his shirt, the kiss lingering for what felt like an eternity, his warmth enveloping me. When he finally pulled back, a satisfied smile danced on his lips. "Ah, I can get used to this."

I couldn't help but smile back, my heart racing as if it might burst from my chest. But then his hands moved from my waist, and my breath hitched as he deftly hooked my bra by keeping me pinned in place with his unwavering gaze.

"You ripped my shirt," I murmured, heat creeping up my neck and cheeks as the memory flashed in my mind.

He leaned against the wall, one hand still on my waist. "Been wanting to do that for a long time. I'm not sorry. But I could probably buy you more shirts as compensation."

I narrowed my eyes playfully. Though, his confession made my heart to skip a beat, "Oh, you mean with my own money?" I mocked, raising an eyebrow. He laughed, shaking his head, "Now, move. I need to wear something before someone sees me."

His smirk was infuriatingly charming. "Sure. But let me see you first." He looked down, and I gasped, quickly covering myself with my arms. His laughter echoed in the air, light and teasing.

"Adrian, please. You're embarrassing me."

But he didn't let up; instead, he kissed me again without warning. I grabbed his shoulders for support as the warmth flooded back, and this time he held the kiss, savoring the moment. When he finally pulled away, utter satisfaction painted his face, a wide grin spreading across his features.

"Get dressed. I'm waiting," he said, turning to walk away. I bit my lower lip, struggling to control my grin but failing miserably.

Did we really just make out?

I felt giddy, wanting to scream in excitement, but I simply giggled, my gaze drifting to the flower vases in the corner. The smile faltered. The flowers, once vibrant and lively, had withered, losing their color and turning sickly dark, much like how the botanical garden had faded.

Tension gripped my chest, and I scoffed, "I have to learn to keep control over my powers." I shook my head, walking away from the scene, my heart still racing from what had just happened.

# Chapter 38

# Walmart

### Liza's POV

Time, it seems, has a way of running ahead, leaving me scrambling to keep up. This week slipped through my fingers faster than I could have imagined, so fast that I barely had a moment to catch my breath. We've been trying to find the tome, anything that could help us in this situation, but we're only meeting dead ends. In between the break of the treasure hunt, I learn to do magic with Rachel. She's teaching me spells and how to control them, though I'm far from mastering that control. My abilities have started slipping more often lately, and it's getting worse. I used to only make flowers wilt, but now, they crumble to ash.

I'd called my school earlier, extending my leave and giving the excuse that I was terribly ill. I might as well have been, though not in the way they assumed. The truth was, I wasn't ready to return to teaching. There were bigger things at stake now, things that made the trivialities of everyday life seem distant and small. I told them I'd be absent for at least another week, though I wasn't sure how long I'd truly need.

When I left the UK, so much about me was different. I used to be quiet, reserved, a timid. I was the woman who was haunted by her past—by the memories of her hometown, by the weight of everything I had tried so hard to escape. Back then, I couldn't even imagine standing up to any of that, especially my mother. I feared it would swallow me whole if I ever dared to confront it. But now, as I stood in my mansion, I realize I had changed. The past didn't terrify me anymore. The old me was gone, replaced by someone stronger, more confident, *powerful*. I could feel it in the way I held myself, in the way my thoughts weren't clouded by fear but sharpened with purpose.

The last time I had been here, my only responsibility had been figuring out how to send Adrian back to the world he came from. It had felt like a daunting task, an impossible burden to carry. But now, things had shifted. Sending Adrian back wasn't the most urgent concern anymore. Somewhere along the way, that task had fallen to the background, replaced by something far more pressing: The tomes. Someone was after the power they held, and we have to find out who's doing this—and more importantly, why.

Adrian's presence in this world is no longer an anomaly we need to fix immediately. We've found ways to extend his stay, to keep him here for a little longer. But that doesn't mean the danger is gone. If anything, it's only grown. The threat that looms over us hasn't dissipated, and I can't ignore it. The stakes have risen, and it's no longer just about Adrian—it's about the tomes, the witches, and the ancient power that someone is trying to exploit.

I looked up at my grandmother's picture, hanging on the wall. She was alive when I put it here. I loved this picture of hers, it's close to my heart because I had taken it. I gently touched it, smiling. This place holds so many memories, beautiful memories, but I know it also holds secrets—secrets I was finally ready to uncover. This place—the creaking floors, the dusty air, the way the shadows seemed to stretch out and whisper my name—it was more than just my home. It was a labyrinth of secrets, and I was determined to navigate it.

My grandmother, a woman who had always been shrouded in mystery, had lived here once, and I was convinced that somewhere within these walls, she had hidden something important. Something that might help me understand what was happening.

I had been searching the mansion, digging through its dark corners and hidden places. But I'm only receiving disappointment. But I'm not giving up. The answers might be buried here, waiting for me to find them.

"Would you like some coffee?" Rachel's voice broke my focus, pulling me back to reality. I smiled, gratefully accepting the cup she handed me. "Your grandma must have been a beautiful woman when she was young," Rachel remarked, her gaze wandering to the old photo on the wall.

"Yes, absolutely," I replied with a fond smile.

She took a careful sip before whispering, "How do you live here?" Her wide eyes glanced around the mansion. "It's huge... and honestly, a bit spooky."

I let out a soft chuckle. "I've been here for years. It wasn't easy after she passed, but I learned to survive on my own."

Rachel's expression softened. "It must have been hard, living here all alone."

My gaze lingered on the picture again, and I nodded slowly. "It was." A shiver crawled up my spine as memories of those early days—those horrible, tear-filled nights—flooded my mind.

"Liza?" Rachel called gently, pulling me from the past. "Once all this is over, we're taking a trip. We'll drink wine, get wasted, and forget the world for a while. What do you think?"

A smile broke across my face. "I'd love that."

She grinned, and we shared a comfortable silence as we sipped our coffee. Over time, Rachel had become more than just a friend. She was family now, someone I trusted with my life. Amid everything—the life-threatening dangers, the looming uncertainties—we found moments to laugh, to reminisce about silly memories, and to feel human again.

Last night was one of those moments. We, along with Adrian, played charades late into the night, and for a brief time, the weight of our lives lifted. But when the games ended and the night deepened, the anxiety crept back in. I knew sleep had evaded us all. The fear of what's to come, the constant dread that our efforts might not be enough, hung heavy.

Suddenly, I remembered something very important, "Shoot, I completely forgot!" I groaned, running a hand through my hair in frustration. "The groceries. I need to go, like now. There's literally no food left, and Adrian would never let me order takeout again. He hates outside food."

Yesterday, it had taken me a full hour to convince him to let me order dinner. He was stubborn—stubborn like a rock. He kept insisting I should go to the market and get groceries so I could cook something for him. But I'd been too exhausted to even think about it. I just needed something quick, something that required zero effort. And that was a battle with Adrian, to say the least.

"Right," Rachel said with a half-smile that barely touched her eyes. It was the kind of smile you give when you're hiding something. I'd grown used to that smile. Ever since we started staying under the same roof, Rachel and Adrian had been distant—cold even. I wasn't sure what had happened between them, but whatever it was had left a lingering tension in the air. They rarely spoke directly to one another, and whenever they did, the exchanges were clipped and terse. I had stopped asking what went wrong a while ago. It was clear that neither of them was willing to share.

"Alright," I said, shaking the thoughts away, "I'll go get groceries. You coming?" I asked, giving her a chance to break the ice.

She shook her head immediately, "No, I wanna stay in."

I nodded, already knowing that answer. "Cool. I'll take Adrian with me. I'll be back before sunset."

With that, I headed downstairs, hoping to find Adrian quickly. But he wasn't in his room, nor in the backyard where he usually spent hours lost in his own world. My eyes landed on the car. The car that, according to Rachel, was never supposed to show up with Adrian in the first place. It had jumped out with Adrian with some accident. That was what they both told me, anyway. The whole thing made no sense. But then again, after everything I've been through lately, I've learned not to question things too deeply.

The sound of music interrupted my thoughts. Not just any music—piano music. And not just any piano. My piano.

I followed the melody through the hallways, recognizing the room immediately. It was the same grand piano that had sat unused for years, a gift from my grandmother on my seventeenth birthday. I reached the doorway and saw Adrian sitting there, completely engrossed in the music, his fingers dancing effortlessly across the keys. He hadn't noticed me yet, or maybe he had, but he didn't turn around.

I approached quietly, smiling at the sight of him so at ease. He played with such grace and precision, it was hard not to be mesmerized. There was something ethereal about him in moments like these, when his guard was down and he seemed to be part of the music itself.

He finally stopped, fingers resting lightly on the keys as he spoke, his voice gentle. "Since I... jumped out of the book," he said, the phrase still strange to hear, "I think this is the only thing I've found most interesting in this age."

I stood beside him, my eyes locking onto his. His green eyes met my grey ones, and for a long moment, we just looked at each other. In the soft light of the room, his features were flawless, almost too perfect to be real. There was an otherworldly beauty about him that had always captivated me.

"Can you play?" he asked, his tone as soft as the breeze that slipped through the half-open window.

I smiled, glancing down at the piano that had gathered dust for far too long. "I don't know," I admitted. "It's been years since I've touched this. I hardly remember any of the keys."

"I can teach you," he said, standing up and motioning for me to take his place on the bench.

I hesitated for a moment before sitting down, my fingers hovering over the keys. The familiar feeling of the cold ivory beneath my fingertips sent a rush of nostalgia through me. I pressed a single key, the sound echoing through the room. But before I could try another, I felt Adrian's hand gently cover mine from behind. He leaned in, his breath warm against my neck, and for a split second, the world seemed to hold its breath with me.

"Relax," he murmured, his lips almost brushing my ear. "Let the music come to you."

I swallowed hard, my breath catching as I tried to focus on the piano, on anything but the way his presence made my skin tingle. Slowly, he guided my fingers through a simple melody, his hands steady and sure. It was a tune I didn't recognize, but it was hauntingly beautiful, like something from a dream.

I abruptly stopped and pulled my hands out of his grip, making him frown down at me.

"What?" He asked, confused. I replied, "As much as I love this moment, I need to return before sunset," His frown deepened, "We need to get to the market, Adrian. We need to purchase groceries," I said.

He let out a soft chuckle, his breath fanning against my skin. "Groceries?" His voice was smooth, coaxing.

Now, it was my turn to frown, "What's funny?"

"Nothing," He shook his head, the smile still on his face, "I see this era has the kind of wonderful system that delivers the items at the doorstep?"

I smiled, half-laughing, half-melting under his touch. "Yeah, but I haven't left this house in days. I want to get out."

His expression softened as he studied me, "Alright," he said, making me grin, "Let's go."

I grinned, "Perfect."

We headed to Walmart in the car that mysteriously appeared in my backyard—still can't quite wrap my head around that. We parked, and as we entered, the fluorescent lights of Walmart greeted us with their signature hum. The sliding doors whooshed open like we were entering a very different kind of adventure, one filled with bargain deals and endless shelves. Adrian, who looked surprisingly at home in this odd scenario, pushed the trolley alongside me as we wandered through the aisles.

I tossed a packet of raw chicken into the cart and gave it a gentle shove forward.

"Do you think we need anything else for dinner tonight?" I asked, glancing at Adrian. He shrugged, which is basically his way of saying 'I'm just here for the ride.'

"I can't find the bathroom stuff. You mind holding down the fort while I go on a little quest?" I asked, hoping to get his full attention. He nodded, his eyes already drifting off to some random aisle display of oversized teddy bears. Classic Adrian.

I handed him the trolley, making sure to give him my best 'please don't wander off' look, and headed off in search of the detergent aisle. After weaving through what felt like miles of shampoo, paper towels, and clearance electronics, I finally found my treasure—a bottle of detergent with the exact right scent that makes me feel like my laundry is personally blessed by angels.

With a satisfied grin, I turned back to find Adrian.

Or, well, where I left Adrian.

When I got back to the spot, the trolley was gone. So was Adrian. I stood there, blinking for a moment as a sense of disbelief washed over me.

"Adrian?" I called out, probably a little too loud for the other shoppers' comfort. My voice echoed down the aisle, but no response. Just blank stares from people who probably thought I was crazy.

Great. "Excuse me," I asked a nearby couple who were studying discount dish soaps like it was a life decision, "Did you see a guy here? Beige pants? Grey sweatshirt? Might've looked like he was lost or, I don't know, on a secret mission?"

They exchanged glances before shaking their heads, politely edging away like I might ask them to join the search.

"Perfect," I muttered, rolling my eyes. "Of course, he disappears." I pulled out my phone and dialled Adrian's number. Voicemail. Every. Single. Time.

"Wonderful," I grumbled, stuffing my phone back in my pocket.

Determined, I started combing through each aisle like I was on a manhunt. It didn't help that the store was huge, and my mental map of Walmart was only slightly better than my knowledge of ancient hieroglyphics. After fifteen minutes of dodging shopping carts and angry toddlers, I finally turned a corner into the toy aisle, and there he was—Adrian, sitting cross-legged on the floor, deeply engrossed in stacking an army of plush unicorns into a precarious tower. The shopping cart was parked haphazardly nearby, abandoned like an afterthought.

"What... exactly are you doing?" I asked, staring at the wobbly unicorn tower that looked seconds away from toppling.

Without missing a beat, Adrian looked up with a mischievous grin. "Engineering."

I raised an eyebrow. "Engineering?"

"Yeah." He gave the tower a careful nudge. "I'm testing the structural integrity of this unicorn fort. If it survives the next five seconds, it qualifies for military defense contracts."

I crossed my arms, leaning against the end of the aisle. "Pretty sure stacking stuffed animals doesn't qualify as engineering."

Adrian's grin widened. "That's what they want you to think." He gave the plushie on top—Sir Sparkles, according to the tag—a little spin. The entire tower wobbled dangerously.

I stepped forward. "If that thing falls, you're cleaning it up."

"And if it doesn't fall, I'm a genius," he shot back, leaning back on his hands like he had all the time in the world.

Naturally, the plush tower collapsed.

Adrian sat there in the aftermath, surrounded by toppled unicorns, and let out a deep, regretful sigh. "So close."

I couldn't help it—I burst out laughing. "You're a disaster."

He shrugged, clearly unbothered, and started lazily tossing the unicorns back onto the shelves like it was no big deal. I bent down to help him.

When done, he threw one of those plush into the cart, "Sir Sparkles is coming with us." He said, grinning.

I rolled my eyes. "You're weird."

"And yet," Adrian said, smirking as he stood up and dusted himself off, "here you are, still hanging out with me."

I nudged the cart forward. "Mostly to make sure you don't get arrested for weird public stunts."

"Please," he scoffed, falling into step beside me. "They'd give me a medal."

We made our way through the aisles, Adrian occasionally sneaking ridiculous things into the cart—like a tub of neon slime and a rubber chicken.

"You really think we need this?" I asked, holding up the chicken.

He nodded solemnly. "Absolutely. Rubber chickens are essential."

"For what exactly?"

"Good vibes," he said with a straight face. "I felt good when I held it in my hands."

With a laugh, I tossed the chicken back into the cart. Adrian, looking entirely too pleased with himself, grabbed a pack of party hats and tossed it in next.

"Okay, that's enough." I swatted his hand away before he could grab something even more absurd. "We're not buying half the toy section."

"Oh, be grateful, I haven't purchased the whole section and only picking stuff that you can afford. Miss broke."

I gasped, my eyes narrowing, "Says the one who's living on my money?"

He clenched his jaw with a smile, "Thanks for the reality check, you mean, Liza Kirby."

I laughed, shaking my head.

By the time we made it to the checkout, our cart was half full of nonsense—party favors, a glitter pen, and, of course, Sir Sparkles riding proudly atop the groceries.

The cashier raised an eyebrow as Adrian handed over the rubber chicken first, giving her a serious nod like it was a sacred artifact. "This," he said solemnly, "is non-negotiable."

The cashier cracked a grin, and I shook my head, biting back a laugh.

After paying, we loaded the bags into the trunk of the mysterious car waiting for us outside. I slid into the driver's seat, glancing over as Adrian settled into the passenger seat, kicking his feet up on the dash without a care in the world.

"You know," I said, pulling out of the parking lot, "most people don't treat Walmart like it's their personal playground."

"Most people are boring," Adrian replied, arms behind his head, grinning like the troublemaker he was born to be.

I shook my head, a smile creeping onto my face despite myself.

# Chapter 39

# Shameless

*Liza's POV*

I put the document aside and picked another from the safe. Yes, a safe—my grandma's old, dusty, ironclad safe. It was filled with all sorts of important papers—property deeds for the mansion, insurance policies, and a stack of legal documents that might as well have been written in ancient hieroglyphics for all I understood. We'd spent the past three days sorting through everything, hoping for some kind of clue, some key to unravel the mess we'd found ourselves in. But nothing. Just more questions buried under paper trails.

The only significant thing we've uncovered so far? My childhood photo album. And of course, Adrian had found it.

He laughed for hours. And not the polite kind of laugh either—no, he was bent over, clutching his sides, red-faced and gasping for breath. He laughed at every awkward grin, every cringe-worthy Halloween costume, and every unflattering haircut immortalized on those glossy pages. The absolute nerve of him.

I scowled at the memory, but a small smile tugged at my lips. Sure, those photos were mortifying, but they were also... well, me. Innocent moments are frozen in time. Sure, some of them made me want to bury my head in the sand, but that didn't permit him to laugh like it was the funniest thing he'd ever seen. They were cute, dammit. They were natural. And, more importantly, they weren't meant to be seen by the likes of Adrian Scott.

But somehow, in the weirdest way, that night was one of my favorites so far.

We talk more now, and not just about the big, heavy things that were weighing us down. Somewhere along the way, we started sharing the small stuff too. The unimportant things. The things that mattered only to us.

He had this strange fascination with the stars. He'd drag me outside on chilly nights, insisting I needed to see this particular constellation or that shooting star. I'd stand there, shivering in my hoodie, pretending not to care. But secretly, I loved the way his face lit up when he pointed to the sky, the way he talked about the universe like it was an old friend.

Then there was the ocean—his latest obsession. A few nights ago, we stumbled across a YouTube documentary while I was making dinner. I'd been chopping vegetables, only half-listening as the narrator droned on about the ocean's unexplored depths. But Adrian? He'd been glued to the screen, fascinated. I swear, he didn't even notice when I told him dinner was ready—he just kept watching, completely absorbed.

And ever since then, he hasn't stopped talking about it.

"*Do you realize,*" he'd said the next morning over coffee, "*that we've explored less than five percent of the ocean? Five percent. That's nothing! There could be anything down there.*"

*He'd leaned across the table, his eyes wide with excitement.* "*What if there's a giant squid that's smarter than we are? Or some prehistoric shark just waiting for the right moment to show up?*"

*I'd laughed, stirring sugar into my coffee.* "*I think you've been watching too many monster movies.*"

*He ignored me, completely undeterred.* "*No, seriously. Think about it. Space gets all the attention, but the ocean? That's where the real mysteries are.*"

And he was still on about it—days later.

Just yesterday, I walked into the living room to find him sprawled across the couch, watching another ocean documentary with some important paperwork around that he was barely paying attention to. I didn't even bother asking if he wanted dinner, or telling him that we were still under a threat—I just started cooking while he muttered facts at me from the other room.

"*Did you know there are places in the ocean where the water is so deep, light can't even reach it?*" *he'd called out, like it was the most fascinating thing in the world.* "*Can you imagine? A whole part of the planet lives in total darkness.*"

*I'd rolled my eyes, tossing pasta into the boiling water.* "I think you're obsessed."

*He appeared in the doorway, arms crossed, grinning.* "I think I'm enlightened."

And, honestly? I didn't mind. I liked these little moments with him—his ridiculous tangents, the way he filled the silence with half-baked theories about giant squids and lost cities underwater. It made everything feel a little lighter, a little less overwhelming.

Now, as I pulled out another stack of documents from the safe, I couldn't help but smile at the thought of him. Adrian was chaotic, unpredictable, and, at times, downright exhausting. But somehow, he made even the dullest moments feel like an adventure. He could turn a night of paperwork into a debate about constellations, or a quiet afternoon into a full-blown discussion on the mysteries of the Mariana Trench.

And without realizing it, I'd started to look forward to those moments—the ones where it was just us, wrapped up in conversations that had nothing to do with saving the world or fixing our mess.

I glanced at the clock—time for training. I closed the safe and stood to my feet, heading towards Rachel's bedroom where I usually get trained. But as I made my way to it, I felt thirsty. So I decided to drink some water before heading to her.

I got into the kitchen and drank some water but as I placed the glass in the sink and turned around, my breath caught in my throat.

Adrian stood there, his tall, imposing figure leaning casually against the door. He wore a green sweatshirt that matched the intensity of his eyes and dark pants that contrasted his effortlessly cool demeanor. The faint, clean scent of him filled the air.

"You know," he started, crossing his arms, looking entirely too pleased with himself. "your seven-year-old self really had a thing for mismatched socks. Very fashion-forward."

I narrowed my eyes at him. "Don't you have anything better to do than make fun of my childhood choices?"

"Nope." His grin widened. "I live for these moments."

I threw him a fake smile and crossed my arms against my chest too, "And for someone who acts all wise about the universe, you sure watch a lot of fish documentaries."

He gave a mock-serious nod, stepping further into the room. "There's a lot to unpack about the ocean. Like, did you know we've explored more space than the sea? The ocean's hiding stuff." His voice dropped like he was revealing a state secret.

*Not again.*

I rolled my eyes, letting out a frustrated sigh, "Oh, God! How long before this obsession of yours gets over?" I wasn't actually irritated but in this early morning, ocean was the last thing I wanted to talk about.

He narrowed his eyes slightly, taking a deliberate step toward me. My heart raced, and I instinctively stepped back. "What?" I whispered, my hands pressing lightly against his chest as I tried to stop his advance.

But he didn't stop. His arms caged me in, bracing against the sink behind me. I felt the heat rise to my cheeks, turning them a deep crimson. These past few days, everything had shifted between us. He'd become more daring, more direct, constantly pushing the boundaries. He didn't care if Rachel or anyone else might catch us. He was shameless. And, despite everything, I found myself drawn to him more and more.

"Do you know how gorgeous your eyes are?" he whispered, his thumb brushing softly over my jaw.

I gulped, lost in the depths of his eyes, completely hypnotized.

"They're like the rarest gems, Liza. The kind of beauty you could lose yourself in for hours and never regret a second."

My heart fluttered, blooming under the weight of his words.

"And your lips?" His voice dropped even lower, his eyes darkening with an intensity that made me gasp. "Every time I see them, all I want to do is kiss them."

I looked down at his lips, forcing myself to breathe. "What about now?" My voice came out shakier than I intended, but I held his gaze. "Or do you prefer imagining it?"

His smirk faded slightly, his fingers moved down and wrapped around my neck, sending a thrill through my body as he yanked me closer to him a bit roughly, making me wince.

"You have no idea what I imagine, Liza," He whispered near my lips, "Kissing is... nothing compared to the things I dream about when it comes to us."

Heat surged through me, pooling between my thighs. Without another word, he lifted me effortlessly, placing me on the counter. My breath hitched as he stepped between my legs, his hands gripping my thighs, spreading them around his waist.

"Adrian... What are you doing? I need to get to Rachel. She must be waiting," I protested weakly, trying to push him back. But he didn't budge.

"She can wait longer," he murmured, his voice filled with a dark amusement as his hands slid up my thighs, parting them further. I gasped. I knew my face was flushed, my body betraying every hint of desire I felt. His hands were dangerously close to where I ached for him most. "Let me look at you... or maybe," his hand trailed higher, grazing my inner thigh, making me suck in a sharp breath, "I'll do more than just look," I looked down at his hands. His strong, huge veiny hands.

"Eyes on me, baby," He ordered. I obeyed, my gaze snapping back to his, heart pounding, "Good," His hand hovered over the sensitive heat of my body, fingers teasing dangerously close. He leaned in, kissing my neck while his thumb traced slow, deliberate circles over the fabric. I gulped, curling my toes at the sheer intensity of it.

My eyes fell shut, surrendering to the moment as his lips brushed against the curve of my neck. Each kiss felt like a deliberate promise—soft yet scorching, tender but laden with an intensity that made my breath hitch. My hands gripped his sweatshirt tightly, holding onto him as though he were the only thing grounding me in the whirlwind of sensations spiraling through me.

But then, the sharp, unmistakable sound of my zipper being undone sliced through the fog clouding my thoughts. My eyes snapped open, panic flooding my senses.

"A-Adrian?" I stammered, my voice trembling as I realized where it was going.

"I can stop if you tell me to," He said, his voice was warm and low, like velvet, coaxing me into stillness.

I was nervous. Too nervous. But I didn't want him to stop. Not anymore.

His hand moved with calculated precision, slipping past the waistband of my jeans and resting just above the thin fabric of my underwear. The heat of his palm seemed to burn through the barrier, and I froze, my breath catching in my throat. The realization of how close he was sent a rush of embarrassment and something far more dangerous coursing through me. My cheeks flamed, and I bit my lower lip, my fingers wrinkling the fabric of his sweatshirt.

He applied a gentle pressure with his thumb, and an involuntary arch of my back brought me closer to him, seeking more. His lips moved against my neck, his teeth grazing the tender skin in a way that should have stung but instead sent a jolt of sensation through me.

Then, as if testing my resolve, his hand dipped lower. His fingers slipped into my panties, and my eyes widened as a gasp escaped my lips. The vulnerability of the moment made my pulse race.

"Adrian, I—" I began, but before I could form a coherent thought, his lips crashed down on mine.

The kiss was wild, demanding, and unapologetically possessive. His teeth tugged at my lower lip, sending sharp, electric shivers down my spine. My hands clung to him, torn between pushing him away and pulling him closer. His free hand slid to the back of my neck, tilting my head to deepen the kiss, while his other hand ventured farther.

When his finger pushed inside me, a sharp pain tore through me, and I flinched, the discomfort pulling me back to reality. I winced against his lips, but he didn't stop, didn't let go.

Instead, he murmured against my mouth, his tone dark and teasing. "Oh, baby. Do you want Rachel to hear what I'm doing to you?"

The weight of his words made me shudder. My cheeks burned hotter, and the mortification of being overheard made me instinctively press my lips harder against his, stifling the sounds that threatened to escape.

He withdrew his finger, only to thrust it back in, his movements deliberate and unrelenting. My breath hitched, and a strangled moan escaped despite my best efforts to contain it. Desperate to silence myself, I kissed him harder, my lips moving against his with a ferocity I didn't know I possessed. He groaned into my mouth as I bit down on his lip, the taste of blood faint on my tongue.

The initial pain began to fade, replaced by an unfamiliar ache that sent waves of heat coursing through me. His finger moved expertly, coaxing responses from my body that I didn't know I was capable of.

"Part your legs wider, baby," he rasped, his voice thick with desire, the words brushing against my lips like a command I couldn't disobey.

I hesitated, the vulnerability of the request paralyzing me, but the authority in his voice left no room for resistence. Trembling, I shifted, parting my legs just enough to grant him better access. He pressed a kiss to the sensitive spot just below my ear as a second finger joined the first.

A sharp gasp escaped my lips, my body tensing at the stretch, but his movements were patient, coaxing me to adjust. His thumb began circling a spot that sent jolts of electricity through me, each motion drawing me closer to an edge I didn't fully understand.

The tension in my stomach tightened, coiling like a spring about to snap. My breaths came quicker, each one more labored than the last.

"Oh, my God," I whispered, the words slipping out unbidden.

"I can feel you're close," he murmured against my skin, his voice laced with satisfaction. His lips captured mine in another searing kiss, his tongue teasing and exploring as his fingers continued their relentless assault.

And then it happened. A wave of euphoria crashed over me, stealing the breath from my lungs as my body convulsed against him. The release was overwhelming, a sensation so intense that it left me gasping for air, my limbs trembling from the aftermath.

He pulled his hand away, and I watched, stunned and speechless, as he brought his fingers to his lips, his eyes never leaving mine. His tongue darted out, tasting me with a slow, deliberate motion that made my already overheated skin burn brighter.

I stared at him, unable to form a coherent response, my mind spinning from what had just happened. My body felt foreign, as though it had been awakened to sensations I never thought possible. The weight of the moment pressed down on me, leaving me stunned, overwhelmed, and undeniably changed.

"You're going to need to change," he said, his voice teasing, a smirk playing on his lips, "And close your legs unless you want my lips now."

I gasped at his bluntness, my face heating as I glanced down. My legs were still parted, my jeans barely preserving my modesty. Embarrassment surged through me, and I quickly pulled my legs together, biting my lip to suppress the whirlwind of emotions coursing through me.

He stepped closer, commanding my attention with the intensity in his eyes. His presence was magnetic, and I couldn't look away. Without breaking our gaze, he reached down and tugged my jeans back into place, the metallic sound of the zipper being drawn up making my breath catch.

The simple act was intimate, almost reverent, and left my heart pounding in my chest.

"You're shameless," I muttered, my heart racing.

He chuckled, "Baby, I'm more than that."

I smiled and lifted my chin to kiss him but a sound from outside broke through the haze. It was Rachel's voice. My heart jumped as I abruptly pulled away, shoving him back in panic. I scrambled off the counter, hastily adjusting my clothes while Adrian just chuckled, clearly unfazed.

But before I could take another step, his hand shot out, grabbing my wrist and pulling me back into his arms. He captured my lips again, this time for a soft, teasing kiss, making my knees weak all over again.

I smiled against his lips, kissing him back.

Breathless, we pulled away. He winked at me, and I rolled my eyes. But then my smile vanished as my eyes fell on the flower vase behind him—in the place of lilies, remained ash.

"All this training and I still can't control my powers," I muttered, frustration bubbling inside me. Adrian followed my gaze to the dead flowers, his brow furrowing slightly. His suspicion lingered, but he turned back to me with a small, reassuring smile. "How long before I finally learn to control it?" I asked, the impatience creeping into my voice.

"Patience, Liza. You'll learn," he said gently. "Now go. Rachel's waiting for you, and you know she's not the most patient person." We chuckled lightly, "Go. I'll keep up the treasure hunt in the house."

I nodded, turning away from him and heading toward the door. As I stepped into the hallway, I found Rachel waiting, arms crossed, her face tight with frustration.

"Where have you been? We don't have time for this, Liza. We're losing precious hours," she scolded me, sternly.

"Sorry," I mumbled, searching for an excuse. "I was grabbing something to eat."

Rachel stared at me for a long, hard moment before sighing and letting it go.

"Alright. Come with me."

"I'm just behind. I just need to pee first." I said, making an excuse to change. There's no way I can stand normally with wetness all over my thighs.

"Okay. I'm waiting outside. Come quick." Saying this, she turned on her heel and walked towards the exit, her boots echoing sharply across the floor. I let out a sigh of relief and glanced back over my shoulder at Adrian, who stood there, waving at me with a mischievous grin.

I smiled but that wavered when the fact that he was destined to return twisted my heart. I looked away.

Don't think about it. Don't think about it. Don't think about it. Don't think about it. Don't think about it. Don't think about it.

"Alright," Rachel said, her tone brisk and businesslike as we stood by the table in the backyard, "we're trying something different today." She placed a large, rough stone on the table in front of me. "Break it."

"Break it?"

"Yes. We've been practicing simple magic, but you need to push yourself if you're going to handle what's coming. The people who want the tomes won't give you second chances."

Understanding the seriousness of her words, I nodded. Taking a deep breath, I raised my hands instinctively, ready to channel my energy.

Rachel sighed loudly. "Liza, how many times do I have to tell you? You're not Iron Man. Hands down. Focus your mind on the stone and say... Confractus."

Feeling slightly embarrassed, I lowered my hands and focused on the stone. The air around me began to stir, picking up leaves and dust as my concentration deepened.

"Liza!" Rachel's sharp voice cut through the growing wind. "Don't lose control. Focus on breaking the stone. Keep your energy contained."

I nodded, breathing deeply to steady myself, and turned my full attention back to the stone.

"Confractus," I whispered, and in an instant, the stone cracked and shattered into several pieces. I smiled at the success, glancing up at Rachel. She nodded approvingly.

"Good. Now, fix it," she said.

"Alright. What's the spell?"

"No spell," she said simply. "Fix it without one."

I frowned, uncertain. "Can that even be done?"

"Yes," Rachel said firmly. "You're more than just a witch, Liza. You have power beyond words. Use it."

I stared at her, then back at the broken pieces on the table. Could I really do this? I swallowed the knot of doubt rising in my throat.

"You believe I can?" I asked, my voice hesitant.

"I do," Rachel replied. "Now, focus."

I nodded, turning my gaze back to the shattered stone. The pressure in the air thickened as I gathered my focus. Without thinking, without speaking, I directed my energy toward the pieces, willing them to reassemble.

Slowly, they lifted into the air, floating back together, and in a matter of moments, the stone was whole again. No cracks, no breaks—just as it had been before.

I stepped back, my breath catching in my throat. I couldn't believe what I'd just done.

Rachel smiled, "See? You're learning control. You're not perfect yet, but I trust you won't hurt yourself or anyone else during magic. Now, just learn the spells."

Her words didn't ease the unease stirring inside me. I stared at the stone, feeling the weight of something much larger than my magic settling in.

"Rachel..." I began slowly, my voice trailing off as my thoughts unraveled. "Whenever I'm with you, it feels like I have control. But earlier... when I was with Adrian... the flowers—"

Rachel tilted her head, her expression confused. "Flowers? What happened to the flowers?"

"They withe—" I stopped, the word stuck in my throat as a wave of realization began to form in the pit of my stomach. My heart skipped a beat, then another, until it was pounding so hard I thought it might burst.

The truth crashed over me, sudden and undeniable. My pulse quickened, my breath shallow and uneven, as the pieces began to fall into place.

Rachel was watching me, her brows furrowed, concern etched into every line of her face. She could see it—the panic, the fear—but she didn't understand. How could she? I barely understood it myself.

"Liza?" Her voice was soft, tentative. "Are you alright?"

I didn't answer. My mind was spinning, racing through every moment, every small sign I had ignored. The flowers—they only died when I kissed him. That wasn't an accident. That wasn't some rookie blunder with my magic—it was the universe itself retaliating.

Adrian and I, we don't belong to the same world. We are opposites in every possible way. A kiss between us was more than just a moment of passion—it was a violation, a sin committed against the very fabric of existence. The universe, in its mysterious, unforgiving way, was sending a message, showing us the consequences of our actions.

The flowers—their withered, lifeless state—were the first signs. The universe's subtle attempt to warn us that what we had done could have far-reaching, catastrophic consequences.

Deep down, I knew from the moment I allowed myself to feel anything for him that it would lead to blood and chaos. But now... seeing the universe reacting this way, is concerning.

Rachel took a step closer to me, "Liza?"

"The flowers..." I finally spoke, my voice wavered, the words sticking in my throat as I tried to make sense of it all. "It wasn't some rookie blunder."

Rachel's face shifted, her concern deepening into confusion. "What are you talking about?"

I could barely find the words. "They withered... it was a sign. A sign of destruction," I paused, trying to steady my breath, trying to make sense of the storm raging inside me. "No. The universe is reacting to us. It's... it's pushing back. Because I'm breaking a rule, crossing a line that I'm not supposed to," I trailed off, the full weight of the situation crashing down on me.

Rachel stepped closer, her voice filled with concern. "Liza, what are you hiding from me?"

The silence that followed was heavy, suffocating, and the truth loomed over me like a storm cloud. I could feel it—the pull of fate, the pressure to do what was right, to let him go. But I wasn't sure I could.

"That I'm falling for him," I finally whispered, the confession leaving my lips like a fragile secret I wasn't ready to face.

## Chapter 40

# The Evil Zephyr Valtor

*Rachel's POV*

Fear.

I've been consumed by it for so long-Zephyr's presence has poisoned my mind. I hate him, loathe him with every fiber of my being. But today, it's different. Today, there's no room for fear. Only rage. Burning, searing rage that coursed through me, unstoppable.

How can anyone be so selfish, so heartless?

Liza is falling for him, and with every step deeper into this dangerous affection, the fabric of our world will unravel. Their connection isn't just emotional-it's elemental. They are two opposing forces, bound by laws. If they continue to defy these laws, if they dare to cross the boundary, the consequences will be catastrophic. Decaying flowers is nothing compared to what could happen. The balance will tip, unleashing a storm of chaos that no one will escape unscathed.

My blood boils every time I think about what he's doing to her, how he's pulling her in with that easy smile, that false kindness as if this is some kind of game to him. But it's not a game. Not for her. Liza doesn't realize what she's walking into. She's blinded by whatever she thinks she sees in him-something worth saving, something worth loving. But I see the truth. I see the mask he wears. And when it slips, it won't be just her heart that shatters. He'll leave her broken in a way no spell, no time, no love could ever mend. And when that happens, when the pieces of her soul scatter to the wind, he won't care.

Damn him. I want to rip that smug look off his face every time he plays at kindness. Every word, every smile, every glance-it's all calculated to keep her under his spell, to make her believe there's something real between them. But there isn't. There can't be. If they keep going down this path, the world will pay for his lies, but Liza will pay the highest price of all. And I won't stand by and watch her be destroyed. Not her. Not when I care about her too much to let that happen.

I have to stop him. I have to make her see him for what he truly is a threat, a force of chaos that will only bring ruin to everything she holds dear. She thinks she's in control, but I know better. Once she's too far gone, once she's given him every part of herself, he'll leave her to drown in the wreckage. And when she tries to pick up the pieces of who she used to be, they'll cut her so deeply she might never find her way back to herself.

I won't let that happen. Even if it means making her hate me. Even if it means tearing her apart. I'll do whatever it takes to protect her, even if it's from herself. Because if no one stops him now, it'll be too late. And Liza... Liza will never survive what's coming.

I stormed through the door, my fingers tightening into fists, and found him standing by the window, nonchalantly holding a photo album. Liza's childhood photo album that we found last night. The sight of him, calm and smug, sent waves of anger through my veins.

His brows lifted slightly when he noticed me, "Hello?" he began, a mocking tone in his voice.

But I was done with words. I closed the distance between us in two strides and slapped him, hard, across the face. The sharp crack echoed through the room, and the sting shot up my arm, but it was worth it.

His face jerked sideways, his jaw tightening. Slowly, very dangerously, he turned back to me, and his green eyes-those blazing, inhuman eyes flared with fury. But he stayed silent. For a moment, we just stood there, his glare matching my rage. I knew what I had done could cost me, but I didn't care. Not anymore.

"How can you be so evil, Zephyr?" I spat, my voice trembling with emotion. "That child has been through enough, and you-" my voice cracked with disgust, "you decided to play this twisted game of feelings. Do you even realize what you're doing to her?"

He didn't answer. His silence was infuriating, but I wouldn't be intimidated by it. I wouldn't be intimidated by him.

"That's worse than killing someone!" I snarled, stepping closer.

Suddenly, the door behind me slammed shut, hard enough to make the walls shake. I flinched but quickly swallowed the moment of fear. No, not this time. I wouldn't let him win. I squared my shoulders, staring him down as he stepped forward.

"Evil?" he whispered, his voice low and dangerous. He took another step toward me, and instinctively, I stepped back. But I refused to break eye contact, meeting his gaze with defiance. "If I were evil, you wouldn't be standing here breathing after slapping me. If I were evil, you wouldn't have the courage to order me around like you do."

He moved closer, his voice like ice. "If I were evil, I would've killed your husband for disrespecting me, or to put you in your place. If I were evil, I would've done things to make you all beg for death."

My heart raced, but I forced myself to stay rooted, chin raised defiantly. His words sliced through the air, but I wouldn't let him see my fear. I wouldn't give him that satisfaction.

"Evil?" he repeated, his voice softer but more menacing. "Evil is your so-called savior, Archon." The mention of Archon offended me, and I opened my mouth to retort, but Zephyr held up a hand to stop me. "What do you really know about him? About the past?" Zephyr's voice turned bitter. "Archon, the great spellcaster, yanked characters from their worlds, using them when it suited him, only to shove them back without a second thought. Do you know the truth, Rachel? Zephyr, yes, I, became a problem. A problem so big that your precious Archon had to sacrifice his own life to send me back. That's the story you've been told, right? The legend of Archon and the villainous Zephyr who killed people in a fit of wrath. Children included."

He paused, his eyes searching for mine for a response. I said nothing, my fists clenched so tight my nails dug painfully into my palms.

"Let me take you to the time when your great Archon became the hero, Rachel," Zephyr said, his voice a dangerous whisper. "Let me show you what really happened so you can decide for yourself who was the true evil."

Before I could respond, Zephyr's hand shot forward, grabbing my wrists. A blinding light exploded before my eyes, and for a moment, everything went silent-utterly still. The brightness enveloped me, distorting time. When it finally faded, I blinked, struggling to focus. The room I had been standing in only minutes before was gone. Instead, I found myself in the middle of a ruined landscape.

Smoke filled the air, swirling around the remnants of what must have been a village. The dying embers of a great fire flickered in the distance, casting a dull orange glow over the charred ground. I turned, my heart hammering as I took it all in. This wasn't an illusion. This felt real. Too real.

"Where are we?" My voice was hard, though my heart pounded with uncertainty. "What is this place?"

Zephyr stood beside me, his eyes fixed on something far ahead. "The 8th century," he said evenly. I followed his gaze and took in the scene. Two figures standing amidst the ruins, the tension between them thick even from here. "See the man in white armor? That's me-The evil Zephyr Valtor. The one facing him in tattered robes is Archon Astralis, your 'great' spellcaster. This is the moment I was first summoned."

"You expect me to believe this?" I asked, my voice cutting through the oppressive atmosphere. "I won't fall for your pathetic illusions, Zephyr."

Zephyr didn't flinch, his gaze fixed on me, "I'm not inside your head, Rachel. If I wanted to control you, I could compel your mind-bend your thoughts, your will. But I don't need to. I don't want your submission; I want your trust." His voice dropped lower, more serious. "That's why we're here."

I clenched my fists, unwilling to let him manipulate me, but my instincts whispered a truth I didn't want to accept. My psychic powers, always sharp, tugged at me, hinting that what I was seeing wasn't a fabrication. Despite myself, I found my resolve wavering.

"Shall we?" Zephyr gestured toward the figures ahead. I walked past him, though every step felt heavier as I moved closer to the gruesome scene. My stomach churned at the sight that awaited us.

The ground was littered with corpses, or rather, what was left of them. Bodies turned to ash, scattered like forgotten remnants of a once-living village. In the midst of it all, stood the old Zephyr. His face was a mask of indifference, the destruction around him seemingly nothing more than an inconvenience. He inhaled deeply, then turned to face Archon, who, despite the devastation, remained tall and regal, unshaken by the carnage.

"What happened here?" I asked, my voice barely a whisper as my heart twisted at the sight.

"Some 'bad' people slaughtered these innocent villagers, desperate to display their power. I was summoned to deal with them," Zephyr answered, his tone as casual as if he were discussing the weather.

I took a deep breath in, turning my gaze to Archon, who faced Zephyr fearlessly.

"Speak," Zephyr ordered, his voice dripping with authority. The arrogance in his tone was palpable.

I bristled. *Narcissist*. He wore his pride and ego like armor, wrapped so tightly around himself that no emotion-no empathy-could penetrate. I couldn't see a shred of humanity in him, and I doubted Archon could either.

"We require your help," Archon said, his voice careful, measured. The old Zephyr raised a brow, waiting. "He paused as if choosing his words precisely. "These people you see were murdered by the Shadows. A coven tainted by dark magic. We need you to protect our village. Avenge our fallen."

For a long, painful moment, the old Zephyr said nothing. His gaze, cold and unfeeling, fixed on Archon with an intensity that made the air around us grow colder. I felt my skin prickle from the drop in temperature.

Finally, Zephyr spoke, his voice as icy as the silence before. "What do you think I am?" His lips curled into something that could've been a sneer. "I'm not your soldier, Archon. I am a god. If you summoned me thinking I'd fight your battles, then you're even more of a fool than I thought. Perform the ritual again. Send me back. I have no interest in this world or its problems."

I felt the shock ripple through the room, and my stomach twisted in disbelief. I glanced at the Zephyr beside me, but his expression was unreadable, though something dark flickered in his eyes-rage, perhaps? I frowned and followed his gaze. He was glaring at Archon. But why?

"Seven witches sacrificed themselves to summon you," Archon's voice cracked, his composure slipping, rage and desperation battling for control. "You owe them this, Zephyr."

The old Zephyr's eyes flashed with a violent green light as he stepped forward, the weight of his presence intensifying. "I owe no one," he growled, voice low and dangerous. "I don't belong in this world. You are meddling with forces beyond your comprehension. Send me back before you regret it."

Archon's face twisted with barely contained rage. "How can you be so heartless?" he spat. "People are dying. Families are being torn apart. You could help them."

Zephyr's expression didn't change. His cold, emotionless gaze locked onto Archon. "Blame your fate, not me. I wasn't born to fix your broken world."

Without another word, the old Zephyr turned and walked away, leaving Archon standing in stunned silence. The scene left a suffocating weight in the air, and I couldn't keep my emotions at bay any longer.

"What are you trying to prove?" I demanded, whirling around to face the present-day Zephyr. "That you're truly heartless?"

He met my eyes but said nothing. Instead, he turned and followed his past self. I trailed after him, my mind swirling with confusion and anger, and curiosity.

We continued walking in silence, the remnants of the village still heavy around us. The old Zephyr's footsteps slowed as he wandered, his hand grazing the foliage as though absorbing some of the life around him. His face was no longer indifferent but contemplative, almost peaceful.

"I felt real here," Zephyr said suddenly, his voice softer, more distant. "More alive than ever. I wasn't just a figment of someone's imagination. I was real. This was real."

I snorted, the bitterness in my tone evident. "Is that what you're trying to show me? The moment you became obsessed with 'reality'?"

Zephyr chuckled, a low sound that felt more thoughtful than amused. "You misunderstand me."

Before I could question him further, the soft rustling of leaves caught my attention. The old Zephyr had heard it too. A small child, no more than five, stepped timidly out of the shadows. Her face was streaked with dirt, her eyes red and puffy from crying. My heart clenched at the sight.

"Hello, little one," the old Zephyr said gently, his steps slow and deliberate as he approached her. The girl gazed up at him with tear-filled eyes, her lower lip trembling. Zephyr knelt before her, his expression calm, watching her with what I feared might be cold indifference. I tensed, ready to intervene, though the reality of my powerlessness loomed over me.

"Mother said you would protect us," she whispered, barely able to hold back more tears. "She said you'd take away our sorrow and bring us joy. Will you?"

Her words pierced through me. I expected Zephyr to laugh at her innocence, to tell her the harsh truth that he wasn't there to help, that he didn't care. But to my shock, he gently wiped the tears from her cheeks. "I don't like cowardly children," he murmured, his tone soft but firm.

"I'm not a coward," she protested, her voice weak but determined. She squared her shoulders, standing tall despite her small frame. "I'm brave."

"Then why are you crying?" Zephyr asked, his gaze intense yet not cruel. "Brave children don't cry."

"I am brave," she insisted, wiping her tears with the back of her hand. "And I'm not a child. I'm a lady. A strong lady, like my mother says."

A genuine smile broke across Zephyr's face-warm, soft, and entirely unexpected. "A lady, you say?" The little girl nodded, a hint of pride in her posture. Zephyr chuckled again, a sound so foreign to the cold god I thought I knew.

"So, will you protect us?" she asked, her big eyes filled with hope that made my heart ache. For a long moment, Zephyr said nothing, just gazing at the girl. Then, slowly, he nodded, and the girl's face lit up with joy.

"Yes, little angel," Zephyr said softly. "I will protect you. I'll take away your sorrow. I promise."

Without hesitation, the girl threw her arms around Zephyr's neck, and he lifted her into his arms, holding her close. There was no darkness in his expression, no malice. Only warmth, a tenderness I never thought he was capable of.

"Evil, huh?" The present-day Zephyr's voice cut through my thoughts, pulling me back. He was watching me closely, and for once, there was no arrogance in his gaze. "Still think I'm heartless?"

I stared at him, speechless, the image of the old Zephyr cradling the child was something I couldn't believe. Maybe-just maybe-there was more to him than I had ever imagined. I took a step forward but halted when everything and everyone around me turned to dust, and we were thrust into another fragment of his memory. At least, that's what I thought it was.

I blinked as the new scene came into view. The place was different-better. People were smiling, children were playing happily. The sun bathed the village in a golden light, and a slow, calming wind brushed past us. Everything was peaceful, almost surreal, after what I'd just witnessed.

"What's happening?" I asked, my voice quieter than I intended.

"This is five days after my confrontation with the Shadows," Zephyr replied, watching the scene with a small, almost fond smile.

I glanced at him, confused. "What did you do to them?"

His smirk returned, and his eyes gleamed with something dark as they locked on something behind me. I turned to follow his gaze and saw two figures in the distance. They were laboring in the dirt, dirty and humiliated, while children ran by, throwing mud at them. The men-once proud and dignified-were now reduced to this.

I couldn't help but chuckle in disbelief. "You didn't kill them?"

Zephyr shook his head, his eyes never leaving the men in the yard. "No. Death was too merciful for what they did. They had too much pride and too much arrogance. Now, they get to live every day in shame, humiliated by the very people they once wanted to rule over. Isn't that so much better than death?"

I swallowed, trying to suppress a shiver at his words. "You're cruel," I muttered, though a part of me understood his reasoning. A punishment like this seemed fitting for them.

Zephyr smiled at my response, a smile that didn't reach his eyes. "Cruelty is subjective."

I shook my head, trying to rid myself of the unease. "Where's Archon?" I asked, scanning the area for any sign of him.

Zephyr's smirk faded slightly. "Come with me," he said, turning on his heel and walking away. I followed, my mind racing with everything I'd seen so far.

We walked through the village in silence until we reached a small hut. Zephyr pushed the door open, and I stepped inside after him. The room was dimly lit, but I could make out Archon, standing near the centre, his back to us. He was arguing with a woman. His wife, I assumed.

"Archon, get back to your senses," she pleaded, her voice strained. "You don't speak like this."

"Senses?" Archon's voice was bitter, laced with resentment. "I am in my senses, Marcella! You saw it. Those people out there, they worship him. They worship him, not me. And I'm the one who brought him here. I, Archon Astralis!"

Marcella looked around in fear, lowering her voice to a harsh whisper. "Archon, lower your voice! If anyone hears you, God knows what will happen."

I felt Zephyr's presence beside me, his voice dripping with amusement as he whispered, "The great Archon Astralis is jealous? And of me? The 'evil' Zephyr?"

My stomach churned at his words, my beliefs about both men shifting in ways I didn't want to admit. Could this really be the truth? Was this who Archon truly was? My mind rebelled against it, but deep down, my powers- my instincts- told me it was all real.

"I deserve it!" Archon's voice boomed, his anger erupting. "All this celebration, all this worshipping-it should be mine, not his! He's nothing but a fragment of imagination, destined to return to the void. I'm real! I'm the one who should be worshipped!"

Marcella's eyes widened in shock. "Archon, stop! If anyone hears you, you'll be damned!"

Archon's fury boiled over. His eyes flashed red, and before I could even react, he lunged at Marcella, grabbing her throat and slamming her against the wall. She gasped, choking in disbelief, fear etched across her face as her hands clawed at his arm, struggling for air.

My heart leaped into my throat, and I clamped a hand over my mouth in horror.

"I'll send him back," Archon snarled, tightening his grip on her throat. "That scoundrel will go back to his realm, and I'll do it tonight."

Beside me, Zephyr watched the scene with cold indifference. "The great Archon, abusing his wife," he remarked with a chilling casualness. His eyes flicked to me, and he smiled. "Great, isn't he?"

I was speechless, my mind spinning. This wasn't the Archon I had heard about-the noble, powerful spellcaster. This man was twisted by jealousy, consumed by his own pride. And Zephyr-he had known all along.

I didn't know what to believe anymore. Everything I thought I knew about him was unraveling. The kindness-the tenderness-wasn't something I expected. Not from him. And for the first time, the hatred I held onto so fiercely began to slip away and now I wanted nothing more than to know this man.

The real Zephyr Valtor.

# Chapter 41

## *Hidden Chest*

*Liza's POV*

Ever since I realized how I feel about Adrian, the fear hasn't left me. It lingers in the back of my mind, haunting every moment we share, reminding me that he's not meant to stay. He doesn't belong here, in this world, with me. He's from somewhere else, a realm I can't touch or truly understand. The thought that one day, I'll have to let him go, that he'll vanish, slip away like a dream, is unbearable. I feel like I'm constantly standing on the edge, knowing that any second I could lose him. And I'm terrified of that.

I know it's wrong to want him to stay. I know it's selfish. I know it's crazy. But I can't help it. I need him here. He's more than just a person in my life; he's become a part of me, woven into my heart in ways I didn't expect. Before him, I was lost, adrift in a world where I felt like I was constantly fighting to keep my head above water. But Adrian... Adrian makes it easy to live, he makes me feel alive. When he smiles at me, the storm of my heart calms, when he looks at me with those eyes that see right through my defenses, I feel... Whole. He makes me happy, he makes me feel seen and heard. And I'm not ready to lose that. I'm not ready to lose him.

But I can't ignore the truth either. In this world, there are people I care about, they matter too. I'm not blind to that. I know there are consequences and dangers of my feelings for him. The world could fall apart around me because of it. But I can't accept that it's a choice between saving the world and keeping him. It can't be. I refuse to believe that. There has to be a way to save both. There has to be a solution, something we haven't discovered yet.

I don't know how I'm going to do it, but I'll defy fate itself if I have to. I'll tear down the boundaries between realms if that's what it takes to stay together and save both worlds. I don't care what the cost is-I won't lose him. Not now, not ever.

I'll find a way.

I swung open the door to my grandma's bedroom, the old hinges creaking under the force, and hurried inside. My eyes darted around the room, scanning the familiar surroundings, desperate for something-anything-that might help. This was the tenth time I'd been here, scouring every corner, pulling open every drawer, searching through every book and box. But this time was different. This time, desperation gnawed at me like never before.

When I realized the universe was pushing back, sending signs of destruction, I didn't feel fear. If anything, I felt a strange, burning resolve. The signs weren't warnings to stop. They were challenges to overcome, obstacles in my path. I wasn't going to back down. If the universe thought it could keep Adrian and me apart, it was wrong. I wouldn't let it.

Rachel's reaction was exactly what I expected-concern, disbelief, and anger. I could see it in the way her eyes flickered, the tension tightening her jaw. She wasn't just worried-she was mad. Furious, even. She couldn't believe what I'd just admitted, and the weight of my words hung between us like a storm about to break.

She didn't need to say anything. Her anger was written all over her face, in the way her brows furrowed, the way her mouth set in a thin line, as if she was holding back from lashing out. And beneath that anger, there was something else-fear. She was terrified of what would happen next.

She wanted me to think practically, to pull myself back from the edge, but I could see it in her expression as the realization hit. She saw it-the fear, the recklessness, the stubborn determination brewing inside me.

And I didn't care.

This was the first time in my life I was doing something for me. Not for duty, not for others, but for my own happiness. I'd spent so long being afraid, holding back, hiding from what I wanted, but now-I was done with that. I deserved to be happy too. For once, I wasn't thinking about consequences or risks. I was thinking about what I needed. And I needed him. It's crazy, it's wrong, it's disastrous but I need Adrain in my life.

I tore through my grandmother's things, yanking open a dusty old chest in the corner of the room. Inside were remnants of her life-old photographs, journals, and charms. Somewhere in here had to be a clue, a hint of the magic she once wielded.

My hands shook as I rifled through the contents, but my heart burned with fierce determination. I was going to find a way to keep Adrian here, no matter what it took. The universe could throw every warning, every disaster at me, and it wouldn't matter. I was ready to fight for this. For him. For us.

I deserved this happiness. I wouldn't let anyone, not even fate, take it away from me.

The search grew desperate, my hands no longer just sifting through my grandma's belongings but violently tossing them aside. Papers, trinkets, and books hit the floor with a dull thud. My frustration bubbled up until I was throwing things across the room. A pile of clothes flew onto the bed, and an old vase shattered against the wall, but I barely noticed.

With each useless item I uncovered, the fury within me grew. My jaw clenched so hard it ached, my fingers curling into fists as my breaths came in ragged gasps. A table clock, a small, harmless thing, sat mocking me on the bedside table. Without thinking, I grabbed it and hurled it against the wall. It smashed into pieces, the sound sharp and unforgiving, but even that wasn't enough to ease the ache inside.

My heart pounded, my body trembling under the weight of endless disappointments. Every time I thought I was getting close, the universe seemed to slam a door in my face.

I could feel the tears welling up, blurring my vision. Taking in a shaky breath, I tried to calm myself, but it only made the emotions worse.

"Nana," I whispered, my voice breaking as I squeezed my eyes shut, letting the tears slip free. "Please, show me something. I need you. Please lead me."

The silence that followed was deafening, only the sound of my uneven breathing filling the room. For a moment, I felt completely alone, as if the universe had turned its back on me. But then, a flicker, a whisper in the back of my mind.

*"We have a secret chest in our home?"*

I snapped my eyes open as a distant memory about a chest hidden somewhere in the house flashed before my eyes.

I tried to grab hold of it, tried to pull the memory into focus, but it was distant, slipping through my fingers like sand. I closed my eyes, pushing my mind as hard as I could, willing the memory to return. I could almost hear her, almost see her face, but the details were hazy, scattered fragments of a moment long forgotten.

"Come on," I muttered to myself, my fists clenching as I tried to piece it together. "Come on, Liza, remember."

But it wouldn't come. The memory, the key to something, hovered just out of reach, taunting me. I forced myself to breathe, to calm the storm inside. Maybe if I gave myself a moment, if I stopped pushing, the fragments of the past would reveal themselves.

The room went quiet. The only sound was my shallow breathing as I stood there in the wreckage, waiting. And then, like a thread being slowly unraveled, the memory began to piece itself together.

I was young-barely six-and I could see myself sitting at the kitchen table, my legs swinging in the air as I ate. The faint taste of something sweet lingered on my tongue as I spoke, my voice muffled by the food in my mouth.

"Legacy?" I had asked, curious but confused. My childlike innocence seeped through in my tone, unsure of what the word meant.

My grandmother's face softened with a smile, her hand gently brushing my hair back. She looked at me with that warm, knowing gaze she always had. "Yes, honey. Our legacy. Something that you will preserve, something very precious."

"What's a legacy, though?" I asked, squinting at her like I always did when I didn't understand.

Her smile deepened, and she leaned down to my level, placing her hands on my tiny shoulders. "It's one asset, Liza. Something so valuable, that it's passed down from generation to generation. And one day, you'll keep it safe. And when the time comes, you'll pass it on to those after you."

A legacy. Something passed down. Something I had to protect. It must be the tome.

I tried to remember more, desperately grasping at the fleeting fragments of that long-ago conversation.

"Where is it, then? The thing I'm meant to protect and pass on?" I had asked, my voice a blend of curiosity and urgency.

She chuckled softly, a warm, melodic sound that seemed to wrap around me. "Well, it's exactly where it's meant to be-hidden away. So well hidden that you keep it safe without even knowing where it is."

*"Nana!" I whined dramatically, frustration creeping into my voice as I pouted. "Please, tell me where it is. Just show me!"*

*Her gaze softened, filled with love and a hint of mischief as she picked me up in her arms. "Alright, but you must promise me something. Never speak of this to anyone, and you can never, ever step inside that room again. Do you promise?"*

*With wide eyes and a beaming smile, I nodded vigorously. "I promise."*

The chest.

I snapped my eyes open, adrenaline surging through my veins as I remembered everything in fresh pieces. Without a second thought, I bolted out of the bedroom, almost stumbling in my frantic haste, propelled by the instinct that the key to everything I was searching for lay hidden in that secret place my grandmother had guarded for so long.

As I entered the room, the weight of yesterday's fruitless search still hung heavy in the air. But this time was different. I was driven and determined. I didn't hesitate as I made my way to the far corner, the exact spot where my grandmother had once taken me, years ago.

The room was old, untouched for what seemed like decades. Cobwebs clung to the corners like veils of a forgotten time, and the layer of dust that coated the floor kicked up with every step I took, swirling in the dim light like ghosts of the past. The scent of age and mildew filled my lungs, making me cough, but I pushed through the discomfort. I couldn't stop now, not when I was this close.

My hands trembled slightly as I knelt and began to pull away the heavy, moth-eaten carpet that had concealed the floor for so long. My fingers fumbled at the edges, but eventually, I peeled it back, revealing the floor beneath it-except it wasn't just a floor. My pulse quickened as the wooden boards gave way to something else-an old, weathered trapdoor, almost hidden in the shadows.

My breath caught in my throat as the memory came flooding back, the memory when my nana told me that it was down there but refused to take me there, telling me about a monster. A lie.

I ran my fingers along the edge of the door, feeling the rough texture of the wood beneath my skin. My heart pounded harder, the rhythm matching the intensity of the moment. I could hear it thudding in my ears, a frantic beat that only seemed to grow louder with each passing second. I forced myself to breathe, to steady my hands as I pried open the door with a creak that echoed ominously through the room.

Beneath, there was nothing but an abyss-darkness so thick it seemed to swallow the dim light filtering through the windows. A chill crept down my spine as I peered into the blackness. It wasn't just dark-it felt wrong, like the space itself had been forgotten by time, left untouched for so long that it now existed in some strange limbo, trapped between then and now.

I gulped hard, a nervous tremor passing through me as I scanned the room for something, anything that could shed light on the void below. A torch would be ideal, but I couldn't find one among the clutter of old furniture and discarded belongings that filled the room. Panic threatened to rise in my chest as I fumbled for an alternative.

Then it hit me. My phone.

I rushed out of the room, my steps quick and uneven as I bounded up the stairs two at a time, the urgency coursing through my veins. The house seemed unnaturally quiet as I grabbed my phone from the table, the cool screen lighting up in my hand. Back downstairs, I retraced my steps, my breath shaky but resolute. The room loomed ahead, darker now, more foreboding than before. The trapdoor yawned open, a gaping void that seemed to pull at me, daring me to descend into the unknown.

With a flick of my thumb, I turned on the phone's flashlight, the beam slicing through the thick blanket of darkness as I pointed it into the basement below. The light barely penetrated the blackness at first, as if the shadows resisted it, but slowly, inch by inch, the details began to emerge. Dust particles floated lazily in the beam, and the faint outlines of stairs leading down into the unknown came into view.

*Should I call Rachel and Adrian?*

I swallowed the lump in my throat and, with my heart hammering against my ribs, I descended into the basement.

*It's alright. I can do this alone. I'm not afraid of darkness.*

The temperature dropped instantly as I went lower, the air growing colder and denser, as though I were stepping into a place untouched by warmth, untouched by life. The faint scent of damp stone and earth filled my nostrils, the silence oppressive, broken only by the creak of the old wooden steps beneath my weight.

With each step, the beam of light revealed more of the space, the room much larger than I had anticipated. The stone walls were rough and uneven, carved by hand long ago, now slick with moisture, and draped in the same thick webs that covered the room above. There was something ancient about this place, something that felt far older than my grandmother, far older than even the house itself.

I've never been afraid of darkness, but here, I am. My mind is screaming at me to turn around, to stop, to leave before I uncover something I can't handle. But I can't stop. Something unexplainable pulls me forward, drawing me closer to whatever secret my grandmother hid here. I'm so close. Too close to turning back now. But it's not just the tome I feel waiting for me in the shadows—it's something more. Something beyond my imagination.

The light flickered, and my heart skipped a beat. For a split second, the thought of being trapped down here, alone in the pitch-black void, sent a wave of cold terror washing over me. But then, the light steadied, and I let out a breath I hadn't realized I was holding.

I looked up and ahead of me, something caught the light-something metallic, gleaming faintly through the dust. I stepped closer, my pulse quickening again. There, half-buried beneath the rubble, was a chest. An old, ornate chest, the wood darkened with age, its metal clasps rusted but still intact.

This was it. The secret my grandmother had hidden from me. The legacy she had kept safe all these years. This must be it.

With trembling hands, I reached for the chest, my fingers brushing against the cold metal. The weight of what lay inside pressed down on me, and for a moment, I hesitated, the enormity of it all crashing down around me.

Then, with a deep breath, I cast the spell I had learned. The chest lifted in the air and I smiled. I took it upstairs and placed it on the table, not before pushing everything down.

I brushed the dust off it, coughing, and unlatched the chest, lifting the lid. A huge grin spread across my lips as the light from my phone caught something in the chest. There, nestled among dust-covered objects and forgotten relics, lay ancient grimoires, arcane texts, and at the centre of it all, the *tome*.

My hands trembled as I reached out, brushing off the layers of dust that clung to the worn leather cover. I found it. I found the legacy. But my grin faded as soon as my eyes landed on the text engraved on the tome's cover.

"Flame's Dominion."

The words were etched in a fiery orange, glowing faintly against the deep red leather.

I frowned, trying to find where I'd seen or heard the name. It felt like something important, just on the edge of my memory, teasing me. Picking the tome back up, my fingers brushed against something tucked between the pages-a thin, old sheet of paper. I carefully pulled it out and unfolded it, revealing a list scrawled in faded ink.

The list was meticulous. It contained the names of tomes, the covens responsible for protecting them, and the characters who lived within those pages, along with their powers.

A wave of admiration washed over me. "Wow, Nana," I murmured, a bittersweet smile pulling at my lips. "Looks like you were organized and knew everything... probably even how to send him back."

I turned my attention back to the list, scanning the names. The first tome was Flame's Dominion. The very one my grandma had kept hidden all these years. The character listed beneath it was Atlas Dupont, a fire wielder.

I paused, reading it again.

"Fire?" I repeated, frowning. I looked at the tome, then back at the list. But Adrian is the fire wielder. My grandma was very clear when she said that each character held unique powers tied to their book. Then, how come two men possessed the same power?

To clear the confusion, I continued reading, my eyes moving swiftly down the list until I reached the last name.

Arcane Flame. The book I found. Adrian's book.

I looked for his powers and my eyes widened when I saw the name of the character who lived within the pages of this tome.

*Zephyr Valtor.*

My breath caught in my throat. The name echoed in my mind, each syllable dripping with the weight of dread. The paper and tome slipped from my trembling hands, hitting the floor with a muted thud, but I barely registered the sound. My heart pounded, my chest tightening as panic took root.

Zephyr Valtor.

I staggered back, the truth crashing into me with suffocating force. He's Zephyr. He's been Zephyr all along.

# Chapter 42

# The revelation

### Rachel's POV

I watched the old Zephyr among the children, his once-dreaded presence now a source of pure happiness. The kids adored him—especially the little girl, who seemed to claim the biggest part of his heart. Their laughter floated through the air, light and carefree, wrapping around me like a warm breeze. It was surreal. Zephyr, the monster we all feared, was crouched down, letting the children braid his silver-streaked hair, putting flowers in his hair, his rough hands cradling the girl with a gentleness that felt unnatural for a being like him.

For a moment, I let myself smile, caught up in the simplicity of it all. This wasn't the cruel, calculating creature I knew. This was someone else—someone softer, someone... human. It didn't fit the image I'd burned into my mind.

The little girl chuckled, her laughter ringing like delicate chimes in the air. "You look like a garden fairy princess," she teased, a playful glint in her eye as she watched the other kids giggle.

Zephyr raised his brows in mock disbelief, a smile tugging at the corners of his lips. "A princess? Because I'm wearing flowers? How rude!" The girl's laughter only grew louder as she continued to decorate his hair with blossoms, each petal a gentle reminder of innocence and joy.

In that moment, the love he held for the little girl was as clear as day, brightening his usually brooding features. It softened the hard lines of his face, revealing a warmth that was unbelievable to witness.

But when I turned my gaze toward the present-day Zephyr, bracing myself for his usual smirk—the familiar mockery that had become a permanent shadow in his expression—I was met with something altogether different.

Pain.

Raw and unfiltered, it lay heavy in his eyes, threatening to pull me under like a whirlpool. It made me hesitate—just for a second.

"What happened?" I asked, my voice came out softer than I intended like a whisper carried on a breeze.

He met my gaze, and for the first time, there was no mask, no walls between us. He exhaled, the sound heavy with exhaustion and something else I couldn't quite place.

"He's coming for a civil talk," Zephyr murmured. His words were cryptic, but before I could ask what he meant, I felt a presence sweep past me like a gust of wind.

Archon.

The old Zephyr—the one playing with the children—noticed him immediately. He set the little girl down gently, his hands lingering as if reluctant to let go. Straightening, he turned to face Archon with an expression I couldn't read.

"Good afternoon," Zephyr said politely, "How may I help you?"

Archon gave him a small, measured smile, but there was no warmth in it. "You've gotten along with my people better than I expected."

The smile Zephyr returned was different—forced, thin, and hollow. It wasn't the kind of smile he gave to the children. No, this one was sharp-edged, a shadow of the genuine joy I'd just witnessed moments ago.

"We need to talk," Archon said curtly, his tone carefully neutral, though I could sense the displeasure simmering beneath the surface. He motioned for Zephyr to follow, stepping away from the children to ensure their conversation wouldn't be overheard.

"Speak plainly," Zephyr said, crossing his arms. "I don't like people who beat around the bushes."

Archon's gaze hardened. "Very well. The spell that brings fictional beings into reality has a rule: every character must return to their realm once their task is complete. Failure to do so will disrupt the balance between both worlds—potentially causing both to collapse."

Zephyr didn't flinch. He nodded as if he'd already known this. "I'll speak plainly, too. Find a way for me to stay here. *Permanently*."

Archon's composure cracked, his expression shifting from cold indifference to disbelief. "What?"

"You heard me," Zephyr said, voice steady, almost casual. "I want to remain in this world. I've made my decision."

Archon's jaw clenched, his face pale. "That's impossible. No such spell exists."

A dark chuckle rumbled in Zephyr's chest. "And yet here I stand—a fictional being, living and breathing in your reality. Bringing tales to life was supposed to be impossible too, wasn't it?" He stepped closer, his presence suffocating. "If there isn't a spell to keep me here, then create one."

Archon's eyes narrowed, his fists tightening at his sides. "Do you even understand what you're asking? It's not just about you. The consequences—"

Zephyr cut him off with a dismissive wave. "Ah, the consequences. I know how terribly it could go down if... You won't find a way to keep me here permanently. Because there's no way I'm going back."

I swallowed hard and asked, "So... you really did get obsessed with reality?"

Zephyr's gaze flicked to me, and for a fleeting moment, something softer crossed his features—a flicker of vulnerability buried beneath all the bravado.

"It's not just obsession," he muttered, almost as if he were admitting it to himself. "It's freedom."

Archon's expression darkened further, his patience wearing thin. "This world isn't yours. If it's anything, it's a prison—one that will collapse if you stay too long."

Zephyr's grin faded, and the weight of his resolve settled in the space between us. "Maybe." He shrugged, the motion lazy, but there was steel in his voice. "But it's a prison I choose. And I'm not leaving."

Archon clenched his fists, his control slipping for a moment. "You're asking for the impossible."

Zephyr's gaze darkened, and a dangerous edge crept into his voice. "Then make the impossible happen. Because Zephyr Valtor isn't going back. Not anymore."

The air between them crackled with tension, heavy and suffocating, but I didn't flinch. Zephyr wasn't just fighting for his life—he was fighting for his right to exist on his own terms. And I couldn't help but admire the sheer audacity of it. My entire viewpoint on him has changed. I can understand him now.

This wasn't about obsession or power anymore.

This was about freedom—his freedom.

"Zephyr—" Archon tried to argue, his voice edged with frustration, but Zephyr dismissed him with a flick of his wrist, the gesture casual yet commanding. He returned his focus to the little girl and scooped her up into his arms, whirling her around. Her laughter pierced through the tension like sunlight breaking through clouds.

I smiled but then my surroundings disintegrated into dust once again, drawing me into another fragment of his memory.

It was a ritual site, ancient and foreboding, cloaked in smoke that slithered along the ground like restless spirits. Two towering pillars stood at the far edges, their tops engulfed in flame, crackling and spitting embers into the murky air. Strange symbols, carved deep into the stone pillars, pulsed with a faint, ominous glow. Beneath them lay a circle of jagged black rocks, arranged in a pattern that radiated power—dark, unnatural, and tainted. The ground was charred, the earth scorched as though something monstrous had crawled from its depths.

I could smell the burnt offerings—ash, copper, and something far more sinister, a metallic stench that made my stomach turn. The air was heavy, oppressive, and pressing against my lungs as if the very place resented my presence.

My chest tightened, panic squeezing my throat shut. "Where are we? What's this?" I whispered, afraid that raising my voice might awaken whatever evil lingered here.

Zephyr stood beside me, cold and still. His face was devoid of emotion as if he'd already made peace with the horrors of this memory. There was no sorrow, no rage—just a void. I stared at him, searching for some fragment of the man I thought I knew, but his gaze was locked ahead, distant, like he was bracing himself for what was to come.

The smoke began to lift, dissipating slowly, and as it thinned, I saw a shadow emerge from the haze. A figure took form, and my breath caught in my throat.

Zephyr.

Not the Zephyr who stood beside me now, but the one from the past. His back was to me, broad shoulders slumped as if the weight of the world had crushed him.

I walked closer to him. Each step felt like dragging my body through water, as if some unseen force wanted to hold me back, warning me not to see what lay ahead. But I kept moving, drawn by something I couldn't explain.

And then, I saw him clearly.

Zephyr was kneeling in a pool of blood, the scarlet liquid lapping against his waist. His hands—so strong, so capable— held something small and fragile against his chest.

My heart stopped. It was a child in his arms. I gasped, the air catching painfully in my lungs as the scene struck me like a hammer. The coppery scent of blood filled my nose, sharp and nauseating. I couldn't tear my eyes away from the scene, no matter how much I wanted to.

Her lifeless body rested limply in his arms, cradled with an almost unbearable tenderness. Her small face—so serene, so heartbreakingly innocent—was pressed against his chest. Blood stained her tiny dress, pooling around them in waves of crimson, thick and endless.

The girl he held close was the same girl he had stayed for. The child whose laughter once softened his sharp edges, the girl he had cherished the most.

Earlier she was giggling and laughing and now she lay in his arms silent and lifeless.

The worst part was that there were more children—twelve in total—their small bodies scattered around the pool like discarded dolls, their faces pale and lifeless, their eyes closed forever.

Zephyr clutched the girl tighter, rocking her gently as if the simple motion could somehow undo the horrors that had unfolded. His tears fell silently, mingling with the blood beneath him. Not a sob escaped him—only the silent grief of a man broken beyond repair.

A sharp pang tore through me, and I turned to look at the Zephyr standing beside me now.

Tears glistened in his eyes, but his expression was rigid, his jaw clenched tightly. He stared at his past self with an agonizing stillness, as if frozen in time. His hands twitched at his sides, fists curling and uncurling as if the weight of his guilt were too much to bear.

I forced myself to speak, though my voice came out cracked and unsteady. "Did... Did Archon—?"

Zephyr didn't meet my gaze. His eyes remained fixed on the past, on the broken man cradling the child in the pool of blood.

"A ritual," he whispered, his voice raw with old sorrow. "A ritual for power. It required the sacrifice of twelve children."

I stared at him, the weight of his words suffocating. "He... He killed them... for power?" Disbelief was clear in my tone.

Zephyr gave a bitter, broken laugh, but there was no humor in it—only rage and despair. "For mere power," he said, his voice trembling with fury and grief. "He slaughtered those innocent children... for something as empty as strength."

The silence that followed was unbearable, heavier than anything I had ever known.

I couldn't move. I couldn't breathe. The weight of the scene, of Zephyr's past, pressed down on me like a crushing tide, threatening to pull me under. Every story I had ever heard, every tale whispered over generations, shattered into fragments around me. We had been told the wrong story.

A lie.

Archon—the name that we revered, the legend we believed in, the savior we worshiped—was none of those things. He wasn't a god. He was a monster. A cruel, twisted creature who had stolen not only the lives of innocent children but also the truth from the world. The weight of that realization crushed me, leaving me gasping for breath.

My gaze drifted back to Zephyr. The man everyone had warned me about. The villain in every tale. The monster I was supposed to hate.

But now, standing here, with his past laid bare before me, I saw him for what he truly was.

Not a villain. Not a monster.

A broken man.

A man who had carried the unbearable burden of grief and guilt for far too long. A man whose heart, though shattered, still beat beneath the weight of that sorrow.

A man with a soul.

Zephyr wasn't the merciless figure the stories made him out to be—he was a man who could love. And he did love someone, adorned her. But he lost her.

He stood still now, his shoulders stiff with the weight of the memory, as though carrying it for so long had fused it with his very being. His gaze was distant, locked on his younger self kneeling in that pool of blood.

A tear slipped down my cheek, though I barely noticed. I couldn't imagine the agony of holding that child in his arms, knowing she was gone, knowing that her death—and the deaths of eleven others—had been for nothing more than power. All because he was more powerful.

And for the first time, I understood.

"You're not the villain," I whispered, more to myself than to him. "You never were."

"You're wrong," Zephyr said, his voice low but laced with an edge sharp enough to cut. "I wasn't the villain for those who suffered..." His eyes shifted over my shoulder, and I felt the hair on the back of my neck stand on end. "I was the villain but for those who caused those innocent people to suffer." Slowly, I turned to see what he was looking at.

And then I saw him—the Zephyr of the past—rising from the pool of blood, the children now laid around the corner of the pond.

His clothes clung to him, drenched in crimson, the sticky liquid trailing down his arms and dripping from his fingertips. His expression was hollow, his eyes lit with the same burning green fire, but this version of him was colder, more dangerous. A storm in human form. Flames danced on his fingers like restless spirits, flickering with barely contained fury.

I felt my breath catch in my throat.

"The calamity will start from here, Rachel," He murmured, snapping my attention on him, his voice hauntingly calm, like the final breath before an explosion. "The story you've heard about my cruelty wasn't fake."

His words carried a heavy, undeniable truth. I could feel it—the weight of the devastation that was about to unfold.

"The people who were involved in this will die—die in the cruelest way possible!"

Rage, an electrifying force that coursed through my veins like wildfire. This was the first time I stood beside Zephyr, not as someone who loathed him but as a fierce supporter, reveling in the chaos he unleashed as he slaughtered those before us without an ounce of mercy.

Archon had built his own army-a twisted legion of dark sorcerers, each one believing themselves invincible. I couldn't fathom how they were all so ready to die at Zephyr's hands. But there was no reprieve for them. He showed no hesitation, no flicker of remorse as he dispatched them one by one, each death more brutal than the last.

He was a force of nature, burning in the flames of revenge, grief, and wrath that had been stoked to a raging inferno. The most astonishing part of this fight was that Zephyr wasn't relying on magic; he was dismantling these dark sorcerers with his bare hands. He snapped necks like twigs, plucked hearts from chests with the casual ease of a child picking fruit, and shattered bones as if they were mere glass. They were nothing more than obstacles to his fury.

A man lunged at him, his fists crackling with dark energy. But Zephyr was faster, seizing the man by the throat with an iron grip. The sorcerer struggled, his eyes wide with terror as Zephyr leaned in, his voice a low growl, "Where is that bastard?" He asked, but the man didn't respond. In a heartbeat, Zephyr unleashed a torrent of fire, engulfing the man in flames. The scream that erupted was a visceral sound of desperation, a haunting melody of anguish that echoed across the battlefield. The flames consumed him, burning flesh and hair until he was nothing but ash, swirling away in the wind.

I watched, captivated, as Zephyr released his hold, the remnants of the sorcerer drifting away like forgotten memories. He turned to the next enemy, a sorcerer paralyzed by fear, standing frozen in shock.

Zephyr took a step forward towards him. The terrified sorcerer raised his hands to cast a spell, but it was too late. Zephyr was upon him, faster than the eye could see. He grabbed the man's arm, twisting it until the sickening sound of breaking bone filled the air. The sorcerer howled in pain, but Zephyr didn't stop there. With a swift, brutal motion, he drove his fist into the sorcerer's chest, his fingers plunging deep into the flesh. I could see the terror in the sorcerer's eyes as Zephyr's grip tightened, plucking his heart out as easily as one would pull a weed from the ground.

The man fell to his knees, blood pouring from his gaping wound, shock painted across his face as he sputtered and died. Zephyr looked down at him, a chilling calmness in his expression before he turned the heart to ash with a flick of his wrist. The body slumped to the ground, lifeless and defeated.

As the relentless army advanced, Zephyr spread his hands, unleashing a torrent of green lightning that arced from his body like vengeful serpents. The crackling energy engulfed his foes in a blinding flash, turning them to ash in an instant, their screams swallowed by the chaos.

Then, suddenly, a shimmering rope shot through the air, ensnaring Zephyr's neck with a cruel jerk that yanked him backward. He hit the ground strongly. I jumped and followed the glowing line to its source, where Archon stood, a stark contrast to the man I saw earlier. Clad in black, his eyes burned a sinister red, and a wicked, grotesque smile twisted his features.

I looked at the present-day Zephyr and found him watching the scene without an ounce of emotion in his eyes. He knew what's gonna happen next and he was replaying it all to show me. I looked back and flinched in horror as Archon twisted the rope, forcing Zephyr into a brutal collision with a gnarled tree. The sickening thud echoed in the charged air, and my heart raced. Yet, beneath the weight of grief, Zephyr's fury surged. The very fabric of his being pulsed with vengeance, amplifying his power.

In one swift motion, Zephyr seized the rope, but Archon stood firm, a dark glint in his eyes as he prepared for the inevitable clash. With a surge of raw power, Zephyr redirected the energy of the rope, throwing Archon off balance and sending him sprawling into the underbrush. Without wasting a second, Zephyr lunged, his grip tightening around Archon's throat. The air crackled with electricity, waves of light swirling around them like a tempest. With a brutal punch to Archon's gut, Zephyr sent him flying back into the tree, which splintered and exploded from the impact, sending debris cascading like shrapnel through the air.

As Zephyr approached, every step resonated with deadly intent. He grabbed Archon by his hair, lifting him effortlessly from the ground, and plunged his hand deep into Archon's chest. Archon's eyes widened in terror, a choked gasp escaping his lips as flames ignited at his feet, creeping up his body and devouring him slowly.

"Four. She was just four!" He seethed, the flames getting stronger as they ate Archon hungrily, "They were only children, you bastard!"

"You can't kill me!" Archon spat, blood oozing from his mouth as he writhed in agony, the flames licking hungrily at his skin. "If you do, the worlds will collapse!"

The weight of those words hung heavy in the air, and Zephyr hesitated, withdrawing his hand. Archon crumpled to the ground, gasping for breath, a pained expression etched across his features. But Zephyr's loathing was palpable as he healed Archon just enough to keep him alive, a cruel flicker of mercy in his dark eyes.

"I have created the spell. To keep you here. To save our worlds."

Zephyr clenched his jaw and lifted him by his throat, "You think you can fool me?" He growled, his grip tightening around Archon's throat.

"You have to trust me," Archon pleaded, desperation flooding his voice. "If you let me live, I can perform the ritual to-" He paused as a wicked grin crept across Archon's face, a sense of dread washed over me.

Zephyr's eyes narrowed, and in a flash, he turned, just in time to intercept a dagger aimed at his back. He caught it in his hand, the blade slicing through flesh, blood spilling onto the ground, but healing as quickly as it flowed.

Archon seized the moment, summoning a dark incantation that ignited a circle of ash around him. Zephyr's jaw clenched in defiance, glaring at Archon.

Archon laughed, blood dripping from his mouth and unhealed wounds as he watched Zephyr fade into a bright blue glow with wickedness but that laugh died when the ground split open and massive roots snaked upward, ensnaring Archon, trapping him in a painful embrace.

I smiled with utter satisfaction as Archon fell to his knees, struggling against the binding tendrils.

"No!!" He screamed, struggling against the roots.

A smirk played on Zephyr's lips as he witnessed Archon's plight. The once-mighty sorcerer clawed at the earth, howling in desperation, summoning spells that fizzled against the roots. With a final, desperate scream, Archon was swallowed by the ground, the last remnants of his power dissipating into the earth, while Zephyr's essence flickered like a dying flame, retreating into the tome that lay among the trees.

I gasped as I was plunged back into the present, my heart hammering in my chest, shock, and revelation intertwining like vines around my throat.

There was utter silence between us.

"Now tell me, Rachel," he said, his voice dripping coldness, "Who's truly evil?"

I stared at him without blinking. The revelation was too much to handle. All of it. We've been misguided and given the wrong information. Whatever we know about the past is not true.

I took a step forward to Zephyr and asked, "Can I hug you?" My voice is as soft as the breeze. He froze. His eyes fluttered slightly as shock enveloped his form. I raised my eyebrows, waiting for his approval. He, very slowly, gave me a curt nod. I didn't waste a second and engulfed him in a warm hug, "I'm sorry for everything, Zephyr."

"It's alright," He said, I felt him smiling, awkwardly, "I nearly killed you. I deserve it."

I pulled away, "Yes, you did. And you're not evil. But you're a fool!" He stayed mute, "Why didn't you tell me all this before? Why keep it from us? And why subjecting me to the torment when you could have simply told me the truth?" My voice turned rude as frustration bubbled over. He could have nicely done this rather than choosing the bad way, "We've been worshiping a monster-all of us. I can't believe this!" I stammered, my mind spinning. "We were lied to. Manipulated. And we-" I let out a shaky breath. "We're fools. Fools!"

Zephyr's lips curled into a smile-sharp, cruel, and mocking. His expression was that of a predator savoring its prey's misery. "Fool, you say?" His voice was low and sinister, dragging each word out slowly. "If you think this is bad, wait until you hear what I say next."

I froze, my chest tightening as the air seemed to thicken around us.

"That bastard," he whispered, pausing to savour the tension. "He's alive."

The world tilted beneath me. I stared at him, wide-eyed, a chill creeping down my spine. "What?"

"Alive," Zephyr repeated, his gaze unwavering. "Zach told me. He's the one behind the tomes. Every theft. Every death. It's him. He's after the power they hold-all of it."

I shook my head slowly, as if denying the words could make them untrue. "Oh my God," My voice was barely a whisper. I clutched my arms tightly as if that would somehow keep my mind from unravelling. No one could make me turn against Zephyr now, not after everything. I had already crossed that line.

"But-" I hesitated, feeling the weight of the impossible. "You killed him."

"I buried him ali- he paused as his expression shifted as if he was hurt.

"What happened?" I asked, concerned.

He shook his head, bracing himself, "Nothing. I was saying I buried him alive but there's a possibility that he escaped. He's been alive for over centuries-he paused again and winced as he dropped to his knees. A deep frown etched between his eyebrows.

"Zephyr," I called him, rushing forward. My heart pounded harder, panic rising as I knelt beside him. "What's happening? Are you okay?"

He didn't respond, his gaze fixed on something on the floor. Then I saw a glowing white circle etched beneath him, shimmering faintly at first, but growing brighter with each second.

My heart stopped. "Oh, my God," I whispered, dread pooling in the pit of my stomach. "What... what is that?"

The circle pulsed ominously, like the slow, rhythmic beat of a heart. I reached out, desperate to touch it, to understand what was happening, but the moment my hand neared the edge, the light flared violently. A sharp hum filled the air, vibrating through my bones, forcing me to jerk my hand back.

"Zephyr..." My voice wavered as I looked at him, his fingers. They were dissolving, fading into the air like smoke caught in a breeze.

His gaze locked onto his hand, eyes wide with disbelief and something dangerously close to fear. "It's Liza," he said hoarsely, his throat working painfully. "She's... she's sending me back," My heart nearly stopped.

"What?"

# Chapter 43

# The Final Chapter

*Liza's POV*

A sob escaped my lips as I hugged my knees tighter against my chest, trying to hold myself together as the weight of it all crashed over me, dragging me under like a tidal wave. The betrayal struck like a knife plunged deep into my chest, twisting with each memory that surfaced- his laughter, his touch, the way his voice softened when he said my name. All of it, every moment, every glance, every word, every touch has been a lie. A facade crafted to trap me. To *use* me. The truth coiled tight in my chest like a viper, hissing with venom. It whispered that I was a fool for trusting him, for opening myself up, for hoping. He was never Adrian. He was never the man I thought I knew. The man who kissed my scars, who made me feel alive, who looked at me like I was his salvation. He wasn't mine to love. He was Zephyr all along-a villain wrapped in charm and promises, weaving fantasies only to shatter them.

Another sob tore from my throat, raw and uncontrollable, the sound of my soul unraveling. I clawed at my chest, my nails digging into my skin, I was desperate to pull the pain out, but it was everywhere- inside me, wrapped around me, suffocating me. I couldn't breathe. I felt like I was drowning in the very air I breathed.

How could he do this? How could he look into my eyes, touch me, whisper those words, and feel nothing? How could he make me believe that there was something real between us?

I closed my eyes and let the tears fall inconsolably, curling tighter into myself as if I could disappear into the darkness.

I should have seen it coming. I should have known. But I didn't, and now I was paying the price- my heart is shattered, my soul is hollowed out by the lies I let myself believe.

"No," I shook my head, voice cracking under the weight of my grief, "No, I won't let him win. I won't let him destroy me," I wiped at my face furiously, smearing tears across my skin as they kept falling faster than I could clear them. My heart was hurting, terribly, and all I wanted was to get rid of it but I couldn't. But I could, at least, save the world and people from him. From a monster like him.

I looked at the chest and reached for it. My fingers trembled as I grabbed it, searching for anything-something, anything that could fix this, that could make it right.

And then I found it—the spell. Though the language was foreign to me, its power was unmistakable. I couldn't fully decipher the intricacies, but the symbols etched across the parchment spoke volumes.

Everything I'd learned, every moment of training and practice, had prepared me for this. The unique markings, the subtle curves of the runes, and the arrangement of the glyphs left no doubt in my mind. This was it—the spell that could change everything.

I picked it in my hands. The parchment felt fragile in my hands, like my heart, brittle, ready to break. This was it. This was how I would send him back to the realm he belonged to, back to the world of fiction where he could no longer hurt me or anyone else.

I stared at the paper, his image burned into my mind-those piercing green eyes, the way they seemed to see right through me, the way they looked at me like I was his entire world. A fresh wave of tears spilled down my cheeks, unstoppable. My heart burnt as if put in flames.

He only wanted a way to stay. And I was stupid enough to give it to him. I almost did.

I let out another cry, violent and relentless, and I sank to the floor, clutching the spell to my chest as if it could stop my heart from breaking apart. My eyes burned, my heart burned, my very soul burned and everything around me seemed to eat at me, tearing me apart.

*Why did it have to feel so real?*

*Why did it have to hurt this much?*

I wiped my tears once again and dragged myself to my feet, my legs shaking beneath me as I stumbled toward the door. I have to get to Rachel. I have to tell her about his lies. I have to protect her. I couldn't let him stay in this world. Not after knowing everything. No. I tightened my grip around the spell and ran-ran as if ghosts were running behind me.

The mansion felt haunted, every room filled with his presence, every shadow shaped like his memory. The scent of him still lingered in the air, pulling me deeper into a whirlpool of grief and pain. I couldn't move without stumbling into reminders of him. I passed the chair where he'd lounged, his smile lazy and wicked. The hallway where he kissed me, his hands gentle as they held my face. The fireplace where we sat in silence, finding comfort in each other's presence.

Lies. All of it.

I stopped, my breath hitching as the memories stabbed deeper, twisting the knife inside me. My knees buckled, and I fell to the ground with a broken gasp, the spell slipping from my fingers.

"Why?" I whispered into the silence, my voice barely audible, "Why did you do this to me?" The tears didn't stop, and I let them fall, unable to stop the flood. It hurts so much.

The walls seemed to close in, suffocating me with the weight of everything unsaid. I had given him everything-my heart, my trust, my soul. And he had ripped it all away, leaving me hollow and bleeding.

But I couldn't stop now. I wouldn't. He has to go.

With determination, I scooped the spell off the ground, clutching it like a lifeline. The tears might keep falling, and my heart might never stop hurting, but I would not let him destroy me. I would not let him win. I would not let him stay here, not when everything is bare in front of me.

His cruelty, his wickedness, his facade. I would send him back. Even if it killed me.

I ran through the corridors, desperation clawing at my throat until I finally found her-but she wasn't alone. My heart dropped, eyes widening as I took in the sight before me: Rachel stood frozen like a statue, and Adrian loomed in front of her, gripping her hands. Their eyes glowed with an unsettling, bright white light, an unnatural aura that sent chills down my spine.

"Rachel!" I shouted, rushing towards them, but as I reached out to touch her, she remained rigid, unresponsive, as if trapped in a spell. My gaze snapped to Adrian, and a wave of despair crashed over me, tightening my chest. Tears streamed down my face, hot and bitter.

"What are you doing to her?" I croaked, my voice cracking under the weight of anguish. The words felt heavy, laden with accusation, "I won't let you do anything to her," Determination surged through me, fuelled by desperation and hatred.

I turned on my heel and sprinted back to the room where the spell ingredients lay, remnants of my training. I hurriedly grabbed Adrian's tome, my hands trembling as I set it on the ground. I chose the same room where I found the chest to perform the ritual. Following the incantation inscribed in the spell page I found, I circled the ash around Adrian and made a small cut on his palm, letting his blood spill onto his tome and within the confines of the circle. I couldn't bear to look at him; the sight alone twisted my insides.

Whatever magic he is casting on Rachel, I'm glad that he's unconscious too because I would not have been able to get his blood for the spell if was awake.

My heart twisted as I glanced at Rachel, her face was pale and her glowing eyes seemed like someone was ripping her soul away. "I will save you," I said and ran back to the room where I had prepared for the ritual.

The atmosphere grew frigid, wrapping around me like a shroud as I sat down before the tome, placed in the centre of a circle, surrounded with symbols and ritual ingredients.

I took a breath in and sliced my palm, allowing my blood to drip onto the tome. A tear slipped down my cheek, just as warm as the crimson in my palm, but the physical pain was nothing compared to the ache he had inflicted on my heart. I let out another breath to calm myself and opened the spell.

"Omni nequam, da potestatem ut redeat ficta quo pertinet." I started. The candles flickered as if there were air, their flames dancing in rhythm with the rising tension. "Omnibus impiis," I continued, my voice stronger now but still tinged with hurt, "Rogo te, ut mihi potestatem fictionem remittas quo conveniat!"

As the final words left my lips, the candles erupted into a vivid blue flame, illuminating the tome with a fierce intensity. The air grew thick and charged as a chaotic storm of magic was awakened that threatened to consume everything in its path. The room trembled as objects jerked violently; my heart raced, pounding like a drum against my ribcage. Windows rattled ominously, the glass threatening to shatter under the pressure. A voice inside me whispered doubts, warning me of the danger inherent in the ritual, but I couldn't stop now. I had to see this through.

I spoke the spell aloud, the wind whirling around like a hurricane, my hair danced around my face, my body almost crumbling against the force of this spell, but I stood rigid, determined.

The tome trembled before me, light exploding from its pages with blinding brilliance, forcing me to squint. I put my arm above my eyes shielding my eyes as the room descended into chaos. Objects spun wildly through the air, slamming against the walls. The windows groaned under the pressure, cracking as if the spell's power was trying to rip reality apart. The walls trembled, their foundations threatening to crumble under the sheer force I had unleashed. I felt it all, magic, raw and unrestrained, clawing at my skin as though it wanted to peel me apart.

And then, above the tome, a gust of bright air spiraled into form, swirling violently like a vortex. My heart almost stopped beating as I understood it was him... *Adrian*. He was going.

The journey that had begun with a mistake was now ending with grim determination. I never wanted to send him back. And yet, I was the one doing it now. The weight of my own choice crushed me, a betrayal of my heart's deepest desires.

I looked away, my vision blurring as tears threatened to spill again.

The glowing air roared, spiraling faster, tightening into a storm of blinding magic. Pages from the tome fluttered wildly before the air was sucked into it with terrifying speed, spinning into the book like a cyclone desperate to devour him whole. Then like a switch, it was over. Everything stopped, the vortex, the chaos, even the breath in my lungs. The light was gone, swallowed by the tome. Silence descended like a heavy, suffocating fog.

A lone tear dropped down my cheek as the realization hit me like a physical blow-a deep, soul-crushing agony. Adrian was gone. For good. He was... *Gone*.

I crumpled to the floor, hugging my legs to my chest as more tears spilled out of my eyes. The pain in my chest was unlike anything I'd ever known, a wound so deep it felt as if my heart had been ripped from me, leaving only a hollow void in its place. A torrent of emotions built in my throat, raw and uncontrollable, until I couldn't hold it back anymore. I threw my head back and screamed-loud, broken, my body shaking with the force of it. I had done what I had to do, but at what cost?

The door to my room burst open, slamming against the wall with a violent jolt. Rachel staggered in, her face pale with terror, eyes wide and wild. I looked up at her through tear-streaked eyes, my heart drowning so deeply in pain that even seeing her alive couldn't stir joy within me. It was a bittersweet relief, like gasping for breath under crushing waves.

"Oh my god, Liza, what have you done?" she said as she knelt beside me, her hands gripping my trembling shoulders.

"I did what had to be done. I sent him back," I looked into her eyes, barely able to speak between the sobs that continued to escape my mouth, "He wasn't Adrian. He was never Adrian. He was Zephyr-Zephyr all along."

Rachel's expression didn't shift, no shock, no disbelief. Just resignation.

"Oh, sweetheart," she said softly, "I knew he was Zephyr."

My heart stopped for a moment, cold confusion flooding me. I blinked at her, mouth agape, "You knew?" she nodded, her eyes softening, "Why didn't you tell me?"

Before she could explain, the tome lying in the centre of the ritual circle trembled violently, grabbing our attention. With a deafening whoosh, it flew into the air as if possessed, alongside the tome my grandmother had safeguarded for so long. The air shimmered with unseen power as both tomes floated, glowing with unnatural light. Rachel and I looked toward the door, the way where the tomes flew but we couldn't see anyone. We both stood up to our feet, heart pounding.

An eerie silence filled the room, thick and suffocating-until a voice sliced through it like the hiss of a blade, "Good evening," the voice alone sent a shiver down my spine. Itwas low and jagged, dripping with venom and amusement.

A man stepped into the light, cloaked in black, his aura steeped in malice. He moved like a shadow given life, his wicked smirk curling at the edges of his pale lips. His eyes gleamed with something far worse than hatred: *satisfaction*.

"Archon..." Rachel breathed, more to herself than anyone else. Her voice was brittle, disbelief cracking through it.

My heart dropped, eyes wide. Archon? The same Archon who had sacrificed himself centuries ago to banish Zephyr and protect our world? How can he be alive?

He laughed. His laugh was a low, twisted sound-like the creak of a coffin lid opening. But that laugh wasn't for Rachel. It was for me. His attention was on me, his eyes burning with something sinister.

"You made it so easy, Liza," He said. My skin prickled at the mention of my name from his mouth, "You trapped him back in the tome, gift-wrapped, just for me. You did all the hard work," His grin widened, "How thoughtful."

I gripped my palms tight, panic spreading like wildfire through my veins. Then, with a flick of his hand, he chanted a spell in ancient words. The wooden chest behind me erupted in flames, fire roaring to life with an insatiable hunger. The heat stung my skin, and I let out a terrified scream.

"No!"

Archon's eyes gleamed as he watched the blaze consume everything in it. "Now, nothing can stop me," he declared, his voice dark with triumph. "In this world, I will rise as a god. You will all worship me, bow to me, whether you want to or not."

I looked at Rachel but she stood frozen, her eyes wide with disbelief. *How had she recognized him so easily?* The question gnawed at me, but there was no time to ask.

Archon's gaze shifted back to me, and his smile darkened. "But I want no obstacles," he murmured, his tone almost bored, "Ensure you are reborn as something ordinary next time. Before I could react, he lifted his hand, and whispered "Mors animae," As the words left his mouth, black tendrils of magic snaked through the air, curling toward me.

Time slowed.

I gasped, bracing myself for the impact-certain this was the end. But just as the magic lunged toward me, Rachel shoved me aside with all her strength, causing me to hit the ground and the dark magic striking her like a death blow.

"No!" I screamed, my voice breaking as she hit the ground, eyes wide and vacant, her limbs limp and lifeless.

For a moment, the world seemed to tilt, the air thick with disbelief.

"No, no, no," I got up and rushed towards her, my heart splintering with every second. "Rachel, no... Please, no," I pulled her onto my lap, shaking her desperately. "Rachel! Rachel, wake up!" My voice cracked under the weight of my grief, but she didn't respond. She stayed lifeless in my lap.

I sobbed, shaking her.

Behind me, Archon chuckled, a sound so vile it made my stomach turn. "Ah, such a pity," he said mockingly, watching my anguish with twisted delight. "Too much goodness in one place. It's nauseating."

"Rachel," I clutched Rachel tighter, my tears soaking into her lifeless skin. My sobs echoed through the room, raw and unrelenting, but I could barely hear them over the pounding of my shattered heart.

Archon crouched slightly, his cold gaze locking onto mine. "I'll spare you," he said with a sneer. "Not out of mercy-don't flatter yourself. I just want you to be a living warning." His grin deepened, sinister and gleeful. "Let everyone know: whoever dares stand in my way... will meet the same fate."

With a final, mocking glance, he vanished into thin air, leaving behind nothing but silence and the stench of burnt wood. I held Rachel's lifeless body close, rocking back and forth as my cries filled the empty room.

In a single night, I had lost everything, my love, my trust, my friend, my hope, my sanity... Me.

Will I ever be the same after this?

*To be continued...*

www.ingramcontent.com/pod-product-compliance
Lightning Source LLC
LaVergne TN
LVHW041222080526
838199LV00083B/2154